House of Brian

 **Barry Tyrrell**

Produced by:

FriesenPress

Suite 300 - 990 Fort St
Victoria, BC, Canada, V8V 3K2

www.friesenpress.com

Distributed to the trade by The Ingram Book Company

Table of Contents

Acknowledgements

The task of creating a book, especially over an eight year period, requires the talents and patience of many hardworking individuals pulling together to meet almost impossible demands.

For their gallant efforts and commitment, I wish to thank those outstanding people responsible: First, to my wife Gail, whose selfless devotion and encouragement made this book possible. To my son Jonathan, University of Alberta graduate, who performed the first real, edits of the work; to my daughters, Christine and Tracy, who provided so much inspiration. And a special thanks to my mom, Mrs. T, who has always been so proud of me; for no valid reason.

CHAPTER ONE
The Escapade

The gusting wind and the driving rain buffeted the old Ford truck and drowned out the throbbing of the diesel, as it idled at the crossroads in the darkness.

Brian sat peering through the rain-streaked windshield out into the night, his knuckles white as he gripped the wheel, his jaw clenched shut with nervous anticipation. Wild images raced through his mind like a whirlwind. He fought desperately to cope with a cascading barrage of improbable 'what-if' scenarios that could so callously and brutally demolish his carefully prepared plan. Brian's heart beat fast and heavy in his chest as his anxiety and frustration grew. Waiting was always the hardest part.

There were two beers left out of the six-pack on the seat by his side. Brian cracked one and gulped down half the can in a vain attempt to bolster his courage. The nervous tension that wracked his body with anger and sudden irritability was too much to bear. He pressed his flushed face against the cold, damp glass of the driver's side window and strained to see through the void.

There was nothing to see.

But Brian need not have worried; he had done his homework well.

His staring eyes suddenly caught the faint glow of headlights beyond the hills; below the rain-swept horizon. His breath caught in his throat in panic, as severe anxiety threatened to overwhelm him.

Brian cursed his fear and his startled reaction. He angrily threw the truck in reverse and backed up to the fence line and halfway into the flooded ditch. He switched off the engine.

The glow in the sky emerged into a blurry point of light confirming the approach of a lone vehicle traveling along the old road from Bolton to Edmonton.

★★★

Inside the approaching vehicle, Fred Parker was stressed out and sick of the whole situation. The office politics, the poor pay and most of all, the worst courier route in the whole damn company.

"I'm an old man", he lamented bitterly to himself, his voice dull in the clattering din inside the van. "Everybody says so. I don't need this crap any more."

Fred peered blindly ahead at the dismal, ill-kept road, gauging the black shining tar-filled cracks in the pavement that snaked back and forth across his path. May weather could be evil in Alberta. Fred strained to see through the sleet and the rain that splattered incessantly at the windshield: the wipers could barely keep up. The van bounced from one gut-wrenching rut to another as he tried to follow the narrow yellow beams of the headlights through the darkness.

Fred Parker had been driving for Kyle's Courier Services in the last two years and it seemed that his workload had doubled. He was getting too damned old to drive such long hours, and the pickup and delivery deadlines were ridiculous.

Kyle's younger brother, George Bishop, was Fred's supervisor, his self-appointed mentor, and most importantly, his immediate boss. George Bishop had gone to great pains to explain to Fred that cutthroat competitors had forced the company to restructure. The resulting cutbacks had meant that everyone had to "step up to the plate" and to "carry the extra workload" — along with a "small cut in benefits" of course. With a total of one courier van, and Fred and George the only two drivers in the company, it meant Fred Parker had to "step up to the plate."

What a crock!

Fred hated that tired old expression and wished he could have a little talk with the bastard who invented it. Fred's thoughts drifted to other things.

The only other local courier service in Bolton had folded the previous month and all the bank courier business in Bolton had been taken over by Kyle Bishop. It seemed to Fred that someone had pulled a few strings there. The takeover had happened very quickly and Kyle Bishop had been very well prepared for it. Fred later learned from George that Kyle had some very influential friends in the bank's hierarchy, somewhere in the city.

If the truth were known, it seemed to Fred that Kyle's Courier Service was in fact the "cutthroat competitor" George was talking about.

"Oh! Bloody hell," Fred muttered aloud, "I really don't give a damn anyway."

The new corporate philosophy of doing more with less did not sit well with him. Fred had paid his dues a long time ago in a world of hard knocks and punishing schedules, but somehow he still managed to end up as the sucker who had to drive the bloody awful thirty-six miles cross-country to Edmonton to meet the delivery schedule.

"On a dirty-black night like this! On a stupid deadline! And in this weather!"

Fred groaned. He consoled himself with the knowledge that he could return home using the main highway, even if it did take twenty minutes longer.

His mind soon drifted to Maude, his wife of forty pretty-good years. He was thirty-three when they married, and she was twenty-three. Maude would be biting on him again for working so hard when he got home. She was always biting on him.

"Silly old Moo," he smiled, muttering to himself and fighting to keep the violently chattering van on the road as it ran over another corrugated section.

Fred and Maude Parker lived in 'Maude's Cottage' a little two-bedroom house in Bolton, which he had built for her 20 years ago. The mortgage had finally been paid and now the house just needed some tender loving care. He had precious little time or energy to putter around the house; and that, he thought, was sad.

Fred had been a successful civil engineer. Adventurous, he had worked on many international contracts; however he had been somewhat financially and physically reckless. Fred Parker had saved very little for his retirement. Living frivolously from day to day, he had been totally unprepared for the sudden, and relatively unexpected onset of old age; it came as a total shock to him. Fred fought what he considered life's great tragedy for a long time and refused to acknowledge his limitations, but time and illness finally caught up with him.

Asbestosis, brought on by exposure to asbestos fibres in a dozen hazardous demolition sites, had robbed him of some of life's enjoyment.

No longer able to work as an engineer due to the irritating lung disease, Maude convinced him to retire and Fred became a content, but emotionally restless senior citizen at the age of sixty-nine. Then out of the blue, Maude too had taken ill. Somehow, suddenly they had become a part of what Fred referred to as the 'Canadian Seniors Soap Opera.'

Because of the long waiting lists at the hospitals in Canada due to doctor shortages, Maude would have to go to a private clinic in the United States to be treated, and that would cost more than they could afford on his pension. Maude would not consider allowing Fred to mortgage the house again. When he suggested it, she nearly took his head off. He wouldn't go there again!

With only a modest pension to support the two of them, Fred had taken a part-time job with Kyle Bishop to earn the extra money. What Maude really wanted him to do was to quit his job and just hang around the house until he died; she got her point across by lecturing him every time he was late for dinner.

Fred sighed. He would be seventy-three years old in June; twenty-two days to go.

"Way to go girl," he grumbled allowed, thinking about Maude scolding him for his own good. "But not just yet, another six months or so and then we can afford for you to see that specialist in the States."

Fred decided that he would buy her six yellow roses in the city before he headed back home, which usually calmed her down. His spirits were lifted — but not for long.

With a resounding crash, the van hit another huge, invisible pothole with the left front tire. Water cascaded over the windshield, blinding him totally for a few awful seconds and shocking him out of his musings. Fred swerved the van from the edge of disaster and back to the center of the road in the nick of time.

"Damn this road!" he muttered through gritted teeth. "And damn their stupid deadlines!" he cussed for the tenth time that night. Gradually, his heart settled back to its normal rhythm.

Fred slowed down a little, as he peered through the driving rain hammering against the glass, and tried to ignore those angry black road serpents, shimmering and dancing in the headlights.

★★★

The main highway, completed some five years before, bypassed Bolton completely and the turnoff was almost eight miles long.

Neglected and full of jarringly painful potholes, the old road was barely navigable; nevertheless, it was still the shortest distance to from Bolton to Edmonton, shaving twenty minutes off the trip. The narrow country road was seldom used, except by farmers and the occasional tourist who went astray. The dusty trail rose and fell as it carved its way through the rolling grassy hills of south-central Alberta.

Brian also knew the road very well. He had planned his little escapade based on the knowledge that there would probably be no other traffic on that stretch of road at night. The only thing Brian had not anticipated was the abysmal weather. He reassured himself that the storm would probably work to his advantage. Only fools and desperate men would be out on such a night.

Trying frantically to calm his nervous stomach and the ruminating thoughts spinning aimlessly in his head, Brian drained the last of the beer and carelessly threw the can onto the floor on the passenger's side of the truck. Gritting his teeth, he forced himself to calm down and concentrated on the events which lead up to the present moment.

He took another shuddering deep breath as he watched the flickering yellow lights of the approaching van, pitching and plowing through the night like a small boat on a stormy sea.

★★★

When, during Easter Sunday dinner a month earlier, the anxious little man disclosed to the members of his family that he intended to sell a part of his business, Brian had been unmoved and only mildly interested. He had idly listened to only parts of the conversation. Brian seldom paid much attention to what Graham Andrews had to say anyway.

"… an analysis of our profit projections to maintain the new courier service proved totally inadequate," Graham was saying. "Our gross profit margin would be negative unless the bank helps pay to cover the costs of an armored vehicle to carry all that extra cash currency…"

"Armored vehicle?"… "Cash currency?" Brian was suddenly very interested.

Brian had learned a long time ago that the one thing that really mattered in the world was money; the more you had, the better life you had. He had seen what money could do, and what men would do to get it. He felt a tingling at the base of his skull as he strained to hear the rest.

"…the bank will loan us the money," Graham continued sarcastically. "guaranteeing a return on our investment over umpteen years…." He was going off at a tangent and Brian was beginning to lose patience with him, then, "…So I have no idea how Kyle Bishop will transport the bank receipts to Edmonton; his operating profit margins must be similar to ours." Graham paused for a moment to think, staring up at the ceiling. He nodded as he reached a conclusion. "In his courier van, I expect. An unacceptable risk…"

Graham droned on and his voice faded into oblivion as Brian focused on the astonishing possibilities.

For the following two weeks, Brian was a regular visitor in Bolton. To his great annoyance, he was recognized by a number of people in town. He returned their greetings grudgingly, and only when he absolutely had to.

He had followed the courier van on his bicycle as inconspicuously as possible through the streets and alleys of the little town, all the while carefully documenting the routes and routines of Kyle's Courier Service in his notebook.

9:30am … Kyle's Courier Service security doors opened at graystone warehouse. Courier van — light gray GMC van with Kyle's Courier Service in big red letters on doors.
9.35am… Maude's Donut Shop. Driver in there talking to Maude and other old people.
10.00am… Van went to Bolton Dry Cleaning. Picked up courier bag.
Brian followed a mosaic pattern of criss-cross pick-ups and deliveries between offices, stores and shops all over town.
12.00pm… To Kyle's Warehouse.
1.00pm… Van left warehouse.
1.10pm… Went to Bolton Framing. Driver went in and put courier bag in back of van.
1.30pm… Bolton Hardware. Driver went in and put envelope in bag in back of van
2.00pm… Boston Pizza. Driver put box in bag in back of van
3.00pm… Bolton Pharmacy. Driver put package on front seat of van
3.30pm… Standard Bank. Driver and bank guard unloaded packages and bags and took into bank
5.30pm… Back to Kyle's warehouse.

The same pattern was repeated, more or less, on Monday, Tuesday and Wednesday — but Thursday afternoon was different.

After the normal pick-ups and deliveries, the van arrived at the Standard Bank much later that afternoon — around four-thirty p.m. After a thirty-minute wait, the bank officer helped Fred Parker load two canvas bank bags into the van. As Brian watched, his breath caught in his throat and his chest swelled to bursting.

Kyle's Courier Service's van, driven by old Fred Parker, took off out of town on the old road to Edmonton.

★★★

Brian spent the following week confirming what he had learned the week before. He had taken great care to remain unnoticed, by changing clothes twice a day and sometimes wearing a hat or a different jacket, he was confident that nobody had noticed his surveillance activities.

On Wednesday morning, Fred Parker parked around the corner from the Donut Shop and out of the direct line of sight from Maude's Donut Shop windows. It had not been a coincidence.

All the parking spots directly in front of the shop were suddenly out of service, due to half-a-dozen strategically placed orange traffic cones which Brian had 'borrowed' from a road construction site the previous night.

Nobody ever bothered to lock their car doors in Bolton. Brian had taken the opportunity to take a good look inside the van while Fred Parker was otherwise occupied with his cronies. There had been nothing particularly unusual about the vehicle. It was a custom-line cargo van with letter and parcel boxes on the floor and wire racks on the walls. Some spare coveralls and an old jacket hung on hooks in the back. The van had smoked rear windows and standard manufacturer's equipment. An expired fire extinguisher was clipped behind the passenger seat. There was no alarm system. Brian took down the name and number of the two-way radio mounted in the front dashboard.

Later that day he checked with the manufacturer. The maximum reception range of the radio was five miles.

The next day, Thursday, Brian sat as quietly as he could between four or five other customers in the waiting area of the Standard Bank, reading a magazine. He had been waiting for almost half an hour. He fidgeted impatiently, pretending to be engrossed in his reading.

A vehicle stopped outside the front doors of the bank, and Brian glanced at his wristwatch: it was four thirty-five p.m. A few minutes later, Fred Parker walked into the bank and was greeted formally by Mr. Hiller, the assistant bank manager. They talked quietly for a while, then the assistant manager turned, lifted the counter gate and the two walked to the rear of the bank and out of sight.

Brian stood up and strolled casually over to the information booth. He extracted a number of deposit slips, moved to the counter near the flip-up gate and began filling out the forms.

"Can I help you?" a pretty young teller asked, with a helpful smile.

Brian jumped. Totally engrossed on the task at hand, he had not noticed her approaching.

"No! No thanks! I…I'm good. I'm fine, thanks…. No!" He finished angrily.

His response surprised her. She flushed as she murmured an apology and moved away, glancing at him over her shoulder. Brian gritted his teeth.

"Chill!" he admonished himself under his breath, trying to quash his anger. He pretended to concentrate on the deposit slips. He knew instinctively that he had handled that badly. He began to sweat. Too wound up, he thought. Must act normal! With a start, he realized that he did not know how to do that.

Inner tension caused a mood swing that made him chuckle aloud. Inadvertently, he relaxed somewhat; he liked that. He laughed a little louder.

The young teller glanced at him from across the room. He ignored her. She flushed again, embarrassed and a little annoyed; she assumed that he was laughing at her.

Meanwhile, Fred Parker stood leaning against the vault door watching Mr. Hiller and Ray Dowd, his chief accountant, carefully count and stack the week's receipts. They stuffed the money into three official bank bags and sealed them.

"There you go, Mr. Parker," Mr. Hiller said. "Sign here."

He passed Fred the clipboard. Fred scrawled his signature, grabbed two of the bags and headed out the door. Mr. Hiller picked up the last bag and followed.

When they reached the counter, Fred stopped to allow Mr. Hiller to open the gate with his free hand. Mr. Hiller hesitated, he glanced around the room. Satisfied, he said:

"That mini-carnival is in town next week, Mr. Parker." Fred's questioning look told him he was at a loss. Mr. Hiller was not one for casual conversation. Slightly irritated at having to explain himself, Mr. Hiller continued crisply.

"There will be more than the usual cash receipts next week…and considerably more work for the bank," he continued. "Pick-up here is at six-thirty p.m. next Thursday, Mr. Parker. The main bank in Edmonton has been notified and expects delivery by seven-thirty p.m., sharp." Mr. Hiller looked at Fred expectantly.

"Yeah, okay." Fred sighed. "I'll let George Bishop know."

Mr. Hiller opened the gate, and with Fred following respectfully, they crossed the floor, passed through the front doors and out to the waiting van.

Brian, standing hunched over the counter, had heard every word and could not believe his luck. He concentrated, writing furiously on the deposit slips in front of him.

Brian kept his face buried at the counter until he calmed down and Mr. Hiller had returned to his office. Nevertheless, his hands shook with excitement and his face was very red when he finally left the bank.

The young teller frowned a little as she watched him leave. She walked to the counter and gathered the deposit slips he had left there. Most were just scribbled, but one read:

Name: Brian Andrews
Deposit: $200,000.00

She dropped the spoiled deposit slips into the wastepaper basket.

★★★

The next day, Friday, Brian scouted the old Bolton to Edmonton road five times until he finally found the exact spot he was looking for.

Seven miles from Bolton, in the hills above Poplar Creek, the road took a sharp turn to the right and cut right into the hillside. Bushes and small trees had grown down to the edge of the road so that the driver could not see all the way around the corner. His vision was obscured even more as the road ran uphill as he rounded the bend.

It was perfect.

On the other side of the road, a steep bank of clay and rocks with some grass and shrubs poking through ran unchecked down to the heavy bushes beside the rocky creek some fifty yards below. There was a barrier rail running along the edge of the road above the creek, but the support posts were practically rotted though.

Brian had calculated that for his plan to work, the courier van had to be at that exact point on the road after nightfall. He had checked the newspaper; sunset was at 6.15 p.m. the following Thursday evening. That had been a real problem, since according to Brian's calculations the van would have arrived at that spot at 6.30 in the evening. That would have been a full half hour before full darkness.

He had retrieved the traffic cones from the parking lot in front of the donut shop and devised a crude and risky plan to send old Fred Parker on a little detour through the hills. Because of the later pickup time, Brian had no need to do that now.

Brian spent Saturday morning scouring the junk and second hand furniture stores on the outskirts of Edmonton. He paid cash for a large old dresser and scribbled incomprehensibly when he signed the sales receipts. He loaded the dresser onto the truck and drove back towards Poplar Creek. He came to an intersection two miles from the curve and turned onto a gravel farm road. He drove the five miles down the winding road to a remote area overgrown with spruce, poplar and birch trees.

Brian stripped the two large mirrors out of the dresser, and dumped the remainder of the furniture into the ditch. Nobody would care. Brian had noticed that people often dumped sofas, mattresses, even washing machines along ditches in rural areas. Why not an old dresser?

He loaded the mirrors onto the truck and headed back to the old Edmonton road. He returned to the curve on the road above Poplar Creek. Brian parked the pickup on a deserted approach and began his preparations. He was concealed from any casual passers-by by the scrub willows and bushes that grew down to the roadside.

Clouds were beginning to gather and a hush fell over the sparsely inhabited, rolling prairie countryside. It was as if God was holding his breath. A storm was coming.

★★★

Fred Parker arrived at the Standard Bank in Bolton the following Thursday evening for the six-thirty pm. pickup as instructed. All was well as Ray Dowd, Mr. Hiller and Fred Parker walked into the vault. The 12 foot square room was well lit; grey safety-deposit boxes lined the walls from floor to ceiling. A beige, rectangular table stood in the centre of the room surrounded by four black leather and chrome office chairs. A water cooler was positioned just behind the door. In the centre of the table beside the empty bank bags, was a pile carefully stacked bills of various denominations. Phyllis, the teller, was counting out the last of the $312,250.00 on the table. Fred nearly choked. That *little* pile would solve a lot of his and Maude's problems. He shook off the bad thoughts, grudgingly.

To get by Ray, Fred opened the door of the vault a little too wide and bumped the water cooler; in the scramble to catch it, Ray lurched, shoved the table with his hip and knocked the money onto the floor along with the bank bags. Both Ray and Fred had to endure a five minute lecture on bank protocols from Mr. Hiller, before life could go on. Everything had to be recounted. Five official bank bags were eventually loaded into the van; by the time they were done, it was almost 7.00pm.

Fred shook his head in frustration. He was going to be late, and George was sure to raise hell when he got back.

★★★

Fred Parker, driving the Kyle's Courier Services van, approached the curve above Poplar Creek in the driving rain on that pitch-black Thursday night in May, at 7.15pm precisely. He knew the old Bolton to Edmonton road quite well, and despite the wind buffeting the van and the incessant freezing rain pelting down on the windshield, he was not all that concerned as he negotiated the turn above the creek. He saw the headlights suddenly appear in front of him and was totally unprepared for what followed.

Fred's surprise turned to shock as he realized that the other vehicle was on a collision course. He instinctively swerved to the right and hit the brakes; his tires lost traction as he hydroplaned on the rain soaked road. Fear welled up in his throat as he saw the lights follow him across the lane. In a sheer panic, Fred threw the van against the barrier rails, In a shower of sparks and screaming metal, two headlights collided in the darkness.

Fred heard a crash of shattering glass and saw the explosion of light frag-ments, but incomprehensively, there was no shock! No impact! For two seconds nothing happened. His mind screamed trying to comprehend the impossible, illogical happening — but he had no time to recover. The weakened barrier posts, incapable of taking the tremendous load of the careening van, collapsed and the galvanized railings corkscrewed through the air like demons in the night. The van reared, flipped over, and plunged nose-first down into the ravine.

At breakneck speed and upside-down, Fred stared helplessly, horrified, as the light from the remaining headlight illuminated his terrifying plunge down the rock-strewn embankment. The van hit a bolder protruding from the bank and the windshield imploded in Fred's face. The force of the collision sent the van ass-over-tea kettle but scarcely slowed its decent. In a peal of thunder, the van tumbled through the last of the entangled scrub-brush and willows and came to a sudden, jarring, screaming stop — almost upright among the rocks and bushes at the bottom of the gorge.

Everything went black. All around, dead silence, except for the gurgling black water and a high-pitched scream that would not stop. After a while, Fred Parker realized it was he.

★★★

Brian crouched down in the Ford and watched as Fred Parker and the courier van flashed by in a blinding mist of spray. Winding down his window, he breathed through his mouth as he listened to the receding vehicle above the wind and the rain. He watched as the blur of red tail-lights disappeared around the curve in the road. Apart from the skin prickled on the back of his head and the fact that his mouth was dry, and despite the numbing effects of the alcohol and the cold rain lashing his face through the open window; at that moment, Brian felt nothing at all.

★★★

It had taken him a long time to set up the two mirrors earlier that afternoon, and it was almost dark by the time he was done. Eventually though, Brian found that by setting the mirrors twenty feet apart, right in the curve of the road, with the closest mirror in the right lane, it was almost impossible to escape his own reflection. Brian had gotten the idea from watching a television program, 'Mythbusters,' he thought.

Brian practiced driving up the road towards the mirrors until they were per-fectly aligned. He then parked the pickup at the crossroads a quarter-mile away, where he watched and waited, shivering in the darkness.

He was still very afraid, but Brian was only afraid for himself. It seemed that the overwhelming fear of failure and hopelessness that engulfed him periodically would not diminish, no matter what he did. He gave no thought to others, or to the possible deadly consequence of his actions.

Anything Brian had anticipated and prepared for dissolved in a flash when the van hit the guardrails. The glistening beams of the headlights ripped through the rain-streaked sky, dancing briefly like cosmic sabers in the void and faded into oblivion.

A seasoned soldier would have grimly clenched his jaw on hearing those sickening, hollow sounds of metallic destruction ringing through that awful night. It seemed to go on forever, but it was over in an instant, and for Brian, almost before it began.

"Yessss!" Brian screamed with glee.

His exuberance unchained, his face beaming, Brian fired up the engine, floored the pickup and sped up the road towards the curve above Poplar Creek, to the place where he had set his cruel and merciless trap.

At the scene of the devastation, Brian slammed on the brakes and brought the truck to a sliding stop. He jumped out, staring in dismay. His joy evaporated in an instant in the pouring rain. In the glare of his headlights, Brian could see that the courier van had struck one of his mirrors.

In the glow of the headlights, he quickly gathered as many pieces and shards of broken glass as he could find and threw them all into the back of his truck along with the other unbroken mirror. Brian grabbed his flashlight and turned his attention to the van.

He had acquired a new 9V battery in Bolton earlier that day, and in the powerful beam of the flashlight he could make out the lighter silhouette of the van through the rain-soaked tangle of bushes at the edge of the creek. With his excitement returning, Brian headed down the bank.

The slope was sheer, slippery clay and mud. Brian's feet came out from under him, and he went skidding down the bank as if he'd been greased. The flashlight was jarred out of his hand by a sharp crack on the elbow and it tumbled down the hill and rolled under the stricken van. Water shorted the switch and with a sizzle, the light went out.

Brian plowed feet-first, deep into the willows and tangled scrub brush at the base of the hill. For a moment he panicked, having no idea where he was in the darkness. Recovering his footing and sobbing with fright, Brian fought his way out of the tangled underbrush and stumbled through the mud and bushes in the hellish gloom to where he thought the van should be.

He was scratched and bruised and tears of frustration ran down his face, when ten minutes later he finally reached the van. In the dim light he could just make out that one of the rear doors had been blown open in its plunge down the embankment. Groping inside the door, Brian located one of the moneybags and his heart lifted. He climbed into the van out of the freezing rain as his eyes slowly adjusted to the darkness.

There was a soft groan from the front of the van. Brian jumped.

The outline of Fred Parker slumped to the side still strapped in his seat sprang sharply into focus.

His heart pounding, Brian crawled a little farther into the van and felt cold water cover his hands. The front of the van was immersed in the creek and Fred Parker had water up to his navel. Brian saw that one of the moneybags had landed on the radio. He reached across the passenger seat and grabbed the bag just as Fred moaned again. Brian sprang back with a yelp.

Brian was trembling violently from the cold, fear constricted his throat and numbed his thinking, but he still managed to focus on the layout of the van from his earlier excursion at the donut shop. He fished around until he found the remaining bags, strapped them around his shoulders and bailed frantically out of the back of the van. He was glad to leave that place.

Brian tried to climb the bank but kept losing his grip in the mud and slid right back down again. Four more times he tried until he was nearly exhausted. Finally, he decided to make his way around the side of the slope alongside the swollen creek. In the darkness he tripped over a branch and fell headfirst into the rushing water with the five bank bags still tied around his neck.

Brian panicked. He couldn't swim!

He rolled over onto his back and sucked in some air as the turbulent waters swirled him out to the middle of the stream. The bags were buoyant and more or less kept him afloat in the black waters that propelled him brutally over rocks and boulders. A hundred yards downstream, the surging current flipped him out onto the bank, half drowned — and ten feet from the road at the bottom of the hill.

Bruised and battered, Brian staggered up the road to his truck. He opened the passenger door and threw the bags inside. An empty beer can rolled out and fell into a puddle on the road. Brian crushed it with his boot.

Sobbing with relief, Brian climbed into the truck, cold and soaking wet, he turned on the ignition. When the engine sprang to life, he slipped the truck into gear, turned up the heat and started slowly down the road towards Edmonton.

Brian Andrews began to hum tunelessly. He was rich; it was all good; he didn't have a care in the world. It was the middle of May, and there were still months of summer holidays ahead. He had just turned fourteen.

★★★

CHAPTER TWO
The Boy

Brian Andrews headed down the gravel farm road to where he had dumped the dresser. The rain had stopped but the road was a greasy mess of gumbo-mud. Six times, Brian had to power through heart-stopping stretches of flooded ruts in the darkness. He got stuck twice on the way in. Breaking off spruce branches from nearby trees with his bare hands, Brian shoved them under the wheels for added traction, and lurched on down the road.

When he reached his destination, he unloaded the mirrors and shattered glass into the nearest ditch and stomped the larger pieces to break them up. While trying to turn the truck around on the narrow road in the darkness, Brian misjudged and dropped the rear left wheel into a mud hole. Howling in anger, he pounded on the steering wheel with his fists.

After many fruitless attempts to raise the vehicle, and buried up to his knees in the mud, Brian finally resorted to using the spare tire as a base for the jack. Somehow he managed to lift the truck up high enough to shove enough deadfall and branches under the wheels.

With the engine screaming, Brian cursed the old Ford truck until it finally lurched out of the ditch and up onto the road in a cloud of smoke; the pungent stench of burning rubber filling the air around him. Totally exhausted and with tears of frustration rolling down his cheeks, Brian fought his way back to the main road, leaving the spare tire buried deep in the mud. It was four a.m. in the morning and he still had much to do. The storm had passed; it began to rain again.

Brian drove home through the dark, rain-swept night, his stomach in a frightened knot. He relaxed with a grateful sigh when he finally saw the familiar lantern lights mounted on the stone walls beside the driveway gates.

Brian lived with his family on an estate two miles east of Bolton. An impressive, two-story red-brick, Victorian-style house stood in the middle of a landscaped ten-acre property. A gravelled, tree-lined driveway ran up to a circular yard in front of the house.

The three-car garage stood separated from the main house on the left side of the yard, and across the way a yard-light illuminated the front of the property. A sensor controlled the light, which turned on automatically in the evening, and shut off again at dawn. The light was still burning with its bright yellow glow, when Brian arrived at the gates.

Immaculate lawns covered the grounds which ran down to the rustic iron fence at the bottom of the driveway. Trees and shrubs and the manicured flower gardens completed the landscaping. Tucked away in the left front corner of the garden, were four old wooden grain sheds, relics from a time when the land was farmed some 30 years before. The twelve-foot square sheds were partially hidden by overgrown shrubs, ivy and willows and added to the aesthetic value and privacy of the property.

Brian turned onto the grass, and, with absolutely no regard for the garden drove straight across the soaking wet lawn to the sheds.

Three of the sheds were used by the family to store material things; junk too valuable to throw out but of no use to anyone in the house. The fourth shed was filled to the rafters with yellow five-gallon pails. The pails, also relics from the farming days, had long since lost all traces of the chemicals they once contained. Some even had the lids removed.

After collecting the bank bags from the truck, Brian selected five of the open pails and stuffed the bags into them one at a time. He gathered up some of the metal lids, sealed the pails and stacked them neatly in a corner of the shed. Satisfied, he got back into the truck. He drove back the way he had come across the lawn and up the gravel driveway to the house. Brian yawned. He was very tired; it had been a long, long day.

★★★

Mary D'Laney-Andrews stood sadly at the rain-streaked window of her upstairs bedroom, her arms folded, watching her son walk across the yard towards the house. She had seen the flash of the headlights a short time before and now wondered what was taking Brian so long to drive up to the house. Mary watched in dismay as Brian tore across the wet lawn to the driveway, perplexed at his total disregard for the damage he was causing. She bit her lip, then, shook her head resigned. That was the careless nature of her son.

★★★

Mary realised by the time he was eighteen months old that Brian was different. He had not liked being held or cuddled. He was not interested in playing children's games and displayed none of the care and affection that her eldest daughter had at that age.

She remembered back to when he was four: she and her husband, Graham, had taken him to a specialist who had diagnosed conclusively that their son was merely overactive and perhaps a little autistic "…from eating the wrong foods," he said.

"Brian's total disassociation and lack of concern for the feelings of others and even for his mother, is probably due to a dysfunctional family environment," Dr. Brown, the specialist, intoned bluntly, after a little discussion, "It is a common trait among children in materialistic societies, especially among the aristocracy, where children are often raised by nannies — or left to their own devices." He stared down at her judgementally over the top of his bifocals. "Indeed, the practice still prevails where children are required to be seen — but not heard."

Mary was livid.

For him to insinuate that she was a materialistic mother, one who should pay more attention to her child's needs, was, to say the least, insulting. And to further suggest that she and Graham neglected their family and were in pursuit of social status was preposterous. What social status? They lived in Bolton, Alberta, for crying out loud!

"You arrogant prick," she had told him coldly, storming out of his office.

As time went by, Mary adapted to Brian's special needs. She lavished love and attention on him. As a consequence, she had, in some respects, even sacrificed much of her relationship with her eldest daughter, Kelly.

But, the specialist's words were an educated diagnosis proffered by a medical professional, and the damage was done. Over the next ten years, Graham Andrews became distant, unwittingly blaming his wife for Brian's undisciplined behaviour, while believing that everything would eventually return to normal.

As Brian grew older and more active, the Andrews family often came under considerable stress because of his increasingly dangerous antics. In an environment of growing frustration, loneliness and persecution, Mary's depression grew and self-doubt crept in. Only when Brian turned thirteen years old and his mood swings and violent behaviour were becoming too unpredictable, did she finally manage to convince her husband that they should seek a second opinion.

The new specialist, Dr. Adams, did some tests and a month later made an appointment to see Mary and Graham in his consulting room in the city. They arrived at his medical office, and she and Graham sat down on the wooden chairs in front of the desk like parents at a PTA meeting. A terrible feeling of foreboding overwhelmed her; Graham grasped her wrist.   She   glanced around frantically, looking for an escape. There was none.

Mary knew that she would never forget that untidy room, with its oh-so-typical certificates and charts on the walls, books on the shelves and a plastic skeleton in the corner. That bleak room, where her dreams were crushed and her nightmares were confirmed.

"Your son is autistic," Dr. Adams told them bluntly, cleaning his glasses. "He has a relatively mild type that is called *infantile autism*," he said, continuing to explain his diagnosis. "What does concern me is that in addition to the autism he has all the typical early warning signs of *childhood-onset-schizophrenia.*

"The disorder can develop over a number of years or, be very rapid. I believe the latter to be the case, especially since we have had the opportunity to observe Brian for the last month, and you have also noticed significant changes in the last six months. Change in behaviours, mood swings, cognitive and communication problems, delusions and hallucinations are all key symptoms. Schizophrenia onset is typically between the ages of 14 and 30, and Brian fits the pattern perfectly." The doctor saw the shock on their faces and tried to soften the blow.

"Brian has a form of schizophrenia characterised by acting out his fantasies — which he perceives as reality. In his case, this is accompanied by a total withdrawal from human emotional attachment." The doctor rubbed his jaw as he continued.

"At the same time, we have also determined that Brian has above-average intelligence. And, as an adult, with high-functioning autism, there is every indication that he will be able to live independently and be successful in his chosen profession.

"Medication can help with the schizophrenia; we caught it in the early stages of onset. Brian can lead a normal life."

What followed was the usual kind of numb questioning.

"Is there a cure?"

"No."

"What causes it?"

"We don't know, we think it's genetic."

"What can we do?" Mary inquired desperately.

"With most families," Dr. Adams offered, "I would recommend using respite care — a family support service, as well as joining a help group with families in similar situations. I can refer you to some if you wish."

Mary began taking Brian to help groups, but when Brian persistently kneed other boys in the groin without provocation, and then stood by watching them curiously as they rolled on the ground in agony; she withdrew him from the program.

Medication helped for a while, but the serious side effects, such as dry mouth, constipation, blurred vision, muscle stiffness and spasms resulted in Brian refusing to comply; so try as she might, Mary could not control him, and Brian relapsed.

Graham had gone into denial, refusing to accept that Brian was engaged in anything more than typical childish fantasies and daydreams.

"Appropriate behaviours for one his age," he insisted, "and behaviours he will likely grow out of."

Graham immersed himself in his businesses in town, spending eighteen to twenty hours a day in the office and leaving the domestic responsibilities to Mary. She, in turn, had focused her energy on her gardens.

By the time Brian turned thirteen he was totally uncontrollable and came and went as he pleased. School was a rare, sporadic occasion, depending on his mood.

One bitterly cold evening in January, Brian had stormed out of the house in a rage over some trivial incident without his coat. (He thought his sisters were spying on him.) Brian had returned home exhausted and hypothermic four hours later after walking back from town. On hearing of the incident, Graham had exacerbated the problem by teaching the boy how to drive — and gave him the keys to the Ford pickup.

"He's only thirteen," Mary had protested to no avail.

"Boys must have wheels," Graham told her, not realizing how chauvinistic he sounded. "And besides," he said with a wink at the boy, "he'll only drive on farm roads."

And so Brian became totally independent; seldom home for regular meals, and often not seeing or speaking to his mother or the rest of the family for days at a time.

★★★

Standing at the bedroom window, Mary stopped her deliberations of the past and snapped back to the present as she watched her son tear across the lawns in the pickup and spin up the driveway to the house. Brian misjudged the distance and slammed the truck into the garage doors. She watched him get out of the truck and kick the damaged door in annoyance. He crossed the yard and glanced up…Seeing her, he stopped, arms hanging loosely by his side, sparkling like an angel in the pouring rain under the yellow glow of the yard light. He smiled.

He broke her heart.

As many mothers had done before, she buried her face in her hands and wept for her son. When she looked for him again, he was gone.

★★★

Fred struggled back to consciousness again through a red mist of pain and racking nausea. He knew that he must stay awake. When the hero was mortally wounded, the rule was that he had to stay awake or he wouldn't make it. All the books said so.

He fought hard to stay alert all that first night, while the freezing water rose up to his armpits. Fred had some vivid hallucinations of a slim ghost climbing in and out of the van as he faded in and out of consciousness. He fought all that day and the next, and yelled himself hoarse hoping someone would hear. No one did. The old Bolton to Edmonton road was rarely used, and never right after a storm.

As evening approached once more on the second day, the water receded down to his shins. Fred shook the fog from his brain and took stock of his injuries.

The van's frame had twisted, pinning his legs under the dashboard. His right leg was totally shattered below the knee; he could see the bone protruding in two places. His knee was crushed between the frame and dashboard and the two were acting as a steel tourniquet. That was the only reason he had not bled to death.

The steering column had punched into his chest, compressing him into the seat. It was hard to breathe. Fred knew that he had probably broken some ribs, maybe even punctured a lung. His stomach felt huge, swollen. Internal bleeding? He wondered.

In his semi-conscious state, it took a little while for Fred to comprehend the full severity of his plight, but eventually he realised that he was mortally wounded. He knew that he would not live to see another day. When the reality finally set in, the feeling of hopelessness, claustrophobia, entrapment and panic washed over him like a wave and his eyes and his mouth opened wide with horror.

The scream of the dying man, which caused the night creatures of the creek to still their chaotic cacophony, was made all the more dreadful because it was gasped and …almost silent.

★★★

CHAPTER THREE
The Police

Inspector Claude DuBois, Operations Commander, Fifth Detachment, Bolton, Alberta, was playing with his two-year-old daughter on the carpet in front of the television set. He was chasing her around the room on all fours, a blanket over his head and making a terrible racket. The child squealed in terror as she scrambled away from the charging bundle of noise, turned, and came back for more.

Susan, Claude's wife, stood in the doorway with a wooden spoon in her hand, shaking her head slowly from side to side, wondering how she was ever going to settle Meagan down at bedtime. It never ceased to amaze her to see the big tough cop playing on the floor like a child. Well, she had something special planned for her hubby tonight; just because it was Thursday. She would let them play a little longer.

She had cooked his favourite dinner — roast leg of lamb with mint and roasted potatoes. And for after, when Meagan was asleep, she had warmed up the Jacuzzi. They would finish the bottle of Chardonnay and then, who knows…

The telephone rang. Startled out of her daydreams, she grabbed the receiver and said a quick hello.

"Hi Susan, is the Inspector there?" Her heart sank. It was Corporal Patrick D'Laney, and the call was serious. Whenever he called their home, Patrick always asked after her and Meagen first, and he always asked jokingly for Claude as 'the Sarge,' even though Claude had been promoted to Inspector two years before.

The special evening she had planned would have to wait for another time.

"Sure, Patrick…hang on."

Claude took the phone from Susan with Meagan on his arm. He slowly lowered her to the ground as he listened to his corporal's report. Susan scooped her up and carried her into the kitchen to find her favourite pot-toy.

"Inspector," the corporal said, "the courier from the Standard Bank didn't make his scheduled delivery in Edmonton."

"What time was it supposed to be there?" asked Claude, suddenly focused.

"7.30 this evening", answered Patrick. "Mr Hiller and George Bishop are here at the precinct right now."

Claude glanced at his watch. It was 8.15 p.m. "Okay. Put three cars out to cover the route," he said tersely. "Alert the Edmonton police, and put out an APB for the courier van and the driver, what's his name… the driver?…Oh yeah, Fred Parker. I'm coming in."

Claude hung up the phone, and looked across at his wife standing resigned in the doorway with the child on her hip. He shook his head, bent down, gave Susan a kiss on the cheek and reached for his coat in the closet.

★★★

Down at the Detachment, Inspector Claude DuBois was literally pulling his hair out. It was Saturday night and it had been more than twenty-four hours since the courier van was reported missing and… Nothing! There was not a sign of it anywhere, not along the highway, or in the ditches, or even on or off any of the side roads. They had checked all the abandoned buildings, farms and houses along the route. Maude Parker had not seen him either, she was genuinely worried. Nobody had seen anything.

Edmonton Police had seen no sign of the courier van in the city, and it had been a quiet night. Claude himself had taken a car and helped in the search through that awful storm and right into the morning hours. Still nothing.

Mr. Hiller, Kyle and George Bishop walked into his office. Claude groaned inwardly as Kyle Bishop got right to the point.

"Inspector," he said, leaning over with his hands on the desk. "It's damn near 26 hours since my van disappeared and I bloody well hope you're bringing in reinforcements."

"I've got five officers on this case, including myself, Kyle," Claude said patiently. "We will find your van and Mr. Parker… eventually."

"Eventually doesn't cut it!" Kyle yelled. "The money will be long gone! Eventually? Bloody Hell, Claude! Get a chopper out there!"

"Clouds are on the deck; the pilot wouldn't see a thing, even if he could get off the ground," Claude said evenly.

"You've got to do better than that!" Kyle was getting red in the face. "I demand…"

"Kyle, get the fuck off my desk and sit down!" Claude said grimly, as he stood up, kicking back the chair.

Everybody jumped. Claude was tired and getting a little cranky. His visitors played musical chairs for a minute. When they had settled down, Claude continued.

"Let's go over this again. Mr. Hiller, do you have anything to add to your earlier statement?"

"Like what?"

"Well, did you notice any change in Parker's behaviour, his attitude? Was he agitated?"

"Well," Mr. Hiller said thoughtfully, drawing out the word. "He looked, uh, he looked impatient. That's it, impatient, especially when Ray knocked the money on the floor. I remember looking at him. Can't say that I was particularly happy with the situation myself."

"That's it?"

"Yes, except that he mentioned something derogatory about deadlines." Mr. Hiller looked miserable.

"I don't see how…" Kyle began his voice fading as he saw the look on the inspector's face.

"George?" Claude asked.

"No. Like I said, the last time I spoke to Fred it was at about six o'clock Thursday evening, before he went to the bank. I figured that with the storm coming, Fred would likely take the main highway to Edmonton." George forgot to mention that he had threatened Fred not to be late…or else.

"Fred just told me about a kid following the van around town on a bike." George said miserably.

Claude sat back in his chair and cupped his chin in his hand. He felt a prickle behind his ears. Parker had a choice of routes? If Parker was on a tight deadline, he might choose a shorter route. The revelation hit him like a thunderbolt.

The old Bolton to Edmonton road!

"Michelle!" He roared at the dispatcher. It was 8.45 p.m., Saturday night, twenty-five and a half hours after the accident.

★★★

The flashlight that Brian dropped had rolled under the courier van out of the rain, and was perched against a rock. The water in the switch slowly dried, until electrodes flowed freely through the contacts once more. The light flickered, and came on. It shone all Saturday afternoon and into the evening.

"Dad! There's a light down there."

Pete Morgan and his fifteen-year-old son, Josh, were returning home. They had passed this way just that morning on their way to the north quarter but had not noticed anything unusual.

"A light? In the creek?"

Pete slid the '57 International grain truck to a stop in a series of sliding hops on the side of the road. They scrambled down to the creek and followed the shaft of light to the wrecked van. Josh reached underneath the van and retrieved the flashlight. He climbed up into the back of the van through the open door.

"Holy shit! There's a guy in here!" Josh yelled, as searchlights from approaching police cars illuminated the scene.

Inspector Claude DuBois and Corporal Patrick D'Laney came sliding down the bank. The Cavalry had arrived.

★★★

Julie Martins kneeled, crouching over Fred Parker in the front of the van. The interior was lit up like day by the torches held by her partner and two firemen at the side windows. They waited patiently for her instructions.

The prognosis was not good. She knew that her decisions over the next few minutes would mean life or death for this man. Julie felt the panic well up in her throat. There was no hope! *This man was going to die in her hands!*

Julie Martins had been a paramedic for two years now. Attached to the Number 4 Fire Station in Edmonton, she was a credit to her unit.

Julie had been a junior-high school teacher before joining the Canadian Army Reserves as a Medic. Prior to joining the 4th, Julie served six years as a Medic in the Canadian Armed Forces, which included two six-month tours overseas in Kosovo.

Corporal Julie Martins had distinguished herself as a fine soldier; that was, according to the official manifest. In fact, Julie had seen and felt the utter futility of war and its incomprehensible aftermath. She had seen the depravity, the plight of the sick, the starving, the blind and the crippled and had done what little she could for the people of that wretched country. The little ones had crushed her. Julie had wept every day and every night of her tour of duty.

Privately, she had prayed and cried aloud with helpless rage and frustration at her own human limitations. She had witnessed the outer limits of man's inhumanity to man, but when called upon to do so; she had gone back for a second tour. When she returned home, she became ill. The doctors diagnosed her condition as PTSD: Post-Traumatic Stress Disorder, and she was soon discharged from the service.

Julie Martins gathered herself and took a deep breath, crushing the panic in her breast. Now, all her training, knowledge and experience came into play, as she focused on the task at hand. Julie automatically gave Fred Parker two shots of morphine and hooked up the oxygen mask. She checked his vital signs and did a quick assessment of her patient's injuries in the confined space without moving him.

"Right," she said. "We have to get him out *in* the chair, vertical as he sits right now. If we lie him down, he'll be dead in less than five minutes."

They brought the compressor down with the 'jaws of life', and jammed them between the chassis and the dash.

"Wait!" Julie said.

"Matt," she turned to her partner, "put a tourniquet around that leg. If we take the pressure off, we'll never stop the bleeding in time."

Matt Finch, a 10-year veteran with the unit, did not argue. He had developed a great deal of respect for this woman with the nerves of tempered steel. When it came to the really tough jobs, everyone in the unit turned to Julie Martins.

"Tighter, Matt. Dammit!"

They pried the leg loose. Matt blanched as he saw the blackened destruction of the leg below the knee. He glanced at Julie, checking vital signs and readjusting the oxygen mask and tubes. She never turned a hair.

"Okay, get the angle grinder and cut off the bolts holding this seat," she instructed the fireman, as she strapped Fred into the seat with stretcher straps. "And keep him upright all the way to the hospital," she reminded everyone curtly.

She held a bag of saline solution connected to the IV tube over the injured man's head as she dodged the shower of sparks from the grinder.

★★★

Dr. Paul Jacobus Strydom, Head of Microbiology and Surgery at Edmonton City Hospital, took personal charge of the case.

X-rays taken with the patient in the vertical position had confirmed the paramedic's instincts. Laying the patient down would have killed him. The first surgical incisions to repair and remove broken bones and vessels in the chest cavity had also been performed with the patient strapped upright on the table.

Dr. Strydom had relished the challenge.

Although he was a highly trained specialist, Dr. Strydom was also quite competent in general surgical procedures and appreciated the opportunity to practice his skills. There is no doubt that without the particular knowledge and experience of Dr. Paul Jacobus Strydom, Fred Parker would have died on the operating table within the first hour.

During the operation, Dr. Strydom had made only one error. At one point during the procedure, a surgical nurse had called for another unit of blood.

"Type?" the nurse asked.

"AB-negative," the surgical nurse confirmed, reading the band on Fred Parker's wrist.

Dr. Strydom started and dropped the scalpel. It rang like a bell on the white tiled floor. He quickly regained his composure and continued with the operation.

★★★

Fred Parker opened his eyes. Everything was blurred.

The biggest nurse he had ever seen came into fuzzy focus. Her tawny brown hair flopped down over her concerned chubby cheeks and her big brown eyes stared into the depths of his as she checked his vital signs.

He spoke his first word.

"Damn." he said.

The nurse standing over him was disappointed. Anybody else would have asked:

Where am I?" or "What day is this?"

"You're in Edmonton City Hospital. You had an accident last Thursday night. It's Monday, two o'clock in the afternoon," she told him anyway. "Your wife and a police officer are here to see you," she continued, as she straightened the covers and checked his intravenous.

She met them at the door.

"He's in stable, but critical condition," she told them briskly. She addressed the officer. "Please be brief," she instructed him. Constable Patrick D'Laney nodded.

Maude rushed into the room. "Hello, Fred," she said.

"Hello, Miss Piggy," he croaked. He always called her Miss Piggy when they had been apart. She burst into tears.

"It's been 4 days since the accident, Fred," she told him, when she recovered her breath. "You've been in and out of surgery four times. We thought we'd lost you."

"Now, Maude," he consoled her. "I'll be okay now." But he knew that he would not. Patrick D'Laney moved to the side of the bed. "Mr. Parker, can you answer a couple of questions regarding the accident?"

Fred felt the pressure build behind his eyes and his blurred vision suddenly began to clear. Then slowly the light began to fade away, as the darkness once again began to engulf him.

"Saw headlights... hit something... no impact...," he said. His voice trailed away.

Bells rang! "Code Blue!"

Nurses and interns scrambled in response to the emergency, shoving everything and everyone aside. In a tangle of intravenous tubes, hoses and wires, Fred Parker was hoisted onto the gurney and rushed to the operating room once again. Fred's internal organs were systematically shutting down, his liver, his kidneys, his pancreas. Only his big heart kept him going.

Maude sat crying quietly beside the empty bed, and the police officer put his arm gently around her shoulders.

***

CHAPTER FOUR
The Investigation

Corporal Patrick D'Laney walked into the office to find Inspector Claude DuBois of the 5th Detachment at his desk staring red-eyed at the mountain of paper in front of him. It was 5.30am., the Saturday morning after the accident.

They had done what they could in the darkness the night before and roped off the scene of the accident. He had also stationed a junior Constable at the barricade.

"Patrick," the inspector said, "I'm assigning the Parker case to you."

"Yes, Sir."

"I'll work with you as the Operations Commander," Claude continued, "so keep me posted."

"Yes, Sir." Patrick waited expectantly. There had to be more.

"Well get with it man!" Claude yelled. "Put your plan together and let me know."

"Yes, Sir!" The corporal turned to leave, but stopped as the inspector spoke again.

"Take Monair with you. Let me know on Monday if you want to keep her on as your partner."

"What? Oh come on, Claude!"

"She needs the experience, Patrick," Claude shrugged. "And who better than you to show her the ropes?"

"Yeah, but Sarge...the rookie?" Patrick protested.

"Do it!" Claude roared, bracing himself in the chair with his knuckles on the desk. Patrick got the hell out of there.

★★★

Corporal Patrick O'Sullivan D'Laney, a policeman for the last 6 years and at 26 years of age, was born to be a police officer.

His father was presently a police officer in Edmonton, his grandfather had been a police officer in New York City, and his great grandfather had been a policeman in Caulfield, County Cork, Ireland. Patrick was proud of his heritage, and he loved his job.

Corporal Patrick D'Laney, accompanied by Constable Michelle Monair, went to the crash site at first light and had made their way down to the van. It had stopped raining scant hours before. A watery sun was scattering its warming rays through the gaps in the trees, but it was still a mud-bath on the ground below. Michelle had gotten her office shoes so stuck in the mud that she ended up walking barefoot in the gumbo. Patrick just shook his head and said nothing. She seemed to like it.

The accident site where the van came to rest did not reveal many clues. There had been at least ten people churning up the mud down there the previous night, climbing in and out and all over the vehicle.

They scouted the banks of the creek for a hundred yards downstream on both sides but found nothing unusual. The official bank bags containing three-hundred and twelve thousand two-hundred and fifty dollars, were gone.

They stood on the road on the top of the bank and looked down on the crash site beside the creek. Despite all the traffic since the accident, Patrick was still able to identify the skid marks of the van, and determine exactly where it had hit the barrier rail. He concluded that the driver had indeed swerved into the barrier to avoid something.

But, what? A deer perhaps?

He shared the information with Michelle. She photographed and documented the findings and made sketches of the area. She picked up a flattened beer can and put it in a bag. Flashes of sunlight reflecting off the road caught Patrick's eye.

"What's this?" he asked. Michelle came over to his elbow.

"Side mirror?" she offered, peering at the fragment.

"Maybe," he said cautiously. He walked a little farther around the curve and stood on the edge of the road looking down the embankment. "And,.. maybe not."

Sparkling in the early morning sunshine lay hundreds of bits and pieces of a shattered mirror, spread out in a great arc fifty feet below his feet.

★★★

They had taken statements from the Morgans the night before, but Patrick decided to review the circumstances following the accident again while they were still fresh in everyone's mind.

He and Michelle were sitting at the wooden table in the kitchen of the Morgan farmhouse, and the three golden retrievers were vying for attention from Michelle. It was late afternoon and they could see the sun just beginning to set behind the trees.

After going through some of the preliminaries over a cup of coffee, Patrick turned to his host.

"Pete, you said you saw a light?"

"Actually, Josh spotted it first, but I saw it after."

"After what?"

"After we got down there."

"Did you see where the light came from?" Michelle asked.

"Nope. Josh got there first."

"Josh?"

Josh was a big boy of fifteen. Over six feet tall and two hundred pounds, he took after his father. Josh shuffled uncomfortably as attention shifted to him.

"It was shining under the van."

"Was it a taillight?" Patrick inquired.

"Flashlight," Josh said.

Patrick scratched his head and asked carefully, "Josh, where is the flashlight now?"

Josh looked up at the two officers and then at his father. He was a little startled as everyone leaned slightly forward and held their breath in anticipation.

"In my room," he blurted. "Want me to get it?"

"Yes, please, Josh." Michelle answered gently, as everyone exhaled.

"Its material evidence from a crash scene," she explained unnecessarily, as Josh left the table.

Josh lumbered off to his room and retrieved the flashlight that had saved the life of old Fred Parker. He brought it to the table and reluctantly handed it to Constable Monair who put it in a plastic bag.

★★★

On Monday, 4 days after the accident, they pulled the van out of the creek, loaded it onto a truck and took it to the police yard. There, forensics went over it with a fine-toothed comb. They found nothing that could tie anything to the missing bank bags, although they concluded that the van was mechanically sound prior to the crash.

Corporal D'Laney and Constable Monair spent the entire morning on the phones tracing the whereabouts of known criminals and interfacing with other police departments on the case.

Patrick went to Edmonton that afternoon, hoping to speak with Fred Parker in the hospital. Michelle was left at the precinct to hold down the fort.

Constable Michelle had something to prove, and she made no bones about it.

Petite, blonde and twenty-five, she had sat as a dispatcher in three different detachments for four years and she felt that she had paid her dues.

Michelle had watched impatiently as other officers had been given the assignments because they were men. The memory of the last occasion flashed across her mind and she quickly shook it off.

Her ultimate objective was to be a forensic pathologist. She had taken every prerequisite upgrading course available, and she had excelled in all of them. She was smart and would make corporal as soon as she had put the years in. But that wasn't the point. Michelle needed the field experience to match her qualifications.

How could she be taken seriously if all she did was sit behind a desk? Now finally, after only one month at the 5th Detachment, she had been given the opportunity. She would learn everything she could from Patrick D'Laney, even if it killed him....her. Figuratively speaking of course, she thought soberly, reining in her enthusiasm.

A call came in from the new dispatcher.

"Constable Monair," he said, "I just had a call from Constable Clark at the scene. He answered a complaint from a local farmer. "Apparently someone dumped some furniture out that way on range road 31 south of township road 470. Constable Clark said you might be interested because of some broken mirrors?"

"On my way," she said, barely able to contain her excitement. "Tell him not to touch anything."

Michelle walked carefully around the area where the dressers and mirrors had been dumped, photographing everything. The sun had been warm the last few days and the mud had dried as hard as concrete.

It was obvious that someone had been there during, or shortly after the storm. It was also obvious that whoever it was had gotten really stuck in the gumbo. Tire marks cut deeply into the hardened mud. The footprints puzzled her. She could see the imprint of someone kneeling; it was short like a child. She took plaster moulds of the clearest of both the tires and the boot prints. She also collected pieces of the mirror and bagged them.

Walking back along the road, she paused as she saw 5 small holes in the mud where the ground had been torn up the most. Poking around with a stick, she soon realised that there was a rim and tire completely buried in the mud. Nobody else had noticed that. She was good! She thought elated.

"Dig it up, and bring it to the Detachment," she told the rookie, Constable Clark, casually, as he gazed at her in awe.

She walked nonchalantly back to her car trying very hard to act calmly; it was just another day at the office. She was bursting at the seams.

★★★

Patrick had returned from visiting Fred and Maude Parker at the hospital. On hearing that Michelle was out on a call, he made his way down to the police yard, leaving instructions for her to join him there when she returned. He had just gained access to the garage where the van was kept when Michelle arrived.

"So, what have we got?" Michelle asked, out of breath. Patrick looked at her and his eyes narrowed thoughtfully.

"I think I know how they pulled it off," he said, pulling on a pair of latex gloves and walking around to the front of the van. Michelle followed him into the garage. Patrick knelt down and inspected the right-side headlight. The glass was smashed but the reflector was still intact. Glass particles resting at the bottom of the reflector bowl caught his attention.

"Michelle, pass me those small forceps and the magnifying glass," he said.

As Michelle looked over his shoulder, Patrick carefully lifted out a piece of glass the size of a large button from within the shattered headlight. It was the colour of dulled aluminium. Patrick turned it over and saw the reflection of her blue eyes in the mirror.

★★★

"They had a mirror set up on the road?" Michelle exclaimed her eyes wide with astonishment. Patrick nodded.

"Fred Parker told me that he saw headlights and that he hit something '…*but no impact…*,'" Patrick explained. "It adds up. Pieces were strewn all over the bank, and pieces of the mirror was still inside the van's right-side headlight."

Michelle nodded. "And I think that I found the dumpsite where the bad guys ditched the evidence," she bubbled, "and I found a tire, and I found their tracks, and I got plaster casts and I found the dresser and the rest of the mirror," she said, counting them off on her fingers. She looked up at him, rocking from side to side. She was flushed and beaming with pride.

Patrick was amused, and more than a little enchanted by her passionate outburst.

★★★

It was Wednesday, 6 days after the accident, and Patrick and Michelle were having lunch at Maude's Donut Shop in 'Beautiful Downtown Bolton.' They were seated in the solarium, partially shaded from the bright sunlight by a large ornamental fig tree.

"Let's go over what we have once again," Corporal D'Laney said thoughtfully, munching on his turkey sandwich and sorting through the notes and papers on the table in front of them.

"Whoever did this probably drove a '92 to'98 Ford pickup," Michelle said, checking her notes while nibbling on a French fry. "The rim on the tire I found matches that bolt pattern only."

"A Ford pickup with a missing spare," Patrick reflected.

"The alleged robbers may be beer drinkers," Michelle offered. "We found that empty beer can at the crash site."

"I don't know about that one," Patrick said, watching her hair reflecting in the sunlight. "A lot of people think it's cool to drink beer when driving on country roads and just fire the empties out the window."

She wrinkled her nose at him. He made himself concentrate on the checklist.

"The robbers probably dropped the flashlight," she said. "It was switched on and underneath the van."

"Forensics is checking it for prints," Patrick added, but he did not sound hopeful. That flashlight had been through a lot.

"And, based on footprints at the dumpsite, one of the alleged robbers is either a small man or a woman," Michelle said.

"I think it's local," Patrick said suddenly. "Whoever it was knew about the old road, the schedule, and the route Kyle's Courier Service's van took. He also has a sound knowledge of the surrounding area." He stopped speaking. Michelle was staring at him intently, her lips slightly parted. They made solid eye contact for a moment. A little startled, he looked down at the table, clenched his jaw and pretended not to notice the sudden tightness in his chest.

"We're back to questioning the last people to see Parker and that van," Patrick said a little too firmly, as he finished his coffee. He stood up, stretching. "The bank personnel, the courier personnel and whoever else knew the courier's schedule."

Michelle was enraptured, and a thought crossed her mind.

Patrick D'Laney is more than just hot — he's sharp too!

She was shocked at herself and her cheeks flushed. How could I think of him that way?

"Let's do it," said Michelle a little flustered, as she quickly gathered the papers on the table. She glanced cautiously in his direction. Patrick had apparently not noticed her reaction.

The officers spent the rest of the afternoon questioning Kyle's Courier Service's staff at Kyle's warehouse. There were seven employees in all, and their whereabouts could be accounted for on the previous Thursday. No one except George and Kyle Bishop knew the courier van's schedule.

Corporal D'Laney insisted on going over Kyle's and George's statements again — much to Kyle's annoyance. He voiced his objections loud and clear. Patrick listened patiently until he was spent.

"Look, Kyle," he said finally, "we can either do it here or down at the Detachment. And, you just know what Inspector Claude DuBois will have to say." Kyle settled down immediately and the interview continued.

"George," Patrick said, "you mentioned in your statement that during your last meeting with Parker, he had noticed a kid following him?"

"Yes."

"Did he say anything else, like whether it was a boy or girl?"

"Not really. He just said that he saw someone tailing him on a bicycle all over town for a couple of days," George said. "Except…."

"Except what, George?"

"Well," George answered, looking a little bewildered. "I remember Fred said he only noticed the kid because he kept changing his clothes."

★★★

Mr. Daniel P. Hiller, B.Com. CA., Assistant Manager of the Standard Bank in the town of Bolton was not a happy man. The last week had been extremely unpleasant, and the last three days had been sheer hell!

Mr. Hiller was the central figure in the 'Root Cause Investigation, file number CAN. 1112-12,' investigating 'Security Procedures Pertaining to Bolton-Edmonton Weekly Cash Receipts.'

Mr. Hiller had been called before the International Board of Directors of the Standard Bank in Edmonton. Director Phinias Muldoon, a most sarcastic and unpleasant man, had grilled him mercilessly on bank procedures for three consecutive days.

Mr. Hiller had heard via the grapevine that someone was always fired at the conclusion of such an investigation. He had an awful feeling that it might be him this time. And now, to add to his misery, Corporal D'Laney was here 'requesting' that he close the bank—in the middle of the day—for two or three hours while he and his partner conducted, essentially, the same investigation!

Mr. Hiller's eyes bulged a little behind his thick spectacles as he stared into the face of Corporal D'Laney.

"Very well," he said finally, expelling his breath and resigning to his fate with a sigh. "Phyllis," he called to one of the tellers, "please close the doors and stand by. Allow no more customers inside." He glanced across the floor and saw a familiar customer. "When Mrs. D'Laney-Andrews has concluded her business, lock the doors and return to your station."

Patrick turned to greet his sister. "Hello Mary," he said. He was pleased to see her again. "How are you, love?" He bent to kiss her cheek. "How's the family?"

"Hello, Patrick," she said, smiling up at him. "Fine, everyone is fine. I'm just in town to do a little shopping." She squeezed his arm.

They had not seen each other for several weeks and generally only saw each other on chance meetings such as this. Graham and Mary seldom entertained.

He tried not to show it, but Patrick was shocked at her appearance. Mary, just 34 years old, had dark shadows under her eyes which she had never had before and her pallor was grey despite heavy makeup. She looked like she had been crying.

"Brian?" he inquired. Mary smiled sadly and turned as Michelle walked over to join them.

Patrick introduced the ladies.

"Constable Michelle Monair, my sister, Mary D'Laney-Andrews," he said. "Mary, my new partner." He cocked his head.

Michelle turned to him as if to say something. She flushed a little, but said nothing.

Mary noticed the exchange. "Pleased to meet you, Michelle," she said with a little smile.

★★★

Patrick questioned each of the staff individually regarding the day in question, but no new evidence had come to light. Before calling it a day, Patrick and Michelle sat alone in Mr. Hiller's office and reviewed their notes.

"There's nothing pointing to any unusual activity in the bank on that day," Patrick said, speaking his thoughts allowed. "But someone must have learned of the schedule somehow." He studied his notes thoughtfully. "Mr. Hiller said that when he told Parker the pickup time, they were standing at the counter gate and he had not noticed anyone close enough to overhear them." He sat back in the big leather chair, tapping his lips with his index finger.

"That was the Thursday afternoon, prior to the accident," Michelle said, checking her own notes. Her brows furrowed. She got up from the chair in which she had been sitting, walked thoughtfully across the room and perched herself on the corner of the desk, and turned to Patrick.

"Did anyone overhear Mr. Hiller and Fred Parker talking at the counter?" She asked.

Patrick sat up slowly. He and Michelle stared at each other across two feet of desk for three seconds, until the penny dropped.

"Let's ask them!" They yelled in unison, and scrambled for the door.

★★★

"We know it was a while ago," Patrick said, addressing Mr. Hiller and the six staff members a short time later. Everyone was standing on the marble floor in front of the service counter, where they had been asked to assemble. "But if any one of you can remember seeing anyone, anyone at all, near to where Mr. Hiller and Mr. Parker were talking last Thursday afternoon, it may help us a great deal."

There was dead silence, and then a small voice spoke.

"There was a boy…"

Everyone turned to look at the pretty young teller.

"Marnie, do you know the boy's name?" Patrick asked again.

Patrick and Mr. Hiller had escorted the girl back to Mr. Hiller's office, where Michelle joined them a minute later. She closed the door and stood for a moment beside Mr. Hiller. Marnie was seated on one of the visitor chairs in the corner and Patrick was sitting on the edge of the desk looming over her like a vulture. The girl looked scared to death.

"What did he look like?" demanded the corporal.

"I…I don't know," Marnie said, wringing her hands in her lap.

Michelle strode across the room, took Patrick gently by the elbow and led him back to the big leather chair on the other side of the desk. She gave him a little shove as he sat down.

The girl giggled nervously.

"Marnie," Michelle said kindly, sitting beside her and gently holding her hand, "how do you remember the boy?"

"He wrote a deposit slip for $200,000.00," she answered.

"Did he write his name on the slip?" Michelle asked softly.

"Yes, but I threw it away."

"Think hard, try to remember, Marnie," Michelle pleaded. "It's very important."

"It…It was a boys name," Marnie said, desperately searching her mind. "Two boys names…Andy…Andy…Andrews! That's it! Brian Andrews!" Marnie squealed with anxious relief.

There was a stunned silence. Patrick flew out of the chair, sending it crashing against the bookshelf. Everyone jumped.

"We have to find Mary," he said coldly, as he headed out the door, his face like granite-stone.

Michelle shivered. *"There is a tide in the lives of men…"* she said quietly to herself, remembering a quote from Shakespeare.

★★★

Constable Monair, found Mary D'Laney-Andrews in Jenny's Department Store. Mary was looking for a coat for her youngest daughter, Beth. "Nine year olds are so easy to shop for, don't you think?" Mary asked a little too brightly, digging deeper into the rack and holding up a winter coat as Michelle came into view. "Kelly, my eldest, is sixteen and so fickle. When we go shopping for her, I just stand aside and she shops." "Hello Mary," said Michelle kindly, "We've been looking for you all over town."

Mary looked up from the rack, momentarily losing her composure.

"Why are you looking for me?" For a moment, her anguish showed in her eyes and then it was gone as she gathered herself once again.

Michelle looked at the woman whom she had only just met and her heart went out to her. Bolton was a small town and the private lives of its residents were like an open book. Mary D'Laney-Andrews' was no exception.

Michelle had listened to the stories, of the Andrews' family in earlier, happier times; and of the gradual alienation of her husband, Graham, and the family's heartaches due to the antics of her son, Brian.

Michelle stiffened her chin. This is my partner's sister, she thought, as of today, Mary has a new friend.

Michelle was escorting Mary across the street, when they saw Patrick just leaving Kang's Chinese Restaurant. He stopped and looked up and down the street with his hands on his hips.

Mary nearly choked. That was the last place on earth she would be.

"Trust Patrick to look for me in there," she muttered.

The growing angst in her chest came face to face with the ridiculous. She began a nervous giggle. That set Michelle off, and the two of them staggered across the street choking and spluttering, tears running down their cheeks, trying to hold back the laugh-bubbles, like two little girls forbidden to laugh in church.

Patrick D'Laney stood on the sidewalk and watched in amazement as the two hysterical women lurched towards him.

★★★

Corporal D'Laney sat at his favourite table in Maude's Donut Shop, grasping a cup of hot coffee and reflecting on the day's events.

The two women had composed themselves and quickly retired to the washroom for a little redecorating. A flash of light from a passing vehicle drew his attention to the window and he relaxed his grip a little. It was beautiful at this time of the evening.

The sky was an orange dome as it reflected the setting sun. The long wispy branches of the weeping birch with its new spring buds, brushed gently against the glass panes of the solarium as they swayed to the rhythms of the evening breeze. Traffic was light in the little town, and there were only a few quiet customers in the donut shop. There should always be such peace, he thought. He knew that this case was too close to home and he should pass it to another officer. He also knew that he would not.

The ladies returned and Maggie, their waitress, brought them coffee. She chatted for a while, then left to serve another customer. Patrick rose and sat across the table from Mary. He put his arms on the table as he leaned towards her. This was going to be difficult. He decided to be blunt.

"Mary, we have reason to believe that Brian may be involved in the Kyle's Courier accident." Mary looked blank. Patrick was stunned. She had no idea what he was talking about. Mary was living in a cave — a gilded cage, she had no idea what was happening in the world outside her home.

"Kyle's courier van ran off the road last Thursday night," he explained. "Money is missing and Fred Parker is in the hospital in critical condition."

"I had no idea…" she began. Then she remembered, and her face went very pale. "Oh Patrick," she said. "That was the night it rained so. Brian came home after four-thirty in the morning. I was so worried. I stayed awake all night waiting for him."

"How did he get home? Did someone drive him?" Patrick asked, his brow furrowing.

"No, Graham gave him the keys to the pickup three months ago," she explained nervously. "He only drives on the farm roads," she finished lamely, not believing it herself. Patrick needed a few moments to collect himself. He stood up and went to get some coffee.

"Is Brian at home right now?" Michelle asked, when he returned.

"I think so. He hasn't left the house…his room, since last Friday," Mary said hesitantly, her eyes widening. "He does that sometimes, preferring to be alone in his room…" her voice trailed away.

"We'd better go out there," Patrick said, standing up and slipping on his jacket. "We need to take a look at that truck."

Darkness had again descended upon the little town of Bolton.

Mary looked up at him through anguished tears that were forming in her eyes. She remembered that untidy room, with its oh-so typical certificates and charts on the walls, the books on the shelves, and the plastic skeleton in the corner, where her dreams were crushed and her nightmares were confirmed.

★★★

The sky was dark and overcast when they drove into the yard of the Andrews' estate. The brilliant sodium bulb of the yard-light bathed the scene with its golden glow.

The truck was still parked in front of the garage, where Brian had left it that early Friday morning, and it was still covered in the mud of its fateful journey. Mary vaguely remembered that Graham had told Brian to wash the vehicle but he had obviously not done so. Michelle swung the headlights of the police cruiser onto the pickup and took a deep breath. It was a '92 Ford.

Without touching the vehicle, Patrick shone his flashlight through the side window into the cab. He peered cautiously though the dried mud plastered on the window. On the back seat he could see an unopened can of beer still fastened in the plastic six-pack ring. The brand was clearly visible, printed on the side of the can, and it was the same brand as the can that Michelle had found at the crash scene.

Michelle got down on her knees and checked for the spare tire tucked under the box. The supporting rod hung down loosely, covered in dried mud. The wing nut was missing and the spare tire was gone.

Patrick and Michelle checked the rear of the truck together. Twin beams of the police flashlights pierced the gloomy interior of the dirt-splattered box simultaneously. The three onlookers gasped in amazement as the reflection of a thousand tiny glass mirrors gleamed like a carpet of diamonds in the back of the pickup.

★★★

CHAPTER FIVE
The Suspect

"You two did a good job," Inspector Claude DuBois said, addressing Patrick and Michelle in the briefing room of the Detachment. It was Thursday, one week after the accident. He had just gone through their completed reports with them in some detail.

The Andrews' pickup truck had been loaded and taken to the police yard for forensics soon after Michelle had called it in.

Inspector DuBois recalled the incident at the Andrews' estate. Apparently young Brian had caused quite a scene; he had even attacked one of the loading crew.

"Brian Andrews must have really been attached to that truck," the inspector said thoughtfully. Patrick nodded.

A week after the pickup truck was loaded and taken to the police yard; all the forensic reports were in. The reports confirmed police suspicions for the most part, though there were no identifiable fingerprints on the crushed beer can, the flashlight, or any of the mirror pieces.

"You are both to be commended," Claude told them with a nod, "you'll make a great team." He was quite pleased with himself; after all, he had put them together.

"Thank you, Sir." Michelle said. Patrick bit his lip, the jury was still out.

"I've set up a meeting with Graham and Mary Andrews along with the boy, Brian, for this afternoon," he said. "I want you two to be there." He looked at Patrick thoughtfully.

"You okay with that Patrick?"

"Yes, Sir."

"Okay." He nodded. "Now, get out of here. I've got work to do."

"Just one thing, Sarge," Patrick said, as they were leaving. "Could you ask Mr. Hiller to be at the meeting?"

Claude nodded, picking up the telephone.

★★★

The six of them sat around the long conference table in the briefing room at the 5th Detachment. Mr. Hiller had another appointment and would be a little late. The Inspector nodded, and Constable Monair turned on the tape recorder.

"Do we need a Children's Advocate?" Graham asked, testily.

"I don't think so," Claude answered. "This is just an informal get-together to try and find out how Brian fits into the picture and hear his side of the story. If you're uncomfortable with my questions, you don't have to answer — and you may leave at any time."

"Are you sure he's involved?" Graham asked, turning to Mary.

Claude glanced at Brian. "We'll lay out some of the evidence for you."

Brian sat in his chair not hearing a word. He was totally consumed by the knowledge that these people had taken away his beloved truck. The fire burned in his chest, settled in his gut and rose up in his throat and the back of his neck. He did not recognise the emotion as rage, but he liked it.

He had sat brooding in his room since that 'Black Friday', coming out only for meals or when he had no other choice. He was not aware of the passage of time, only that his beloved truck had been taken away from him; and along with it all his dreams, his focus, his fascination, the reason for his being.

He had made plans, many plans...but now...without his beloved truck to take him where he needed to be... the fire burned hotter.

"Pieces of the same mirrors were found in four places," Inspector DuBois continued. "The road where the mirror was set up, inside the courier van's head-light, at the dumpsite, and inside the box of Brian's truck. We found a beer can at the crash scene, the same brand as the one found in the back seat of the truck. A spare wheel, which fitted that particular truck has a matching tyre, and possibly belonging to the truck, was left at the dumpsite. We also found tire tracks that match the truck, and boot prints matching Brian's size at the same dumpsite."

"That's totally circumstantial," Graham said. "There could be a thousand reasons why those pieces of mirror got into the truck. You may be able to place him at the dumpsite, but not at the accident scene." He added triumphantly.

Claude sighed.

"You're missing the point, Graham," he said patiently. "We know that Brian is involved. We just don't know to what extent. And that's why we're here." He looked at Brian.

"Can you help us, Brian?" he asked. "Can you tell us how the mirrors got into your truck?"

Brian did not hear him.

Now they'll take my money! Now they'll take my money!
How I planned it, how I did it. That's my aim, my protection from
the deep places.

"…The money? Brian? …Do you know where we can find the money?
Brian? Brian?"

Ah ha!

Brian flew out of the chair like a cat, and jumped across the table, clawing
straight for the startled eyes and face of Inspector Claude DuBois. Mary
screamed. The boy's nails bit into Claude's eyebrow and cheek, his wild eyes
inches from Claude's. Brian opened his mouth to bite, his teeth bared.

Claude instinctively pulled away, tearing more skin off his face. He knocked
the boy aside and covered his eyes as the hot blood stung his pupil.

Patrick jumped up to grab the boy and in that two-second-melee, received
a head butt in his face and a wildly thrashing knee in the groin. He went down
like a rock.

Brian whirled around, his feet planted firmly on the table. He instinctively
focused his rage back on the injured inspector and, like the wild animal he was,
he pounced. Gaining a firm handhold of the inspector's hair with one hand,
Brian's fingers poised to strike at Claude's throat.

A lithe form streaked across the table. Grabbing Brian's shoulder, controlling
the momentum of her leap, she spun him over and pinned him deftly, face down
on the table like a bug. The pair slid to a squealing stop, inches from the edge of
the table. Constable Michelle Monair had nailed him good.

"You can't have my money! You can't have my money!" Brian screamed over
and over again, struggling to get free.

"But…the money's no good!" A voice called from the doorway. "You can't
spend any of it, anywhere!"

No good? The money's no good? Counterfeit!

Brian stopped screaming and went limp with shock. There was a deathly
silence in the room.

Everyone stood up very slowly, eyes cautiously watching the boy still pinned
under Michelle. They glanced questioningly at Mr. Hiller standing nervously in
the doorway.

"No." Mr. Hiller said. "The bills are marked — all of them. If one note
shows up anywhere, anywhere at all, the authorities would know instantly."
He clutched his briefcase nervously. "I…I thought you knew that." Mr. Hiller
looked at the officers.

"I did," Claude said, holding his bloody eye as he stood up, "but I didn't want
anyone else to know…still don't, so keep it to yourselves," he said gruffly.

He nodded to Michelle and she released the now placid Brian. Brian sat up
and began tapping on the table with his fingers, calm as could be — as if nothing
untoward had happened. They all stared at him.

Suddenly, a muffled, heart-wrenching cry came from the one person still
seated at the table. Everyone turned to the sound. Graham Andrews had come

face-to-face with a stark, raw reality. He covered his face with his hands and moaned in indescribable pain. Slowly, he leaned forward in his chair. There was no denying what his eyes and his ears had just witnessed, and 15 years of denial was unleashed all at once. The curved blade of human suffering pierced the heart of a good, gentle man. His pride, his hopes, his dreams, had burst like a bubble. His only son was mentally unbalanced.

The pain wracked his body and tore at his very soul. He would gladly have given all that he had at that moment not to know the truth — not ever to have known the truth.

Mary, who had always known, rested her head on her husband's shoulder and caressed his neck with her fingertips. His heart would heal with time. He would be fine...just fine... She would see to that. They would work through it together; she was no longer alone.

Brian got up from the table and slowly, absently, walked around the room, tapping quietly on the furniture and the walls with his fingers. His face was expressionless. Tapping, tapping, he was totally ignorant of the people in the room, the chaos that he had caused, or the tormenting aftermath. He came to the open door and walked out. With attention focused on the wretched Graham, nobody noticed that he had left, and by the time they did, he was gone.

★★★

Brian went home.

He picked up his bicycle from behind the donut shop and rode the two miles along the paved road to his house.

He opened the gate at the bottom of the driveway and rode up into the yard. He climbed the marble steps to the front porch, opened the great oak door and walked down the long hallway to his father's study. He entered the room, closed the door calmly behind him and walked across the plush Persian carpet to his father's desk. Brian found the keys in the top desk drawer where they always were, and removed a box of shells from the bottom drawer. He walked over to the gun case, unlocked it, took out his grandfather's bolt-action .22 rifle, and loaded it.

Brian sat down on the black leather couch, put the stock on the floor and the barrel in his mouth, and pulled the trigger.

★★★

CHAPTER SIX
The Doctors

"Oh, Matt!" She turned, and her hand flew to his chest. She looked up at him, her eyes pleading. Julie Martins and Matt Finch had been called to the scene.

He nodded his understanding. His eyes narrowed as he walked into the room and opened his trauma bag to begin the primary survey and ABC checks. They were a team, he and Julie, and they had been partners for almost two years. He was not concerned. He knew what she was made of.

Matt recalled a month earlier; there had been a terrible accident on Highway 111 just north of the city. A semi-trailer loaded with logs had struck a mini-van with a family of five on board. The semi driver had fallen asleep at the wheel and crossed over the median.

The father who was driving the van had tried to avoid the collision, but the semi struck the driver's side door, killing him and the baby in the back of the van instantly. The mother and daughter were knocked unconscious and suffered concussions, broken bones and lacerations.

A 12-year-old boy had been disembowelled by a metal splinter and was still conscious. He was writhing and screaming in terror inside the mangled, blood soaked van when they arrived on the scene. Julie had him calmed down and strapped onto the stretcher within five minutes. The boy survived.

They had received the call at the fire station in Edmonton, and within twenty minutes had sped to the Andrews' estate.

"The victim has a gunshot wound to the head," dispatch had said. There had been no mention of a child.

Everyone has nightmares, and Julie's were always about the children. She had dreams of children dying and their innocent blood spilling onto the rubble of their shattered homes. Children wounded and disfigured by mines, bombs and guns, and of orphaned children, with the look of raw fear and confusion on their faces. The difference was that when everyone else woke up, they realised that they had been dreaming; when Julie woke, she knew that it was real.

Matt looked at the boy slumped over the arm of the couch and saw the rifle lying at his feet on the carpet. The room still smelled of burnt powder. He looked over at the three police officers standing beside the couch. Their grim faces told the story.

"He's still alive." Inspector DuBois said.

★★★

Dr. Paul Strydom studied the x-rays carefully. The young man had been brought in half an hour ago with a gunshot wound to the roof of his mouth, and there was no apparent exit wound. The bullet had not had enough velocity to penetrate the top of the skull.

A small calibre round, he told himself thoughtfully. This was not a typical .22 gunshot wound. Probably a .22-short cartridge.

"There it is!" Dr. Bryce pointed excitedly to the dark form of the bullet lodged in the left frontal lobe as he clipped the x-ray plates on the light table in the operating room.

Dr. Strydom glanced at the intern as he washed up.

"This one certainly had a gift for stating the obvious," he muttered, loud enough to be heard.

"Let's just try to determine the trajectory of that projectile, shall we," Dr. Strydom said, sarcastically. The intern flushed.

Brian had been stabilised, though he was having trouble with some involuntary body functions, specifically respiratory, body temperature and heartbeat. He was hooked up to life support systems, but complex operations of the autonomic nervous system were beginning to shut down, and Dr. Strydom was concerned.

"I think judging from this plate, that the bullet somehow missed most of the limbic system, except for the hypothalamus, right here," Dr. Bryce said confidently, pointing to another x-ray. "That would account for the patient's current symptoms."

"Yes," Dr. Strydom agreed. "Except for tearing the amygdala right here," he indicated. "And at the top of the hippocampus, right here."

Dr. Bryce studied the x-ray plate, ignoring the sarcastic tone. "Yes," he said, "and that would mean that the bullet must have passed between the left and right hemispheres of the brain," he concluded. "There is a chance!"

Dr. Strydom looked at the intern in disgust. He was getting too hopeful.

"Through the corpus callosum," Dr. Strydom said, "to the back of the skull, where it bounced back like an eggbeater through the cerebrum and cerebral cortex to the frontal lobes, as you so kindly pointed out."

Dr. Bryce started, studying the x-rays again.

"He'll be brain dead!" Dr. Simon Bryce exclaimed, crushed.

"Let's operate." Dr. Strydom said, his ego satisfied. He glanced at the chart, and froze.

Blood type: AB–negative.

He turned slowly, purposely, towards the lights, the nurses and the bright shiny instruments, and to the 14 year old boy waiting quietly, unconscious on the operating table.

★★★

Dr. Paul J. Strydom had immigrated to Canada from South Africa 5 years earlier. He had earned degrees at the University of Stellenbosch, in the Eastern Cape Province, where he was born and raised. He had also attended the University of Witwatersrand where he earned his Ph.D. in Medicine. He had interned at the Good Hope University Hospital in Cape Town. It was at Good Hope where he had built his reputation as a brain surgeon over the following 22 years.

Brilliant and ambitious, Dr. Strydom had worked hard at his chosen profession. In South Africa, he had been taught by the best, and learned from the best. He had been ruthless with any opponent in his political drive to the top.

He joined the 'Brotherhood', the secret 'White Rule' society in South Africa, aimed at preserving and promoting the pure Master race in the Apartheid era. He rose to a prominent position in the ranks of the organisation and was widely respected — and feared. It was that fear that enabled him to intimidate subordinates and superiors alike. It was what gave him carte blanche to all medical facilities at Good Hope Hospital in Cape Town, and considerable control over the allocation of numerous, lucrative medical research grants. Dr. Strydom kept meticulous records of his research, produced sufficient generic data for the hospital files to keep his tenure, and kept his private files locked up in a safe at his home in Blaauberg, South Africa, a suburb across the bay from Cape Town.

★★★

Dr. Strydom stared at the ivory telephone on the glass–chrome coffee table, then at the big brass clock on the wall over the brick fireplace. Impatiently, he got up and walked through the uncovered French doors of his seventh floor apartment and out onto the patio.

There was a 9-hour difference in time zones between Edmonton, Canada, and Cape Town, South Africa.

I'll have to wait another hour anyway, he thought.

He leaned on the patio rail and stared out across the expanse of the twin golf courses resplendent in all their shades of green. His eyes followed the meandering North Saskatchewan River, up the valley towards its glacial origin in the Rocky Mountains. The sun was setting over his right shoulder, casting its golden hue on the hospital buildings across the valley. The mists forming in pockets in the lower areas, drifted like white spectres over the river. It was late May; summer was just around the corner.

Dr. Strydom saw none of the scenic beauty; his mind was occupied with other things. Having two critical patients, Parker and Andrews, with their particular physical conditions and matching blood-types, here at his hospital at the same time was amazing good fortune.

The coincidence was uncanny, surreal, he thought, — maybe even destiny!

At 57 years of age, Dr. Paul Strydom had never married, being far too self-centred and ambitious in his work to ever consider sharing his life. Lack of taste and the female touch was strikingly evident, judging by the décor in the sparsely furnished, 1700 square-foot apartment.

White-leather furniture was spread helter-skelter across a green-gold carpet, too large for the room. A blue La-Z-Boy chair faced a large television set. The components of a high quality stereo system were piled on shelves and boxes. Speakers were distributed randomly around the room. An untidy computer station occupied one corner of the living room. Dr. Strydom's personal journals were filed away in an oak-veneer file cabinet against one wall. The place was awful.

Dr. Strydom didn't care; his research and his work were his life. He was driven by an insatiable, inner privation to find the answers to his quest.

His masculine needs were easily met by the numerous escort services in the city, and quite simply, he preferred it that way — uncomplicated; not that he didn't have his favourites. Nevertheless, he seldom entertained at home, professionally, or otherwise.

★★★

The operation on the boy had gone as well as could be expected. Dr. Strydom had removed the bullet and found it to be intact, as he had expected, with little deformation due to the lighter charge.

He cauterised the wound and removed all the damaged brain tissue. He had been extremely careful using an electron microscope in the forebrain area, specifically around the limbic system where the controls for emotions, memory and thought processes were situated. Brian Andrews was stable, comatose and on minimal life support when all was done.

Dr. Strydom had ordered a PET scan for the following week, to determine just how much damage had been done. Positron Emission Tomography recorded biochemical changes in the brain. He did not hold out much hope that there would be any neurological activity in at least two of the four regions of the cortex.

The phone rang. He walked back into the apartment, waited, and lifted the receiver on the fourth ring.

"Hello?" Dr. Strydom answered casually. Dr. Colin Arthur Montgomery was on the other end of the line.

★★★

The relationship between Dr. Colin Montgomery and Dr. Paul Strydom began some 22 years before this particular telephone conversation took place; it started when Dr. Montgomery met Dr. Strydom on the first day that he arrived at Good Hope University Hospital in South Africa. The experience held no pleasant memories that Dr. Montgomery could recall.

Early on in his medical career, Dr. Montgomery found that he had more of a propensity towards the administrative side of the hospital than the surgical, and had focused his efforts on the former, by earning his MBA at Cape Town University.

Dr. Colin Arthur Montgomery, Chief Executive Officer, MBA, Ph.D., a graduate of Cambridge University, and of Cape Town University, was eminently qualified to run the institution.

In short order, Dr. Montgomery was promoted as 'Assistant to the Chief Operating Officer.' He was given a considerable amount of responsibility and influence with respect to the hospital's annual budgets and the distribution of research grant moneys. It was about that time that Dr. Strydom became his best friend.

Dr. Montgomery was no fool and recognised the precariousness of his situation at Good Hope University Hospital. He did not belong to the 'Brotherhood'.

Though officially responsible, Dr. Montgomery often bowed to the dictates of Dr. Strydom. He was prepared to bide his time: Dr. Montgomery knew that a change in government was inevitable and that he would win in the end — after all, he thought, he was British.

The good doctor had used his contacts in Scotland Yard, and through a relatively simple process and a little foreign currency, he had persuaded Dr. Strydom's trusted housekeeper to make copies of all Dr. Strydom's private files stored in the safe at his home in Blaauberg..

By then Dr. Paul Strydom had become a research scientist and was the Chief Medical Officer at the hospital. He had written a number of papers aimed specifically at the metabolic processes of the brain and had conducted extensive research into new, controversial surgical procedures using brain, and stem-cell tissue from aborted human foetuses.

As a scientist, Dr. Strydom was entitled to certain grant monies enabling him to perform his research. Dr. Montgomery had observed and even assisted in one of Dr. Strydom's earlier experiments. Dr. Strydom had primarily confined his research to animals such as rats, cats, dogs and later chimpanzees.

As time went by, and Dr. Montgomery rose to the position of Chief Operating Officer. Dr. Strydom used their friendship to obtain blanket approvals for his budgets. Gradually he became more and more aggressive, demanding access to unallocated grant moneys and even to Management Emergency Funds.

Finally, Dr. Montgomery had to draw the line.

"No, Paul!" he told him, on one particular occasion when Dr. Strydom had cornered him in his office. "That money was donated to the hospital specifically for AIDS research, by the patriarch of a very prominent Cape Town family. It's in

Arthur Hayward's will for crying out loud!" Dr. Strydom looked surprised for a second and lifted an eyebrow.

"This trust fund could help eliminate an AIDS epidemic, not just here, but throughout Southern Africa," Dr. Montgomery continued hastily. "Your research is revolutionary and controversial, and despite that, you have always received good funding. I cannot justify funding your research into what may help man in the future, compared to funding AIDS research that may save thousands today; those who are dying right now, and the millions that it will save tomorrow.

"And besides," Dr. Montgomery added. "You have an excellent research grant already, better than in previous years."

To Dr. Montgomery's surprise, Dr. Strydom didn't buy it. His impassioned speech had meant nothing.

Over the following two weeks, Dr. Strydom continued to pressure Dr. Montgomery for the Hayward grant at every opportunity — as a friend, of course.

★★★

Major Pieter van Zyl, head of the secret police in Cape Town, was a noticeable social figure in the city. He frequently attended functions at the hospital and other prominent public gatherings. The local pub near the hospital was frequented by regular hospital staff, so when Dr. Montgomery caught a glimpse of the Major as he crossed the floor and seated himself in a rear booth, a few days later, he was curious, but paid no more attention.

It was better not to be too involved with the secret police. He was told that they were easy to spot because they always wore *veldskoen*, shoes made from raw leather, and that they wore them everywhere regardless of the occasion — from the beach to the ballroom.

Dr. Montgomery had arranged to meet with Dr. Strydom and a couple of lady friends for a drink and a game of cards. He enjoyed a social evening once in a while.

Dr. Montgomery had been married once, a long time ago, and had a daughter, Terry. She was eighteen now, and lived with her mother in England. Dr. Montgomery's sister, Kathy, was married to a South African sugar-cane farmer named Jannie Stein, and lived somewhere in northern Kwa-Zulu Natal province, on the east coast of South Africa. They seldom saw each other.

He and Dr. Strydom played squash every Saturday morning and every Thursday afternoon; it was their only regular extracurricular activity. The two met at the pub once in a while on a Friday night to unwind and mingle with the 'peasants', as Dr. Strydom referred to the working class.

Dr. Montgomery glanced around the traditional British-style pub, but did not see his companions, though there were many there from the hospital that he recognised. He returned their greetings casually. No one would intrude on his privacy without an invitation. He ordered a pint and sat alone at the bar enjoying the ambience.

The pub was called 'The White Knight,' and portrayed a knight carrying a lance, seated on a rearing stallion. The white outline of the figure was super-imposed on a black marble background and hung on plaques on the walls all around the softly lit room. The cherry-wood bar ran half the length of the room and swivel high-back barstools overhung the heavy brass footrest beneath the bar.

Dark blue backlighting reflecting on the mirrors, glasses and the bottles behind the bar created the mood. Black wooden tables and chairs were strewn randomly across the floor. Privacy booths set along the back wall were bathed in shadows and hidden from view from the main room by strategically placed, large tropical plants. The band played the blues — not very well, but the place was packed every Friday and Saturday night anyway.

An hour went by and nobody turned up. Dr. Montgomery finished his beer and was just about to leave, when two burly individuals in dark brown suits settled down on the barstools on either side of him.

Dr. Montgomery looked down.

Veldskoen shoes. His blood ran cold — this could not be good. He tried to turn away but they blocked him in.

"Mr. Montgomery?" the one on his left said, with a thick Afrikaans accent.

"Dr. Montgomery," he corrected bravely.

"*Mister* Montgomery, the man repeated insolently, we got a problem."

"What kind of problem?" His mouth was dry.

"We hear you're taking money from the hospital and giving it to terrorists."

"What? How?" Dr. Montgomery was really startled. A man could be hanged for that!

"Donations from Mr. Arthur Haywood's estate."

"That money is going to AIDS International!" Dr. Montgomery exclaimed incredulously.

"They are terrorists," the man on the right said, matter-of-fact. He had bad breath as well as a thick accent. "Better to keep the money in the hospital." He casually raised his hand, and thumped the muscle above Dr. Montgomery's knee with the protruding knuckles of his clenched fist. Dr. Montgomery winced with pain.

"Maybe you got a friend who's not a terrorist," the thick accent said, his face very close to Dr. Montgomery's ear.

Dr. Montgomery was so scared he could not speak.

"See you later *Mister* Montgomery." They got up very slowly and left the pub.

Dr. Montgomery sat there with his arms on the bar, breathing hard; his heart pounding in his ears. He glanced around the room. Nobody had even noticed. His leg hurt.

At that moment, a match flared in the shadowed private booth as Major Pieter van Zyl lit a cigarette. In the flash, Dr. Montgomery saw the unmistakable features of Dr. Strydom, sitting beside him at the table.

***

"You want to do *what* with the grant money?" Dr. Montgomery said, shocked and amazed at the audacity of his companion. He rose from his chair and stared at Dr. Strydom.

They had been sitting comfortably in Dr. Montgomery's office discussing the distribution of Arthur Hayward's estate. Dr. Strydom inspected his nails as he lay back in the red leather easy chair.

"I tell you I'm fed up with it, Colin," Dr. Strydom said frowning. "These people tying up the operating rooms with their elective surgical demands, while I have important work to do.

Liposuctions, abortions, breast implants, penis enlargements — it just goes on and on."

He swung around and faced Dr. Montgomery with a smile.

"I want to have my own, completely outfitted, operating room," he repeated slowly.

"Out...out of the question!" Dr. Montgomery stammered. "A total misappropriation of funds." He shook his head, trying to stay calm. "Maybe if you submitted a proposal for long range capital expenditure next year, we could consider it."

Dr. Strydom stopped smiling. He sat up. His voice hardened.

"That would take years. I don't think we can afford to wait while our funding is being siphoned away, do you?"

Dr. Montgomery blanched as if he had been struck. He sat down heavily in his chair. Dr. Strydom grinned at him. He knew that he had won. He settled back in his easy chair and continued.

"I want the operating rooms right next to my research lab," Dr. Strydom continued. "Oh, and there will be a small recovery room attached. Oxygen, EKG, dialysis, all that sort of thing. I'll send you a list of equipment." He waved his hand, rotating his wrist absently. "I'll probably have some human patients down there as well."

Dr. Strydom stood up and walked to the door. "The contractor will bring the plans around for your approval this afternoon." He glanced over his shoulder and stopped at the door. He looked down at his shattered friend.

"Colin, so glum!" he said brightly. "We must celebrate. Your place, tonight! I'll bring some people over and a case of fine Stellenbosch wines." He closed one eye, pointed a finger at Dr. Montgomery and left the room, closing the door behind him.

Dr. Montgomery stared blindly at the closed door for a long time. He turned towards the telephone, picked up the receiver and dialled a long distance number.

"Hello? Christopher, is that you? Yes....Colin Montgomery ...good...good. Tell me Christopher; are you still with Scotland Yard...MI-6?"

Within the next six weeks, with the help of his old friend Christopher Barkley, Dr. Colin Arthur Montgomery, code name 'Catcher,' became a mole at Cape Town University Hospital on behalf of Scotland Yard, for the following two years.

★★★

Scotland Yard of course, saw a much bigger picture. Their objective at that time was to set up as wide an information network as possible, in light of the imminent change in the South African government.

Scotland Yard had little interest in the individual activities of Dr. Strydom. Their concern was directed at the stability of the country, the maintenance of law and order, and the safety of British Citizens in the event of civil war. That meant being forewarned in the event of catastrophe. Colin Montgomery was a very small piece in the puzzle, a footnote in the file.

In the two years that followed, except for providing Christopher Barkley access to Dr. Paul Strydom's personal files, Dr. Colin Montgomery had done nothing even remotely covert. Nevertheless, the charade did give Dr. Montgomery a much-needed boost to his ego.

He was a British spy in the service of his country. Dr. Montgomery laughed heartily at the designation, and even harder at the code name, "Catcher." He had made it abundantly clear that he felt that Christopher was taking his job far too seriously.

Dr. Montgomery and Christopher Barkley were old school chums, having gone through high school together and had later roomed together at Cambridge University. Christopher's brother Andrew and his family lived near Cape Town. They were a close family. Dr. Montgomery visited his own family back in England only once a year.

Dr. Montgomery and Christopher's paths crossed frequently, and on one particular occasion the two met for lunch at the city zoo.

Later that same afternoon, Dr. Montgomery walked briskly into his office where his secretary had delivered his mail, already sorted and categorised. He sat down and idly shuffled through the pile, his mind still lingering on an amusing anecdote that Christopher had portrayed during the lunch meeting.

Suddenly, he stopped short as something caught his eye. He picked up a bundle of hand-written envelopes and letters tied together with a yellow rubber band. They were addressed to him, or at least to The Director, but the address had been crossed out with a thick red marker and re-addressed to Dr P. J. Strydom. He called his secretary on the intercom and asked her to step into his office for a moment.

"Sarie, why have these letters been re-addressed," he asked.

"Oops! You're not supposed to get those," she said with a smile, a little embarrassed.

"Just got them mixed up with your mail. Sorry, Doctor." She quickly stepped up to the desk and was about to take them away.

"But, wait a minute, Sarie," he said, placing his hand over the letters. "These letters are addressed to me. Answer my question."

She looked confused. "It's always been like that, Doctor," she said. "I open all the mail, and if there's a letter regarding one of Dr. Strydom's patients, I forward it to him."

"On whose authority did you do that?" Dr. Montgomery raised his voice an octave. "How long has this been going on?"

Sarie gulped and went beet red. "It's always been like that," she blurted, squeezing her fingers.

Dr. Montgomery took a deep breath and sighed. "Very well, Sarie," he said. "That will be all.... Leave these," he added sternly, as she moved to collect the letters.

"But... but Dr. Strydom said..." she stopped. She looked awful. Dr. Montgomery nodded to the door and she left the room.

She was wrong, no matter which way she turned, Dr. Montgomery thought. Catch 22. He dismissed her discomfort from his mind, and concentrated on the letters.

The plain yellow paper had been carefully printed on in pencil, the letters bold and uneven as if written by a child. He frowned as he read the words.

Dear Boss Director of the hospitaal,

My name is Maria M'Babani. My daughter came to your hospitaal to fix the pain in her head. My daughter is named Loni and is 17 years old. We brought her down from the Swartberg.

We spoke to boss doctor Strydom when we got to the hospitaal. Boss doctor said she would be fine in a few days. We have come to the hospitaal two times from the Swartberg and can not find her. Three months and we can not find her. We talked to the policeman. The policeman say talk to the boss Director.

Boss Director, Please give my daughter back to me.

Maria M'Babani.

And another:

Excuse me Sir,

My wife came to your hospital. She doctor said she had the AIDS. Doctor Strydom say he would try to correct the sickness in her head but she died.

Can I claim the body of my wife, please sir. I have asked six times and nobody tells me when.

I must bury my wife at home by her child.

Thank you Sir,

Moses N'ugoni

And another:

Dear Sir Director

I am writing to you about my brother Mango who went last month to the hospital because he had a very painful earache inside his head. Doctor Strydom say he will fix him but he died. My brother is 9 and me too. I have a earache too. Will I die too?

Sandra XhuKosi

And another…and another…. He read them all, carefully, one at a time.

When he was done, Dr. Colin Arthur Montgomery squeezed his eyes shut and sat back in his chair, but the fierce tears would not be stayed. He felt the waves of hopelessness and shame ebb and flow through his very being. He did not try to stop the pain but let it run its course.

He was the Chief Executive Officer, responsible for the entire hospital, yet he had no control of the situation. He had no control because he was afraid of Paul Strydom, a common bully with connections in the dreaded secret police.

Now even patients in his hospital were at risk, used as human guinea pigs and some had already paid a terrible price because of his cowardice. He shuddered again with agony of his guilt. For years he had slowly buckled down under the bullying of Paul Strydom, accepting each level of degradation, until he was almost an empty shell.

Almost, but not quite!

Dr. Montgomery lifted his trembling chin, clenched his teeth and a glint of grim determination came into his eye that had not been there for a long time. His shame helped him summon up the remainder of his courage.

It was time to take a stand!

Dr. Montgomery re-read all the letters. He then scanned them into his computer and sent an e-mail complete with the attachments to Christopher Barkley, care of Scotland Yard.

★★★

It was midnight by the time Dr. Montgomery finished, but a hospital never sleeps. He took the master keys from his desk, left his office and walked down the hall to the elevator. He used his keys and rode the elevator to the lower basement floor level.

He walked down the narrow, darkly lit green-painted stone corridor. Pipes, cable trays and ventilation ducts ran the full length of the tunnel to the door marked

Research Laboratory. Authorised Entry Only.

This was Dr. Strydom's private domain. Dr. Montgomery opened the door and walked in.

There was no one in the laboratory. Dr. Montgomery sighed with relief. He had hoped that there would not be anyone there at that time of night. Colin had not been down to the lower level in quite some time. He stared in amazement at the sophisticated equipment, far more than when he had first toured the facility two years before. He shuddered at the cost.

Dr. Montgomery walked into the operating room, switched on the light and was utterly astonished. The equipment displayed in the facility, though smaller, was far more superior to anything that they had in the rest of the hospital.

A great stainless steel door at the other end of the room caught his attention. He walked over to it, pulled the handle and the door swung open.

It was a cooler, and it was packed from floor to ceiling with jars, bottles and tanks, all neatly labelled — and filled with human brains.

"What are you doing here?" Dr. Strydom asked from the doorway. He was distinctly hostile. Dr. Montgomery jumped. For a moment, his newfound courage teetered on the brink, then gathering his resolve, he turned.

"Just snooping around, Paul," he said with a smile. "I thought that you might be here. Let's go and have a drink." Dr. Montgomery walked past him and strolled over towards Dr. Strydom's office, deliberately ignoring the fine beads of perspiration on his forehead. Dr. Strydom followed suspiciously.

★★★

"You're going to do what?" Dr. Strydom exploded, vaulting out of his chair and spilling his drink on the table.

They were seated in Dr. Strydom's rather ostentatious office attached to the laboratory. Dr. Strydom had poured them each a generous brandy as they had made themselves comfortable on the green leather chairs.

"I'm going to have to shut down this facility," Dr. Montgomery repeated calmly. He was not about to be intimidated any more as his smouldering anger kept his emotions in check. With a superhuman effort, he picked up his drink without a tremor. "As of the end of this week," he said, saluting his host with the glass. He took a sip. '*Oude Meester.*' He nodded approvingly, recognizing the brand. He replaced his brandy glass on the table. Dr. Montgomery's confidence was rising.

For the first time that he could remember, maybe for the first time ever, he had the upper hand over Dr. Paul Strydom. A heated one-sided discussion ensued in which Dr. Montgomery remained calm and undaunted in the face of a tirade from Dr. Strydom. When Dr. Strydom finally resorted to veiled threats, Dr. Montgomery had had enough.

"I'm sorry, Paul," he said, shrugging as he rose to leave. "It's too expensive. The hospital just can't afford it anymore. This experiment is over." He was not in the least bit sorry. Dr. Strydom stood there, barely hiding his fury, unable to speak. He watched silently as Dr. Montgomery bid him goodnight and casually walked out into the corridor, closing the door behind him without a backward glance.

Dr. Paul Strydom picked up his empty glass, replenished it and drained the contents in a single swallow. He sank back into his chair and stared across at Dr. Montgomery's brandy glass half empty on the table. He drank that too. After a time he reached across and picked up the telephone. He dialled a local number.

"I would like to speak to Major Pieter van Zyl, please. Yes…. yes… it is a matter of National Security," he said.

★★★

Dr. Colin Arthur Montgomery was arrested the following night at 3.30 in the morning in accordance with the custom of the secret police at the time. He was then held in detention for six months without any charges being laid, and during which time Dr. Montgomery was treated the same as any other political prisoner in the Apartheid regime.

It was not good.

★★★

Sergeant Frikkie Marais of the South African Police Force was put in charge of investigating the allegations against Dr. Montgomery. Sergeant Marais was a good police officer and justly proud of the fine reputation of the institution to which he belonged. He did not concern himself with other misguided factions of the force.

Sergeant Marais, on being handed the file on the second day after the arrest of Colin Montgomery, immediately requested a meeting with Major Pieter van Zyl of the secret police.

Major van Zyl had taken a personal interest, and was well acquainted with the case. He had long ago seen the opportunity to make significant political and social inroads into Cape Town high society by being closely associated with the celebrated Dr. Paul Strydom. He had been quick to take advantage when the opportunity presented itself.

"My agents have been following a known British espionage agent named Christopher Barkley, from Scotland Yard's MI-6, for years," he told Sergeant Marais. "And just last week, he was seen meeting covertly with Montgomery at the Cape Town City Zoo."

"What did they discuss?" Sergeant Marais asked.

"We don't know that yet," Major van Zyl answered. "But we do know Montgomery's code name is 'Catcher'."

"How do you know that?"

"We picked Barkley up the same night we arrested Montgomery," said the Major, protruding his chin. "We have ways of making them talk."

Sergeant Marais shuddered. *Now where have I heard that before?* He thought.

"Can I talk to the prisoner?" he asked.

"No."

"Can I see the arrest file?"

"No."

Sergeant Marais spent the following weeks going through Dr. Montgomery's house and office. Both locations had been sealed off shortly after his arrest. He found nothing incriminating. He went through all the phone records and found that Dr. Montgomery had called Christopher Barkley quite frequently at his home in London as well as at his office in Scotland Yard. He also found out that they had been school friends and had attended Cambridge University together.

The sergeant had Dr. Montgomery's computers packaged up and sent down to the Department for analysis. All the files were printed to hard copy and he went through everything, piece by piece. Sergeant Marais was impressed; Dr. Montgomery was articulate, meticulous and precise in his work.

Sergeant Marais was beginning to think that someone had made a terrible mistake, when he found the e-mail addressed to Christopher Barkley, care of Scotland Yard. He checked the date that it had been sent. The sergeant was puzzled.

Why had Montgomery sent an e-mail to Barkley in England when he knew that he was still here in Cape Town at the time?

Barkley had not even seen the message. He had been arrested before returning to England. Sergeant Marais read the e-mail, and his eyes widened.

Christopher:

I am sending you this information so that you might add it to the Strydom file.

I am now convinced that Dr. Paul Jacobus Strydom used his position and the freedom at this hospital to perform illegal, unauthorised experimental surgery on human patients. Please see the attached letters from the families.

Strydom selected patients with relatives who would have had little influence should they complain to the authorities; and his connections to the secret police even kept me out of the loop until just recently. There are no records of these individual patients or any acknowledgement of them even being admitted in the official hospital files.

I have remained closeted in my office at this hospital for years in fear for my own personage — ignoring any suggestion of impropriety. In doing so, I have neglected a most sacred duty to the patients who placed their trust and their very lives in my hands.

I now know that I must share the responsibility for these crimes, due to my apathy and cowardice. I see no alternative but to challenge Dr. Paul Strydom and his criminal network directly and face the consequences.

Sincerely yours,

Colin.

Sergeant Frikkie Marais concluded that Major Pieter van Zyl and Dr. Paul Jacobus Strydom had framed Dr. Colin Arthur Montgomery.

Sergeant Marais submitted his report through normal channels. He was honest, accurate and corroborated all the facts. He also sent a copy to the highest-ranking officer in his department. The report essentially absolved Dr. Colin Montgomery of any seditious wrongdoing.

Major Pieter van Zyl saw the report and dismissed it. He saw no reason to inform Dr. Strydom of the Barkley e-mail. Sergeant Frikkie Marais was not a fool. The report did not implicate Pieter van Zyl in any way.

But the wheels of justice turn slowly, and though the sergeant inquired periodically to ensure that the wheel did not stall altogether, it was a full six months before Dr. Colin Montgomery was free again.

On the day that Dr. Montgomery was released, Sergeant Marais was there to greet him, and escorted him to his hotel. Following the normal pleasantries, and finding that Dr. Montgomery had no specific plans, Sergeant Marais assured Dr. Montgomery that his position at Cape Town University Hospital was secure.

"Thanks sergeant," Dr. Montgomery smiled ruefully, "But I can't go back there."

"The hospital needs you, Dr. Montgomery; the country needs you." Sergeant Marais pleaded, but to no avail; he could not convince Dr. Montgomery to change his mind.

"Sooner or later Dr. Strydom and I would clash again," said Dr. Montgomery, "I am terrified of him, he is a very ruthless, sadistic man and I will lose."

They rode in silence for a while.

"Let me see what I can do," said the sergeant, after a thoughtful moment, "I know some people, who know some people, who may be able to help us.

"Have you ever met the Zulu Minister of the Interior, Dr. Moshessa Dingaan?" He asked.

★★★

Life slowly returned to normal at the hospital following Dr. Colin Montgomery's arrest. Various senior faculty members were appointed temporarily to perform his duties; none interfered in the affairs of Dr. Paul Strydom.

Dr. Strydom was in his element. He was close, very, very close to his life's ambition. It had been a long 15 years since he had made the first connection.

While conducting a lesion method experiment on a living patient, which involved the removal of sections of the brain and then observing the effects, he had found that patients with AB-negative blood produced endorphins that functioned as neurotransmitters under stress. In turn, this led to the generation of a growth-promoting protein, which produced new neurons — brain cells which continued to divide and multiply.

In essence, the protein tried to grow back more brain tissue to correct the damaged areas. Not enough, of course, to regenerate a major section of the brain such as a lobe, but with the help of a little dopamine-producing brain tissue (grafted from aborted, living foetuses with AB-negative blood) along with carefully balanced levels of biochemicals such as serotonin and acetylchlorine, cuts, tears and transplanted tissue in the brain would heal and regenerate itself over time.

Dr. Strydom had performed the same operation (unsuccessfully) on 15 living patients to date. The last patient, operated on just one week ago, had been stabilized and lived a full forty-six hours after the operation. An autopsy had shown that a ruptured suture had caused an embolism. They just hadn't caught it in time.

He summoned the entire Department Operating Team in the conference room adjoining the laboratory. They poured over film footage of the latest operation surrounded by charts, reports and computers displaying and analysing anatomical and biochemical changes in the patient's brain. Dr. Vanderberg made his report.

"The electroencephalogram, or brain-wave recordings, taken by the EEG machine, produced patterns that were combined and enhanced with the very latest computer technology," Dr. Vanderberg said. "Thus suppressing all background noise in the brain, leaving only the electrical response, which was stable throughout the procedure as you can see here." The laser light in his hand pinpointed the area.

"And you can see from the PET scan that biochemical changes were active only in those areas where they should be," Dr. Harley noted. "The medulla and the pons, which govern breathing and heart rate and other automatic functions, as shown by the glucose consumption of the nerve cells."

The analysis and discussions lasted another 6 hours, and concluded that everything had been progressing exactly according to plan. There was just that one error that had been the cause of the fatality.

"A ruptured suture for crying out loud!" Dr. Strydom spat, as he cast a jaundiced eye about the room at his team. "Why didn't your magnetic resonance imaging pick it up, Dr. Margery?" he demanded bitterly. "Isn't your machine supposed to detect blood flow?"

"Yes," the doctor answered calmly, "but the MRI works indirectly. It detects blood flow by picking up magnetic signatures from blood that has given up its oxygen to active brain cells." Dr. Margery unrolled a tape to identify the affected area.

"Besides," she continued, "we didn't pick it up because our MRI is too slow to map an activity in real time."

"Not good enough, doctor," Dr. Strydom said coldly, glaring at her across the table. "I will not tolerate incompetence! Your services will no longer be required in this program. And that goes for all the nursing staff on duty as well," he added spitefully, as an afterthought. He felt a little more compensated for the failure.

Dr. Margery gathered her materials, rose, and left the room without a word.

Dr. Strydom dismissed the team and retired to his office, where he poured himself a stiff drink. Darkly, he sat staring at the bare wall pondering his next move on the road to immortality.

He would have to be just as selective next time. That boy with the damaged auditory cortex had been a perfect specimen. Probably got that from getting cracked on the side of the head for not listening to his master, he thought, not realising how prophetic his thoughts were. And that girl with the small, operable brain tumour was irreplaceable.

Dr. Strydom smiled to himself as he realized his mistake.

"Irreplaceable? With all these 'kaffirs' around here? Yah, right!" he muttered, referring derogatorily to the poorest segment of the South African black population.

Dr. Strydom sighed. Still, he really would have liked to have those last two specimens back. Too bad they didn't live through it. He stretched, got up and poured himself another glass of brandy.

A few weeks later, Dr. Paul Strydom received a message requesting his presence in the executive boardroom the following day. The main item on the agenda was to meet the new CEO of the hospital. The new majority government had been in power in the New South Africa for five months and the change had not affected Dr. Strydom in any way; his life and work had carried on as usual.

The catastrophic civil war predicted by the foreign media had not materialised. The peaceful transition of power was due entirely to the phenomenal foresight and efforts of De Klerk and Mandela. Dr. Strydom had however lost contact with his friend, Major van Zyl, of the secret police, some three months before.

Dr. Strydom walked into the executive boardroom at the appointed time. He was greeted by the sight of 26 other department heads standing around drinking coffee and snacking on the catered sandwiches laid out on the tables at the back of the room.

The room was huge. Warmly-lit by two chandeliers, one at each end. The mood in the rectangular-shaped room was balanced by pale yellow sconce lights on dimmer switches, which ran along the length of the rosewood-panelled walls. The most striking feature in the room was the great yellowwood conference table, surrounded by 30 deluxe black leather swivel chairs.

"Colonial extravagance," Dr. Strydom muttered, totally unimpressed. These meetings were excruciatingly painful to him. As far as he was concerned they were unproductive — a complete and utter waste of his time. He switched off, his mind already focused on neurotransmitters. There was one particular epilepsy patient with abnormal gamma-amniobutyric acid and glutamate levels — and type AB-Negative blood.

"Gentleman!" called Dr. Bernard de Lange, "Would you please take your seats." Everyone settled down. Dr. Strydom was seated farthest away from the speaker to his right.

"First order of the day," Dr. de Lange continued brightly. "I would like to introduce our new acting Chief Executive Officer, Dr. Philemon Thlabati"

Dr. Paul Strydom, irritated at having had his thought pattern interrupted, glanced towards the head of the table and was instantly shocked out of his day-dreams. He propelled himself out of his chair and reeled backward until his back hit the wall with a resounding thump.

At the podium, before a room full of eminent senior scientists, doctors and professors stood a young man, around twenty-four years old. Dr. Thlabati smiled confidently in his new domain.

Dr. Strydom could not believe his eyes. A black boy was his new boss!

***

Philemon Thlabati was the son of a Zulu sub-chief. He was born and raised in the Valley of a Thousand Hills in what is now northern Kwa-Zulu Natal, on the west coast of South Africa. He had walked the 5 miles from the mud hut in the hills that he called home, every day, rain or shine, to attend Zululand High School (for blacks only) in Eshowe, where he graduated top of his class. (He had been the only student from the area to graduate that year, out of 187.)

Philemon decided in his final year of high school that he would like to be a doctor and confidently applied to Eshowe Hospital for a position as a Junior Doctor. Since he was the son of a sub-chief of the Zulus, he was hired immediately, but with the understanding that he should start at the bottom. Philemon agreed, and for 2 years he took out the garbage.

Towards the end of his 2nd year, during one of his rounds collecting the garbage, he met a patient, a young white boy around his own age. Philemon met the boy for two reasons:

One: the boy spoke to him.

No white person ever spoke to him in the hospital.

Two: the boy spoke to him in perfect Zulu.

No white person in the hospital spoke perfect Zulu.

"Good day to you, honourable Zulu man," the boy said, recognising the traditional scarring on the face of the son of a Zulu sub-chief.

"Good day to you, young white man. I'm sorry you are dying," Philemon replied. The boy had a hereditary heart disease and was confined to a hospital bed indefinitely. He had come to Eshowe Hospital to end his days.

Formalities over, the white boy continued.

"What the fuck are you doing down there in the shit like a kaffir?"(Black servant.)

"Hauk! Baas?" (What?) Philemon was astonished.

Philemon told the white boy of his ambition to become a man of medicine and that he had almost 2 years now as a Junior Doctor. The white boy listened attentively to his story, injecting only the obligatory clicks and grunts of acknowledgement.

When Philemon was quite done with his story, the white boy kindly explained the facts of life in the white man's world. And when he had finished, Philemon rose slowly up off his haunches.

"I will get my *assegai* and my *panga*, and I will kill that black son-of-a-bitch janitor who hired me," he said passionately, referring to his tribal spear, with the foot long blade, and his machete.

Petrus Stein, for that was the boy's name, nodded in agreement. It was the honourable thing to do.

"And I will help you, since I am dying anyway," he said, "but, we must plan this despicable janitor's humiliating death very carefully."

Philemon spent as much time as he could with Petrus over the next few weeks, as they perfected their plan to ambush and slaughter the despicable janitor.

Doctor Markus, the resident doctor, was much impressed with Petrus's progress as a result of the boy's relationship, so when the janitor tried to fire Philemon Thlabati for dereliction of his garbage duties, the doctor appointed Philemon as Petrus's full time nurse, and doubled his salary.

Philemon learned that Petrus lived with his mother and father and two younger sisters. They owned a three thousand-acre sugar-cane plantation in the rolling hills near the town of Amatikulu, about forty-five miles from Eshowe. Petrus was born on the plantation, and ever since he could remember, he had had a Zulu nanny. Mabel, for that was her European name, who carried him around slung on her back and tied with a blanket, while still attending to her household duties.

To his mother's dismay, Petrus had learned to speak Zulu long before he spoke English. He even spoke Zulu at the provincial primary school in Gingingdlovu attended only by white children. He spoke Zulu, not only because of Mabel, his beloved nanny, but because there were very few white children around on the wild north coast at that time, and they all spoke Zulu.

Zulus have lived in their traditional kraals, villages of mud and thatch huts, in the hills and forests surrounding the plantation for two-thousand years. Zulu children were everywhere. Petrus learned to play Zulu games, and to fight like a Zulu with sticks and a shield. Most of all he learned to respect the Zulu people — their ancient history and their traditions.

Petrus taught Philemon the white man's ways, about white man's values, of commerce, business and education. Philemon taught Petrus how to live. Together they researched the steps Philemon needed to take, and the qualifications he would need to become a medical doctor.

Both Philemon and Petrus were amazed and bewildered at the sheer volume of what Philemon needed to know, but they were not discouraged. Philemon was unwavering in his quest. As soon as he had saved enough money, he would apply for admission to the University of Zululand in Empangeni — right after he murdered the despicable janitor, of course.

The boys worked long, hard hours in the hospital library preparing Philemon for his journey. Even Dr. Markus took an active interest in the curriculum when he recognized their determination.

Finally the day came when Petrus Stein could go home. He had been in hospital almost a year and a half. Petrus considered his options. He would not be physically strong enough to work on the farm for a while, and quite likely, never would. He made his decision and discussed it very carefully with his parents.

"So you would like to study medicine?" his father said thoughtfully, pursing his lips. "Well, if that's what you want, my boy, we are here for you." Jannie Stein turned to his wife questioningly. Kathy Montgomery-Stein smiled and nodded quietly in agreement.

"Papa?"

"Yes, my son."

"Philemon Thlabati saved my life," he said. "He wants to be a doctor too."

"I know," his father replied, with a lump in his throat. "I will ask the headman if I may speak with Philemon's father, the witchdoctor and the elders."

The Stein family had lived in that land for four generations. Jannie Stein was well versed in the customs of the Zulu people. He had often witnessed the power of the witchdoctors of the village and he respected the nobility and dignity of the elders and the sub-chiefs of the Zulus.

A year later, Philemon Thlabati and Petrus Stein attended the University of the Witwatersrand in Johannesburg, where they began their studies in medicine together.

Philemon Thlabati sliced off a piece of the ear of the despicable janitor with his machete. The janitor considered that a fair price for insulting the honour of the son of a sub-chief of the Zulus and never, ever complained.

★★★

Dr. Philemon Thlabati, first year intern, and acting Chief Executive Officer, sat in his new office at Good Hope University Hospital and stared at the desk, trying to concentrate on the reams of paper in front of him. It was no use; after just three months in the position, Dr. Thlabati knew that this job was not his calling. He threw himself back in the comfortable black leather chair, hands behind his head, stretched, yawned loudly and looked around the room.

The walls were painted a hunting red from the floor to a deep, curved cove moulding, which in turn was painted to match the cream ornamental 11 foot high ceiling. Red oakwood wainscot, with matching vertical panelling below, ran all the way around the room, hidden only by two great oak bookshelves against the side and rear walls.

Plush, red-maroon carpets covered the floor. The heavy maroon velvet curtains were drawn back from the windows by a black sash, allowing the bright afternoon sunshine to permeate the shadows.

Original oil paintings by Gibson Mokhachani and Charles van der Merwe decorated the walls, orchestrating the Cape's incredible scenic beauty. There were paintings of Cape Town with Table Mountain in the background; others of the windswept beaches at Blaauberg, where the artists stood with canvas and brushes in hand, of False Bay, Simonstown, and the cold rugged coastal mountains, where the baboons thrived.

Some of the paintings depicted gently rolling hills and vineyards nestled in beautiful sunlight valleys. Two distinctive portraits featured Good Hope University Hospital in the early days.

Plush, black leather couches stood back from the desk at oblique angles, and a red leather chair faced the desk to the side. Two colonial-style upright chairs dressed in red and gold corduroy stood directly in front of the desk. The fine yellowwood desk completed the décor.

Philemon cast his mind back over the last few years: the four hard years that he and Petrus had spent earning their stripes at *'Wits,'* the University of Witwatersrand, and to the changes that had engulfed South Africa while they were there.

Freedom! Apartheid was no more! Freedom!

And now we shall face the aftermath, he thought — reality.

★★★

It was mind-boggling. An oppressed people who have never had any power whatsoever, suddenly have power thrust upon them; more power than they ever dreamed of — just dropped into their laps.

Of course patronage appointments and nepotism would be rife; he himself was evidence of that, he thought

His uncle, Dr. Moshessa Dingaan, was appointed Minister of the Interior because the new government needed more Zulu Nation representation. Philemon in turn was given this job because his uncle pushed the right buttons on his behalf.

Philemon sighed. He was young, but not blind. It was one thing to promote a man to a position beyond his level of competence, and quite another to expect him to perform satisfactorily at that level.

His biggest concern was that the business community maintain confidence in new government. Unless the profit conscious 'International Business Community' believed that the risk was worthwhile for the long term, they would simply not invest in the country — no matter what the western politicians promised. Foreign governments cannot dictate investment policies to their citizens. That's why they called it democracy.

We will learn from the mistakes of other African countries, Philemon thought. If not, we will inevitably fall into the same pattern.

He ticked the highlights off in his mind.

One: Hold officials accountable,

Two: curtail corruption, and

Three: Prosecute offenders to the full extent of the law.

Everything was now churning about in the washing machine. It had been loaded by well meaning people. Everything, they say, comes out in the wash. It remained to be seen if it was true. He wished them luck.

There was a knock on the door, breaking his chain of thought. Philemon swung around as Sarie poked her head into the room.

"Dr. Strydom is here to see you, Dr. Thlabati," she announced.

"Thank you, Sarie," he said with a sigh. "Show him in."

★★★

Earlier that same day, a delegation of hospital hierarchy led by Dr. Thlabati had inspected Dr. Strydom's operating rooms. Philemon had subsequently instructed the guards to affix a large padlock on the door to the facility. Little did Dr. Philemon Thlabati know of the power that he wielded as acting Chief Executive Officer of Good Hope University Hospital in the New South Africa. The chambers were sealed, and it would almost take an act of parliament to undo the chains 5 years in the future.

"Should we try to salvage some of the equipment, Dr. Thlabati?" Dr.Bernhard de Lange had asked, as they strolled through the facility. Dr. Thlabati pretended to consider the question for a minute or two.

"No," Dr. Thlabati replied finally. "The cost of moving it out of here and relocating

it would probably exceed its value." He knew differently of course. He glanced at Dr. Strydom.

"What do you think, Paul?"

"You're probably right," Dr. Strydom answered through clenched teeth.

★★★

After the tour, Dr. Strydom went straight back upstairs and sat down on a couch in the doctor's lounge. He put his hands over his eyes and held them there for a long time, reliving the last few hours in his mind. The decision Thlabati had made regarding the equipment was ludicrous. They had both known that it was crap. A $2,000,000 machine was well worth moving, especially if it only cost fifty thousand Rands (about $10,000.00) to relocate.

And where the hell does he get off calling me Paul! Dr. Strydom thought bitterly.

His whole world was coming apart. He didn't even have an office any more, though he had been assured that he would have one soon. Slowly he removed the documents from his inside coat pocket and stared at them without really seeing. He knew them by heart. He had started the process six months previously — just in case.

One was a letter from Edmonton City Hospital in Alberta, Canada, accepting the terms and conditions for his appointment as Head of Microbiology and Surgery. The others were standard, approved emigration papers.

A group of interns came noisily into the lounge, saw Dr. Strydom seated there and quieted down immediately. They greeted him and went about their business. Dr. Strydom crushed the documents in his hand. Gritting his teeth, he stood up and walked out of the lounge without a word.

The five young black interns just shook their heads resignedly and said nothing.

Dr. Strydom sat in the red chair in Dr. Thlabati's office, his mind finally made up. He knew that he was probably being headstrong and foolhardy, but a lifetime of prejudice and bigotry does not just evaporate from a bitter soul overnight. His pride and his ego could not, would not, accept the inevitable changes in the New South Africa. Dr. Strydom tried once more, producing realms of new reports validating the need for his operating theatre.

"I'm sorry, Dr. Strydom," Dr. Thlabati said ruefully, going over the documentation once more. "Neither you nor I can justify this personal sanctuary of yours any longer — either financially, ethically, or by evidence of a significant scientific breakthrough. It's right here in the papers that you yourself have filed with the hospital." He flipped the file casually across the desk. Dr. Strydom did not move.

"You still have access to all other facilities within the hospital — on a priority basis of course," Dr. Thlabati concluded with a smile.

Dr. Strydom rose, threw his resignation on the yellowwood desk, scattering the papers in the file folder. He turned abruptly and walked out of the room.

★★★

Later that afternoon, Dr. Thlabati looked up from his paperwork a little worse for wear. The door to his office opened and two people walked in, over the protestations of his secretary. Relief flooded his face as he got up to welcome them with a broad smile.

"Hello, Philemon," his old friend Dr. Petrus Stein greeted him warmly, shaking hands. "How did it go?"

Philemon picked up Dr. Strydom's written resignation and waved it in the air.

"He's gone," he said simply. "I think those interns we sent up to the doctor's lounge were the last straw." He smiled broadly as Petrus shook his hand warmly.

"And this must be your famous uncle," said Philemon, turning to the distinguished gentleman waiting patiently to one side. "How do you do, sir? I'm very pleased to meet you at last," he said. "And, I am so very happy that you are here to take over the reins from me," he added enthusiastically, gesturing towards the piles of paper on the desk.

"Three months in that chair nearly had me climbing the walls," Philemon growled. "I'm actually looking forward to the three more years of internship after that." They all laughed.

"I'll be glad to hit the books again too," Petrus said, pursing his lips. "Especially after cutting sugar-cane for three months. That's bloody hard work!"

"How do you feel about the situation now, Uncle Colin?" He asked.

"It's good to be back," the gentleman replied with a smile, folding his arms behind his back. "Especially now, that I know Dr. Paul Strydom will no longer be here to torment me. Thank you…both of you," Dr. Colin Arthur Montgomery said, with an appreciative nod.

★★★

CHAPTER SEVEN
The Operation

Dr. Colin Montgomery was, to say the least, astonished, when he picked up his phone messages as he entered his office at six-thirty that morning. He had never expected to hear from Dr. Paul Strydom again. He collapsed into his chair.

How long has it been now? 5..no!..nearly 6 years since Paul left the Good Hope University Hospital in Cape Town. And I still get a twist in my stomach when I think about him. Dr. Montgomery shuddered at the thought. He had not expected Dr. Strydom to leave the country permanently, but he was relieved that he had.

Sergeant Marais had dropped by following Dr. Strydom's abrupt departure and asked that if Colin should ever hear from Dr. Strydom again, to let him know. That was a long time ago, but…Dr. Montgomery dialled the local police precinct.

Much to his surprise, Sergeant Frikkie Marais arrived at his office within thirty minutes. Dr. Montgomery shook his hand warmly, and asked him to be seated.

"The message just asked that I call him, that he had a very unique case and wanted to perform the operation here at Good Hope," Dr. Montgomery said, raising his hands as he shrugged.

The sergeant was sitting across from him, smartly dressed in his beige uniform, a notepad on his knee.

"Did you call him back?" Sergeant Marais asked.

"Not yet. I thought I would call you first."

The sergeant nodded his approval. "Where was he calling from?"

"He didn't say," Dr. Montgomery said.

The sergeant thought for a minute. "Are there any legal concerns if he were to perform the operation here?"

"No. Not really," Dr. Montgomery answered. "We would have to exercise our due diligence with respect to liability and…Are you suggesting that I agree to this?" He stared at the sergeant incredulously.

The sergeant nodded. "Do you have a problem with it?" he asked.

"Well, of course I do!" Dr. Montgomery said, rising from his chair. "I really don't want to associate with him again."

"I do," the sergeant said quietly.

They talked for a time and when they were done, Dr. Montgomery dialled the number.

"Hello, Paul," he said cheerfully. "How the hell are you?"

★★★

Dr. Strydom reviewed Maude Parker's medical record carefully. He was standing at the window in his office at the Edmonton City Hospital. It was 2:00 pm in the afternoon, three weeks after Fred's operation.

Ovarian cancer.

He shook his head, rubbed his forehead and sat back in his chair again, deep in thought. After a while he sat up and called a colleague at a private clinic in Los Angeles. They discussed Maude's case at some length and he hung up the phone. Dr. Strydom called his secretary.

"Set up a meeting with Mr. and Mrs. Parker right away," he instructed her bluntly.

★★★

They met later that afternoon in Fred Parker's room at the hospital. Maude sat next to the bed holding Fred's arm. Fred was propped up to a half-sitting position, barely cognisant and connected to half a dozen machines. He did not look too good.

"Please consider what I am about to tell you very carefully," Dr. Strydom said patiently. "You too, are very sick, Mrs. Parker," Dr. Strydom said, "and you are on a long waiting list for an operation at this hospital. To be brutally honest, you can't afford to wait any longer. I have arranged that you be short-listed in a clinic in Los Angeles."

He held up his hand when she began to protest.

"There will be no financial obligation, and it's not charity," he lied, "there is a special fund for special cases. Besides, this special case includes Fred going to South Africa." They both looked a little startled.

"I believe that I can make Fred well," Dr. Strydom continued kindly, "but not here in Canada. Some of the drugs and procedures I propose to use are not legal here…yet," he added, rubbing his forehead. "I'll leave you two alone to discuss it," he walking to the door. "I'll see you both a little later." He nodded, smiled encouragingly and left the room, closing the door behind him.

Fred and Maude looked at each other in shocked concern.

"Sounds good to me," Fred said finally, settling back for the long haul. He knew what was coming. Maude would have to analyse the situation to the nth degree before she said, "No!"

Maude started with the day they got married and elaborated in some great detail. She expounded on how they had promised to be together for the rest of their lives, on the sacrifices they had made, on the children they had never had, on how she had quit good jobs, abandoned family and friends and followed him, literally to the ends of the earth.

She summed it all up, reached the inevitable conclusion, and expressed emphatically that she was not about to stay in North America, alone, while he went to the other side of the world, again!

When she was all done, he looked up at her and smiled. He squeezed her hand encouragingly.

"Miss Piggy," he said, "if I don't go, we will be separated by more than just half a world.

> 'How do I love thee? Let me count the ways.
> I love thee to the depth and breadth and height
> My soul can reach, when feeling out of site.'
> He quoted her favourite poem from Elizabeth Barrett
> Browning.
> 'I love thee with a love I seemed to lose
> With my lost saints, — I love thee with the breath,
> Smiles, tears and all my life! — And, if God choose,
> I shall but love thee better after death'.

She burst into tears.

Fred sighed. She was going to LA and he was going to SA.

★★★

Dr. Strydom met with Graham and Mary Andrews in his office. He had been correct in his prognosis following the operation on their son, Brian. The PET scan and EEG had revealed electrical patterns consistent with severe damage to both parietal lobes and the somatosensory cortex, which receives information about pressure, pain, touch and temperature.

The ricocheting bullet had spun like a windmill through to the frontal lobes and destroyed the motor cortex, which controls voluntary movement and the ability to think. It was a wonder that he was still alive.

The doctor had followed up with extensive drug therapy and used needle electrodes to record electrical activity. He had to stimulate Brian's brain with weak electrical currents in order to keep the automatic functions such as breathing and heartbeat rate operating. The results were conclusive. The boy was, to all intents and purposes, brain dead. Dr. Strydom was not about to tell the Andrews' that.

"Mister and Mrs. Andrews," he said kindly. "I believe that I can make Brian well, but not here in Canada. Some of the drugs and procedures I propose to use are not legal here…yet," he added, rubbing his forehead.

★★★

Dr. Colin Montgomery walked through Dr. Strydom's lower level operating rooms at Good Hope University Hospital in Cape Town, South Africa, in a daze, as the memories came flooding back. Everything had remained sealed and untouched — even the cooler was still working. He did not open it.

Colin shook his head. Once or twice he had tried to persuade the authorities to allow him access to the facility, but to no avail. His predecessor, Dr. Philemon Thlabati, had permanently sealed the rooms for unspecified health reasons. Sergeant Marais obviously had some very powerful connections to clear that obstacle in such a short time.

The two young doctors with him were fascinated. Though at least 5 years old, some of the prototype equipment was so unique that they had only read about it in hi-fi medical books, brochures and periodicals.

Dr. Montgomery had decided to keep the entire operation as confidential as possible. He had handled most of the proceedings himself, along with a few trusted individuals.

Each piece of equipment had to be thoroughly cleaned, tested and upgraded by the manufacturers and technicians, after which the whole facility had to be cleaned and sterilised. As he looked around him in wonder at the elaborate layout, Dr. Montgomery promised himself that he would reallocate the equipment to other facilities within the hospital directly following the operation.

The costs were exorbitant, and for a time Dr. Montgomery was concerned about his budget. He was pleasantly surprised when he received the bank draft from Dr. Strydom in an amount that almost doubled the projected costs. Colin sat back in his chair and stared at the generous grant for a long time.

Then the realization struck him; the hairs on the back of his neck stood up and the perspiration broke out on his forehead. Slowly, surely, Dr. Montgomery felt the familiar old knots come back in his stomach. This was far more than a unique operation to be performed in familiar surroundings. To Dr. Paul Strydom, this was an obsession. Dr. Montgomery suddenly had serious reservations about the whole thing.

After Dr. Strydom's unscheduled departure to Canada five years earlier, his medical team had been dispersed throughout the hospital. Since all were eminent scientists and highly qualified technicians, the other departments had snapped them up gratefully. Individually, they had seemed to settle comfortably into their new positions.

Dr. Montgomery was able to locate all but one of the team members and summoned them to the conference room. Initially they all looked very uncomfortable, especially so, when they recognised their old colleagues present at the meeting. The usual chit-chat was notably absent and some were stone-faced, staring straight ahead, saying nothing.

Dr. Montgomery was taken aback by this departure from the norm but nevertheless greeted everyone in turn. He introduced the two doctors accompanying him as Dr. Petrus Stein and Dr. Philemon Thlabati. He continued with the meeting and explained the situation regarding Dr. Paul Strydom and the upcoming operation. The atmosphere in the room changed dramatically. Ex-team members glanced at each other with knowing smiles and a low murmur buzzed excitedly in the room.

"Dr. Strydom asked for each of you specifically," Dr. Montgomery continued. "If anyone does not wish to be part of the program, let me know now." Nobody said a word. The excitement was building in the room like an electrically charged capacitor.

"Very well," Dr. Montgomery continued. "You will begin training in your new duties and refresher courses on the equipment will proceed immediately. Dr. Strydom and his patients will be arriving next Monday."

There was general applause and cheers of approval.

"Dr. Thlabati and Dr. Stein will be joining your team," Dr. Montgomery added through the din. "I believe the experience will benefit them greatly."

The room went silent. Their faces became masks. The smiles so evident a few seconds before were instantly wiped off the faces in front of him. They stared at him without emotion.

The knot in Dr. Montgomery's stomach tightened a little more as he came to a terrible realisation. These were the people personally selected and chosen by Dr. Paul Strydom. They had no room for outsiders; they were the chosen ones — they alone shared his dream — his cause. Dr. Strydom was their Ulysses, Odysseus, on an odyssey of intellectual and spiritual wandering, on the quest for immortality.

They sought the Holy Grail. They were…fanatics!

★★★

Sergeant Frikkie Marais stood unnoticed in plain clothes on the balcony at Johannesburg International Airport in South Africa. He watched as Dr. Paul Strydom and his entourage swiftly cleared customs and caught the connecting flight to Cape Town. Dr. Strydom's patients were transported from one plane to the other by ambulance with little disturbance. When they were on their way, Sergeant Marais left the terminal and hopped into the waiting police car.

"Back to Pretoria Penitentiary, constable," he notified the driver.

★★★

"But, he is a British espionage agent, convicted by the High Court of this free land, South Africa," Captain M'Twe'Twe said, exasperated. "We cannot just let him go free."

They were seated in the governor's office at the penitentiary. Sergeant Marais had presented his case for the release of Christopher Barkley.

"Scotland Yard has something we want," the sergeant said.

"And what is that?" the captain asked.

"Secret files implicating a very subversive element in illicit activities," the sergeant said. "There may even be a conspiracy."

"Huh?"

Sergeant Marais repeated himself in fluent Xhosa. The captain smiled, nodded and unconsciously touched the tribal marks on his cheek. The Sergeant switched back to English for the governor's benefit.

"And let us not forget that Barkley was convicted without proper representation,"

he paused for effect. "Under Apartheid and the shadow of the Secret Police."

"Where did you get this information? Is your source reliable?" the Governor asked. Sergeant Marais nodded.

"It was revealed in a conversation that I had last week with the Chief Executive Officer of Good Hope Hospital in Cape Town," he said, "in a conversation I had with Dr. Colin Arthur Montgomery."

"We'll see what we can do," said the Governor.

Scotland Yard were only too happy to provide the New South African government, and Sergeant Marais, with Dr. Strydom's secret files, in exchange for the release of one of their agents, Christopher Barkley.

***

Within a week of his telephone conversation with Dr. Montgomery, Dr. Strydom had chartered a Lear Jet equipped with all medical supplies and equipment necessary to accommodate his patients. The passports had taken just three days. Fred was impressed.

Fred Parker was a white-knuckle flyer. In his job and throughout his career as a civil engineer, it had been necessary to fly everywhere. He didn't like it then; he didn't like it now. The fact that his internal organs were in a fast downward spiral and that he was only being kept alive by machines was not relevant. He was a double-scotch and soda flyer. When his persistent begging and whining finally got to them, the doctors turned up his IV.

The twenty-six hour flight from Edmonton to Cape Town, via New York, Cape Verdi Islands and Johannesburg, took its toll on both Fred Parker and Brian Andrews.

Dr. Strydom, who travelled with them, was relieved when his patients finally arrived at Good Hope University Hospital.

Dr Montgomery, accompanied by Dr. Strydom's team, was there to greet them.

"Hello, Colin," Dr. Strydom said anxiously, shaking his hand briefly. "It's nice to see you again, but my patients are critical. I'll see you later."

In a whirl of white robes and curt instructions, Dr. Strydom gathered his team and his patients and headed for the elevators. Dr. Colin Montgomery just stood there — stunned. Dr. Paul Strydom had come back and just taken over his hospital once again.

★★★

Fred Parker awoke on the gurney in Dr. Strydom's private sanctuary. His vision was fuzzy and his mind half doped up. Nevertheless, Fred was coherent enough to realise that he was being prepped for an operation that was supposed to save his life. This operation was the reason why he had come all this way, and the only reason that he had left Maude to fend for herself.

Despite the drugs, he suddenly felt uneasy.

Something was wrong! These people were strange.

Everyone, nurses and doctors alike, went about their business efficiently and mechanically. No one smiled. No one spoke to him or offered any encouragement.

This was not right! He knew people were paid to be friendly in hospitals — he had had his appendix out once!

He looked over at the bed beside him and squinted to focus. That kid Brian was being prepped too.

They're going to operate on both of us at the same time?

"Now wait a minute…" he began. A nurse shoved a mask over his face. *"Shit!"* he muttered, and went to sleep.

★★★

The two young doctors stood watching in amazement as Dr. Strydom's team swung into action. Dr. Petrus Stein and Dr. Philemon Thlabati had been given specific instructions during the previous week's training and were assigned some minor tasks to be performed during the operation. That all went out the window in the blur of activity they were soon caught up in.

Brian was brought in first. A scalpel flashed and the skin fell back from the top of his head, exposing his skull. They removed the thick bone from the top of Brian's head with a surgical saw and exposed his brain — a damaged, putty-coloured, wrinkled glob of matter.

Connecting blood vessels to a miniature plastic manifold as he systematically severed them, Dr. Strydom pulled back the motor cortex and, using a monitor and an electron microscope, removed the frontal lobes from Brian's forehead. He removed part of the pariental lobes and of the somatosensory cortex from the top of the brain as well.

During the entire process, computers continuously mapped brainwaves and microelectrodes probed and monitored every major circuit. The operation went on and on. Dr. Strydom moved deftly, quickly, without hesitation. His team was well trained, precise and efficient.

Suddenly Dr. Strydom stepped back, his bloodstained hands in the air.

"Go!" he said. Doctors and technicians scrambled.

Fred Parker was wheeled into the theatre. The top of his skull had been removed and his exposed brain was positioned a foot from Brian's.

Petrus and Philemon watched dumbstruck as Dr. Strydom and his team performed a similar procedure on Fred to what they had performed on Brian minutes before. In a forest of tubes, machines, probes and computers, the operation moved into the realm of the incomprehensible.

Dr. Strydom carefully lifted out both hemispheres of the frontal and pariental lobes, from Fred's skull, still attached to the corpus callosum and complete with the frontal cortex, he then inserted them carefully into the empty cavity he had made in Brian's head. He overlapped the three millimetre thick cortex, laying grafts of living foetus tissue as he went.

"Sixty seconds!" A doctor monitoring the computer began a tense countdown.

They had one minute to reattach the nerves, arteries and veins, to reinitiate the blood circulation, or the brain cells would begin to die.

The team worked feverishly, precisely, connecting nerve endings and blood vessels.

"Twenty seconds," the doctor continued. "Ten…nine…"

"Done!" Dr. Strydom said, his forehead soaked with perspiration.

The operation had taken only one hour, twenty-two minutes and forty-four seconds.

***

A short while later, Petrus and Philemon sat hunched on the bench in the change room — mentally exhausted.

One of the patients, the young boy, Brian, was stable and lying in the recovery room. The other, old man Parker, was on his way to the morgue.

They were both still in shock at what they had witnessed. Petrus looked at his friend. He looked sick.

"We have just seen the first brain transplant," Petrus said. "What are we going to do?"

"You will do nothing," Dr. Strydom said calmly from the doorway. He leaned against the doorjamb, pulling off his mask.

"You will do nothing, and you will say nothing," he repeated, as the doctors began to bristle. "You see," he continued, "you are both implicated just by having been here." The young doctors said nothing, staring at him coldly.

"And not just you two, of course, but the entire hospital and Dr. Colin Montgomery as well," Dr. Strydom continued. He walked into the room and put his foot up on the bench, smiling down at the doctors indulgently.

"Who would believe that this facility, and especially its chief executive officer, did not know the nature of the operation? Dr. Montgomery himself recommended his two best young graduates to assist with it — and that is why I let you stay." He stepped back and stretched his arms.

"Ethically," he continued, looking up at the ceiling, "remember that I had 2 patients who were definitely going to die soon. And I saved both of them — in a way.

"The evolution of the human mind and body and our very existence is based on symbiotic relationships over millions of years. Organ transplants are practically a routine occurrence today, so why not specific parts of the brain?"

Dr. Strydom stood up, still smiling down at the bewildered young men. He stretched his arms, shrugged, relaxing. "The concept of self is a mirage, an illusion," he added philosophically. "We believe we are capable of thought, simply because one verbal module in the left hemisphere tells us we are. Without that verbal module telling us we can think, and making sense of what goes on around us, we are nothing but a collection of perceptions, concepts and feelings, changing from moment to moment to match the circumstances. Like animals". He walked over to the door, stopped and turned to look at the young doctors once more.

"Besides," he said. "Who died? Was it the old man with the clear mind and failing organs, or the boy with the scrambled brain? And, more important, who lived?" He walked out of the room, leaving the two doctors looking at each other in stunned silence.

Dr. Paul Jacobus Strydom was confident — elated! He would release his discovery to the world, in his own time, from his own podium. But not now, the world was not yet ready for this. The world was not ready for *immortality*.

★★★

Dr. Paul Strydom was deep in his own thoughts as he walked across the marble floor towards the elevator. It was a month after the operation, and all seemed to be well. He had agreed to meet Dr. Colin Montgomery at the 'White Knight' for lunch.

He seems to have gotten a good handle on things, thought Dr. Strydom, referring to Colin Montgomery. Maybe, it's time to move back home, develop some old friendships and regain control of the situation.

Since Maude Parker had not yet returned from Los Angeles, he saw no point in shipping Fred Parker's body home to be buried. He had therefore had the remains cremated in the hospital crematorium. Dr. Strydom had arranged for Fred's ashes be sent back to the town of Bolton in Alberta, Canada.

The humanitarian thing to do, he told himself modestly.

His other patient was stable, thank goodness, after a couple of good convulsions the previous night. Dr. Strydom smiled to himself as he recalled his patient looking like a spaceman with all those thin glass tubes and microelectrodes sticking out of his head.

The recommendation by Dr. Petrus Stein to elevate the levels of the biochemical serotonin, norepinephrine and dopomine, and then to inject them directly into the brain across the blood-brain barrier had been a touch of brilliance he had to admit. His brow furrowed in thought for a moment, and then he nodded to himself, his mind made up.

Dr. Petrus Stein would be his next protégé. He would make a valuable contribution to his team, and perhaps some day …

Dr. Strydom had arranged a series of tests to be performed on Brian over the next few months, including biopsies to measure the exact rate of regeneration of brain tissue. The boy would be his permanent living model, his guinea pig, paving the way for all future operations. Future generations would come to celebrate Brian Andrews' sacrifice and the dedication of the brilliant Dr. Paul Jacobus Strydom, of course.

It shouldn't be too hard to convince the parents, so far away, that their autistic son was not ready to return home. Too bad, he would never again be well enough to go home, and as the years passed, they would become accustomed to their loss.

Deep in thought, he stopped as a figure in a beige uniform barred his way. He looked up, a little annoyed, directly into the stern eyes of Sergeant Frikkie Marais. Four constables accompanied him.

"Dr. Paul Jacobus Strydom," the officer said. "You are under arrest for the murder…"

Dr. Strydom was startled, but recovered quickly.

"Don't be ridiculous," he said his mind racing. "An operation is a dangerous procedure. People, regrettably, sometimes die. If you're referring to the unfortunate situation with Mr. Parker last month, my team…"

"Your team is already under arrest," the sergeant informed him coldly. "You are not charged with the murder of Mr. Parker."

"I'm not? Then what the hell…?"

And then he saw her and Dr. Strydom's heart sank. Standing beside one of the constables was the MRI technician he had forgotten about a long time ago — the technician he had so summarily dismissed after the last botched operation before he left the hospital and moved to Canada.

The sergeant braced himself confidently. Along with the e-mail from Dr. Colin Montgomery to Christopher Barker and the eye-witness testimony from Dr. Elisabeth Margret, Sergeant Marais had just that day received Dr. Strydom's secret files from Scotland Yard, in exchange for freeing Christopher Barkley.

"Who, then?" Dr. Strydom yelped desperately, as Sergeant Frikkie Marais spun him around and handcuffed him.

"You are under arrest for the murders of Mango Xhakosi and Loni M'Babani," recited the sergeant. "You have the right…" Dr. Strydom was still confused. He had no idea who they were.

He had not bothered to learn the names of his 'kaffir' patients.

★★★

CHAPTER EIGHT
The Homecoming

Fred opened his eyes and stared at the picture of the yellow spotted giraffe on the ceiling. The colours and the contrasts were incredible. He could see the giraffe's eyes were blue and it had long, black eyelashes. The sucker was smiling at him. Fred tried to smile back, but the tubes down his throat blocked the side of his mouth.

"Hot de' huck?" he said, and was surprised at the sound of his own voice.

The baby monitor on the table near his head beeped once. The biggest nurse he had ever seen thundered down the hallway and dove into the room in three seconds flat.

Her tawny brown hair flopped down over her elated chubby face, as she stared into his eyes and checked his vital signs. She was beaming from ear to ear and her big brown eyes were moist as she cooed and prodded and tucked him in.

In the next two minutes there were 6 very happy nurses and doctors in the room, chatting and bustling and fussing over him. They removed the tubes from his throat and the patches from his head, fluffed up his pillows, adjusted monitors, hooked up new ones and changed his IV.

Now this is what these guys get paid for! Fred thought, smiling contentedly.

"Where am I? What day is this?" he asked in a husky, high-toned voice, surprising himself again. The nurse standing over him was delighted. He had asked the right questions.

"You're in Edmonton City Hospital, you had an operation. You've been asleep for a long time," she told him, still beaming. "It's a beautiful day in late September. Now, you go back to sleep, little lamb, and the doctors will be in to see you in the morning." She clucked over him like a mother hen, tucking him in and checking his IV for the tenth time.

Little lamb? he thought, drifting off to sleep. She deserves that 15 percent raise.

Fred drifted in and out of happy sleep over the next three days until they cut back on his morphine. When he woke on the morning of the third day, he was still a little dazed as he looked around the room.

The walls were covered with posters of Spiderman and Superman and all kinds of action figures he did not recognise. The ceiling was plastered with pictures of funny cartoon characters. Brightly-coloured model aeroplanes hung down on strings and moved gently in the soft air currents.

In one corner of the room sat a huge brown teddy bear with very sad eyes. Next to the bear, on a small round table, stood a lamp with a large yellow shade; it had green ducks embroidered on it. Fred's spirit lifted. He had always liked ducks, ever since he was a child.

He was staring groggily at the lamp wondering why he was in a kid's room, when a familiar voice interrupted his thoughts. Two white-coated doctors walked into his line of view. A battery of machines, computers and technicians accompanied them into the room.

Fred looked up and refocused his squint. He was startled to see the two young doctors from South Africa smiling down at him. He was amazed at how clear they were. An avalanche of vague, frightful memories flooded his mind, so he closed his eyes again and tried to shut them out.

With little formality, they connected Fred to the machines and ran a battery of tests until he was nearly exhausted.

"Reaction time is still a little slow in this area," Dr. Philemon Thlabati said, studying the computer monitor. "Probably due to the gradual development of myelin sheath over the longer axons."

"W...what?" Fred said.

"Your neurons, or nerve cells, are still developing," Dr. Petrus Stein explained. "But, they are communicating in electrical and chemical language and firing at threshold when they're supposed to.

"Your neurotransmitters are exciting and inhibiting on schedule, but the message is just a little slower than normal getting to the synapse right now, that's all." He turned to Philemon.

"The cells are intelligent," he exclaimed. "And they're growing!" Philemon nodded.

"Okay, if that's all," Fred said alarmed, not getting it at all but desperately wanting to. "So now I can get back to my wife and my life, huh?"

The doctors stopped what they were doing immediately. Their exuberance evaporated in an instant. They turned and stood looking down at him without any expression.

"Okay, everybody out," Dr. Thlabati said suddenly, shooing everybody along with his hands.

"Pack it up. Everyone out, please. Thank you. Thank you!" He added, as some nurses would have objected. He shut the door when they were gone.

Dr. Thlabati turned and put his hands behind his back. Looking down at the floor, he walked slowly over to the bed, his stethoscope hanging loosely around his neck. Fred knew that doctors did that when they were serious.

"You have been in a coma for more than three months," Dr. Thlabati said, as Dr. Stein settled down in the visitor's chair. "The Andrews' brought you back to Canada right after the operation in South Africa, and you've been here ever since." He glanced at his companion. "Dr. Stein and I flew out as soon as we heard that you were awake."

"Your wife is still in Los Angeles. There were complications, and she must stay there for a while yet," Dr. Stein added.

Dr. Thlabati walked over to the table and picked up a large hand mirror. He came over to the side of the bed and handed it to Fred.

"Mr. Parker," he said, as Fred stared at his reflection in shock. "You are not Fred Parker any more, you are Brian Andrews, and you are fourteen years old."

★★★

Fred thrust his head back on the pillow and closed his eyes tightly. He peeked at the mirror through one eye, flinched, squeezed it shut again. He fired the mirror across the room. The teddy bear quietly caught the flying mirror in the chest and it dropped unbroken in his lap.

"That was childish," Fred muttered, a little startled at himself.

He grappled with his new reality in a sea of misery and frustration. His seventy-three year old intellect had been transplanted into a fifteen-year-old!

How could he possibly cope with this? And Maude, what about her...the two of them? His heart ached in his breast when he thought about Maude. Their dreams of eventually retiring quietly in Bolton and of getting old gracefully together were toast!

The doctors had tried to explain the operation to him.

"We only know as much as we do because Dr. Stein here managed to 'borrow' one of Dr. Strydom's journals before Dr. Strydom left the country," Dr. Thlabati said. "We subsequently studied his procedures to some extent." He added as an understatement, glancing surreptitiously at Dr. Stein.

For the most part Fred was appalled, but what really caught his attention was the part where some sections of Fred's brain had been transplanted into Brian's.

"Which sections?" Fred asked in a tiny voice. "In layman's terms," he pleaded, holding up his hands as Dr. Stein took a deep breath.

"Okay," Dr. Stein said. "Essentially the frontal lobes in your forehead were transplanted into Brian's forehead. These lobes, containing the prefrontal cortex and motor cortex, are responsible for voluntary movement of the six hundred muscles in your body. They control your social judgement, personality, emotions and behaviour; your ability to make plans and follow through with them. In other words, your *will* to do, or not to do something."

"That's it?" Fred asked, too alarmed to understand.

"Not quite," the doctor continued, concentrating. "There are partial transplants of your parietal and temporal lobes. These are involved in perception, memory, higher learning and understanding language."

"The rest of Brian's brain is apparently still intact and operational," Dr. Thlabati added. "All the automatic and involuntary motor functions of the cerebellum, thalamus, olfactory which control smell, auditory, visual, breathing, heart rate and survival instincts, appear to be normal." He hesitated, a little unsure how to put it.

"What? What?" Fred asked, starting to panic.

"Well, the whole amygdala in the limbic system could not be replaced entirely, as it controls too many other involuntary functions. There may be some latent memories and emotional outbursts."

"Wait a minute," Fred said, perking up. "So some of the stuff I do in the future can be blamed on Brian?"

"Well, yes, and no," Dr. Stein said. "You can't tell anybody about this. You *are* the recovered Brian Andrews."

"What!" Fred was flabbergasted.

Dr. Stein explained the situation regarding the reputation of the Good Hope University Hospital in Cape Town, Dr. Montgomery, and the fact that Dr. Strydom and his team had been arrested.

"We cannot even inform Dr. Montgomery," Dr. Stein said. "He has such high ethical standards that should he ever become aware of the true purpose of the procedure, he would immediately tender his resignation to the institution. We really cannot afford to lose him at this critical time."

"What critical time?" Fred asked.

"This is a critical time for all New South Africa," Dr. Thlabati answered. "A time for forgiveness, tolerance and the integration of our national heritage and our people. It is a fragile peace between the races and the tribes. A revelation of this magnitude and of the sacrifices of those it took to get you to this point could destroy that peace and throw the entire country into civil war."

"So, if you were to tell anyone else about this," Dr. Stein added. "They would take you away in a straight jacket. We are the only ones who know and for the sake of everything we hold dear we could not corroborate your story," he said regretfully, pursing his lips.

"However," Dr. Stein continued in a lighter tone, "you have two of the most dedicated doctors at your beck-and-call...Us!" he said, with a pained expression as Fred stared at him blankly.

"I'll give you a number where you can reach us, day or night." He smiled ruefully.

"Don't worry, even on your worst day, you'll just be another misunderstood teenager."

He turned with a smile as Dr. Thlabati walked across the room with his hands behind his back again.

"Now it's time to meet your family," Dr. Thlabati said, dropping the final bombshell.

"We explained to the Andrews' that your accident caused you to lose your memory and that memories you do experience are actually a jumble of miscellaneous thoughts, some real — some fantasy."

Fred was dismayed. He had to adopt a family as well?

"Like an inverted protection program?" He asked. "I'll be living undercover every day?"

He begged for time… lots of time. They had agreed to put the Andrews family off … but just until later that evening.

Fred smacked his head into the pillow again. There was no way he could fit in with that family; there was no way that he could adjust to this situation.

It's absurd — it's crazy — it's impossible!

Fred knew of the Andrews family, of course. Bolton was a small town; on one of his delivery rounds, Fred had once mentioned to Mr. Andrews that he needed a truck to take some junk to the dump and Mr. Andrews had loaned him one. The Andrews family were said to be totally dysfunctional, never doing anything together, like attending church or community functions.

Fred remembered that the Andrews lived on an estate just outside the town, Graham Andrews was a successful businessman, owning Bolton Hardware among others, and business was all he seemed to be interested in. His daughters, Kelly and Beth, were not socially friendly girls and kept to themselves most of the time. The mother's name was Mary, a proud but unhappy woman, probably because of her son, Brian.

And what about Brian?

He had been…was… a sullen young man. It seemed like he was always getting into trouble.

Fred searched frantically for an answer. The doctors had made it very clear that coming clean was not an option.

I could run away. Of course! And go where? Another runaway kid on the street? Why not add to the burden of an already understaffed police service and child search groups? He thought bitterly, I'm not into this…I can't…no way.

Someone knocked softly on the door and in a panic, he turned towards the sound.

The door slowly opened and the Andrews family filed in. First to enter was Beth and then Kelly, followed by Mary. Graham came in last of all. They looked terrible.

No one said a word and nobody would look directly at him, except Mary. They stood in a row against the wall and he saw Beth shivering.

They want less to do with me than I do with them, he thought, a little shocked. *They are afraid of me!*

"What the hell did you do to this family Brian?" Fred asked himself, ashamed.

He looked at Mary. She raised her chin proudly, resigned to accept whatever cruel barb fate was destined to throw.

He searched his mind for a way out. There was none. There was only one thing that he could do, or deliberately destroy this family, and probably himself as well.

He held out his hand.

"Can I please have a hug?" he asked, in his husky, high-toned voice.

Fred's departure from the hospital a month later in the middle of October was quite emotional.

The biggest nurse he had ever seen considered him her personal jewel and she fussed over him constantly. Fred could not help but love her, as her tawny brown hair flopped down over her tearful chubby face and her big brown eyes wept crocodile tears as they wheeled him out the door.

The drive home from the hospital though, was quite a different story. Fred was uncomfortable and remained quiet sitting next to Beth in the Andrews' SUV.

The family thought he was brooding and left him alone. Fred had taken the first step, but he had no idea what to do next.

How is a fourteen-year-old supposed to act? This was a very awkward start to his new life. He knew that for the Andrews to accept this new Brian he had to fall into some predictable adolescent pattern.

Quiet! That was it! Be a quiet kid; those were the best kind, he thought. He felt a little better.

The red brick, Victorian-style house on the estate impressed Fred, but he said nothing. Late October. It was an early winter and the grounds were covered with a blanket of snow. The branches on the flowering crab apple tree beside the front porch were loaded down with new powder snow. Fred couldn't help giving the branch a little nudge as he passed under it showering the girls behind him. Beth squealed in panic, but Kelly just gave him the death-stare.

They walked into the lounge to find Corporal Patrick D'Laney and Constable Michelle Monair waiting to greet them. Fred had the distinct impression that they had an ulterior motive for being there.

The lounge was a huge rectangular room dominated by a central charcoal-sandstone fireplace with heavy wooden mantles. The walls were painted lilac with a beige trim. Pillowy beige leather chairs and couches were strategically placed. Cherrywood coffee tables and end tables with antique lamps completed the décor. Prints of paintings by Monet hung in heavy gilded frames on the walls. It was a beautiful, well-lit room, functional — but without warmth.

A short time later, Inspector Claude DuBois and his wife, Susan, arrived, followed by the two paramedics Julie Martins and Matt Finch.

Everyone seemed very glad to see him, and it was "Brian this, Brian that," a pat on the head, a pat on the shoulder and even a hug from Julie. Fred didn't mind that.

The unaccustomed fuss and physical show of affection by others made Fred feel quite uncomfortable and confused. He needed a drink. He fished a beer out of the cooler on the dining room table, which Mary instantly took away from him and replaced with a coke. Fred bit his lip. He had to concentrate.

"Do you remember anything before the accident Brian?" Patrick asked casually. The room went very still.

Here we go, thought Fred. The third-degree.

"Not very much," he said casually, sipping his coke as his mouth went dry. "I don't remember what happened."

"Do you know who I am?" Patrick asked.

Fred did a double take. Now what? "You're Officer D'Laney," he said slowly.

"I'm also your Uncle Patrick."

"Oh! Hi, Uncle Patrick," Fred said cautiously. He walked over and shook his hand.

"Just call me Patrick," he answered with a smile.

Everyone was amazed. Brian had never spontaneously done anything like that before. Fred misunderstood the looks and started to sweat.

Small talk continued for some time. Fred tried to avoid answering questions as much as he could without being rude. The strain started to get to him after a while, and he sat hunched in a chair. It had been a long, emotional day.

Mary came up behind him and placed her hands on his shoulders. Fred jumped. Mary quickly dropped her hands.

"Is there anything you would like before you go to bed, Brian?" she asked.

"Yes, there is," Fred said, pausing for a moment, his mind churning. Who the hell was he, Brian or Fred?

Everyone looked at him expectantly.

"Please, call me Bred," he said.

★★★

Corporal Patrick D'Laney scuffed his toe in the gravel as he stood in the yard in front of the Andrews' house, which they had just departed. With him were Constable Michelle Monair and Inspector Claude DuBois. The Inspector had something to say.

"It's a homicide investigation now, since Fred Parker officially died on the operating table," Inspector DuBois said seriously, gauging the metal of his officers.

"That boy is involved. It is our duty to find out how, when, where and why. We cannot afford to lose focus. Is that clear?"

"Yes, Sir." Patrick said solemnly.

Michelle gazed up at the house and wondered about the strange young man and the change that had come over him since the accident.

★★★

Bred was standing buck naked at the washbasin brushing his teeth a few weeks later, when he noticed that he was pretty skinny for his age.

He had been thinking a lot lately, and though it grieved him to have to go through school, puberty, pimples and the whole damn works again, it didn't seem that he had much choice, so he resigned himself to make the best of it. Mary had decided that he should stay home this winter, and start school again next year with a full semester. According to Kelly, he was probably going to get his butt kicked when he got back to school next fall as well. Brian was apparently not a very popular kid.

He had tried to make friends with Kelly, but all those years of emotional detachment had taken its toll on her and she wanted nothing to do with him. It bothered him though, that she was such an unsociable sixteen-year-old. She was quite attractive when she chose to be, but she had no friends or active hobbies that he could see, and she stayed in her room most of the time. Mary had once mentioned something about her wanting to save the whales.

Beth, on the other hand, being only nine years old, seemed happy to accept the new Bred more openly and was becoming quite an ally.

"What's wrong with Kelly?" he had asked Beth one sunny Saturday afternoon when Kelly had gotten up from the lunch table and immediately barricaded herself in her room.

"She does that when she gets a new CD," Beth answered. "She drowns herself in her music, sometimes for days. Kelly even thinks she can play the tenor saxophone," she added with a giggle.

Bred studied his adolescent body in the mirror. He sighed as he rinsed his toothbrush under the tap. He was going to have to work out if he wanted to survive his high school years, again.

He raised his arms and posed his muscles in front of the mirror. Bred was not too impressed. However…a few curls might develop the triceps. Maybe…sit-ups for the abs…

His dandling private accidentally touched the cold sink and he felt a tingle. Surprised, he looked down, and stared in wonder. Private…Sergeant…up through the ranks as he watched in astonishment…Lieutenant…Captain… Holy Shit!…Major!

Bred looked into the mirror at his exhilarated, red-faced reflection. This was the happiest moment of his new life!

★★★

Spring break! It would be his 15th birthday in a few weeks. Bred and Beth left the house that afternoon to ride their bicycles into town. Spring was definitely in the air and the snow was almost gone. School was out and Bred had missed the entire school year. He would have to go back to school in the fall. As they were about to leave, he realised he was missing something. He turned to Mary.

"Is it okay that we go to town, Mum?" he asked.

Mary was startled. He had not asked her for permission to do for anything in a long time.

"Of course," she answered, flushing with pomp. "Be careful of the puddles on the roads. The snow is melting."

Bred nodded slowly as she spoke. *Gottcha!* He thought.

"And could we have our allowance, please?" he asked innocently.

Bred and Beth sat in Maude's Donut Shop. Bred ordered jelly donuts and a strawberry milkshake for each of them, and a coffee for himself. Beth was a wealth of information, well acquainted with the little people and the everyday lives of practically everyone in town.

"…And George Bishop has been seen out at the Sunshine Motel at midnight with Betty, his brother Kyle's wife …"

"Where did you get all this stuff from?" Bred asked, in awe after she had prattled on for ten minutes.

"Listening to Mum," Beth answered matter-of-fact, tugging at her shoe.

Maggie, their waitress, was a pretty girl. She had a slightly plump figure and light-brown shoulder-length hair, which she normally drew back into a ponytail. She wore a knee-length uniform frock of light green cotton, which fitted a little too snugly. Large round tortoise shell glasses kept slipping off her nose as she refilled his coffee cup. According to Beth, Maggie had been working for Maude for the past three years after school. Bred was surprised. He hadn't realised it had been that long since he hired her.

"Aren't you a bit young for all that coffee?" she asked Bred, giving Beth a smile.

Bred looked around the Donut Shop. Maggie was working alone. "You run this whole place all by yourself?" he asked avoiding the question. Some habits were hard to break.

"Maude asked me to look after the place for her while she's away." Maggie answered.

"When do you expect Maude back?" Bred asked casually. He saw the look on Maggie's face and remembered he was just a kid now. "Mrs. Parker, I mean," he corrected.

"I just spoke with her the other day," Maggie said. "She thinks probably in another two or three months. They found another cyst," she added, her brows furrowing in concern as she wiped the table. Bred started involuntarily and accidentally knocked a glass off the table where it smashed onto the tiled floor of the solarium.

"'*Break, break, break, On thy cold grey stones,*'" Maggie said resigned, looking at the shattered fragments on the ground.

Bred quickly recovered his wits. He had been racking his brain, wondering how to get in touch with Maude. This girl was in contact with his wife!

"'*And I would that my tongue could utter, The thoughts that rise in me,*'" he answered, rising to help clean up.

She stopped, surprised. Maggie turned and studied his face. He was as tall as she. "You know Tennyson?" she asked, amused.

"Lord Alfred?" he asked innocently. "We've shared a few lyrics," he added modestly, gazing at his nails.

Maggie would not allow Bred to help clean up and brought them each a fresh milkshake.

While she was away, Beth filled him in.

"Maggie's the youngest daughter of Mr. Hiller, the assistant manager for the Standard bank in Bolton," she said, "she tells everyone that she's seventeen so she can look after the ordering and finances of the donut shop, but actually she's only fifteen.

"She plays an alto sax fairly well," Beth added. "I saw her once at a school gig." Bred was interested.

"What instrument do you play, Beth?" He regretted asking the question as soon as the words were out of his mouth.

"Don't you remember?" She looked upset, and her bottom lip came out.

"He's teasing you, Beth," said Maggie over his shoulder. "He told me you play the clarinet beautifully."

"Oh, Bred!" said Beth shyly, smacking him gently on the arm.

Bred turned, smiling at Maggie gratefully. "Would you like to join us?" he asked. She hesitated.

"Please," he said. "*'There is sweet music here that softer falls, Than petals from blown roses on the grass,'*" he said, quoting from Lord Alfred Tennyson's, The Lotus-Eaters.

"*'And in the stream the long-leaved flowers weep, And from the craggy ledge the poppy hangs in sleep'*" Maggie finished with delight and dropped into the chair next to Beth.

"Stop that! You guys are kinda hokey!" Beth cried.

"Are you entered in the music talent contest, Maggie?" She asked, getting back on topic. "At the Summer Fair," she explained when she saw Bred's curious look.

"No," Maggie said looking down at the table, "the contest is for groups only."

"And ten thousand dollars to the charity of your choice," Beth finished brightly.

"I don't care about that," Maggie said, with a mischievous smile. "I'd just want to win!"

Beth shook her head, excused herself and went to talk to a school friend.

Bred sipped his coffee thoughtfully. He had to make friends with this Maggie girl somehow. How the hell does a fourteen-year-old boy impress a fifteen-year-old girl? He wondered. Maturity! He had to appear mature.

"Beth tells me you play a pretty mean saxophone," Bred said. "But I don't know very much about jazz I'm afraid," he added, feigning regret. "I've been up in the barn at midnight with Mike Murley and Don Palmer," he continued quickly, as she seemed about to leave. "And I listened to *Benghazi Sax; Night Time Uptown*, and stared up at the sky 'til the dawn took the stars away," he mused a little sadly. "But I still don't know very much about jazz."

Maggie settled back down again, and looked at Bred curiously.

She had always been led to believe that this boy was troubled, reclusive, even disturbed. Maggie had simply avoided him in the past. But now before her she saw a smart, sensitive individual — and he seemed very mature.

"Have you heard *On the Lam?*" She asked, referring to *Benghazi Sax's* second CD. Bred smiled. He'd met Sayyd Abdul Al-Khabyyr, Buddy Rich and Wayton Marsalis at the Montreal Jazz festival twenty-seven years ago, but he didn't tell her that.

They discussed Michael Brecker, the brilliant tenor saxophone player, Lord Alfred Tennyson and Maude Parker until it was almost dark and until Beth practically dragged him away.

"What do you know about whales?" he asked Maggie, as he was putting on his coat.

★★★

Mary watched as the two of them rode up the driveway. She could hear Beth chattering all the way. She greeted them at the door and helped Beth remove her coat.

"I had a great time with my friends," Beth was saying, "thank you for taking me, Bred. Kelly never goes to town for fun, not even to the Summer Fair." Beth gave him a quick hug.

"Say, Beth," he said, as he removed his coat. "Why don't you ask Maggie to play in the talent contest with you? I'm sure Mum wouldn't mind if you practised here."

"Why, no, of course not," Mary said, not quite sure what she had agreed to.

"Do you think Maggie would?" Beth asked, a little wide-eyed.

"We can ask her," said Bred, grinning.

Mary was shocked. Who was this boy? Brian would never act this way. Not in her wildest dreams!

The last few months of winter had been relatively uneventful. Brad had kept to himself for the most part, working at his computer which he got for Christmas, or reading quietly in the living room and talking with Beth. Meals were either eaten in silence; or each one in the family did their own thing, seldom were meals eaten together.

Her mind raced as she tried to grasp the incomprehensible; to hope when she knew it was hopeless. She was suddenly very alarmed and — very afraid!

Despite her emotional denial, Mary's very being refused to accept her son's complete change in character and personality. Her maternal instinct rebelled against this — *imposter!*

Mary took him roughly by the shoulders and stared deep into his eyes.

"Who are you?" she demanded hoarsely.

He stopped, arms hanging loosely by his side, his blond hair sparkling under the golden light from the lamp in the foyer. He looked up at her and smiled.

The blood slowly drained from her face. She stood frozen, trapped in his smile like a bee in pure nectar. The memories of a time long ago and of her deepest sadness flooded unbidden into her mind.

Then, one by one, the memories of that time long ago swirled in the mists of relevance, faded — and were gone forever. In her mother-heart she now knew that Brian her only son, the child she had born into this cruel, cruel world, was gone.

With her worst fear confirmed, her sorrow rose slowly in her breast; silently she bore her pain and found her peace. And, as her youngest daughter gazed on in amazement, a wise mother wept and hugged her new son on the threshold.

★★★

CHAPTER NINE
The Teenagers

Graham Andrews was perplexed. It was May, Victoria Day, and the family was seated at dinner in the blue dining room. It was a rare occasion indeed, when the whole family was gathered together for a meal, even on a holiday.

Graham had been elucidating on the complexities and synergies of co-ordinating and managing his businesses. Graham's work was his life. That was where he channelled his energy. Work was all that had kept him going through the difficult years and all he could talk about these days with any passion. The family listened attentively and nodded when it seemed appropriate. Nobody had understood a word that he had said, except Bred.

"I'm still having a problem with our cash flow at the new bakery," Graham said. "I paid cash for the new equipment, but even with depreciation I'm still losing money," he lamented.

Bred was unable to contain himself any longer. "I assume that your income statement emphasises that the depreciation is a non-cash expense," he said, looking over at Graham at the end of the table. Graham stopped with the fork halfway to his mouth.

"Why…no…uh…yes!" He answered, nonplussed.

"Well, then, you also recognise that the cash purchase of the equipment actually represents an exchange of assets, and therefore the depreciation expense that allocates the expense over the life of the equipment requires no cash outlay."

"I suppose so, but…" Graham began.

"So adding that expense to your income will give you actual cash flow," Bred said. "Check your projected balance sheet for the end of the year."

Bred picked up his fork and continued with his meal. Everyone had stopped eating and sat looking at him a little dumfounded. Bred looked around the room.

Barry Tyrrell

"What?" he said. "It's in Dad's *Finance* magazine."

The rest of the meal was consumed with higher than normal chatter around the table, except for Graham, who seemed quite distracted with what Bred had said.

After dinner he turned to Mary.

"I think we should sit down to dinner together more often, Mary," he said thoughtfully, "at least on Saturdays and Sundays."

"Yes, dear," she said. She looked at Bred with a raised eyebrow.

★★★

"A killer whale is not a whale," Maggie yelled laughing, as she chased Bred around the room, threatening to smack him with a cushion. "They're dolphins. Just ask Michael Bigg." She was referring to the late Canadian researcher.

"Michael Bigg is no longer with us," Kelly said coldly from the stairway. No one had heard her coming down.

"Then ask K.C. Balcomb III," Maggie answered, undaunted. She did not really care for Kelly.

Beth had persuaded Maggie to enter the competition with her, and Bred had clinched it by offering to look after the shop while they practised. They had just finished their practise for that evening and were seated in the lounge at the Andrews' residence. Bred had closed up the shop and arrived home a short time before.

Maggie was determined to show off her newfound knowledge and was appalled to learn that Bred knew nothing about whales.

"Then why did you ask me if I did?" she asked surprised.

"It seemed like a good idea at the time," he replied, dodging the cushion.

"You know about whales?" Kelly asked suddenly, standing in the doorway.

"Not a lot," Maggie replied. "But enough to know that cetaceans, all cetaceans, are seriously threatened, and that one hundred years ago the oceans were teaming with whales. And now, due exclusively to human activities — and human greed — they may very soon be wiped off the face of the earth."

Beth looked up at her in surprise. "Not another one!" she groaned.

"Did you know," Maggie continued, ignoring Beth, as she warmed to her theme and turned to lean over the back of the couch to address Kelly directly. "That the grey whale in the North Atlantic is already extinct, as well as the bowhead whales between east Greenland and Novaya Zemba.

"The North Pacific, right whales are almost gone; there are only 25 females left, and there used to be millions of them!" she said. She beat her fists on the back of the couch, exasperated. "Industrialised countries poison them with chemicals, oil and noise pollution and fishermen kill them with indestructible nylon nets and civilized countries allow the largest ships and freighters to go barrelling through known calving grounds. And still some ignorant countries like Norway, the Faroe Islands and *enlightened* Japan, continue whaling even today — for pure greed, but under the pretext of 'scientific' purposes!"

"Even Iceland is planning to start killing minke whales again," she concluded passionately, as she turned back and hugged a pillow. "We have to do something — soon."

Kelly stared at her for a minute, then walked across the room and took her by the arm.

"Come," she said, softly, "let me show you something."

She led Maggie up the stairs to her room, with its books on National Oceanic and the New England Aquarium, and to where the beautiful posters of wild dolphins, orcas, and right whales were framed on the walls.

"Do you think that you and Maggie could use a tenor sax in your group?" Bred asked casually, as he helped Beth pack away her clarinet.

"You mean Kelly?" Beth asked, glancing towards the stairs. "What do you think?"

"What do I think about Kelly playing in tune? I think it would be a good thing". Bred said, bending his head to one side and pretending to bump notes out of his ear. Beth laughed at him.

"I'll ask Maggie," she said, closing the clarinet case.

Mary stood quietly listening at the kitchen door with a dishtowel in her hands. Even she was not allowed in Kelly's private sanctuary. And when last had she heard Beth laugh so? Mary felt tightness in her bosom; she took a deep breath and turned back into the kitchen.

★★★

Over the next few weeks, while Kelly and Beth were at school, Bred spent a lot of time in the town of Bolton, mostly at the donut shop talking to Maggie. She was his direct conduit to Maude.

According to Maggie, Maude had had her last scheduled operation and was responding well to the chemotherapy. It appeared that she was recovering nicely. The doctors considered her prognosis excellent and ventured that she might be able to return home in a month or so.

On a personal note, Maggie had also missed a lot of school that year looking after the donut shop, but planned to make up for it with extra classes that summer.

Bred was suddenly very apprehensive. He would have to go to school in the

Fall and he suddenly realised that he had no idea what his academic qualifications were. He would turn 15 next month, and he had a feeling that he would be in a class with some very short people if he didn't do something about it. He would have to ask Mary about that later.

Bred went to the gym regularly. 'The Gym' was very popular, being the only one in town and adults tended to dominate the facility. It was difficult to gain access to the equipment or even use the benches or free-weights. Everyone seemed to take him for granted: he felt like a single on a busy golf course. He couldn't take his *turn* on the equipment because he didn't officially have one. Bred had to bite his tongue on numerous occasions; the humiliation reminded him that he was not merely playing the role of a young teenager.

He mentioned the problem to Maggie after a frustrating morning where he had done nothing but callisthenics.

"You can work out with me," she offered, almost shyly. Bred raised his eyebrow curiously. "My dad's bank foreclosed on 'George's Gym' last year," she explained. "The creditors and the lawyers haven't processed it yet. I have the key." She raised her eyebrows twice, quickly.

'George's Gym' was perfect. Located off the main thoroughfare and away from the residential areas, the neglected old building would have stood unnoticed forever if left alone. The windows had all been boarded up from the outside and newspapers covered them on the inside.

Most of the equipment was operational and most of the free-weights were still in the racks. The mirrors and the rough red Berber carpets were all in good shape and the building had power, water and heating.

Best of all, the steam-room was fully operational. The ten-by-ten room was tiled with light-blue ceramic, even on the ceiling, and padded wooden benches adorned two sides. A thermostat at the door controlled steam and temperature.

The two of them sat on opposite benches with towels draped around them after their workouts and talked across the room to each other. Maggie liked it really steamy, so much so, they could hardly see each other across the room. They talked about everything under the sun, but mostly they talked about life in Bolton, jazz, Tennyson and Maude Parker.

Bred had always been a good student, but it was hard learning how to be a kid again.

★★★

"My dad is going to be fired!" Maggie wept. "We're going to have to leave Bolton, maybe even Alberta!"

It was raining outside, and Mary, Kelly and Beth had dropped into the donut shop to pick up Maggie for music practice in the family SUV.

"But why?" Kelly asked in dismay, putting her arm around Maggie's shoulder. "Daddy said he was the central figure in an investigation into the security of the Bank's money transfers," Maggie sobbed, wiping away her tears. "He was called before the International Board of Directors of the Standard Bank in Edmonton. "They're sending two Senior Officers of the bank down here to fire him on Friday."

"That's just three days!" Kelly cried, now really upset. She hugged Maggie closer and the tears flowed. Beth started crying too. Mary had her hands full as Bred walked through the door.

"Whoa!" he said, surprised. Maggie ran to him, still sobbing. She hugged him around the neck for a moment, and then quickly ran to the back of the shop to freshen up as two new customers came through the door.

Mary had an appointment and reluctantly left the unhappy group alone in the shop. There would be no music practice that day so she arranged to pick them up later. Bred helped himself and the customers to a cup of coffee and sat down quietly at the table with Kelly and Beth. They finally settled down enough to fill Bred in on the situation.

"What are we going to do?" Beth said desperately. "We've got to help Maggie."

"There's nothing we can do, Beth," Kelly said abruptly, wiping her eyes.

"This is the reality of our dictatorial business world. I detest the whole crass financial institution and its associated greedy commercialism," she added. Beth and Bred stared at her in surprise.

"I overheard Dad," she muttered.

"Bred," Beth pleaded, "can't you do something?" She tipping her head on his shoulder.

Bred had said nothing. He had listened thoughtfully to the conversation, though he was still a little rattled by the revelation.

This unfortunate turn of events he did not need right now. It had taken him a long time to make friends with Maggie and to gain her confidence. He needed her around to keep him informed about Maude. Besides, he liked Maggie and he was just starting to get it together as a teenager again.

Think. Think. Bred taxed his brain. Come on, Brian, do your bit. What was it George had said a while back…? Oh yeah! Kyle had an influential friend at the bank…

Bred took a gulp of his coffee. He looked at Beth and smiled.

"Stone Soup!" he said. Both girls stared at him, startled.

"Stone soup? What's that?" Kelly was the first to recover.

"It's a children's story," Beth said. "It's about three soldiers who trick a whole town into providing them with a wonderful soup meal, including bacon, by starting out with just a pot, some water and some rocks."

"Very good, Beth," Bred said. "That's one version. Ann McGovern wrote the original story a while back."

"But I don't see how…" Kelly stopped. She looked at Bred expectantly.

"Come on!" Bred said, standing up and grabbing a pad and pencil from under the counter. "We'll be the soldiers, we've got work to do."

"Beth," he continued, "make a list of the business people around here and some of the juicy stuff they're involved in. Kelly, let's get your laptop — we've got a few e-mails to write." Bred smiled at their wide-eyed, startled expressions. "We'll put some water in the pot, add the rocks, and light a fire under it," he explained.

★★★

Bred, Kelly and Beth were sitting in the solarium of Maude's Donut Shop at a table beside the window overlooking the bustling main street of Bolton. It was Friday morning on a beautiful, sunny spring day. The streets would normally be empty at that time in the quiet laid-back town, except for the commotion across the street outside the Standard Bank.

"What's going on?" Maggie asked, strolling over and tying her apron around her waist. She looked awful. Her face was puffy from lack of sleep and she looked like she had been crying again.

"Stone Soup," Beth said absently, her attention focused on the street.

"What?" Maggie said. The three of them had agreed not to include Maggie in the plot, just in case their scheme didn't work.

"The bank is the pot," Kelly explained, taking pity on her. "The stones are in the pot, we've added the water," she patted the computer, "and now we're adding the vegetables."

"*What?*" echoed Maggie, even more baffled.

Before anyone had a chance to explain any further, Maggie was called away to serve some new customers.

★★★

Inside the bank, the two senior officers of the Standard Bank were seated in Mr. Hiller's office. They sat erect on their chairs with their thick black briefcases held firmly in their laps. Mr. Hiller sat behind his desk feeling totally intimidated by the two very sombre and very differently proportioned gentlemen, so immaculately dressed in their matching tailored dark suits and turquoise-coloured waistcoats sitting across from him.

Mr. Hiller's eyes bulged a little behind his thick spectacles. He bolstered his failing courage and lifted his chin expectantly. Despite the cruel, unjust fate about to befall him, Mr. Hiller was determined to maintain his dignity.

They look like Laurel and Hardy! The comic characters from the black and white flicks, popped uninvited into Mr. Hiller's head. The images forced a chain reaction of frayed nerves and muscles in his cheeks to create an equally uninvited smile.

"Our visit here is of a very serious nature, Mr. Hiller," *Hardy* said.

The situation was ludicrous.

"Of course," Mr. Hiller said, feeling that despicable laugh-bubble starting just below his ribs.

"We feel that the security procedures and the selection of a conventional courier to transport bank receipts was totally inappropriate," *Hardy* added pompously.

"And you put the bank's assets at serious risk as well," *Laurel* said emphatically, emulating the nodding head perfectly.

Mr. Hiller's laugh-bubble exploded. "Woof!"

He doubled over in his chair and disappeared below level of the desk in a fit of nervous, stifled giggles. The two senior officers were quite astonished and craned their necks to see what was going on.

Mr Hiller physically controlled himself by cutting off his own breathing with his thumb in his windpipe. Regaining his composure, he peeked over the edge of the desk through his tears, only to see *Hardy* opening and closing his mouth like a goldfish. Mr. Hiller slowly sank back below the rim of the desk again, his face turning from crimson to blue as he gradually choked himself to death.

In the nick of time, the bank doors opened and fifty extremely irate citizens surged through and burst straight into Mr. Hiller's office. The room was a pandemonium with everyone yelling at once. The two senior officers stood wide-eyed with their backs against the wall, trying to regain their wits in the midst of the chaos.

Finally, a burly farmer pushed his way to the front of the crowd, flanked by his two equally burly sons. He turned toward the crowd and held up his hands. When they had quieted down, he turned slowly back to address the two senior officers.

"Are you people out of your fucking minds?" Pete Morgan screamed at them, and the whole place erupted again.

"I would have lost my farm if it had not been for Mr. Hiller!" yelled one.

"My business has doubled because of Mr. Hiller's foresight!" shouted another.

"I'm comfortable on my pension now because of Mr. Hiller!" admonish a grey-haired little old lady, waving her finger in *Laurel's* face, as he cringed under the scolding.

"You're firing a man totally committed to his community. You should be ashamed of yourselves!" Phyllis Dowd said, joining in the melee and brandishing a pencil at *Hardy*. And on, and on it went until everyone had had their say.

"It is still a question of security," said *Hardy* regaining his composure when all was said and done. "Mr. Hiller authorised the transportation of the bank's receipts in an unsecured vehicle, resulting, I might add, in the loss of those receipts," he said with finality.

"That is the crux of the matter. Totally unforgivable," *Laural* concluded, nodding furiously in agreement.

Hardy held up his hand, palm out and turned his face away as some of the people would have protested further.

★★★

"Time for the bacon," Bred said, looking at his wristwatch from his lookout post in the solarium.

"Bacon?" Maggie said, still outside the box, having just returned to the table.

"For the soup," Beth said opening the laptop and plugging into the phone jack. "To give it that extra flavour."

"Oh!" Maggie said, wandering off in a daze to help another customer. She didn't have a clue what they were talking about. She would really have to stay away from those people.

"Go!" Bred said. Kelly hit the buttons and the e-mails she had prepared a little earlier sped on their merry, electronic way.

Three minutes and fifty-five seconds later, Kyle Bishop brought his truck to a sliding halt in front of the bank. He jumped out in a cloud of dust, ran up four steps, tripped over the fifth and stumbled headfirst into the bank. Beth howled with laughter.

"The bacon is in the pot," Bred said satisfied, leaning back in his chair with his hands behind his head. "Now we let the pot boil."

"What *bacon?*" Maggie inquired, in real mental distress, coming back to the table and flopping despondently onto a chair.

★★★

Kyle elbowed his way to the front of the crowd in Mr. Hiller's office. He ignored the two senior officers of the bank, if indeed he even noticed them, and confronted Mr. Hiller directly.

"What the hell do you mean by this!" he hollered, holding up and waving the e-mail that he had just received a few minutes before.

"You have absolutely no authority to cancel my courier service contract with this bank," he ranted. "Some very influential people approved this service contract. You voiced your objections about my van a long time ago and you were overruled, Mr. Hiller — *overruled!* You are way over your head, my friend." He stepped closer to Mr. Hiller threateningly, waving the crumpled e-mail in his face.

"This service agreement was drawn up by me and some very influential people who have a vested interest in my business and in the bank's business."

The room was very still.

"And, who might that be?" Mr. Hiller asked stubbornly, not backing down.

His obstinate attitude enraged Kyle further. He was a big man with an evil temper and he towered over the brave Mr. Hiller. "Director Phinias Muldoon and members of the board, for a start," Kyle yelled furiously, his red face almost matching his hair. "As well as…!" He stopped, realising he had gone too far already.

The blood drained from his cheeks, as he turned to look at the room full of shocked faces around him. He stared in turn at the two senior officers standing against the wall and across the room at Corporal Patrick D'Laney. Patrick stood with his arms folded and his head cocked to one side, leaning casually against the doorway to Mr. Hiller's office.

In the Corporal's pocket was an e-mail, informing him that there was a very serious public incident about to take place at the Standard Bank, in the little town of Bolton.

★★★

Maggie came bursting into the Andrews' house at 8.15 the following Saturday morning. It had been raining all night and it was still pouring down. Maggie had ridden the two miles out to the estate on her bicycle.

"Thank you! Thank you! Thank you!" she bubbled, as she came running into the kitchen. Mary squealed when Maggie grabbed her and gave her a big wet kiss on the cheek.

"You're soaked to the bone, child!" Mary exclaimed, wondering what had brought this on, but determined to take care of health matters first.

Mary had wrapped her in a blanket and was putting a towel around Maggie's drenched hair when Beth and Kelly, both awakened by the noise, came stumbling down the stairs in their nightgowns.

Maggie was so excited that she could not stand still. Mary left it to Kelly and Beth to dry Maggie's hair and settle her down on the couch while she made a pot of tea.

"We're staying in Bolton!" Maggie squealed. That got all the girls squealing and dancing up and down on the couch. Bred caught the brunt of it as he came in through the door from his main level bedroom. He stopped and screwed up one side of his face to deaden the ringing pain in his ears.

"My dad had to go to a meeting with the bank directors in Edmonton last night and he didn't get home 'til after midnight," Maggie bubbled excitedly, when they had all settled down in the lounge. "He was commended for his professionalism and dedication to the community.

"He has to fly to Toronto on Monday for a meeting at the head offices of the Standard Bank. He's going to be promoted to Manager of the Standard Bank in Bolton!" She finished on a high note, and the squealing started all over again.

Bred put his teacup down. He didn't want to be blamed when it shattered.

"You guys had something to do with it, didn't you?" Maggie said, squeezing Mary's arm.

"Not me," Mary said, shaking her head. "Why would you think such a thing?" She was genuinely puzzled.

"I detest the whole crass financial institution and its associated greedy commercialism," Beth said, taking her queue from Kelly's earlier rant. Kelly looked at her, quite startled. Bred chuckled and shrugged his shoulders.

"That's excellent news though, Maggie," Bred said with a smile. He rose and stretched, pulling on the belt of his housecoat. "I had better go and get dressed," he said.

"What's for breakfast, mum?"

Kelly rested her elbow on the arm of the couch and cupped her cheek in her hand. She looked up at her little brother as if really seeing him for the first time.

"Stone Soup!" She said, before Mary could reply. Kelly couldn't hold back a smile. Bred grinned at her and left the room.

Beth's pealing laughter followed him until he was way down the hall and out of earshot.

Fifteen may not have to be such a tedious age after all, Bred thought. He had never had a particularly devious mind as a child and it seemed that Brian's parts were becoming somewhat more active, though he had no control over it. Bred smiled, as he opened the door and walked into the bedroom.

That Brian is a sneaky little bastard, he thought.

★★★

The day of the Summer Fair dawned bright and clear; July 1, Canada Day. Bred's sixteenth birthday had come and gone, and to his surprise, Bred found himself joining in the festivities with as much enthusiasm as Beth and Kelly.

He had ridden into town alone on his bicycle, leaving the girls to their stage make-up in preparation for their gala performance. The little town of Bolton seemed to swell with pride.

The population had in fact more than doubled for the annual festive event. Great coloured tents and stalls were packed into the open field behind the community hall and were decked with balloons and stuffed toys. Flags and banners streamed from every pole and light-stand and the music blared as the hawkers cried their wares from every corner.

A local crafts and market-garden atmosphere dominated the fair for the most part, but there was still the inevitable congregation of hucksters and professional rip-off artists competing for the visitors 'fun money'.

Fred had learned the tricks of the carnival a long time ago, and Bred took full advantage. He won a ton of prizes, which he instantly gave away. He had a great time until the thugs and carnies caught on and banned him from playing any more.

Bred wandered over to the tent where the talent contests were taking place and watched some pretty startling performances for an hour or so. He wondered how some folks found the courage to go up there in the first place.

Mary arrived with her entourage and a very excited Beth Andrews in tow, chattering incessantly. Bred came out to meet them and gave Beth a pillow-sized teddy bear that he had won. It was dressed in green dungarees and had a peaked cap with a feather stuck in it.

"A Robin Hood Bear!" Beth squealed delighted. "I always wanted one of these! Ever since I was a child!"

Mary just rolled her eyes.

"So, what piece did your group finally choose?' Bred asked, with a grin.

"Thou Swell," answered Kelly with a deep nervous breath. "A Rogers-Hart tune

from the sixties."

"We wanted something special from the Natalie Cole era," Maggie said, "and not Andy Ratzof and Joe Garland's, *In The Mood*. Everyone plays that."

"I know the one," said Bred. "Theme for '*A Connecticut Yankee in King Arthur's Court*.'"

Mary stopped short, seemed about to say something, shook her head and carried on walking into the tent. While Mary and Bred found their seats, the girls disappeared behind the stage curtain to prepare for their set. A few minutes later, Jenny Tabor announced the group.

"And now," she said, "our own Bolton triplets — '*The Macbeths.*'"

The girls took up their positions in a rehearsed crescendo of firecrackers and smoke. Unfortunately, the young volunteer stagehand had not been warned about the firecrackers and was totally unprepared for the explosions. In his haste to escape what he thought to be certain death and injury, he tripped over a temporary light stand. The structure teetered momentarily before falling, and everyone dived for cover as the lights came crashing down.

Beth watched in dismay as her beloved clarinet was torn from her fingers by the falling pole and dashed to pieces on the concrete floor below the stage. An awful silence settled over the startled audience.

Bred rose from his seat and walked up onto the stage. He took the shaken, trembling Beth by the hand and led her to the piano. He sat down and patted his lap. Beth looked at him strangely and settled on his knee.

"Put your hands on top of mine," he said. Beth complied as she looked at him in anguish.

"Bred," she whispered hoarsely. "You…you don't play the piano."

"I do today," Bred said, nodding to Maggie and began the overture to *A Connecticut Yankee in King Arthur's Court*.

There were many other musical performances scheduled throughout the day and the group watched from the side of the stage.

"Oh, no!" Beth breathed, as one particular group of performers came up onto the stage. "That's Gregory Dowd from my school. He's one of the *Rascals* — and he likes me." She gritted her teeth and shook her head in mock horror.

A brown-haired, chubby boy about ten years old, dressed in an ill-fitting brown suit led the way. He was carrying a violin and was followed by a thin blonde girl in a white frilly dress. She was a couple of years older and carried a flute. Taking up the rear and stumbling up the last few steps came a lanky young fellow in brown corduroy trousers and a white open-neck shirt. He walked over to the piano and settled himself on the bench.

What followed was the most beautiful amateur rendition of *Tchaikovsky's Waltz of the Flowers* that Bred had ever heard. Gregory was magnificent on the violin. The audience sat in stunned silence for a few seconds after the performance, before erupting in thunderous applause, which lasted almost three minutes.

Beth gave Gregory her Robin Hood bear.

Maggie, Kelly and Beth lost the Bolton Music Talent Contest to the *Rascals*, but Beth found her first *real* boyfriend.

★★★

"Grade seven? But I ought to be going to grade ten this fall!" Bred said, aghast.

He, Mary and Julie Martins were sitting at the kitchen table going over Brian's school records. He was a 'D' student at best. "Can't I go to summer school?" he pleaded.

Paramedics Julie Martins and Matt Finch had kept in touch with the family since Bred had come home. Julie seemed to have developed a personal interest in his welfare. Julie had once mentioned in passing that she had once been a teacher, so Mary had asked her to come over, thinking she might be able to help.

"You can do math and language arts," Julie said. "Summer school is available to you for five Saturday mornings starting soon. The only other option open is to pick up the rest of your classes through home schooling."

"Home schooling?" Bred said, hopefully.

"For Social Studies, Science, Art, Music, Health and Home Economics," she said.

"Home Economics?" Bred's heart sank. The women laughed.

Julie agreed to tutor Bred at her apartment, and they worked out a schedule for the two of them to get together once a week.

★★★

Bred attended his first day of summer school in July, with thirty-eight other ne'er-do-wells who really did not want to be there.

Bred's excuse for being there was that he had been ill and missed a year. After that they called him *'Sicko.'* He seriously wanted to kick some butt.

Their instructor, Mr. Gooding, was a sixty-five year old substitute teacher in real life. Frustrated with his chosen profession, no longer able to maintain order by sending the errant student on a trip of the principal's office or by the threat of physical discipline, Mr. Gooding just went through the motions. Those who listened would learn and the rest of the students could just wallow in ignorance for all he cared.

Bred's biggest problem were the students in the class. They were a totally *undisciplined mass of writhing humanity*, sentenced to five weeks of summer school by their holiday-weary parents in desperate need of a babysitter. Bred had intended to idle along nicely for the next five weeks, receive a passing grade and then move on.

There was no way! He just had to move up a few grades — today!

Mr. Gooding scribbled 50 math questions on the blackboard, ignoring the paper darts and spitballs slapping against the board as he wrote.

"This is your assignment for the next two weeks," he yelled through the din, tapping on the board. "Do what you can with them and we'll work on your problem areas after that. "Let me know when you're done."

"I'm done," Bred said loud enough to be heard. He stood up and in the ensuing silence walked to the head of the class and handed his notebook to Mr. Gooding.

Mr. Gooding was taken aback for a minute as he took the notebook. He looked numbly at Bred and then at the class.

"Whooo!" the class said.

Mr. Gooding's jaw stiffened and his face flushed with annoyance. His initial thought was that he was being taken for a fool. He prepared himself to react accordingly. He raised his hand, took a deep breath and was about to admonish Bred when his eye caught the answer to one of his questions. He adjusted his spectacles as he walked back to his desk and sat down, studying the notebook in astonishment.

The minor distraction could not keep the attention span of the class for long and the volume within the *undisciplined mass of writhing humanity* began to escalate once more.

"Class dismissed!" Mr. Gooding said, turning the page. "Mr. Andrews, you stay!"

"You obviously understand the subject matter, Mr. Andrews," said Mr. Gooding looking up from the desk thoughtfully as he flipped through the pages of the notebook with his thumb. "I don't see why we should waste your time here." He reached into his briefcase and extracted a sheet of paper.

"This is the final exam paper, if you wish; you can write the exam right now…we have the rest of the period."

Mr. Gooding smiled as he watched the boy take up the challenge. He reminded himself that, every once in a while, teaching was a pleasure.

★★★

The following week, Mr. Gooding was kind enough to give Bred a passing grade in math and excused him from attending future classes. Language arts, on the other hand, proved to be more challenging.

The class was much smaller, only eighteen in all, and the student body consisted mostly of girls who seemed interested in the class material. Bred found that he was a little rusty on Shakespeare, so he had initiated a lively debate over the great poet's propensity to plagiarise themes: most specifically, Shakespeare's Tragedy, *Romeo and Juliet*, a story likely 'borrowed' from Ovid's *Metamoerphoses,* from Greek mythology, was the tale of doomed lovers Pyramus and Thisbe.

The students were shocked and outraged at the suggestion that the great Bard could actually have cheated. Ms. Stoneway, their teacher, had a lot of explaining to do. In the midst of the furore, she scowled at the grinning Bred. She was not amused.

★★★

Bred took the short transit ride from just outside the school to Julie Martins' apartment, situated in an upscale complex in South Edmonton Plaza.

Bred realised that there was something amiss the minute he walked through the front door. What should have been a pleasant two-bedroom suite, was actually quite the opposite.

Sparsely furnished with utility furniture and matching cushions, the living room consisted of an aged, gold sofa and two matching armchairs. A wood veneer coffee table stood in the centre of the room and on it lay a large scrapbook. Imitation pottery lamps stood on two side tables covered with beige drop cloths.

A small television set was perched on the edge of a plain wooden bench next to a pile of old magazines. Pictures of dull, glass covered wilderness scenes decorated the walls. Julie's apartment was a bleak, unhappy place.

They sat at the plain kitchen table, where Julie reintroduced the fundamentals of a host of subjects, their contents prepared by the crème de la crème of society and intended to mould young minds and stimulate interest in learning. Bred, with his mind already moulded and full of learning, soon became oversaturated. He asked to be excused after a while and went to the washroom to soak his head. Julie got up to make the tea.

Bred accidentally opened the wrong door at the end of the hallway and when he switched on the light, found himself in Julie's bedroom.

The room was furnished with an unmade double bed, a small bedside table with an equally small lamp, an alarm clock and a plain black telephone. No pictures adorned the walls, and no carpets lay on the floor. A blanket covered the window to hide the sun.

Beside the lamp there stood a small picture in a silver frame. Bred walked across the room and picked up the picture. It was a photograph of a younger Matt Finch, Julie's partner, holding a shaggy sheepdog puppy. He replaced the picture and as he did so he noticed a small bottle of blue pills beside the lamp. The label read 'Acetamorphine.'

Bred shook his head. Maude had used those to sleep as well, but only when her pain was intolerable. He opened the bedside drawer, there were more little bottles; 'Lorazepam' and another read 'Zoloft'.

Powerful anti–depressants and anti-anxiety drugs, he thought. They were extremely addictive. He left the room quietly.

Later, while waiting for Mary to pick him up after the lesson, he absently flipped open the scrapbook on the coffee table and was shocked at the images that sprang before his eyes. There were images of children in a faraway land, practically ignored by Western society. There were images of babies and abandoned adolescents, afraid, hungry, mutilated by the ravages of war.

Nothing was held back, the explicit photographs showed the blood and the tears of the children, their health chronically affected by toxic materials, malnutrition and lack of medical care. They depicted the poverty, squalor and the faces of the most wretched of humanity. All was laid bare in the clippings and photographs before him. He turned the page.

"No, Bred!" Julie called in alarm from the kitchen door, quickly crossing the room. "This is not for your eyes. Not until you can understand," she said, closing the scrapbook.

"I have never understood," he said, still appalled. "I will never understand!"

Julie saw only the empathy in his eyes, but could not know, or ever fathom the depth of his own life-sorrow. She hugged him.

"Here's your mother," she said, taking a deep breath and releasing him as the doorbell rang.

Bred was very quiet on the way home. As they came up the driveway to the Andrews' house, he turned to Mary and revealed what was troubling him.

"We have to contact Matt," Bred said. "Julie is suffering from severe emotional distress. She appears to conform to the rules of her community and her working environment. She gets along great with everyone, or appears to, but privately, she's a total wreck. She has all the classic symptoms, anxiety, fear, anger, depression and especially guilt." Bred turned away and stared out the window. Mary was stunned.

"If we don't do something soon, she will do herself a dreadful harm," he said seriously.

Mary stopped the SUV in the middle of the driveway, and turned to stare at her son.

"What happened, Bred?" she asked, recovering from her astonishment at his conclusion.

Bred told her about the apartment, the scrapbook and the little blue pills.

A few minutes later, Mary called Matt on the car phone.

"Matt? I really need to talk to you. It's about Julie," she said. There was three seconds of silence on the line.

"I'll be over right away," Matt Finch said, needing no further explanation.

★★★

Bred had arranged to meet with Maggie in town and could not wait for Matt to arrive. He reasoned that the adults could probably better deal with the matter. On sober second thought, he did not believe that for one minute.

Bred met Maggie and a group of acquaintances at the donut shop. She had good news indeed. Maude was doing well. She would be well enough to travel in two or three weeks and could complete her convalescence at home.

"She'll have to stay in the hospital in Edmonton for a while though," Maggie cautioned.

Bred was ecstatic.

"Yessss!" he yelled, forgetting himself for a moment.

Maggie looked at him out of the corner of her eye.

Matt Finch came through the door and they all greeted him warmly.

Matt was a dark, wholesome, stocky fellow and a popular, frequent visitor to Bolton. Matt and Julie always set up a realistic paramedic display at the Summer Fair, and the kids all milled about vying to be made up as gory crash test dummies.

Matt was not a handsome man by any stretch of the imagination, but he had a great disposition and a ready smile. Matt was thirty-two and had never married, loved his job and he loved Julie Martins, though he could never tell her so, for fear of losing the close relationship they already had.

After the greetings were over, Matt pulled Bred aside and they sat at a table in the solarium away from the others.

"Bred," he said, leaning his arms on the table. "I spoke to your mom and she told me what you had seen at Julie's apartment and what you thought it meant." He rubbed his eye, hoping this would just go away.

"Is it possible that we're overreacting a little here?" Matt dropped his hand on the table. Bred looked at him thoughtfully, would Matt take the advice of a fifteen-year old boy? For Julie's sake, he had to try.

"I'm not a doctor, but I have read the *Diagnostic and Statistical Manual of Mental Disorders* published by the APA. Its primary aim is descriptive, to provide a clear criteria of diagnostic categories." He paused to let it sink in. Matt was staring at him with his mouth open.

"Julie falls into the Anxiety Disorder category — no question." Fred had seen the symptoms before.

Involuntarily he recalled the details of another place, another time, a time of war. Angola — South West Africa. It was 1979, and Fred Parker was working in the Tsumeb mining region just south of the Caprivi Strip.

South African troops were fighting alongside Jonas Sivimbi and his UNITA forces against the overwhelming might of the Soviet Union and its allies, Cubans under Fidel Castro, SWAPO and the Marxist MPLA led by Dr. Agostino Neto.

One night, a terrorist group know as *"Volcano,"* trained in Eastern Europe and commanded by the Russian General Shagnovich, crossed the border into the Tsumeb region and began killing people indiscriminately. Along with SWAPO, they massacred 158 civilians and abducted 450 children back to Angola where they would be trained in guerrilla warfare. Fred Parker was part of the militia that drove off the attackers, killing 76, and joined in the futile pursuit of the children. Every time they got close, the rebels would butcher some of the children in the most brutal manner to slow their pursuers. It worked, and it took Bred a long time to get over his rage. Bred shook his head and focused on the present.

"The pictures she keeps indicate some form of post traumatic stress disorder. Is that possible?"

Matt did a double take, as his mind absorbed the words spoken by the teenager seated in front of him. "Y...Yes," he stammered. "Julie did two tours as a medic in Kosovo with the Canadian Armed Forces, three, four years ago."

Bred nodded. "I don't know where she sends all her money, but I would guess it goes to help children somewhere. She carries a heavy guilt load, Matt."

"Lord knows I've tried, ever since I've known her," Matt groaned. "I know what she's like. But whenever I get too close, she switches off and keeps me at arm's length. She puts on this facade and she won't even see a doctor anymore." He shook his head weakly.

"I've seen it coming," he sighed, "I don't know what to do." He looked at Bred helplessly.

"You can buy her a puppy," Bred said.

"What!"

"A shaggy black and white sheepdog puppy," Bred added. "Like the one you had when you were younger."

"You're freaking me out, Bred."

Bred smiled. "There's a photograph of you and a shaggy sheepdog puppy in Julie's apartment," he explained.

Matt relaxed with a sheepish grin. "That was Max. He's living with my folks out on the island. I gave her that picture a long time ago." Matt thought for a minute. "She won't take it," he said, shaking his head.

"She won't have much choice if you have the pup delivered in a basket late Friday afternoon," Bred answered.

"And by the time the weekend is over, she may…" Matt stopped speaking as he considered the proposal. Finally, he nodded his head and smiled at Bred mischievously. It's worth a try." He said.

Julie was furious. The puppy had missed the newspaper she had just laid out — again!

Bred had come over for his Saturday afternoon lesson and found Julie's apartment in turmoil. The cushions were on the living room floor, a little wet from being gnawed on, and one of Julie's boots was pretty chewed up and lying bedraggled in the corner. The dog had somehow gotten into the laundry hamper and dragged everything all over the place. The puppy was having a great time.

Bred grinned as the pup jumped all over him, while he cleaned up the puddle on the floor with a paper towel.

"Just put him on the paper every time he squats," Bred said, petting the frisky critter. "He'll get the hang of it."

"He's a *she*," Julie said, flopping onto the sofa, "and she gets into everything! Last night I locked her up in the laundry room, but she cried so, I had to let her sleep with me. She burrowed right into my neck, and she whimpers in her sleep!" Julie sat up abruptly and turned to Bred.

"Needless to say *I* didn't get any sleep." She narrowed her eyes. "I'm going to give Matt what-for when I see him again. He's not answering my calls… She's going right back where she came from!" she added angrily, pointing at her soggy boot.

Just then they heard a yelp, and the puppy tumbling out of the bathroom, streaming toilet paper behind her.

Bred broke up laughing. Julie couldn't get any angrier, so she put her hands over her eyes and snickered helplessly. It was going to be a very long weekend. Monday was a holiday, and Matt was nowhere to be found.

Bred was putting on his coat after the lesson, when they saw Mary pull up outside through the upstairs window.

"Would you mind mailing these letters for me on your way out, Bred?" Julie asked.

Bred took the package, petted the pup again as he said goodbye and headed down the stairwell. He paused in the foyer, shuffled through the letters. He selected one and put it in his jacket pocket. He put the rest in the red mailbox just outside the door of the apartment and headed across the sunny parking lot to meet Mary D'Laney — Andrews waiting patiently in the SUV.

Julie watched as they drove out of the parking lot, then absently bent down and picked up the dog bouncing around at her feet. She cuddled the little animal and smiled when the puppy licked her chin.

The silver-green leaves were bursting at the seams as they fluttered in the breeze on the old elm tree in the parking lot, and on the ground, the grass was shaded around its gnarled, bark trunk. The tree stood like pristine, green island in a sea of black, simmering asphalt. Beside the sidewalk, Alberta roses were in full bloom along the picket fence, and robins were strutting around on the lawns.

It was mid summer, and it should have been a happy, melancholy time for all God's creatures, as well as for the people of the little town of Bolton, Alberta.

★★★

Mary manoeuvred the SUV skilfully through the light traffic. She joined the freeway on the outskirts of the city and headed southward on 50th street back toward Bolton.

Bred withdrew the letter from inside his coat and opened it. It was addressed to the Crestfield Institute just west of Calgary; about three hours drive from Edmonton. He inspected Julie's paycheque inside the envelope. The cheque had been endorsed on behalf of the institute.

Just as I had expected, he thought sadly.

Bred turned to Mary. "Would you please drive back to Matt's house, Mum?" he asked. "There's something we have to do." He settled back in his seat and closed his eyes.

Mary glanced at Bred and at the letter on his lap. She nodded and turned off at the next intersection

★★★

Matt hung up the telephone following the call to the institute.

"We have to go to Crestfield," he said, "Sister Marie said to come down right away." Matt informed his guests waiting patiently in the living room of his apartment. "They recognise the urgency, and will wait for us there.

★★★

The imposing, four-story sandstone block building comprising the Crestfield Institute stood on ten acres just west of the village of Crestfield, Alberta. Beautifully landscaped lawns, flowerbeds, trees and shrubs complemented the early nineteenth-century building. Stone pillars stood at the entrance to the estate, and a four-foot high stone wall ran all the way around the property. A long curved concrete driveway ran up from the cast iron gates to a circular driveway in front of the building. The roadway looped around a large stone fountain statue of a father reaching down for his son's hand. Flowers and shrubs, already in bloom, surrounded the statue.

Mary drove the SUV around the garden and stopped in front of the entrance to the building.

Sister Marie, and two other sisters who never spoke a word, greeted Mary, Matt and Bred at the great wooden front doors. They ushered them down a passage and into a comfortable reception room, modestly decorated with mid-American styled furniture. After dispensing with formal greetings and the formalities, tea was served by one of the sisters. Sister Marie turned to Matt.

"Our brief discussion on the telephone did not go very well," she said. "You almost made an unfortunate accusation," she smiled as she continued. "But we thank you for coming all this way on such short notice."

"Our concern is for our friend, Julie Martins," said Mary. "The financial issue is not important." Bred had given the letter to Mary earlier. She handed the cheque to the sister.

"Ah, yes," Sister Marie said thoughtfully, studying the cheque. She rose and walked over to a tall cabinet situated in the corner of the room. She pulled out a file and came back to the table. She extracted four more cheques made out to Julie dated over the last two months and added them to the one Mary had given her. She spread them out on the table in front of Mary. All had been endorsed by Julie, and made out to the Crestfield Institute. The institute had not deposited them.

"This happens once in a while," she added kindly. "Those of us that have been to the brink of despair sometimes feel the most culpable." She lowered her eyes for a moment, and then raised her chin resolutely. "We are sometimes able to recognize the warning signs, and try not to take advantage, as in Julie's case."

"We have been trying to locate Julie Martins for some time," she continued, as everyone stared at her in surprise, "but her contributions have always been without a return address or phone number." She held up palms up in a gesture of helplessness.

"Now tell me her story," she said, sitting down quietly again and folding her hands in her lap.

When they had finished, Sister Marie studied each of them carefully.

"Come," she said, "let me show you something."

They walked down the long passages inside the institute and emerged at the back of the building. They crossed a long stone courtyard, the walls covered in ivy, to a set of heavy black iron gates. The sisters opened the gates and they walked out into a vast expanse of lawns and playing fields.

A hundred children of all ages were playing, running, dancing, jumping, yelling and rolling around on the grass, just doing what kids do on a warm summer day. Some of the parents were sitting on the benches beneath the shade trees, talking and dozing and watching the children play.

A young girl in her teens ran up, flushed from her exertions. She said something to Sister Marie in a strange tongue, looking at Bred shyly.

"Nyet," the sister answered, and she ran off laughing. Sister Marie looked at Bred.

She wanted to know if you were coming to join us," she said, smiling. "All these children are from those war-torn lands you hear about but never see, except in the occasional newsreels," Sister Marie turned to address her guests. "Countries like Somalia, Bosnia, Kosovo, Afghanistan and others.

"And this is the place where the families first come to, after escaping from their homelands. They come here to mourn, to adjust to peace in a foreign land,

and to be integrated into our society." She smiled sadly, briefly holding the hand of woman passing by.

"Its people like Julie Martins who made this possible," she continued. "When they first arrive, they look just as you described in Julie's notebook, Bred. But look at them now." She swept her arm slowly, indicating the field of happy children.

"Bring your Julie down to stay with us for a little while," Sister Marie said to Matt kindly. "It will do her good to know that her efforts and her sacrifices were not in vain."

It took a long time, but Matt finally persuaded Julie to visit the Crestfield Institute. Sister Marie and the other sisters welcomed her with open arms, and Julie cried for a long time.

Eventually, with the sister's help and Matt's love and support, Julie Martins learned to cope with her debilitating illness. Julie moved in with Matt, and took Poochie, her shaggy sheepdog, with her.

★★★

CHAPTER TEN
The Return of Maude

On a Thursday morning in early August a few weeks later, Maggie turned happily to the customers in the donut shop as she hung up the phone.

"Maude Parker is coming back home!" She announced loudly.

A boisterous cheer followed the news and everyone clapped and whistled zealously, even those visitors who had no idea who Maude Parker was.

Bred, who was sitting with Kelly and a few friends, tried to control his enthusiasm. He was aware that Maggie had begun to wonder about his infatuation with Maude but Bred waited patiently, until he saw Maggie heading over to their table.

"I wonder when Mrs. Parker is coming back, exactly?" he asked Kelly casually.

"I don't know," Kelly said. "I'll ask Maggie…. Here she comes.

"Maggie, Bred would like to know just when Mrs. Parker will be back, exactly" she said innocently.

Shit, that didn't work very well, Bred thought, shifting uncomfortably, and seeing the intensely curious look Maggie was giving him.

"Maude arrived at City Hospital this morning," Maggie said, turning her attention to Kelly. "She won't be able to see visitors until Saturday. You can ride in with my dad and me, Bred," she added, looking at him suspiciously.

Bred nodded his head in thanks as casually as he could with a half-smile on his face.

There is no way he was going to wait until Saturday.

Bred looked around the room and saw George Bishop sitting drinking his coffee alone by the window. Excusing himself from the group, Bred wandered casually over to George's table and sat down opposite him.

"I'd like a ride into Edmonton with you this afternoon, George, if you don't mind," he said politely.

Kyle's Courier Service had a brand new armoured truck to transport the bank receipts to the Standard Bank in Edmonton. Insurance was a wonderful thing. George had been appointed the new driver since Fred Parker was gone.

George nearly choked on his coffee. "You're damn right I mind!" growled George, wiping his mouth with his sleeve. "You got some nerve! You caused a lot of grief for old Fred Parker and now you're trying it out on me?"

"Trying what?" Bred said, as innocently as he could. "I'm just a kid asking an old friend for a ride into Edmonton."

"You're no friend of mine!" George said. "Besides, it's against regulations."

Bred smiled inwardly, he knew that George made up the regulations as he went along.

"How can you say that I'm not your friend?" Bred asked, with his best 'injured' look. He took a shot in the dark. "Have I ever mentioned anything to anyone about you fooling around with Kyle's wife, Betty, out by the Sunshine Motel after midnight?" George went white and spilled his coffee. Bred had hit a nerve.

Thank you Beth, Bred thought, remembering an earlier conversation in the donut shop.

"No." Bred continued seriously, pretending not to notice George's discomfort. He held up his hand before George could say anything. "And I never will," he added. Bred rested his arms on the table and stared into George's shocked eyes with his best 'trust me' expression.

"Pick you up at four-thirty outside the bank," George whispered hoarsely, rising shakily to his feet and walking unsteadily to the bathroom. "Don't be late!"

Bred strolled into the atrium of City Hospital at five-thirty p.m. that evening. George had been kind enough to drop him off across the street, and grudgingly muttered something about picking Bred up at seven o'clock and him not being late again. Bred was so excited at the prospect of seeing Maude, he scarcely heard him as he jumped out of the truck and sprinted across the road through the traffic.

The atrium was a vast, lofted cavern, open four floors up to the arched glass roof. Huge gaily-painted air conditionings ducts ran exposed up the walls and were part of the striking architectural features of the ultra-modern facility.

The bustling marble floors of the atrium hosted great open food courts and mezzanine dining areas overlooking the main floor like box seats at a hockey game.

Flower shops and souvenir vendors, surrounded by glass partitions, lined the outside walls. Giant ornamental fig trees in cedar boxes towered above patients and visitors alike. Indoor flower gardens were strategically located to lighten the atmosphere and to take away the sense that this was a place of healing, a place for the suffering, the sick and the dying.

Bred crossed the floor to the hospital reception area. After inquiring about Maude's whereabouts (and having told the nurse that he was related), he was informed that Mrs. Parker was on the fourth floor, Station 6.

Bred took the glass elevator up to the fourth floor and walked past the nursing station without so much as a glance. It was visiting hours. Bred went looking for Maude from room to room, trying not to be noticed and eventually found her alone in a private room. Bred slipped into the room and closed the door quietly behind him. He tiptoed across the room and looked down on the woman he loved and whom he had not seen for almost a year.

She looked just fine, a little pale perhaps. She looked like she was sleeping. He dragged over a chair and sat down beside her. Bred smiled happily, bent down and kissed her on the cheek. Her eyes flew open and she stared at him sideways without moving her head.

"Hi, Maude," Bred said whispering, a joyful grin on his face. "It's me, Fred, but now I'm Bred." Maude's expression didn't change, so he continued. "My brain was transplanted into Brian Andrews' 'cause I wasn't going to make it, and he shot himself in the head anyway, you see," he bubbled excitedly. "I sure missed you while you were in Los Angeles, honey," he added with a tear in his eye. "It seemed like you were never coming back." Bred perched himself on the side of the bed and reached for her hand.

"I've been living with the Andrews family, but now that you're home maybe we can get back together when you get out of here." He smiled, confident that they would work something out together.

Her eyes never left his, her head never moved. Slowly she reached around his shoulder with her free hand and picked up the stainless steel kidney bowl. Maude raised the bowl and smacked him soundly on the right side of the head with it.

Bred went tumbling over the chair and onto the floor. The chair went down with a bang. The flying kidney bowl hit his flailing foot and went smashing into the wall before bouncing all over the place, creating a crescendo like the crashing of a thousand symbols.

The ringing seemed to go on for a long time. It did — the ringing was in his ears. He lay on his back for a few seconds looking up at the ceiling while the fog cleared.

"Holy shit, Maude! What you do that for?" Bred yelled, struggling up on one elbow and checking with his other hand for blood. He had no idea how such a sickly woman could still have such a wicked temper.

The biggest nurse he had ever seen cast a huge shadow over him. Her tawny brown hair flopped down over her angry chubby cheeks and her big brown eyes stared into the depths of his as she lifted him off the floor by the scruff of his neck.

"What are you doing here?" the nurse demanded angrily, recognising him, but not releasing her hold on his neck. "Maude Parker is not allowed visitors, and especially those who disturb the whole floor."

Bred vainly tried to protest the indignity, but to no avail.

"Out! Out!" she bellowed, getting quite red in the face and propelling him unceremoniously towards the door.

The biggest nurse he had ever seen had no love for the healthy — only for the sick and the dying.

★★★

The following Saturday, Maude and Maggie greeted each other warmly when Maggie arrived for the afternoon visit. Maude was pleased to see Mr. Hiller too, who welcomed her back warm-heartedly. Bred was with them.

"Hello Maude," Bred said cautiously, smiling at her apprehensively from the end of the bed.

"That's Missus Parker to you, you little twit," she retorted haughtily.

"Why are you so mad at me?" he asked.

"Last I remember was that you put traffic pillions in front of my shop and nobody could park there for a whole day," she replied.

Bred rubbed the goose egg-sized lump on the side of his head.

" I thought you two were old friends," Maggie said. "Why, Bred has been on pins and needles for months."

Maude nearly choked. "He thinks he's my hus…"

"Keeper!" Bred yelled. "I'm her housekeeper…she forgets," he finished sheepishly. There was an uncomfortable silence in the room for a moment or two.

Mr. Hiller cleared his throat.

"Please excuse me, Maude," he said. "I have to see another patient. One of our directors was just admitted today. Apparently Mr. Phineus Muldoon had a stress attack after receiving some bad news."

"I think that I'll come with you, daddy," Maggie added, eyeing Bred carefully. "I think Bred and Maude have some issues they need to discuss."

"Of course," Maude said graciously. "Do come back and see me before you leave."

As soon as they left the room, Bred skittered across the room and smiled down at her adoringly.

"Maude, it's me Fred," he said pleading, sitting down in the chair beside her bed. He put his hand over his heart. "Ask me anything, anything at all."

"Okay," Maude said. "When's my birthday? When's my wedding anniversary?"

Bred looked at her in dismay…. That wasn't fair!

"Wait a minute, Maude, we were married in…in November! Yes! That's it! November 2nd, and your birthday is in July." He looked at her in triumph.

"What year?" she looked at him sceptically. His face fell.

"Nineteen…fifty…Shit, Maude! I don't remember exactly!" he said, exasperated.

"See my toes?" she asked, pointing with her chin. Bred looked.

"I don't see…?" he began, looking back at her.

Maude nailed him with the kidney bowl right above the eyebrow, and once again. Bred went tumbling out of the chair and onto the floor. He was crawling slowly on all fours towards the door just as Maggie walked in. She watched in amazement as Bred scrambled past her out into the passage. Staggering to his feet, he took off in a series of drunken lurches down the hall with his hand over his eye.

Maggie swung back to Maude with her mouth open. Maude was sitting upright in bed with the kidney bowl in her hand. Maggie had rarely seen a more satisfied grin on the face of a senior citizen.

★★★

The next afternoon, as Mary was putting on her coat, she glanced across the room to where Kelly and Bred were playing backgammon on the floor.

"I'm going to see Maude Parker," she said. "Would either of you like to come with me?"

Bred excused himself from the game and rose. "Sure," he said cheerfully, "I'll come with you."

Mary raised an eyebrow. This was extraordinary. Bred had an egg on his head and a classic black eye after his two previous encounters with Maude Parker, but still took the first opportunity to visit her again. She pursed her lips and said nothing.

When they arrived at the hospital, Bred excused himself to pick up a gift for Maude while Mary went on ahead. She entered the room and was surprised to see that Patrick and Michelle had chosen that time to visit Maude as well.

They were all pleased to see each other. Maude was in good spirits and even had Patrick raise the head end of the bed so that she was in a half-sitting position.

"Fred died in South Africa," Patrick said. "We're very sorry for your loss, Maude."

"I know," said Maude sadly, and tears came to her eyes. "They notified me in Los Angeles soon after he passed away."

"We're still trying to piece together what happened here," Patrick said. "And, were hoping that you could help with events leading up to the accident."

"I'm afraid not," Maude said. "I've thought and thought about it. It was a normal day. Fred mentioned nothing unusual, except…" she hesitated.

"Except what?" Michelle asked, gently.

"Except that he was hoping to catch some kid who was following him around on a bicycle all over town," she said with a puzzled smile.

Bred chose that moment to walk through the door, followed quickly by a very suspicious nurse. Maude's smile faded and she lay very still on the bed, watching him with puckered lips and a jaundiced eye.

He cautiously crossed the room and placed six yellow roses in her arms. Maude was stunned. She stared at the flowers for ten full seconds before she hit the roof.

"Bloody hell, Maude!" Bred yelled exasperated, ducking away from the flowers she had hurled at him. "Those things always calmed you down before."

"That's it!" bellowed the biggest nurse he had ever seen.

She stampeded across the room like a mother bear protecting her cub. Her tawny brown hair flopped down over her enraged cheeks, and her big brown eyes stared down into the depths of Bred's. She grabbed him by the scruff of his neck and propelled him unceremoniously out the door.

"You are banned from this room and from Station 6 …forever!" she proclaimed loudly, for all to hear.

Patrick, Michelle and Mary followed slowly, cautiously. The whole ward froze as she spoke. Patients and visitors watched open-mouthed from the doorways and hallways of that hallowed place of healing as the scene unfolded.

She stood towering over him, glorious and ominous at the same time in her spotless green uniform — a centurion — her arms folded across her ample bosom — a magnificent hulk!

Bred was very conscious of his bruised and aching neck. This is a very forceful nurse caring for Maude, he thought gravely. He stood motionless, his eyes flitting from one side to the other as he surveyed the scene and weighed his chances. There was no way out.

Bred looked up at the 'Mighty She'…and beamed. He was so proud of her!

As the doors closed and the glass elevator plummeted to the floors below, the events of the last minutes crowded in on his mind. Bred frowned and shook his head.

"Damn it, Maude," he muttered. "You always have to do it the hard way."

★★★

Bred sat nursing his coffee in the solarium of Maude's Donut Shop. He slumped next to the window, gloomily staring out across the street and over the false-fronted single-story buildings to where the fields of black soil beyond the fences were drying in the warm noonday sunshine. Farmers would be pleased. There had been a lot of moisture this past year and the early snowfall was melting slowly, soaking into the thirsty ground. They would be fall-seeding soon and their season would begin all over again, not unlike the seasons of his life — beginning all over again.

The sun was warm on his back and shoulders, even though it was late September. Bred hunched over his coffee wondering why he shouldn't just leave things the way they were. Maude didn't need him or even want him around. He could just carry on and do it all over again. No one needed to know. Maggie came over, saw that he was downcast and gave his shoulders a squeeze.

He smiled wanly at her and she left him alone.

The problem was, of course, that he had relied on Maude for so long. She was his partner, his confidante his soul mate. How could he possibly have any fun without her?

Fun! That was the key.

If he had to do it over, he would bloody well have fun doing it… and Maude had no choice, she was a part of it too. He needed an ally and she was it. Bred's depression dissolved.

Come on Bred, he thought. Make a plan.

The next few days Bred spent recuperating from his injuries at the donut shop or at the gym, plotting his next move. He even practised imitating Fred's voice in front of a mirror for hours. Maybe that would help. According to Maggie, Maude would have to remain in hospital for another few weeks before she would be allowed to go home.

Confucius said: "If the mountain wouldn't come to Mohamed…then Mohamed must go to the mountain."

So be it!

On the following Thursday afternoon, George dropped Bred off across the street from the hospital as usual. It was cold and it looked like a storm was brewing. Bred sprinted across the road through the oncoming traffic without sustaining any serious injury.

He crossed the atrium and took the elevator to the third floor, where he found the laundry room marked: 'Hospital Staff only.'

Bred slipped inside and closed the door behind him. He stripped off his clothes, including his shoes and socks, rolled them up and stuffed them into a corner of the rack. He dressed himself in a yellow-green cotton patient smock that tied at the back. He pulled a cotton cap over his head and slipped on a pair of hospital slippers. He completed the disguise by tying a white surgical mask over his nose and mouth. He was ready.

Cautiously opening the door, he stepped out into the hallway and walked slowly over to the glass elevator. Bred rode up the elevator to the fourth floor. He loitered nonchalantly in the hallway until the traffic increased and joined a throng of patients strolling past the reception desk at Station Six. As he passed, he glanced over at the nursing station. Everyone was busy and paid little attention to the stream of patients passing to-and-fro during the visiting hour.

He soon found himself in front of Maude's room. Glancing swiftly up and down the hall to make sure that no one had seen him, Bred slipped inside, quickly checked the hallway again and closed the door behind him.

Maude was a little startled to see the green-clad patient dart into her room. She looked away quickly when she caught a glimpse of his naked derriere through the gap in the back as he checked the hall.

"Maude! It's me, Bred, er… Fred," he called in a harsh whisper, pulling off his mask and cap.

"Oh, crap!" she yelped, looking around for something to throw at him.

"Wait! Wait! Wait! You silly old Moo!" he called desperately, in his best imitation of Fred. He held up his hands as she latched onto the kidney bowl. She wavered, the wind taken out of her sails.

"What did you say?" she demanded.

"It's me, Fred," he said, his eyes pleading. "You were born in 1945 and our wedding anniversary is 1962."

"Cretin!" she hissed. "1965!" She fired the kidney bowl at him.

He caught it, fumbled, caught it again and ended up on his back on the floor.

"Bloody hell, Miss Piggy!" he blurted.

The colour drained from her face.

"What?" she said, lowering the vase with the battered yellow roses she was about to wing at him.

"What did you say?"

"I keep telling you," he said, annoyed, getting up quickly. "I had my memory cells transplanted into that kid, Brian. I'm Fred."

Her eye caught sight of the greeting card that came with the flowers. She picked it up.

"*Get well soon, my dearest Maude.*"

"Who wrote this note?" she asked hoarsely.

"I did," Bred said coyly.

She grabbed a pen off the table and handed both it and the card to Bred. "Write the same thing on the back," she ordered.

Bred looked at her, his head tilted to one side. He sighed, took the card and the pen and wrote the message again.

Maude looked stunned.

He had written with his left hand, and the handwriting was identical to Fred Parker's!

She looked down at the six yellow roses and the card in her hands.

"What was the last thing you told me before you left for South Africa and I went to Los Angeles?" she demanded, her throat tightening. She gripped the vase so tightly that her knuckles turned white.

Bred studied her carefully for a minute. He walked over beside the bed and replaced the kidney bowl on the table. He sat down on the chair and took the vase from her trembling fingers and stood it on the table as well. He took her cold, still trembling fingers gently in his. "Maude," he said tenderly. "I know this is hard for you... it's hard for me too." He looked at her tenderly as he recalled the memory of that last moment.

"I told you that if we didn't have the operations, we would be separated by more than just a world.... and, I quoted your favourite poem by Elizabeth Barrett Browning, remember?"

The colour returned to her face and the tension drained away. An aura of tranquillity illuminated her as she slowly sat upright while the boy quoted the passages from the poem — exactly as Fred would.

"I remember," she said quietly. "It is you in there, isn't it, Fred?" she acknowledged gently, stroking the hair off his forehead.

They talked about the good times they had had and laughed at the hard times they had overcome. They talked about the present and the situation they were in, and they laughed until the tears ran down their cheeks.

The past and the present would do for now. They did not talk about the future.

At 6.45 that evening, Bred left the ward the same way that he came in and shuffled past the nurse's station with a good crowd around him. Two nurses followed the group and noticed that one of the ties on Bred's gown had come loose.

"Nice tush," murmured the younger one to her companion as they passed the crowd heading for the elevators. The nurses headed on down to the end of the hallway and stood idly in front of the huge glass pane window overlooking the busy street and the parking lot. It had begun to rain heavily, and the setting sun cast an eerie glow over the scene below.

Bred tiptoed into the laundry room on the third floor and went to the rack where he had hidden his clothes. They were gone!

"Shit!"

He searched the room; he found nothing. Bred checked his watch. It was five minutes to seven. He had to go *now*, or George would leave without him.

Bred shuffled over to the glass elevator and rode down in full view from the atrium.

He scooted across the crowded food floor to the echo of laughter and the muffled screams of the women. People hopped out of his way and stared after him in astonishment.

By the time he reached the front doors, Bred was in a state of sheer panic and another tie on his smock had come undone. Holding the gaping cotton behind him, he navigated the doors with one hand and clumsily fought his way through the incoming people-traffic and out into the city street. It was raining — that freezing rain that only seems to happen in rush-hour in late September or when you're leaving the hospital dressed only in a thin cotton gown. Bred could not stop now.

George watched the scantily clad figure run awkwardly around the throng of pedestrians and across the busy road through the pouring rain. Bred came tearing towards him, splashing and sliding clumsily through the puddles in the parking lot, vainly holding his gown shut in the rear. George watched as the soaking wet cotton stuck to Bred's body like a wet tee-shirt. He was sorely tempted to leave the scene at that moment.

Lucky for Bred, George was laughing so hard that he couldn't get the truck in gear. It was just as well, the tears clouding his eyes would have made for a very dangerous getaway. George felt vindicated. There was no need for him to seek revenge. With all the punishment Bred inflicted on himself, all he had to do was sit back and watch.

Bred dove head first into the truck through the passenger door and slammed it shut shivering like a leaf. He glared at the red-faced, spluttering, choking idiot beside him through the strands of wet hair and ice plastered to his face.

George was really beginning to like the kid. It took a few more minutes before he was safe to drive.

Up on the fourth floor behind the huge glass pane windows, two nurses stood with arms folded and casually watched the events unfolding below.

"It's amazing how Maude Parker has improved since the boy began visiting," the younger nurse commented. "She should be able to go home soon."

"Yes," nodded the biggest nurse she had ever seen, her tawny brown hair flopped down over her satisfied chubby cheeks and her big brown eyes probed into the depths of the armoured truck.

She turned to her companion. "What did you do with his clothes?" she asked, curiously.

★★★

CHAPTER ELEVEN
The Good Times

Remembrance Day dinner at the Andrews' dinner table was not a particularly fun time. Graham was far more talkative than usual; unfortunately, it was all about work and the company. None of Mary's attempts to change the subject had been remotely successful. Everybody sat with their eyes glued to their plates as Graham expounded on many of his company's standard operating procedures, detailed instructions and checklists compiled in systemised manuals.

The man is worried, Bred thought suddenly. He looked across the table at Mary. Her eyes were pleading with him to say something. Bred sighed.

"Are all procedures within the company controlled by standard detailed instructions and manuals?" he asked.

"Why, yes," Graham answered. "All subject to clarification and interpretation by myself, of course."

Bred sighed again. He just *had* to open that can of worms.

He wiped the corner of his mouth and placed his napkin beside his plate. He turned to face Graham, choosing his words carefully.

"That's all very well in a growing market," Bred said seriously, "which you have enjoyed up to now — since you were expanding and drawing local customers away from Edmonton."

"The company has been quite profitable, up to quite recently," Graham agreed, "but why the sudden downturn?"

"Your company has been profitable through watching your cash flow, general economising and keeping your niche market in a centrally controlled environment," Bred said.

"But nothing has changed from that perspective," Graham argued. "My employees have become stale. What else could it be?"

"Consider this," Bred said patiently, looking at Graham with a frown. "Your customer base is finite. You're stagnant and the competition is moving in. Your employees are not to blame." He rubbed his nose as he thought for a minute while everyone waited.

"You have to restructure," he said finally, replacing his napkin on his lap. Bred glanced over and caught Mary's amused expression as he stabbed a piece of ham on his plate. He looked over at Kelly and Beth who were staring at him open mouthed.

"What?" he said, seeing the looks on their faces, "it's all in Dad's *Fortune* magazines." The rest of the meal passed quietly and most enjoyably.

★★★

Maude moved back home to 'Maude's Cottage' in Bolton, in late November, accompanied by a full-time live-in nurse. All costs were paid by the trust fund established by Dr. Strydom before Fred and Maude were forced to seek their medical destinies in foreign lands.

Brad had convinced Mary and Julie that he should continue with his home schooling program since he was academically positioned between Grade Ten and Grade Eleven.

He challenged the Provincial exams and did quite well, though it was not always that easy. A lot of stuff had changed in the last 60 years, especially in the sciences, and Bred was very thankful for the internet.

His main motivation, of course, was to spend as much time as he could with Maude. Though it was good to be able to see Maude every day, Bred's visits were heavily chaperoned, the dutiful nurse having been forewarned by the hospital staff.

Maggie accompanied Bred on a visit to Maude's house with serious personal reservations, remembering the last time she had seen them together.

She had enjoyed visiting the Parker home in happier times. It was a lovely little two-bedroom house with mature trees and gardens, and grey-blue, ivy-covered stucco walls. The home was decorated with old English and American furniture throughout and some pieces were now genuine antiques. It was comfortable, homey and unpretentious. Wallpaper recalled an elegant period — Grandma's house — and it gave the visitor an immediate feeling of old-fashioned comfort and warmth.

Maggie was happy to see that nothing had changed. It seemed that Bred really was a very good housekeeper. She was surprised to see the strong bond of friendship between Maude and Bred, their obvious display of affection in stark contrast to the way they had behaved at the hospital. When Maggie mentioned that she was pleased to see them getting along so well, Bred smiled.

"She remembered," He explained simply, shrugging his shoulders.

Maude nodded in agreement — but not spelling out exactly what she had remembered.

★★★

Bred explained the situation regarding Graham's business problems to Maude during one of his visits to 'Maude's Cottage'.

"But I really don't want to get caught up in the family business," he lamented, when Maude suggested he help.

"You! You! You!" she admonished him loudly. "What about Mary?" Maude held up her hand, reassuring the nurse at the other end of the room. The latter had dropped her magazine at the sound of the raised voice and had half-risen out of her chair, prepared to injure Bred. She growled and quietly settled back down again.

"Mary?" Bred whispered, eyeing the nurse furtively.

"Wouldn't Graham have more time for his family and *Mary*," she said with emphasis, "if this little problem was resolved?"

"Okay," Bred said, capitulating. "But he'd better take me fishing in the spring."

★★★

A week later, Bred and Kelly were doing homework at the kitchen table, when Graham arrived home early.

"Bred, my boy," Graham said nonchalantly, brushing an imaginary speck of dust off his jacket. "My managers can't agree on a restructuring plan. Any suggestions?" He glanced up at Bred under his hooded brow.

"For what it's worth, sure," Bred said modestly, glancing at Kelly.

Kelly rolled her eyes, excused herself and headed for her room.

Graham sat down, studying Bred's expression and put his arms on the table. Bred practised his 'expressionless' face.

"Let's go to my study," Graham said abruptly, getting up.

Bred, nonchalantly led the way into the study, walked across the room and sat behind the desk. Graham was taken aback but settled himself on the black leather couch against the wall. Bred waited expectantly, laying back in the chair with his finger over his mouth.

Graham had a tug-of-war with himself for a minute or two. It was hard to forget that this confident young fifteen year-old boy sitting at his desk had gone berserk a year before and had finally ended up shooting himself. The operation had obviously been successful and the last few months had been calm and peaceful as far as he knew, *but still…*

But still I have to confide in someone who knows what the hell I'm talking about, and Bred seemed to know! Graham thought, and bit the bullet.

"The company is in trouble and I'm going to have to lay off a lot of people," he blurted out.

Bred studied him calmly. "Do you personally hire every employee?" he asked.

"Yes."

"And you authorise all expenditures, throughout the company?"

"Yes."

"And how close are you to your customers? Do you see them every day? Every transaction?" Bred already knew the answer.

"Well, no," Graham said, already uncomfortable with this line of questioning from this adolescent boy.

"Your company's only real assets are your customers," Bred said seriously. "That's according to Jan Carlzon, CEO of Scandinavian Airlines, in an article in one of your *Fortune* magazines." He rubbed his palms absently.

"He gave his front line managers autonomy," Bred continued, "and the responsibility to utilise their own creativity, ingenuity and familiarity with a particular situation and to respond in the best interest of their customers."

"That makes sense," Graham said thoughtfully. "They're right there on top of it. But I don't see how we can restructure for that in our business." He looked doubtful and his brow furrowed as he considered the proposal.

"I would suggest that you break each department down into smaller cost centres," Bred said. "Make each department head responsible for making a profit in those cost centres." He paused for a minute. "Give him or her, the authority and sufficient financial backing to do whatever it takes to do so, even to using resources outside the company if he or she, can get a better deal out there.

"By all means, share internal resources where possible," Bred continued, anticipating the question and holding up his hand when Graham would have protested. "Economies of scale and all that — but charge the requesting cost centres internally, for those services too."

He was done. He jumped out of the chair and headed for the door.

"That's all I've got," Bred said casually. "Good luck.... If it works you owe me a fly-in fishing trip," he added, looking back over his shoulder as he left the room.

Graham stared after him with his mouth open.

"*Fortune magazines?*" He stuttered.

★★★

"I want Graham to take me fishing in the spring, Maude," Bred said, at one of his afternoon visits to her house a few weeks later. "But it will be awful expensive, so I can't ask him." He was laid back in the rocking chair pondering the problem. Bred had heard that Patrick was an avid fisherman. Maybe he could speak to Graham for him.

Maude was knitting, deep in her own thoughts, and paid no attention to him at all.

"You know that Patrick just needs a little push," Maude said suddenly.

"What?" Bred said, startled by Maude's apparent psychic abilities.

"Patrick and Michelle," said Maude patiently. She had seen the chemistry between them a long time ago.

"Patrick and..." Bred laughed. "It will take more than a little push. No fraternising in the ranks and all that," he mocked.

Maude gave him a dirty look.

Patrick and Michelle had visited Maude earlier that morning, pursuing evidence on the Parker case.

"They still suspect your involvement in the case, Bred, aren't you the least bit concerned?" she had asked, her own concern evident in her tone.

"For what?" he answered with a laugh. "For complicity in staging my own demise?"

Maude berated him severely for making light of a serious matter. Bred flinched at every syllable, but she had given him an idea.

★★★

The snows and cold winds of winter slowly turned to spring, and on a sunny day in March, family and friends gathered for a Saturday afternoon barbecue on the Andrews' estate.

Graham had followed Bred's suggestions for restructuring the business over the past months and it was already evident that earnings were up. He had not had to fire anyone.

Patrick and Michelle had accepted the invitation to join the Andrews to celebrate.

The grey, flagstone patio at the rear adjoined the house and was protected from the wind by flowering trees and shrubs on three sides and by the house on the other. A stone-covered fireplace served as the barbeque and stood on one side. Manicured lawns behind the ring of flagstones lay like a green carpet beneath a raised gazebo made of cedar. Beth's new yellow garden swing hung in the shade of a majestic elm beyond. The adults were seated on colourful patio furniture that Mary had purchased for the occasion. They basked in the afternoon sun, sipped chilled fruit juices, Canadian beer and a fine white cabernet sauvignon harvested from vineyards in the Okanagan Valley of British Columbia.

Bred and Patrick looked after the steaks roasting on the barbecue.

"Have you ever been fishing up at Namier Lake, Patrick?" Bred inquired casually. He had taking the opportunity to ask the question when everyone else was out of earshot.

"Why, yes I have," Patrick answered. He stopped what he was doing and recalled the

adventure. "It's a great lake for fishing, but it's hard to get to. You have to fly in to it on a float plane from Fort McMurray, or snowmobile in the winter." He nibbled on a chip.

Bred nodded, not making any further comment. He had spoken to Mary earlier, and already knew the answer to the question.

Plant the seed… he thought.

Patrick had actually been to Namier Lake twice before. So when Graham asked him a little later if he knew of a rustic fishing lodge where there was a better-than-average probability of catching something, Patrick was quick to recommend Namier Lake in northern Alberta. He elaborated on its attributes with some enthusiasm.

"I want to go too," Kelly pleaded from the swing in the gazebo, overhearing the conversation. She was quickly echoed by Beth. Graham looked across at Mary and then at Bred. They nodded in agreement.

"Okay," Graham said with finality. "Would you two like to come along as well?" he asked, turning to Patrick and Michelle. "We might as well make a week's holiday out of it. It's on me." A successfully restructured business and two beers in the hot sun made Graham generous.

"Where is this place anyway?" he asked.

★★★

Daniel Dobbs, at sixty-nine, was a character. He was also the owner of Namier Lodge on the southern shore of Namier Lake in the Porcupine Mountains of northern Alberta, one of the finest (trophy) lake trout habitats in the province.

Dobbs lived at the lodge throughout the year. The lodge had all the comforts of home: power, running water and flush toilets — at least in the summer time. He owned a 1947 Beaver single, rotary-engine floatplane, and flew guests back and forth from Ft. McMurray. The trip took about an hour and forty-five minutes each way.

Dobbs, as he liked to be called, had once been a field engineer and worked in the oilfields around Ft. McMurray. One day there had been a gas line explosion and Dobbs lost his right leg below the knee. He quit engineering soon after that and opened the lodge on Namier Lake. That had been nearly eighteen years ago.

Dobbs greeted his guests on a strip of water known as the Snye, in downtown Ft. McMurray. He loaded the seven of them into the Beaver, along with their luggage and gear. Dobbs had already loaded all the timbers he needed for a ten-by-ten shed, including the roof trusses. He had also strapped a sixteen-foot aluminium boat and an outboard motor between the pontoons.

"Workhorse of the North, ma'am," Dobbs said, when he saw Mary's look of apprehension and fired up the big rotary engine.

Nevertheless, Dobbs taxied out into the inlet and took the longest run into the light wind that he could get. He jumped the plane out of the water at the last second and cleared the ten-foot earth berm at the end of the Snye by inches and scared the ducks. Dobbs banked the plane over the Athabasca River and headed north to the Porcupine Mountains.

"Nothing to it," he yelled over the deafening roar of the engine, as everyone expelled the air from their lungs.

★★★

Everything was bathed in brilliant sunshine on that fine spring morning in June. Mary stared mesmerised at the infinite rolling canopy of the forest. Suddenly the green carpet elevated a thousand feet and the clear blue expanse of a lake unfolded in the huge crater before her. Mary gasped in wonder at the incredible spectacle; a divine gift from the ice age, formed by retreating glaciers 10,000 years before.

Dobbs had carved his lodge out of the pristine boreal forest on the steep banks overlooking Namier Lake. From the air, the lake looked like a kidney-shaped lagoon as it nestled comfortably between the colossal hills. Vegetation indigenous to the Porcupine Mountains grew everywhere in abundance. Tree-covered islands rose high above the water on either end of the ten-mile long mountain-lake.

In every direction, the green forests of spruce, tamarack, poplar and lodgepole pine rolled out to the horizon. The great boreal forest was broken only by the mirrored splashes of a thousand lesser lakes, rivers and muskeg marshes. There were no other buildings, roads or human beings for hundreds of miles around. Namier Lodge was just a stitch in the fabric of the great Canadian wilderness.

Dobbs cleared the surrounding hills and flew out over the lake. The plane seemed to drop vertically out of the sky as he banked the aircraft sharply towards the lodge. At the last minute he straightened out ten feet above the water, floated smoothly between two islands, and settled gently onto the calm water a hundred yards from the dock. He taxied over and tied off.

Fred had been there a dozen times before, and twice by snowmobile in the dead of winter.

★★★

The Andrews family left Dobbs and his handyman to unload the gear into the trailer behind the quad and walked along the dock and across the boardwalk to the gravel path.

As they climbed the steep path towards the log cabins and the main lodge, Bred noted the heavy ice still clinging to the shore in the shadows.

"Good," he said to no one in particular, "the grayling will still be in the river."

"That's right," Dobbs said, coming up beside him silently on the quad. "You've been here before?"

"I know someone who has," Bred answered truthfully.

"And who might that be?" Dobbs asked.

"Fred and Maude Parker," Bred said.

Dobbs stopped the quad with a jolt and stared after the boy, as Bred continued walking up the path to the lodge without a backward glance. Bred had recognized Dobbs right away, and besides the good fishing, Dobbs was the main reason he was there.

★★★

The log cabins were typically twelve foot by sixteen foot, with a six foot covered porch in the front and surrounded by a wooden safety rail. Stairs lead up to the elevated deck from the side and a door led off the porch into the cabin. All the cabins had a panoramic view of the lake through a large picture window beside the door.

Inside, a single bunk bed rested against a wall, and a double bed was pushed to the other side. The rest consisted of rustic furniture, a table and chairs, gas lamps and a wood stove. The cabins were all wired for electricity. Dobbs had a diesel-powered electric generator, which he ran until midnight for the convenience of his guests.

Beth, Kelly and Michelle shared a cabin, Graham and Mary had another and Bred shared one with Patrick. Dobbs had suggested that everyone gather at the main lodge for lunch after they had settled into their cabins. In the meantime, he would prepare the boats for anyone who wanted to go fishing that day.

Bred followed Dobbs down to the boats. He helped check the oil on the outboard motors and filled them with gas. He then helped to push the aluminium boats down off the beach into the water. Neither he nor Dobbs spoke much.

When they were done, they walked back up the beach across the sand and leaned against the grassy bank. Dobbs pulled out his pipe, filled it with tobacco and lit it.

"So you know the Parkers?" Dobbs asked, as he shook out the match.

"Like family," Bred answered.

"How are Maude and Fred doing?" Dobbs asked, a little too casually.

Bred could detect a little tension. He looked out across the lake, watching the sunlight play off the ripples on the water.

"Maude's doing great," he said. "Fred was killed in an accident last year."

Dobbs looked down at the sand and moved it with his foot. He put his hand over his eyes, rubbed his face and took a deep breath. His hand was shaking as he turned his back.

"Where's she living now?" he asked after a minute or two, his voice tight.

"Maude still lives in Bolton, in the cottage," Bred said, ducking out of the way as Patrick and Michelle came sliding down the bank to join them.

"I should get down and see Maude one of these days," Dobbs said reflectively.

"Maude Parker?" Michelle inquired breathlessly, buoyed up by the slide, and by Patrick. She had caught the last part of the conversation.

"When did you meet the Parkers, Mr. Dobbs?" she asked.

"Just call me Dobbs, ma'am," he said smiling, as he turned to pick up the empty gas cans and headed back up the pathway. "I was the best man at their wedding," he said, looking back over his shoulder, "some 45 years ago."

★★★

They spent the afternoon fishing close to the lodge and just generally fooling around in the boats. Though they didn't see any of the legendary twenty or thirty pounders, they still managed to catch enough smaller trout to have a cookout that evening.

Dobbs employed a young catering crew who lived at the lodge throughout the summer months and they pampered their guests.

They sat around the campfire in front of the main lodge in the cool of the evening, watching the flames dancing and popping on the logs, and marvelled at the sparks shooting high into the night sky.

Their chefs for the evening had chopped up the freshly caught fish, dredged them in flour and spices and dropped them ceremoniously into a huge cast iron frying pan. The aroma was exquisite; everyone was suddenly very hungry. The fish sticks spluttered and sizzled in the hot butter and canola oil mixture for a few minutes. They emerged as golden-brown cubes of ambrosia, the likes of which they had never tasted before. The kids, including Bred, ate them up like peanuts until they were stuffed.

"Got your fly rods ready?" Dobbs asked a little later after supper, addressing Graham and Patrick and glancing at Bred. "Grayling at first light," he added, lighting his pipe.

Bred was surprised.

"Down the Indian trail?" he asked incredulously, before he could stop himself. Dobbs never invited strangers to fish the hidden pools below the cascading Namier River rapids. Dobbs saw Bred's expression and raised an eyebrow.

"The Grayling are already in the mouth of the river," he said. "They're early this year."

The next morning dawned bright and clear, with a light wind from the northwest. They took off after breakfast in three sixteen-foot open aluminium boats, driven by fifty-horsepower outboard motors, heading toward the northern end of the lake. Bred, Dobbs and Patrick were in the lead boat followed by Graham, Mary and Beth. Michelle and Kelly were all over the lake screaming and laughing, unable to control the boat with the rear driven outboard motor, despite practising with Patrick the previous day.

They sped past Pelican Island near the far end of the lake and came to the narrow mouth of the Namier River. Nearby, spectacular waterfalls cascaded down a rocky face fed by an unnamed creek, and piles of broken timbers, driftwood and deadheads lined the northern shores.

"When the *sou'wester* blows," Bred mused, looking at the wreckage. Patrick looked at him curiously.

"That's right," Dobbs said, surprised that Brad was so informed. "When the southwest wind comes up, everything gets blown to this end of the lake. It can get pretty rough."

"Do you still have the cabin on Pelican Island?" Bred asked a short time later, pointing to the island.

"Yes," Dobbs nodded, wondering again how the boy had gotten the information. "If a group should happen to get trapped here, they have somewhere to find shelter. I keep it stocked too… you never know."

They all had a great morning catching the elusive Grayling. The fish only grow to about three pounds, but with that great dorsal fin it thinks it's a sailfish and acts accordingly.

At noon, they had a fish fry on a clear section of sandy shore, about half way between the river and the lodge. It might have appeared spontaneous, except that the catering crew had somehow managed to arrive first and had a fine spread already prepared.

"This is the only fish I know that won't keep," Dobbs said, lying on the warm sand and picking his teeth with a bone. "Has to be eaten fresh too. Goes soggy if you freeze it."

"It's the best fresh-water fish I've ever tasted," Graham said, managing another mouthful.

Later, they set the downriggers and everyone caught their limit in lake trout. Graham caught the biggest that day at twenty-two pounds.

It was a very relaxing holiday, just fishing, tooling about in the boats, hiking in the hills and lying on the beaches. Nobody went in the water. Though it was as clear as a bell, it was also just barely above freezing at that time of year.

Bred and Graham wandered down to the dock on the third day of the trip, to find Dobbs and his handyman fuelling up the float plane.

"Have to go to town for a couple of days," Dobbs said. "If there's anything you folks need, just ask any of the crew."

They watched as the plane taxied out onto the lake. Dobbs revved up the engine and with a thundering roar, tore across the water and lifted gracefully into the air. He circled, gaining height to clear the hills, then, waggling his wings in farewell, he headed south.

The following morning, Bred stepped out onto the porch outside his cabin. He started to stretch and froze halfway, sniffing the air. It was only seven in the morning, the sun was up and there was not a cloud in the sky. The air was muggy; no breeze rustled the newborn poplar leaves and the drops of morning dew on their tips sat waiting in anticipation. There was an expectant hush over the forest. A storm was heading towards their little mountain retreat.

Bred knew that he ought to behave himself, but... he took a deep breath, told himself that he was only a boy, and relieved himself in a great arc off the edge of the deck.

The day stayed muggy until late afternoon. Bred and Graham had gone out, and though the water was calm, fishing had dropped off to nothing. Mosquitoes managed to find them out in the middle of the lake and horseflies followed the boat everywhere, even when they tried to escape at full throttle. Graham was happy to head back to the comfort of the lodge, at Bred's suggestion.

As they floated up to the dock in front of the lodge, Bred glanced up at the sky and saw the tell-tale line of grey cumulonimbus cloud appear on the southern horizon. A zephyr whipped across the water, stirring up a trace of dancing ripples on the surface and blew up into the poplar trees, causing the hushed leaves to hiss sharply. The sound of the wind faded away and the afternoon resumed its unnatural stillness.

Graham, unaware of the transition, pulled the boat up onto the beach and dropped the painter over a log.

***

"Will you help us push the boat in, please," Kelly asked later that afternoon, as one of the crewman came by the beach. "My brother and I are going fishing." She gestured towards Bred loading the supplies.

Bred had promised Kelly that he would take her fishing and had deliberately waited until after everyone was resting, before suggesting they go.

"Where are you guys off to?" the crewman asked as Bred reversed into deeper water.

"Namier River," Kelly said. "We're going to catch some northern pike." Bred put the outboard in forward and gunned the engine.

"Hey! I'm not sure that's a good idea!" the crewman yelled. Whitecaps were forming out on the lake.

"Let Patrick know where we've gone," Bred called as he pulled away. "He may want to join us later."

As they rounded the point and passed out of sight of the lodge, Bred could see the rising southwest wind had already created a two-foot swell and foaming whitecaps out in the lake. The storm was moving in fast and the leading cumulus clouds were already racing overhead.

Bred hugged the west shore in the lee of the land and out of the fierce wind. A hundred yards past the point, he guided the boat into a narrow, almost invisible inlet between two vertical rock outcrops. The inlet opened up into a huge shallow bay as big as a football field.

A creek cascaded down a rocky slope into the bay on the far end, fed by artesian springs and the surrounding marshes. Tall trees ran right down to the narrow rocky shores, completely sheltering them from the wind. New spring flowers, bushes and wild flowering shrubs lined the edge of the shore and covered the forest floor. Kelly gasped with wonder.

"How did you ever find this place?" she asked, marvelling at the serene beauty.

"Fred Parker told me about it," Bred said, dropping the anchor. "That's the Namier River inlet," he said, pointing to the creek. "This spot is reputed to produce the greatest Northern Pike on the lake."

Bred rigged Kelly's line, and with her first cast next to a weed-bed, she hooked a five-pound fish. She was instantly squealing and laughing and hollering for help.

"Get the net!" she yelled.

"I've got it covered," Bred answered confidently, as he rolled up his sleeve.

As Kelly brought the fish closer, Bred leaned over and took hold of it with one hand behind the gills and lifted it into the boat. Not having prepared what to do with it after that, Bred stuck the fish head first into the bailing bucket while he looked around for the cooler box. As soon as he released the creature, it gave a mighty flip out of the bucket and ended up flopping around alarmingly in the bottom of the aluminium boat.

A northern pike looks very similar to a barracuda — snakelike — and all teeth. So when the fish started writhing vigorously towards Kelly, she was at first startled, then absolutely terrified. The blood drained from her face and she jumped up in the bow screaming.

Bred, slightly unbalanced by the shrill sound of Kelly's terror, reached over in the now unsteady craft and tried to grapple the slippery creature with his bare hands. He missed, slipped and sprawled lengthways in the bottom of the boat. Bred's efforts only succeeded in propelling the squirming, snapping beast straight towards Kelly's bare ankles.

She panicked.

Kelly stampeded across the precariously rocking boat, scrambled over Bred and past those snapping jaws to the very stern and turned around only to find to her horror that the monster had followed her.

She had forgotten to let go of the rod. The fish was still attached and she had dragged it with her in her mad dash to safety. Utter chaos ensued for a full thirty seconds until Bred finally flipped the fish over the side with his foot. He barely managed to stop Kelly from abandoning ship.

When she had calmed down enough, Kelly punched Bred as hard as she could in the stomach. She still had the rod in her hand and the fish was still on the line.

"Net!" she said through clenched teeth, her eyes blazing.

Bred groaned, sank to his knees and picked up the fishing net. It was going to be a long afternoon.

★★★

It was later that afternoon when Patrick stepped out of the lodge and was surprised to feel the electrical tension in the muggy air. He and Michelle had been playing cards with Mary and Graham and he had just stepped out for a breather. The wind in the trees had picked up considerably and as he looked up at the sky, he saw the ominous grey-black clouds streaking in low from the southwest.

The Lodge was situated on a small bay off the main lake and protected from the wind to a certain extent by the two southern islands. But the forces of nature would not be denied for long. The fury building on the distant waters would soon engulf even these quiet beaches as the strength of the storm increased exponentially.

Patrick saw the crew scurrying about dragging the boats and equipment up onto the beach away from the surging water. He ran down the gravel pathway to lend a hand.

"Mr. D'Laney," a crewman called, breathlessly, coming up to meet him. "Young Bred and Miss Kelly have not returned yet."

"Where did they go?" Patrick asked, looking out at the wind-whipped whitecaps, evident even at that distance out on the lake.

"To the Namier River mouth," the crewman said miserably. "I tried to warn them but..."

"Get me a boat," Patrick said urgently, grabbing a life jacket from the shack. "I'm going after them."

They dragged the boat down to the lake through the rising wind. Three-foot waves breaking on the shore overpowered them and threw them and the boat back against the bank, time and again. The wind and the waves made the light aluminium craft unmanageable, as it took on a life of its own in the surging water.

A figure scrambled past him and heaved into the bow, as Patrick and the crewman strained to turn the boat into the waves once more. With the added weight in the bows, the nose bit deep into the swell and the keel held its line. With a final, mighty heave, the boat wallowed away from the turbulent shore-waves and out into the swells on the bay.

Patrick scrambled aboard and started the outboard motor, shoved the gear lever forward and opened the throttle. Only then did he look up to see Michelle in the bow fastening her life jacket. He opened his mouth to protest but she beat him to it.

"I'm coming with you," she cried over the wind and the roar of the motor. "Don't argue!" She snapped the last buckle and turned to face the dragon.

Patrick hugged the western shore out of the direct force of the wind. He raced right past the inlet to the bay where Bred and Kelly were fishing. Unaware of their proximity, Patrick and Michelle were bound for Pelican Island and the outlet of the Namier River, ten miles north across the storm-swept lake.

★★★

Bred heard the whine of the outboard motor and the pounding on the hull as the boat carrying Patrick and Michelle bounced off the swells as it raced past the hidden bay. He looked up at the sky, and the rising wind in the treetops.

"We'd better go in, Kelly," he said casually. "There's a storm coming."

★★★

Patrick held to the lee shore in the gathering darkness, until he reached a point about two miles from Pelican Island. He had navigated dry mouthed between the half-submerged deadheads as the little boat pitching recklessly in tremendous swells along the threatening shoreline. From that point on, they had no choice but to head out across the raw expanse of the lake. Patrick looked over his shoulder and his blood ran cold. A black-purple mass of turbulent cloud engulfed his vision as bolts of sheet lightning shimmered in the heavens, …. and the rain fell.

Great sheets of pelting rain drenched them both to the skin in seconds, but the rain went unnoticed when weighed against the freezing spray and gyrating actions of their precarious craft. Kelly and Bred were out there somewhere and probably in real trouble; they had to try to find them. There was no turning back now. Patrick clenched his jaw and headed out into the abyss, and the wind engulfed its prey.

Scarcely had they begun, when Patrick swung the nose of the boat a little too much off the beam and they breached. A tumbling boiling flood of black water caught the boat and whirled it almost perpendicular. Water swarmed in over the side, and the little craft, drunken with the weight, snuggled deeper into the lake like a waterlogged tree trunk.

Instinctively, Patrick opened the throttle wide and twisted the sluggish craft downwind. The rush of the water inside the boat met the next incoming wave from the lake right where Patrick was sitting in the stern. Both he and the motor were engulfed for an instant in a maelstrom. His grip on the tiller was all that stopped Patrick from being swept away in the surging rush. The water was cold… freezing cold, and the shock took his breath away.

"Bless you, Mercury," he mumbled, as the motor spluttered and resumed its rhythmic pulse.

"Yeee-haa!" Michelle yelled exuberantly, and grabbing the bucket, she began furiously bailing out the dinghy.

Patrick was appalled. She actually thought that he was in control of the situation. Didn't she realise they were going to drown?

He clenched his jaw to stop his teeth chattering and took a firmer grip on the tiller with his freezing fingers. Slowly, they picked up speed and raced downwind, barely ahead of the monstrous cresting rollers falling in their wake. The light faded as the driving rain and blanketing clouds of darkness blotted out the shoreline.

There was a thunderous crash and lightning flashed like a strobe light revealing in stark contrast the chaos about them. Alone, they clung precariously to the small boat in the middle of the lake with the tempestuous raw forces of nature all about. Tossed like a seashell in a boiling cauldron, few had witnessed this tumultuous scene from an open boat and lived to tell the tale.

It occurred to Patrick that it would be a real shame when they drowned.

★★★

Bred idled the craft slowly through the swells out of the bay, and into the main part of the lake. He was astonished to see the ferocity of the storm even a mere hundred yards out on the water. A cold shiver ran down his spine and the hairs stood up on the back of his neck. He clenched his jaw in apprehension as the realization struck him. He had seriously miscalculated the storm's intensity. His recklessness may have placed Patrick and Michelle in real danger.

Although partially protected by the rising hills to the west, the wind still managed to buffet the light aluminium boat, making it difficult to steer. The surging swells generated by the storm crashed alarmingly against the rocks on the shoreline a few yards to starboard. Bred nosed the boat carefully along the shore through the weed beds, around the point, and into the bay a half-mile from the lodge.

A crewman spotted them as they rounded the point and the alarm was quickly raised ashore. Graham suggested that they launch a boat to assist in bringing them in, but the crewman hesitated.

"That young fella can handle that boat all right," he said reassuringly, watching keenly from the beach. "See how he rides the waves, straight and clean, tacking into the wind. He's done that before."

"I don't know where," Graham said, looking down at Mary holding onto his arm. She shrugged and smiled, long past inquiring how Bred did such things.

Bred surfed the five-foot swells as he angled across the water, matching his speed and adjusting the tiller to the water and the wind. As he neared the beach he timed his approach to the waves and the blustery weather. He accelerated through the in-shore rollers, cut the motor and lifted the propeller at the last second. The boat caught the wave, and shot smoothly up the beach to where willing hands dragged them the last few feet to safety.

The crewman nodded in appreciation as the family embraced each other. He only prayed that Patrick D'Laney would navigate his craft as safely as young Bred Andrews had done.

★★★

At last, Patrick caught a glimpse of the island through the murky, rain-swept dusk as another flash of lightning confirmed the gloomy silhouette two hundred yards ahead and to starboard.

Michelle was exhausted from the strain of balancing in the bouncing boat and continuously bailing the incoming floodwaters. Twice, they had been swamped by rogue waves in the vicious crosscurrents; the second wave had spun them around and threatened to overturn them.

Only by a supreme athletic effort and good fortune was Patrick able to right the boat and turn downwind again as another rolling wave cascaded over the gunwale and swamped the outboard motor. It spluttered, stalled and started again on the third pull of the line, and the little craft surged gallantly ahead through the lonely depths.

Patrick could see the in-shore rollers heaving sheets of simmering water scudding up the slanting beach as he gradually turned towards the island. He had to land on the west shore; he had to make it there, there was no other choice.

To be blown past the island and then attempt a landing on the mainland would prove disastrous among the deadheads, logs and driftwood piled high on those forbidding shores. He opened the throttle and drove forward.

Too late, he saw the monstrous wave over his left shoulder. Huge, furious, implacable, it fairly enveloped the little aluminium boat and rolled it over and over in a boiling fury of cascading water and froth. The two occupants tumbled simultaneously into the icy waters of Namier Lake.

Buoyed up by his lifejacket, Patrick fought his way to the surface only to be forced back under again as another tremendous black wave broke over his head. Gasping and choking for breath, he kicked up the next incline, broke through the furious crest and swung down the long back of the wave. Completely dazed, he was at first conscious of little but the noise of the water.

Michelle!

Riding up the next crest, Patrick saw the flash of a fluorescent life jacket twenty yards ahead and swam awkwardly towards her. The water was so cold, it was tragic.

Patrick reached out and grabbed Michelle as another wave broke over them. The girl was totally disoriented and barely conscious. Patrick trod water as he tried to catch his bearings. He saw Pelican Island drifting by fifty yards to his right and was afraid that they would be driven right past by the incessant wind and waves, when his foot suddenly touched the gravel bottom of the lake at the base of a swell.

Patrick half dragged, half carried Michelle up the pebble beach of the island towards the trees and collapsed at the base of a path near a fallen spruce. He lay there gasping for a minute and felt his dizziness and disorientation increase. The agony in his chest and limbs slowly diminished.

Hypothermia! The thought flashed through his mind and he scrambled to his knees. Gritting his teeth against the reviving pain, he pulled himself up and forced Michelle to her feet as well. He had to get them both to the cabin right away.

They staggered down the slippery, muddy trail through the pouring rain, branches tearing incessantly at their clothes. Abruptly, they came upon the deserted cabin nestled in the trees. Patrick burst through the door and dropped Michelle unceremoniously onto the floor as he kicked the door shut behind them.

He was shaking like a leaf and almost totally disoriented as he groped his way across the room towards the fireplace. He grabbed the matches off the shelf, and on the fourth try, managed to light the fire in the pot-bellied stove.

He turned his attention back to Michelle, unconscious on the floor. Her lips were blue with cold. She had only been in the water for seven or eight minutes but that was enough — she was in an advanced stage of hypothermia, and he knew that he had very little time to save her.

His hands were too stiff and swollen to undo the buttons as he stripped off her soaking wet clothes, rolled her in a blanket and laid her on the bed. He tore off his own wet clothes rolled himself in another blanket and lay down shivering beside her.

She was still blue, her breathing shallow.

Michelle's core temperature had dropped too low; he knew that she would not be able to recover by herself. Patrick pulled the blanket off her, laid his own naked body against hers, covered them both with the blankets as snugly as he could and wrapped his arms tightly around her.

The storm raged on into the night and their doomed boat was thrown violently against the tangled wreckage on the north shore. A branch protruding from a shattered tree trunk pierced the hull like a spear, and the valiant craft hung vertically like a broken shingle, pounded by the endless, merciless waves. No living creature could have survived in that terrible place, in that terrible storm.

While the thunder crashed and the wind and the rain howled like demons in the trees, the little log cabin slowly warmed, and so did Patrick and the Michelle. They slept, exhausted.

★★★

Michelle floated back to consciousness and her eyes flew open with a start. She tilted her head back until she focused on Patrick's face beside her, and felt a rush of comfort flood through her very being despite her befuddled senses.

Everything seemed surreal as the terrifying memories of the previous day sprang unbidden to her mind. She unconsciously wriggled deeper into the warmth of Patrick's embracing arms. It was dark and cold outside, but the fire burning in the stove cast a warm glow about the cabin. Reflections danced off the logs and the pots and pans in the open cupboards against the wall.

She recalled their reckless dash across the lake, how very afraid she had been, and the incredible stoic bravery of the one named Patrick D'Laney. She remembered, as if through a fog, her being in the water, the awful cold, Patrick carrying her up to the cabin door, and nothing more until this moment. And this moment was the happiest moment of her life.

She loved him.

She started at the revelation and anxiety enveloped her. She loved him, but because they were police officers and partners in the same detachment, he would never be allowed to know how she felt.

Still in a daze she suddenly realised with a shock that she was totally naked.

★★★

Patrick woke slowly, reluctantly, feeling the glowing warmth of the woman close against his skin. If this was a dream, he wanted it to go on forever. He opened his eyes slowly in the flickering firelight, and looked down at the shy smiling face of the woman that he so desperately wanted to protect and care for, for the rest of his life.

A little confused and unsure of himself, he started to rise but she held him close, raised her head and kissed him tenderly before snuggling back into his arms.

"You're not going anywhere, Patrick D'Laney," she said firmly. "I'm still freezing and it's dark outside."

When Patrick woke again it was dawn. He untangled himself from Michelle's embrace without waking her, dressed himself in his still damp clothes and quietly left the cabin.

The sky was still overcast and angry, and though the wind and the rain had abated somewhat overnight, the lake was still very turbulent and unsafe for small craft.

He searched the island for any sign of Bred or Kelly, and checked carefully along the mainland northern shoreline. He found nothing. They were not there.

He recognised the remains of his own craft by the red-painted foredeck and shuddered at the sight of it hung upside down on the logjam. He realised just how fortunate they had been to survive their ordeal.

It had started to rain again and he was shivering with cold, so he headed back to the cabin and found Michelle awake in bed with her arms behind her head, staring dreamily at the ceiling.

"The kids are not here," he said guiltily, sitting beside her on the bed and kissing her brow. "They're probably back at the lodge. I almost drowned you for nothing."

"Not for nothing, my love," she said with a radiant smile, holding her arms out for him. "Now, I think you should take off those wet clothes and let me warm *you* up for a little while."

Bred piloted the rescue launch through the swells and wind whipped waves. The wind, though diminished, had not lost its sting as the rescuers approached the island. Bred smiled and waved when he saw Michelle tucked under Patrick's arm as the two stood waiting patiently on the sandy beach.

Patrick's eyes narrowed as he watched the launch approaching. Bred stood unsupported in the bow of the pitching craft. He was relieved to see Bred safe and sound, but Patrick had also come to realize, as had most of the family, that Bred was no ordinary sixteen-year-old boy.

★★★

"You mean there was another Namier River?" Maggie said, enthralled with the story Kelly had told her. Bred sipped his coffee and helped with the details only when called upon to do so.

They had gathered at the donut shop on a sunny morning a few days after returning home and were telling Maggie about their vacation adventures.

"Well, not really. The river runs in at the south end of the lake and out the north end," Kelly explained, pointing one way and then the other with her hands. "Bred and I were at the inlet close to the lodge the whole time before the storm. Patrick and Michelle thought we were at the north end and went there to rescue us and got stuck."

"And Patrick and Michelle were stuck in a cabin on a deserted island for three days," Maggie said with a sigh, clasping her hands under her chin. "How romantic! How did you know they were okay?"

"Patrick lit a big fire and we saw the smoke," Kelly replied. "On the *second* day," she said, rolling her eyes.

"Got to go," Bred said. This conversation had deteriorated to the girlie stuff, anyway. He wanted to go and see Maude again and it was getting late.

★★★

Bred walked through the town to 'Maude's Cottage'. As he opened the squeaky garden gate he noticed a shiny new silver Buick parked across the street.

Getting smaller all the time, he thought, remembering the Buick Roadmaster he and Maude had owned ten years before.

Bred rang the doorbell, but there was no reply. He was puzzled. Maggie had told him that Maude had been at home earlier that morning. He rang the door-bell again and thought that he heard a shuffle inside. No one answered.

Bred tried the door but it was locked. He walked around to the back yard, but there was no one there either. Bred shrugged and determined that Maude must have gone shopping. He decided to head over to the gym for a while and was just passing under the bedroom window when he heard a bump from within.

Alarmed, Bred ducked down and headed silently across the back yard. He climbed up onto the deck. Something did not feel quite right here.

There may have been a dozen reasons why Maude might not be able to answer the door but she always called out. Bred retrieved the key from beneath the potted *rhododendron* and, hugging the wall, let himself into the house through the back door.

The light was on in the kitchen and Bred paused to look around. Dishes were piled up in the sink and empty beer and wine bottles stood on the counters. There were newspapers and old picture albums strewn across the kitchen table and some were on the floor.

Bred frowned. This was not like Maude at all; she was a meticulous housekeeper.

There was a muffled noise in the direction of the bedroom. Bred turned swiftly and raced down the carpeted hallway. He flung open the bedroom door and his momentum carried him into the room. Bred stopped short, recoiling. He could not believe his eyes. He backed up too quickly and cracked his head sharply against the door jamb.

The room was a disaster area. Red ribbons and streamers hung from the lights and the headboard and flowers were strewn about the room. Champagne bottles and discarded clothing spilled over the chair onto the floor. Pillows and blankets were in a tangled mess on the bed and on the floor.

Bred stood frozen, his arms stiff at his sides.

Maude was in bed — but she was not alone. A surprised face peeked out from under
the covers. It was Dobbs.

"Oh, Bred!" Maude gasped, clutching the sheet to her breast.

Bred, startled out of his stupor, stumbled out of the room, down the hallway and collapsed onto the couch. He sat there, rocking back and forth with his hands over his face, moaning.

Maude came into the room, tying her robe, and sat down on the couch beside him. She put her hand over her mouth and closed her eyes for a minute.

"You must have realised, Fred," she said gently. "That since your operation our relationship could never again be the same as it was. Society would condemn us… me." She turned away, distraught, but she gathered her resolve, lifted her chin and continued.

"From you I learned the comforts of a loving relationship and I missed that so much that for the last few months I cried myself to sleep after your visits. I became a desperately lonely woman!" She turned to him, as he looked at her sadly and lowered his eyes. "All we have are our memories of the past; but there is no future for us." She paused, swallowing hard. "I finally faced the situation and resolved not to give up on the rest of my life. So when Dobbs arrived at my door… it was like the angels had thrown me a lifeline."

Bred stood up shakily and looked down at Maude's pleading eyes, desperately seeking understanding. There were many things he could say; none would have made things easier for either of them.

"I know," he said, his voice choking. "Dobbs is a good man." He took her hands in his. "I wish you both the very best." He squeezed her hands and looked downcast as he headed towards the door.

"Let a little time pass," she pleaded. "We three can still be the best of friends."

Bred nodded, sadly, thoughtfully. He studied Dobbs' Buick parked across the street.

"Tell Dobbs they found out Bier switched materials so he could keep the job going, and that's what caused the explosion." He opened the door and stepped out onto the porch. The sun had passed behind a heavy cloud. It was going to rain again.

Maude was a little confused by the request, as she watched him walk down the stone pathway and open the squeaky garden gate.

★★★

Dobbs stepped out of the hallway from where he had been eavesdropping, walked over to Maude in the doorway and wrapped his arms around her from behind. Together, they watched as the boy crossed the street. She clasped her hands over his arms and leaned against him, tilting her head to one side.

"You heard?" she asked.

"Some of it, yes," he answered, not venturing any further.

Dobbs was in a state of euphoria; he and Maude were together again at last. They had been separated for a long, long time, and he had honestly thought that he had lost her forever.

Forty-seven years ago, in a different world, he and Fred had both courted the girl. Fred had won her hand fair and square, and Fred and Maude were married two years later. He had been Fred's best man and his best friend, until the accident eighteen years ago. Dobbs had kept his true feelings for Maude to himself through all those lonely years and never married.

In the mellowness of the moment, swaying slowly back and forth in the doorway with Maude in his arms, Daniel Dobbs allowed his mind to idly remember the past and to explore the possibilities for their future.

It was an amusing story that Maude had told him.

Apparently, the boy had become devoted to Fred, and Fred in turn had engrossed Bred in countless of his stories. In the process, Fred had imparted a great deal of his life and experiences to him. Bred had then become totally dedicated to Maude, especially after Fred went away and left her alone. Bred considered himself her moral guardian.

Fred had been like that; he was always telling magnificent lies to little kids, just to watch their mouths drop open and their innocent eyes pop out. He and Fred went back a long way, and Dobbs recalled the memories with a sigh.

Age is a tragedy.

Dobbs and Fred had both graduated from the University of Manitoba forty-eight years ago, and despite the difference in their ages had become firm friends. They had worked on many jobs together both in Canada and in South West Africa; that was, until the accident. Dobbs smiled to himself, the times they had had.

Only Fred could have known about the superintendent on his last job — that greasy Saul Bier. Bier had switched a critical pipe spool for another made from an incompatible material — just to make overtime work for himself and his crew. No one caught the switch in time. The chemical reaction in the process caused an explosion during commissioning, and that had taken his leg. Dobbs only found out the truth two years after the fact, and purely by accident.

A company manager, whom he had known quite well, had a little too much to drink one night at a party up at the lodge. That had resulted in a very hush-hush meeting between Dobbs the company executive. The company's reputation would have suffered greatly if the information had been made public. Dobbs had been compensated handsomely for his silence.

And trust Fred to divulge the location of the hidden bay and the inlet of the Namier River to a kid, Dobbs thought cynically. He and Fred had found that bay together thirty years ago and sworn each other to secrecy. Few knew of its location. He lived on the lake, and he hadn't told anyone, not even his most regular clients.

Dobbs scratched the stubble on his chin as he watched Bred stroll up the road. He wondered just how smart the kid was. From what Maude had told him about Bred's involvement in the affair, and of Patrick and Michelle's professional relationship before being stranded on Pelican Island, it seemed quite possible, even probable, that Bred had set Michelle and Patrick up for their little adventure.

"No, no, that's a reach," he told himself with a chuckle. "Then he could just as well have set up Maude and me." He shook his head, smiling at the absurdity.

Amused at his meandering thoughts, he squeezed Maude a little tighter and settled back into his dreamy state.

They watched as Bred shuffled along the dusty road with his head down in gloomy sadness. But as he reached the corner, Bred turned back towards the house, threw a casual salute with his left hand, and his mouth creased in a wry grin.

Dobbs stiffened, shocked out of his daydreams. The hair stood up on the back of his neck as he watched the boy disappear from sight. Fred had always done that too — when he said goodbye to a job well done!

★★★

A few weeks later, near the end of June, Bred sat in his usual spot next to the window, nursing his coffee in the solarium of Maude's Donut Shop. Beth sat across from him chattering like a squirrel. Bred listened absently, amused at her gay prattle. He looked out across the street to the sun-drenched fields of fluorescent-green beyond the town, and to the cattle browsing on the newborn grass shoots in the pastures. He watched the wild geese and ducks splashing happily in shallow lakes created by the melted snow. Sunlight flashed off water, which mirrored the pale blue sky.

Bred knew that the ponds would soon be gone, that they would quickly evaporate in the warm sunshine or be soaked up by the thirsty land. The ducks didn't care. They lived for the moment — any moment. He smiled to himself.

"Next time around I want to be a duck," he said aloud, without thinking.

"Me too!" Beth said smiling, sipping her milkshake through the straw.

Two ladies entered the donut shop, stopped and looked critically about the room. Bred glanced towards the door and did a double take. He hardly recognised them.

Maggie and Kelly were dressed in smart black business suits with knee length skirts, and each had had a makeover. Their hair was drawn back in fashionable buns and they sported thin black briefcases under their arms. Bred stared open mouthed as they tripped across the room towards him in their new high-heeled shoes. He suddenly realized that his friends were now seventeen and no longer children.

"You look *gorgeous!*" Beth congratulated them as they approached the table.

"Yes,….yes, absolutely," stammered Bred, emerging from his stupor, and rising to offer the ladies a seat. Bred was totally thrown off balance and the girls were loving it. They accepted his kindness graciously.

They could barely contain their excitement, and their sober demeanour evaporated as soon as they sat down. Kelly hugged her hands with glee, and Maggie took a big slurp of Beth's milkshake.

"What?.. what?" Bred asked, totally bewildered, as Beth protested the assault of her property in the background. The girls looked at each other, giggling, and turned toward him.

"You are addressing the proud new owners of Maude's Donut Shop!" They pronounced in unison. There was a brief silence as Bred absorbed the startling information.

"Good, then you can get me another milkshake," Beth said, unimpressed.

"Maude is leaving town at the end of the month and told me that she was planning to sell the shop," Maggie said, still highly elated and not at all aware of the successive shocks that she was administering to the more tender parts of Bred's anatomy. "So, Kelly and I spoke to my dad, and your dad," she said, her eyes sparkling.

"We have just concluded our first meeting on the Articles of Incorporation with our lawyers, the bank executive and our silent partners, the dads," Kelly continued, putting on a most sophisticated air. "It's in the Minutes."

"But…but, Kelly, you and business?" Bred stammered, throwing his hands open. "You can't stand it — remember?" he finished lamely, rubbing his forehead. She gave him a haughty look.

"This is different," she said. "This is mine…ours," she corrected, smiling, holding out her hand to Maggie.

Bred raised his eyebrow, shook his head and capitulated.

"Congratulations to you both," he said, standing and raising his coffee cup in mock salute. "On behalf of our quasi-democratic society," he orated, "I welcome you to the realm of business and taxes, politics and taxes, financial enterprise and taxes, and the pursuit of the one true Canadian dream — tax returns."

Beth and the half-dozen customers seated at nearby tables laughed and applauded heartily. Kelly punched him on the arm.

"It'll never work!" He mumbled, as he held back the snicker with a gulp of coffee and choked on it for his punishment.

Later that afternoon, Bred strolled down the road towards 'Maude's Cottage', he noted thankfully that there was no silver Buick parked on the street; he wanted to speak to Maude privately, this one last time. A small moving van was parked in front of the house. Bred was curious, Maude had a lot of stuff in there. He opened the garden gate and paused. No squeak. Dobbs must have oiled it. Bred was involuntarily annoyed for a second. For twenty years that squeak had heralded the approach of visitors to their house.

"Their house!" Bred sighed, and continued down the pathway.

Maude met him at the door as if she had been expecting him.

"I knew that your grapevine would give you the news quickly," she said brightly, ushering him into the living room. Bred sat down on the couch and Maude brought him a cup of coffee.

"I just made it," she said. "I knew you would come as soon as you heard." Bred took a sip of the coffee and waited patiently.

"I'm moving up to the lake with Dobbs," she said. "He promised to keep the power on all the time. We'll come south in the winter — but not here. Dobbs has a house somewhere on the Sunshine Coast."

"I'm sorry, Fred, er, Bred," she said, pleading. "This is the end for you and I… please try to understand."

Bred took a big breath and nodded soberly. He had recognised the futility of their relationship a long time ago. He felt like Humphrey Bogart and Ingrid Bergman in *Casablanca.*

"I've signed 'Maude's Cottage' over to you," she continued, brushing away his protestations. "Dobbs and I are quite well off," she said. "And don't forget Fred's insurance," she reminded him. She looked at him for a minute and dropped her head.

"Anyway," she continued with a mischievous grin, "you don't get possession until you're eighteen. In the meantime I've rented the house, furnished, to Patrick D'Laney, whom I think will soon no longer be the most eligible bachelor in town." She paused for a minute, studying him carefully. Bred practised his 'curiously interested' expression. "He'll move in when his present lease expires in about three months." She concluded slowly, watching him struggle to keep the expression. Her suspicions confirmed, her eyes narrowed. "You know that Dobbs thinks that you orchestrated the marooning of Patrick and Michelle, and maybe even our own reunion, don't you." She said.

Bred winced and looked out the window.

"What about the shop?" he asked quickly, changing the subject. "You turned it over to two adolescent girls with stars in their eyes, fantasies of grandeur, of fame and fortune, and.. and...it'll never work!" he said, resigned.

Maude burst out laughing. "That's exactly what you told me fifteen years ago when I opened the shop," she said, wiping away a tear. "...Fantasies of grandeur...never work...I remember now. Oh, Bred," she said, putting her hand on his arm. "Everything will be fine."

Bred was not convinced.

"Maude," he said, "you have been very ill, and Namier Lake is so remote. A thousand kilometres from civilization, no roads, no...no nothing! Don't you think..."

"I'll be fine," she interrupted reassuringly. "I had my final check-up just last month, and Dr. Strydom says he's confident that I'm totally cured."

Bred sat bolt upright.

"Dr. Strydom?" he exploded. "He's back!"

"Why yes," she said, looking at him sharply. "He's been back for a few weeks now. By the way, he did ask after you. He wants you to go in for a check-up too. I referred him to Mary D'Laney-Andrews of course." She smiled, looking at him curiously.

Bred's jaw tightened as he jumped to his feet.

"He's supposed to be in a South African jail," Bred said exasperated. "Bloody hell!"

He raised his arms and clenched his fists in frustration. Just what did it take to incarcerate a murderer?

"The last time that I was in his care, Dr. Strydom was about to perform a series of biopsies on my brain." He tapped his temple with his finger. "Rest assured that within a day of my being in his clutches my head would have been buzzing with sparks delivered through tiny electrodes drilled into my head." He turned away to stare out the window. "Dr. Strydom would be directly connected to my entire nervous system, making me twitch and jerk like a puppet on a string!" He said coldly. He turned around and saw the shocked expression on Maude's face.

"That's not going to happen," he said with a reassuring smile, forcing himself to relax a little. "I plan to stay as far away from City Hospital as possible in the future."

He was shaken, but not stirred — and very, very thankful for the news. He checked the time.

"May I use your phone, Maude," he asked casually. "I need to call Dr. Thlabati and Dr. Stein in South Africa. I need to get some answers."

Bred walked slowly back towards the donut shop, trying to comprehend the logic of the insane merry-go-round he was on. The sky had clouded over and there was a fine drizzle, which soaked through his nylon golf-jacket. Bred shivered, but not from the cold.

He came to the only bus stop on the main street in town and sat down on the bench, ignoring the rain.

Bred had said his farewells to Maude and wished her well. He knew that they would see each other again from time to time.

Overall, everything has gone pretty well, he thought with a sad smile.

The unanswered questions of the future of their relationship had plagued Bred for a long time, and in the end, he had made up his mind to give Maude a second chance at happiness, if he could.

Fate had definitely played a role, with a little nudge here and there. He had expected her to carry on with her life, but he had not considered that she would leave town. He wished Maude and Dobbs the best, but he couldn't help feeling sorry for himself, now that it was over.

He sighed. This really was the end of an era, he thought.

★★★

His conversation with Dr. Thlabati, however, did not have the same result.

Apparently, the South African government considered the evidence accumulated against Dr. Strydom in the apartheid era to be too volatile to be presented before the free, integrated, democratic people of the New South Africa. In their wisdom, the South African courts had declared all the evidence inadmissible, and had released Dr. Strydom, unconditionally.

Bred and the young doctor Thlabati had had a heated philosophical discussion on the ramifications of pardoning evil for the greater good. At least they both agreed that there was a vast difference between justice for the people, and the manipulation of Imperial Law by omnipotent judges out of touch with humanity.

It was the same in Canada. Bred and the doctor were at opposite ends of a dichotomy. The New South Africa needed stability; Bred needed justice to be served.

The end result, of course, was that Dr. Strydom was back in his old job at City Hospital in Edmonton, absolutely free to pursue his tormented obsession.

Bred could not bring himself to hate the man; after all, he had saved his life — sort of. But that did not justify the road the doctor had chosen to travel in order to achieve his goals. He would do it again; the end did not justify the means.

Dr. Strydom had to be stopped.

Bred shook his head in frustration and put his face in his hands just as the bus pulled up and opened the doors in front of him. Bred was so absorbed he didn't notice.

"Are you gonna get on the bus or not," the driver yelled impatiently. Bred looked up, startled out of his cognitive dilemma.

"What's it going to be, punk?" the driver slurred, his contempt for punks clearly apparent in his voice.

"Fuck off!" Bred yelled, standing up. He was just as surprised at his outburst as the driver was.

"Brian, you little bastard!" Bred muttered to himself, as he walked away.

★★★

The following Saturday morning, Bred and Beth peddled their bicycles into the town of Bolton under a clear blue sky It was early in July and the temperature was thirty degrees in the shade and the trees were beginning to droop in the still, sweltering air.

They stepped into Maude's Donut Shop to be greeted by twenty youngsters between the ages of seven and seventeen milling around the room. Bred and Beth could not help but notice the excitement in the air.

Parents clustered at tables in one corner of the shop for mutual protection, clutching their coffee cups and glancing furtively around the room for glimpses of their offspring, hoping that they wouldn't break anything expensive. Beth squealed, and was immediately drawn into the throng by four or five other eleven year old girls. Bred shook his head with a grin; Beth was really coming out of her shell.

Kelly and Maggie were at the counter across the room talking to a husky six-foot blonde seventeen year old, the size of a small car. He was wearing a grey tank-top vest that displayed his muscular frame. Bred disengaged himself from the doorjamb, and walked over to join them.

"This is Josh," Kelly said a little shyly, holding his arm. "Josh, this is Bred," she introduced them blithely. Bred nodded his acknowledgement and offered his hand.

Josh eyed him coldly for a second as he filtered through a short list of his sworn enemies. A light went on in his head and he stiffened, ignoring Bred's gesture of peace.

"I know you," he said, his face turning red as he stepped closer. "You're the dork that ambushed me the last day of school in Grade Seven." He shook Kelly's hand off his arm as he spoke. "You hid behind a tree and smacked me in the back with a shovel and then took off like a frightened rabbit!"

Josh was getting pretty hot; he tensed his peck muscles and spread his fingers wide as the memory of that humiliating day flushed through his body like hot glycol through a radiator.

The posture nearly doubled the size of the 'car' and Bred knew he was toast.

Damn it, Brian, he thought. You're going to get me killed before I even get back to school.

"Sorry about that," he said hopelessly in a small voice, closing his eyes tightly to avoid witnessing his own inevitable demise.

"No Josh, wait!"

Bred opened one eye very carefully. Kelly had grabbed Josh's arm again with both hands and was looking up into his face, pleading with him.

"Bred is really, really sorry and… and he's my brother!" she said, apologising for him.

"Your brother?" Josh echoed, his anger fading away. He stared at her and then at Bred.

Bred saw the loophole and nodded his head quickly and practised his 'I'm sorry' smile. Bred was delighted. Just one year ago Kelly wouldn't have given him the time of day and today, she was actually trying to save his life.

"I'll let it go for now," Josh said grudgingly, eyeing him dangerously, "but if you ever…" He left the threat unfinished as he turned away and he and Kelly wandered across the room to an open table. Bred took a deep breath and watched with relief as they walked away.

"Kelly just saved your ass," Maggie said with a nervous giggle. "Josh Morgan was going to squash you like a bug."

Bred smiled, whistled quietly and raised his eyebrows. "Don't I know it," he said. "That was huge; I owe Kelly big time."

Maggie looked at him curiously.

Bred changed the subject as he looked around. "What's going on here?" he asked. "Somebody's birthday?"

"No," Maggie laughed. "We're waiting for Matt Finch. He's arranging the annual camping trip to Pine Lake in a couple of weeks." She looked down at her feet. "Are you coming Bred?" As she spoke, Beth and her friends came over to join them. Bred hesitated. He looked about the room at the now somewhat familiar writhing mass of undisciplined adolescents.

"Sure, I'll go," he said with a smile, glancing over at Beth and her group. He was surprised to see the look of concern on Beth's face as he spoke.

"But Bred," she said. "We have a rope swing that goes out over the lake, canoes and rafts and everything."

"That's nice," said Bred.

"But…but you don't swim, and you're terrified of going into the water," she said exasperated.

Bred was surprised. The water at Lake Namier was practically freezing. "That's why I stayed *in* the boat," he said.

The rest of her argument was drowned out by cheers from the crowd. Matt Finch and Julie Martins came through the front doors and into the donut shop.

★★★

Camp Minatonka is a partially cleared track of land on the shores of Pine Lake. Pine Lake itself is a relatively small turquoise-coloured body of water, about two miles long and one mile across, situated in the middle of the Rocky Mountains Forest Reserve. Generally unnoticed by travellers and tourists in the vastness of the western wilderness inundated with greater lakes of equal or greater beauty, this particular lake has one outstanding feature:

Fed by warm springs created deep beneath the lake, the water is always ten degrees warmer than any other lake in the chilly Alberta foothills along the Rocky Mountain Range. The lake never freezes over completely, even in the coldest of winters.

Being on crown land, no one had paid much attention when, some years before, boy scouts found the lake and carved out a campsite among the huge lodgepole pines, poplar and spruce in the thick forest along its rugged shoreline.

As a young man, Matt Finch had been one of those boy scouts, and today, tried to keep the campsite alive by taking the kids out every summer and showing them the wonders of nature. Matt's sister, Paula, lived in Bolton with her family and she had a ten-year-old daughter. Matt took his niece and some of the local kids camping for two weeks every summer up to Pine Lake, in the foothills of the Rocky Mountains.

An old trapper named Zakk (Matt had forgotten his last name) lived in a tumbled down cabin on the edge of the camp throughout the summer; he did a little maintenance and discouraged vagrants and vandals from camping there. The camp directors retained him for just that purpose, but nobody told the kids that.

Zakk kept to himself for the most part, though his cackling laugh echoed across the lake or from the deep woods from time to time. His cabin was off-limits to the campers.

Some said he was crazy and many a timorous group of young people sitting enthralled and wide-eyed around a dying campfire had moved just a little closer to the embers, during the telling of some of his exploits.

The six-hour trip to Camp Minatonka in the small yellow school bus had been a real experience. Packed with twenty excited kids and all their gear, rafts, canoes, paddles, life jackets, food and drinks for a fortnight and along with the five chaperones and a portly German chef, they finally arrived at the camp by mid-afternoon. Bred was exhausted from simply watching the younger kids having fun.

The bus driver dropped them off at the camp and returned to Edmonton, promising before he left to return in fourteen days. Bred was not so sure about that; why would he be such a masochist?

The long wooden bunkhouse accommodated the smaller children and the chaperones, while the older kids pitched their tents on either side of the bunkhouse. The flat ground was covered with a carpet of pine needles beneath the trees.

Julie, along with the girls, had naturally migrated to one area, while Matt and the boys had gone to the other. Bred was assigned to share a tent with Josh.

By the time they had all settled in it was late afternoon. Josh, who had been there before, took a rope from the storage shed and called for Bred to come along. They headed over to an overhanging tree at the edge of the lake.

Forgive and forget, Bred thought, relieved, happily jogging after him.

Some of the little kids tagged along to watch the proceedings, as Josh swarmed up the old poplar and crawled out onto the overhanging limb. Bred threw him the rope and Josh tied it off.

"Okay!" Josh yelled, swinging the rope to Bred. "Give it a try."

Bred surveyed the scene from the top of the bank overlooking the water.

The sandstone-gravel slope ran down twenty feet almost vertically to the edge of the lake. Swinging out on the rope would put him thirty feet out over the water, and if he didn't let go he could simply swing back up on to the top of the bank again.

A well-worn path led from the edge of the water in a series of switchbacks back up to the top of the cliff, clearly made by those that did drop into the water. A smoothly worn patch of ground cleared of vegetation served as the launching platform. It showed signs of having been used by a great number of children over many previous summers.

Bred gave the rope a tug, testing its security as more of the curious campers gathered to watch the awesome spectacle. He was quite confident. Fred was a veteran of the rope swing. As a young man he had developed his gymnastic skills on swings very similar to this one and he had one good trick: Fred could swing upside down and by locking his ankles around the rope, spread his arms out like an upside down crucifix. It was an impressive manoeuvre; always a crowd-pleaser.

More little kids arrived, along with the girls and a couple of the chaperones. They gathered around, whispering excitedly in anticipation. Bred felt the hot pride course through his veins; the rush of a true athlete about to perform a magnificent gymnastic feat before the masses.

He pulled back to gain extra height for his swing, flipped his legs up in a graceful arc and locked his ankles around the rope as his forward motion began. He spread his arms and had just cleared the edge of the bank when the rope broke.

Face down in the dirt, Bred tumbled disgracefully down the bank, skipping and sliding like a demented otter through the mud and the rocks to the edge of the water. He hit the bank and launched headfirst into the flotsam and jetsam and slimy blue algae gathered at the edge of the lake.

Scratched and bruised, waist deep in the water, Bred scrambled spluttering to his feet and struggled to the shore. He was covered in weeds and mud and gore. He was a very sorry sight indeed.

Somewhat dazed, he stood up and looked around. Twenty startled little faces peered down at him from the top of the cliff. A hush fell over the scene as everyone stared down at the sorry heap of misfortune.

In the silence that followed, a quiet voice spoke from the branches:

"That's for the shovel," Josh said with a chuckle.

Relieved or disappointed that he was not dead, the audience roared.

Bred never, ever tried to perform that crucifix stunt again.

The twilight turned to darkness and the night became still as they all sat around the campfire listening to Matt tell ghost stories to the younger children before bedtime. In the kitchens attached to the bunkhouse, the chef had prepared a wholesome meal for everyone and the little kids were just starting to drop off, when Zakk's cackling laugh echoed across the lake. Bred smiled at the theatrics and at the audible intake of startled breaths.

"How you doing, Bred?" Josh whispered over his shoulder. Bred jumped.

"Just fine thanks," Bred answered coolly, composing himself and unconsciously rubbing a bruised elbow.

"Come on then," Josh said quietly, turning away and slipping off into the darkness. Bred followed cautiously.

Barely visible in the starlight, Bred saw the silhouettes of Maggie and Kelly crouched beside the corner of the bunkhouse waiting for them to arrive. Josh paused to whisper something to Kelly as Bred appeared, and headed up into the trees towards the other end of the campsite. They followed obediently.

Silently, they scurried over the carpet of pine needles between the trees, across the campground and up to the edge of the forest. Through the gloom, Bred could just make out the beginning of an overgrown pathway cut into the trees.

"Where are we going?" Bred whispered harshly.

"Shhhh!" Maggie turned and put her finger over her lips. She pointed to an old clapboard sign nailed to a tree beside the trail.

"Do Not Enter — Trespassers Will Be Shot!"

The warning was boldly written in fresh red paint across the gnarled wood.

"To check out Zakk's cabin," she whispered.

Childish pranks, Bred thought with a sigh, but okay, he would go along for the ride.

The cabin, situated on the right side of the short cut-line, was cloaked in total darkness as they crept towards the door. Josh stepped up onto the creaking porch and tried the door. It was unlocked.

They all crowded into the doorway and Josh snapped on a small flashlight, revealing before their startled eyes that which no camper had ever seen before.

A polished wooden table and four matching chairs stood in the kitchen area, with a vase and flowers as a centrepiece. The sideboard and display cabinet revealed clean dishes and fancy china cups stacked neatly together on the shelves. Shiny new pots and pans hung from a copper carousel over the counter, and the spotless stainless steel sink flashed in the torchlight.

A huge stone fireplace rising from floor to ceiling dominated the other side wall, and a solid wooden mantle, high above the set fireplace, was adorned with framed pictures of animals, and some pictures of Zakk together with his old acquaintances. A rifle hung from brass hooks above the mantle and a polished brass antique cartridge box rested on the shelf beneath. The bed was neatly made up against the far wall behind a giant oak chest.

The place was immaculate.

"This guy's got a woman here." Josh whispered hoarsely. Kelly punched him in the ribs.

"Haaarrrrh!" The scream came from the forest close to the cabin, making the hair stand up on the back of Bred's neck. They all bolted for the door.

Josh kept the flashlight on as they jumped off the porch and headed down the trail.

"*Haaarrrr!*" Came the horrible scream again, right behind them, from the darkness.

Josh swung the light around to confront the demon, and the beam caught the flash of a green florescent creature hurtling down at him from the trees. He dropped the flashlight and fled. Everyone took off down the trail at a full gallop, the girls in the lead.

★★★

Zakk launched himself off the tree platform and rode down the stretched cable like Rambo. He was hollering and yelling like a banshee with his green-florescent plastic garbage-bag cape flapping in the wind behind him.

The cable, invisible in the dark, spanned all the way down the trail to six feet above their heads. As he caught up to them, Zakk let go of the pulley and fell in a descending parabolic arc feet first towards Bred. Bred glanced over his shoulder and saw him coming at the last second. He barely stepped aside in time.

"Ho-lay!" He yelled.

Zakk shot past him in full flight and slammed feet first into Josh, ploughing him face down into the dirt and tumbling him into the wild rose bushes at the side of the trail. Josh tripped up Kelly and she collided with Maggie in a midnight chain reaction. The girls scrambled up on their knees and sat holding each other, breathless and shivering in fright in the middle of the trail.

Bred didn't go unscathed. Zakk's flailing arm caught him on the side of the head as he went by and the momentum bounced Bred off a tree.

"*Steeerike!*" Zakk yelled exuberantly, as he came to a sliding stop in the tall grass.

Crazy Zakk's cackling laugh resounded through the forest for ten minutes afterwards, as he rolled on the ground laughing hysterically in the aftermath of yet another, soon to be legendary escapade.

Bred smiled and rubbed his swollen ear. He was really beginning to enjoy the best of his second childhood.

★★★

Camp Minatonka was ideally situated above a wide sandy beach on the edge of the lake. The soft yellow sand ran gradually down into the lake on a gentle grade and the clear blue water was only waist deep some fifty yards out.

Someone had set a rope string of red and white buoys in a semi-circle in front of the beach as a pool boundary for the non-swimmers, the little people, and the cautious. A little beyond the buoys, in the deeper water, a large wooden raft mounted on drums was anchored firmly to the bottom of the lake. Off to the left, away from the beach, a wooden dock extended out into the water and two of the campers red canoes were tied up to it.

It was a beautiful, warm day, with scarcely a cloud in the sky and the light wind off the lake caused little waves to break on the beach where the younger kids were already building castles in the sand.

Bred and Josh had had breakfast and were busy helping Matt inflate the big yellow raft, when Julie came down to see the action. She stopped short, staring at the boys in their swimsuits.

"Have you boys been fighting?" she demanded, coming over to them and inspecting one and then the other. "Shame on you two, setting such a poor example!" Julie was quite irate.

"Whoa, there partner," Matt said, coming between them with his arms up. "They haven't been scrapping, it's just normal wear and tear," he finished lamely as he saw the look in her eyes.

Julie wasn't buying it. The boys were all covered in bruises, cuts and scratches and Josh had two black eyes. She turned on Matt, her eyes blazing.

"I've seen less wear and tear in a war zone! We haven't even been here a full day yet." She turned back to the boys, livid.

"Now you two get over to the bunkhouse where I can dress those cuts and scratches before they get infected." Julie whirled around on Matt.

"*Rhuff!*" She said in exasperation and followed the boys up the beach, leaving the innocent Matt with his hands out wondering what he had done wrong.

★★★

By the time they were all patched up, the raft had been inflated and launched and half a dozen of the older kids were already loaded. Josh and Bred splashed through the shallows and dived aboard. Kelly and Maggie pulled frantically on the ores and the craft careened erratically away from the beach.

Beth eyed Bred anxiously.

It was a soaking, hilarious ten-minute trip out to the raft. Bred finally reached over and grabbed one of the anchor rings and scrambled onto the wooden deck, followed by the rest of the group. Josh tied off the inflatable dinghy and jumped onto the raft.

His sudden considerable weight on one side caused the raft to pitch precariously and everyone hung on for dear life. Bred, on the opposite side, however, experienced the sensation of being on a diving board and was flipped over backwards into the water.

"He can't swim!" Beth screamed. She jumped into the water and wanted to dive beneath the surface, but her lifejacket kept popping her back up. Everyone raced over to the side of the unstable craft and stared anxiously down into the depths for a glimpse of the body.

Bred, meanwhile, let himself plunge deep under the water and even swam down a little to the sandy bottom. He cleared his ears and relished the moment. It had been a long time since he had been swimming and he had almost forgotten the freedom. He was amazed at how warm the water was.

With his father's encouragement, Fred had become an accomplished swimmer at four years of age; he had even competed in his high school swimming gala. As he grew older, Fred had become fascinated with the underwater world and during his vacations had swum and snorkelled in many of the lakes and oceans of the world.

He swam lazily under the raft, rolling over, slowly exhaling through his nose as he looked up at the sunlight glinting off the surface. He rose quietly to the surface on the far side of the raft and propelling himself up out of the water, sat softly, unnoticed on the edge of the raft.

Bred watched Beth curiously for a minute, as she bobbed up and down like a duck.

"What's her problem?" he asked after a while.

Kelly shot upright at the shock of his voice, whirling around and knocking Josh off balance. He spread his arms to regain his balance, lost, and took Maggie, Kelly and two or three others into the drink with him.

When the dust settled, Bred sat astonished and alone on the edge of the bobbing raft.

★★★

Later that afternoon, Bred, Kelly, Maggie and Josh had the raft to themselves, and were just lying about relaxing in the warm sunshine. Beth and the other kids had taken the inflatable raft and were playing over by the dock.

Zakk's cackling laugh echoed briefly once again across the lake.

"He's mocking us," Josh said dourly. "He never does that in the daytime."

"Our children's children will hear the story and be *so* ashamed," Kelly said pouting, and blushed when she realised what she had said. Josh gave her shoulder a reassuring punch. Bred raised himself up on one elbow and stared thoughtfully towards the shore.

"We have to get even," he said suddenly. They looked at him dubiously.

"But, how?" Maggie asked miserably. "This is his domain, his private sanctuary; we can't outfox him." That sounded like a challenge. Bred smiled.

"We can, if we're patient and let nature take its course," he said. "Come on."

Bred dove smoothly off the raft and swam effortlessly through the water in a fast crawl-stroke heading towards the beach. Kelly stared after him.

"How…?" she began, gave up, and dove into the lake in pursuit. The others followed.

Back on dry land they changed into jeans, sneakers and tee-shirts and retired to the bunkhouse to plan their strategy. Bred laid out a sheet of paper on the table and sketched the campsite, the bunkhouse, Zakk's cabin and his outbuildings in plain view and labelled them all carefully.

"Pretty good!" Josh said, admiring the map.

"Okay," Bred said. "And this is our target." He made an X.

"The outhouse?" Maggie exclaimed.

Bred explained his plan, and they all looked at him quite startled for a minute.

"That'll do it!" Josh burst out, and the girls giggled nervously.

"We have to get up to the cabin unseen," Bred said, as they crowded closer. "Maggie, you and Kelly wait here, give Josh and me five minutes, then head up alongside the trail through the trees. Come in from the back side and hide inside this shed." Bred marked their route and destination on the map.

"Josh, you and I will cut through the trees from the other side. There're bound to be trip wires," he warned. "So take your time."

They looked at him curiously.

"That's how he knew we were coming the first time," Bred explained, "he was probably down on this bluff making noises to scare the kids." He indicated the point on the map. "But he got back to the cabin too late and had almost no time to prepare before we arrived." He saw the doubtful look on Kelly's face.

"We were the first ever to see inside his cabin, weren't we?" Bred said, with a grin. "He's slipping! And he'll have to go to the washroom soon."

Maggie shook her head. "You're crazy, Bred," she said with a laugh.

"All right," he said. "Any questions before we take up our positions?"

"How do you know he'll have to go?" Kelly asked.

"He's old, he goes at least six times a day, and a couple of times a night," Bred replied, with absolute authority.

★★★

Kelly sat shivering with Maggie by her side, hidden deep in the bushes beside the trail leading up to the cabin. It was not the cold that made them shiver. The sun would still shine for another hour and she really wished that she were still lying on the beach.

But, it was a matter of Josh's honour! Kelly stiffened her resolve and squeezed Maggie's hands reassuringly.

They waited silently while Zakk walked past them heading down the trail. He paused momentarily, and they held their breath. He continued his journey and they breathed a sigh of relief. He had not seen them. They waited five minutes according to the plan and crept out of their hiding place. The girls made their way carefully through the trees beside the trail and stepped over a tripwire partially concealed in the bushes near the cabin. Bred had been right! They slipped quietly over to the shed behind the cabin and ducked inside. Kelly peered through a crack in the boards; the outhouse was in plain sight.

Zakk's unearthly laugh reverberated in the late afternoon stillness and a chill ran up Kelly's spine. She would never get used to that! Bred waved to them once, from the trees beyond the outhouse. Everyone was in position. She checked her camera for the tenth time. Now all they had to do, was wait.

They didn't have to wait long. Zakk suddenly appeared in front of the cabin and Kelly involuntarily sucked in her breath. She had been watching the trail and didn't see him come up. Zakk stood quietly with his nose in the air, his floppy felt hat pulled tightly down over his forehead and his long grey-black beard waved lightly in the breeze. He glanced around the area suspiciously. Apparently satisfied, Zakk stripped off his grey coat as he walked into the cabin and closed the door. The nervous teenagers settled down to wait again.

The sun had already set when Zakk emerged from the cabin and headed towards the outhouse. The air was crystal clear and the mountain twilight seemed to enhance the contrast, as light and shadows played tricks on their optic nerves.

As Zakk closed the door, Kelly and Maggie slipped out of the shed and sat quietly on the side.

Bred and Josh crept out of the trees and came quietly up behind the outhouse. They held baseball bats raised in their hands. Bred signalled to Josh with his fingers.

One! Two! Three!

They swung the bats and crashed them against the sides of the outhouse.

Deja-vu! Kelly vaguely remembered a movie called M★A★S★H.

Zakk came flying out, nearly tearing the door off its hinges, pants around his ankles. He ran twenty paces like a hog-tied kangaroo, his shredded newspaper still gripped in his hands.

Maggie and Kelly clicked away, taking the pictures that would vindicate them and their offspring forever.

★★★

Their sides splitting, the four delinquents sprinted away down the trail, not pausing until they reached the trees above the bunkhouse.

"That was magic!" Josh yelled exhilarated, mimicking one of Bred's strange expressions. He held up his bat and kissed it, and in the exuberance of the moment, lifted Kelly with one arm around her waist and kissed her too.

"Your little brother is cool," he said a little lamely, as she hung there, limp and wide-eyed with surprise. Bred rolled his eyes, and Maggie laughed, delighted.

The laughter died on her lips and she grabbed Bred's arm in sudden fright. Without warning a familiar rattle became distinctly audible and slowly increased in volume until they held their ears to shut out the sound.

Zakk's cackling laugh pealed through the forest and echoed eerily out on the lake — at the same time. The hairs stood up on their arms and they looked at each other in alarm, their self-confidence melting away at the awful realisation.

Zakk was not alone.

Josh broke first, and they took off running down the hill in the fading light towards the safety of the campfire and the protection of the relatively sane people from the town of Bolton.

★★★

Zakk sat at his table in the cabin and poured himself a cup of tea.

Gotta give the kids their due, he thought with a chuckle. He hadn't seen that coming, even though he had caught the scent of the girls in the bushes as he went by earlier. He would ask Matt to send him a photograph of this group for his mantle.

He was glad that he had saved the rockets and small explosives he had rigged on electrical fuses around the cabin for another time. They, or others like them, would be back.

He hung up the microphone wired to the speakers on the cliff and unplugged the batteries to save power.

★★★

CHAPTER TWELVE
The Bad Times

Peace reined in the remote forest retreat for the next few days; that was, until Josh got restless again, on day eight of the fourteen day trip.

Bred, Josh and the girls had been quite happy lazing around on the beach, canoeing on the lake, or just dozing in the sun out on the raft. The boys had begun to heal nicely from their wounds, and Zakk had kept quietly to himself after that second day.

They had watched in amusement from the raft as Julie remonstrated with him behind the cabin and out of earshot of the camp, with one hand on her hip. Zakk just stood there with his head down, humbly shuffling his feet.

"Serves him right," Kelly said unsympathetically, rolling over on the deck to toast the other side. "He was scaring people."

★★★

Later, Bred paddled around the lake in the canoe and arrived back at the dock in time for lunch. Josh was nowhere to be seen and Kelly was worried. Josh never missed a meal.

They scoured the camp and eventually found him tinkering with an old all-terrain vehicle behind the shed above the dock.

"Where did you find that?" Bred asked, inspecting the old quad.

"Up there in the trees," Josh answered, pointing vaguely in the direction of Zakk's cabin.

Josh was shocked to hear that he had missed lunch and very thankful for the sandwiches Kelly had brought for him.

"I almost got it going," he said, between mouthfuls. "We've got one of these on the farm. What do you think, Bred?" Josh failed to mention that their old ATV on the farm had never run, or that he had never actually ridden on a quad before.

Bred shook his head. He hunched down and looked at the fuel filter. The glass bowl was empty.

"There's gas in the tank?" he asked.

Josh confirmed that there was.

"You've got a clogged fuel line," Bred said.

Josh was stunned. He had been working on the machine for hours. He disconnected the line at the filter and found it to be blocked with straw and other organic matter. He reconnected the hose and kicked the starter. On the third try the machine roared to life. Josh jumped aboard and revved the engine.

"Come on, Bred," he yelled ecstatically. "Let's go!"

Without thinking, Bred leaped up behind him and they tore off down the hill towards the dock.

In the process of fixing the machine, Josh had accidentally disconnected the front brake cable, so when the rusty old throttle jammed wide open; he had no idea how to stop. Bred hung on for dear life as they hit the dock and accelerated the sixty yards to the end of the jetty. Matt and Julie were on the dock and saw the boys hurtling towards them at thirty miles an hour.

Josh had found the horn with his thumb, but the blaring racket only added to the confusion as they bounced over the rattling boards on their mad dash of doom.

Julie grabbed Matt and the two of them jumped into the lake fully clothed just as the screaming machine flew by

They went off the end in a graceful arc and the quad nose-dived into the lake, coming to an abrupt halt in the rock-hard water twenty feet from the dock. Josh went over the top and skipped across the water like a pebble on a pond, Bred firmly attached to his back like a starfish on a clam.

Matt and Julie fished the dazed, bewildered and half-drowned boys out of the lake and dumped them unceremoniously onto the dock.

An hour later the boys, who had almost fully recovered from their ordeal, were standing miserably on the dock with the rest of the campers.

Matt and Julie were not very kind.

★★★

"You couldn't steer six feet to the side and put it in the shallow water," Bred fumed turning on Josh after the ordeal. "No! You had to nail the dock, fly off the end and dump it in the deep end.... *Are you nuts?*"

Josh hung his head in shame, and Julie hid her smile at the sight of the big farm boy so contrite under the scolding from the relatively diminutive Bred. Her shock and fear had subsided and she was beginning to see the humour of the situation.

★★★

They watched as Matt tried to get a grapple-anchor on the submerged quad.

Matt broke the surface, gasping, and swam slowly over to the dock, where he hung on, blowing hard.

"There's no way I can reach it," he said to Julie, shaking his head. "It's twenty feet down and under a shelf." He looked up at her. They would have to find another way. Bred sighed. "I can reach it," he said, stripping off his shirt and sneakers.

Kelly watched in amazement as her little brother tied the line with the heavy anchor around his waist, adjusted his swimming goggles, and despite Julie's protests, took four deep breaths and jumped into the crystal clear waters of Pine Lake.

Bred dropped quickly to the bottom of the lake; clearing his ears as he went. He soon located the quad lying upside down under the rocky ledge where it had come to rest after its fateful plunge. He righted the lightweight machine easily under the water where its buoyancy was increased by the air in the big balloon off-road tires. Bred straddled the unit and tied the rope securely to the front hitch. He placed the anchor on the front carrier and snapped it securely in place with the bungee cords.

Satisfied, he swam slowly back to the surface, exhaling the expanding air from his lungs as he rose. He was surprised to see Matt swimming frantically towards him half way up and waved to him with a smile. Matt stopped cold in a classic pose of 'frozen-in-shock-under-water' and a great bubble of air expelled from his mouth. He clawed frantically for the surface.

Bred continued his leisurely assent wearing a puzzled frown on his brow. Why was Matt so alarmed? He had only been down for two or three minutes.

★★★

Josh and Bred were compelled, on pain of no dinner, to apologise to Zakk for taking his quad. Josh packed his duffle bag along as they made their way slowly towards the cabin.

Zakk tried to keep a straight face as he listened to their tale of woe. He lifted his arm with index finger extended and was about to give them his standard lecture on the sanctity of his personal property, when Josh produced the two-gallon jug of genuine, homemade, Alberta moonshine, from his duffle bag.

Zakk smiled, and all was forgiven.

Josh shrugged when he saw Bred's look of astonishment.

"Never know when you might want to party," he said with a grin.

★★★

Bred lay back on the cushions in the canoe with a sigh and let his fingers drag through the clear cool water.

"A little more twist as you drag to keep the canoe straight, after the stroke," he instructed sleepily.

"But I…" Maggie began.

"You want to learn how it's done, or not?" Bred interrupted loftily.

Maggie fumed quietly. Bred had offered to teach her how to paddle a canoe and *this* had been going on for the last half-hour. They had travelled all the way around to the opposite side of the lake from the campsite and she was getting fed up with it.

"Right!" she said a little testily, digging deep and sending the canoe scooting straight ahead. Bred's eyes widened in sudden alarm.

The plastic canoe rode up on the rocks and turned over in the shallow water, dumping Bred and his cushions into the lake. Maggie was prepared when she slipped into the water, and howled at the look of shock on Bred's face.

"Serves you right, you supercilious prick," she said, laughing. "I tried to tell you I was steering around the rocks." Bred went after her with a vengeance.

★★★

They dragged the canoe up onto the sandy beach and dumped out the water. They loaded the boat and were just about to push off again, when Bred saw the tracks in the sand off to the side. He walked over and knelt beside the imprint of a large grizzly bear.

Water was slowly gathering at its base, and as he watched, a green leaf, which had been compressed under one huge claw, sprang back to its original shape. These tracks were fresh! Maggie came over and looked down at the imprint.

"What is it?" she asked, measuring the track with her palm. She didn't even come close. The hair stood up on the back of Bred's neck.

"Just a bear," he said casually. Standing, he took her hand and led her swiftly back to the boat. He pushed off from the shore and paddled quickly out into the lake. A whiff of the telltale smell of rotting meat invaded his nostrils. That bear was far too close for comfort.

As he paddled quietly back to camp, Bred was in a conundrum. There was an abundance of wildlife in the area and the campers had seen many wild creatures while paddling on the lake. The animals seemed unafraid of any threat from the water and allowed the boaters to approach quite near. However, a bear this close to the camp could be a problem.

Bred understood that the forest was the bear's domain, but human encroachment inevitably spelled nothing but disaster for the animals. In another life, he had witnessed the destruction of many fragile species.

He decided to say nothing. There was no point in alarming everyone. Besides, in four days they would all be on their way home.

★★★

Beth woke slowly in the cold light of the new dawn. It was chilly, even in the bunkhouse, and she snuggled deeper under her blankets. She was thankful that she didn't have to sleep outside on the cold hard ground like the others.

She listened to the patter of rain on the shingled roof and groaned aloud. This was their last day; the bus would arrive just after lunch. She didn't want it to end; this had been the best camping trip that she had ever had.

It had rained all the previous day and the campers had been restricted to playing board games in the dormitory. Some had ventured down to the lake to swim, but the wind and the rain made it a disheartening experience and they had soon returned, shivering, to the shelter of the buildings.

Beth yawned and stretched, wondering why she had awakened so early. She was still pretty tired. She rolled over and wriggled her head into the pillow and closed her eyes with a sigh. She loved the old bunkhouse with its cosy, smelly wood stove and the rustic, hand-hewn plank floors, walls and doors. The rafters were also hand-made, cut from the virgin forest by the early boy scouts with hand-saws and axes. The original plank roof and walls were now covered on the outside with plywood, painted brick-red and sealed with tree-gum to keep out the drafts. About sixteen feet by thirty feet, the building comfortably housed the ten little people and the catering crew.

Beth's bunk was situated against the wall adjoining the kitchens and the shuffling snort next to her ear made her bolt upright, her eyes wide with fright.

Beth screamed as the huge claws ripped through the fragile boards of the partition wall of the bunkhouse. The room erupted in bedlam.

★★★

The portly German chef was the first to react as the huge bear tried to enter the bunkhouse through the hole it had just created. Leaping from her bed with her pink and blue, flowery white nightgown hitched up around her bosom, she was the epitome, the essence of the great white north, a line-camp cook — a lumberjack!

Lifting the whole metal frame of her cot, she charged down the length of the bunkhouse between the bunks shouting vile obscenities in many dialects, and used the bed as a battering ram to repel the angry, roaring beast. The children hushed and gazed in awe at their lively cook. Another elderly chaperone followed suit with another bunk, and then another.

The bear retreated in the face of such resistance, seeking easier prey outside. It turned on the tent where Maggie and Kelly were kneeling inside, holding each other in fear. The bear ripped the tent asunder with one mighty swipe. At that moment Josh came up behind the creature and belted it across the back with a shovel; so hard in fact that the solid hickory handle snapped off like a twig.

The bear whirled around instinctively, raking Josh across the chest with its claws, sending him flying back twenty feet and crashing into a tree. Josh slumped senseless to the ground. Blood ran from his nose and the gaping wounds in his chest and onto the rain soaked ground. The girls looked on in silent horror.

Matt dove out of his tent on the opposite side of the bunkhouse, tripped over a tent rope and sprawled headlong. He scrambled to his feet and dashed into the bunkhouse to check on the kids. The great bear turned to go after him, and Bred pelted the beast on the side of the head with a rock.

The bear turned its attention on its new tormentor. Bred fired two more accurate rocks at the bear and hightailed it up the hill towards Zakk's cabin.

The grizzly took after him with a savage scream of anger. Bred tore up the trail to the cabin yelling his lungs out with the bear closing quickly on his heels. He expected Zakk to appear at any moment with a rifle in his hands.

Bred charged through the cabin door with the bear scarcely six feet behind him. Zakk was nowhere to be found. He tried to slam the door shut behind him, but the enraged animal would not be denied. It crashed into the door, sending Bred skidding across the hardwood floor on his back.

The bear hesitated as it came into the dimly lit room and stood up on its hind legs to a full eight feet. Its great head bowed, the silver-tipped fur bristling on its arched neck and back.

Bred leapt onto the table and propelled himself up onto the mantle, resting on one knee. He grabbed the old .30-30 rifle off the wall and opened the chamber.

It was empty.

He snapped open the brass cartridge box on the shelf and started loading shells into the magazine. The bear roared with savage hate, so loud that the plates fell off the cupboard shelf and smashed unnoticed on the floor of the cabin. The ferocious grizzly lowered itself to all fours and charged across the room like a flash of lightning. Bred closed the breach and swung to meet the menace.

The bear reached him before he could shoot and swatted Bred off the mantle like a fly. The terrible claws on one slashing paw hooked his calf just below the knee and stripped the flesh from his leg down to the bone. Bred flew across the room and into the back of the heavy sofa with a force that splintered the frame and tossed it over with a crash. He sprawled on the wooden floor. Bred felt no pain, but as the shock drained the strength from his body, he knew that he was badly hurt.

The bear roared in triumph and went after him just as Julie came through the door with a tent pole in her hands. Without hesitation, and yelling like a banshee, she hurled the pole at the beast like a javelin. The pole bounced harmlessly off its back, but she did get the animal's attention. The bear turned with a howl of fury and charged down on the pale, defenceless Julie as she stood helpless in front of the doorway.

At that moment, Matt appeared in the doorway behind her. He grabbed Julie's shoulders and threw her aside onto the floor. Matt crouched in front of her like a wrestler with his fingers spread and his teeth bared, prepared to meet the charge of the eight-hundred pound monster with his bare hands. The bear hesitated for an instant when confronted by this new menace, then charged again.

Bred barely registered Matt's presence as he gathered his waning strength and propped himself up on one knee. The two shots sounded as one, as he fired, cocked and fired again with the steady nerve of an experienced hunter. Two bullets struck within an inch of each other and drove deep into the bear's spine just behind the ears.

The creature crashed to a thrashing stop with a mighty groan just five feet from the unflinching arms of the brave and reckless Matt Finch, its eyes open, tongue lolled to the side — stone dead!

Matt stared at the fallen beast for a minute, his nostrils full of its stench, not yet comprehending that he was not going to die that day after all. Slowly, the strength drained from his legs, and in the hushed aftermath, Matt sank to his knees beside Julie, in the broken doorway of Zakk's ramshackle cabin in the woods.

★★★

Zakk sat bolt upright on his bed, hidden and unnoticed behind the shattered sofa. An empty two-gallon jug rolled off the mattress, ran across the floor and came to rest against the far wall. Zakk tried to rise, but the sudden rush of blood from his brain rendered him unconscious. Zakk's eyes crossed and he flopped back onto the mattress, oblivious to the world.

★★★

The sun came out just before the rain stopped falling and a double rainbow appeared in the cloudy eastern sky above the turquoise-jewelled waters of Pine Lake. Bred was the only one to notice, as he peered sleepily through the bunk-house window in wonderful Camp Minatonka.

He smacked his lips.

That morphine was good shit! He really should get the recipe, he thought.

It had taken all the combined skills of Matt and Julie to stop the bleeding and to reduce the shock due to the loss of blood. Josh and Bred were now stabilised. Julie had field dressed their wounds, but both boys needed to be in hospital under a doctor's care as soon as possible.

Matt had contacted the park rangers. They had relayed the emergency, and Edmonton STARS Air Ambulance was dispatched immediately.

Bred moved his head slowly and tried to concentrate on reality through the drug-induced haze. A park ranger was sitting at the table talking to Matt and Maggie. He did not sound happy.

"You say that you saw bear tracks across the lake four days ago and didn't report it?" the ranger asked. Matt did not look too happy either.

"Bred said not to tell anyone because you would just shoot it," Maggie retorted matching his hostility.

Atta girl! Thought Bred with satisfaction.

The Ranger sighed. "We tranquillise endangered animals that venture into areas occupied by humans," he said patiently. "We check them over, tag them and then transport them safely by helicopter far back into the wilderness, where they're released into the wild again." He paused, rubbing his hand over his face.

"We save them from situations such as this," he waved at the scene, "where they usually end up getting killed."

As the words slowly filtered through, Bred was mortified. It was totally his fault. He had really screwed up this time.

Fred had always been critical of those who were so quick to judge the actions of government institutions based merely on their own uninformed perceptions, or worse — unsubstantiated tavern-criticism of authority. Bred was guilty of the same misguided judgement.

Would he ever be old enough to gain a little wisdom and avoid the hard lessons? Bred thought miserably, as his attention span began to fade.

He turned to look over at Josh lying on the bunk beside him. His pallor was grey and he didn't look too good — but at least he was conscious. Kelly was sitting by his side, holding his hand and rocking back and forth. She really liked the guy.

"Kelly has a boy friend..." Bred sang merrily. Julie came over and turned up his IV drip; he started to drift off again.

"The air ambulance will be here soon, Bred," she said softly. "We'll have you back in Edmonton City Hospital in no time."

City Hospital?... Dr. Strydom! Bred's mind reeled with the shock. He *had* to fight the fog closing in on him.

He slapped his leg.

That did it!

Pain shot through him like an electric current.

"Maggie!" he managed to yell out, as Julie and Matt held him down so that he could not hurt himself again. "Find Maude... Tell her where I'm... going... Dr. Strydom..."

The darkness closed in as he heard the throb of the ambulance helicopter circle overhead.

★★★

CHAPTER THIRTEEN
The Full Circle

Bred swam up through the white mists of consciousness and surfaced in a rush. His eyes focused on the picture of a yellow-spotted giraffe on the ceiling with big blue eyes and long, black eyelashes. Bred had the strangest feeling that he had been here before. The giraffe was talking to him. Bred shut his eyes tight and opened them again, slowly.

Concentrate! He thought.

Dr. Strydom stood solemnly at the foot of the bed explaining the situation to Mary and Graham. Kelly and Maggie were standing near the doorway listening quietly to the discussion and looking very sombre.

"Apart from the infection, which is resisting conventional antibiotic treatment," he was saying, "your son has sustained a serious concussion. We believe that the concussion caused disruptions in various neural pathways triggering changes in neurotransmitter or neuromodulator levels."

"But, he seemed to be doing so well," Mary said, distraught.

"With current technology we can only scratch the surface of brain-cell activity," Dr. Strydom sighed, shaking his head regrettably. "And there may be some inflammation and swelling in the brain due to the concussion and scarring from his previous operation." He was pushing and he knew it, but the time was ripe.

Dr. Strydom had been meticulous and diligent during the fifteen-hour operation on Bred's wounded lower leg. A team of his best surgeons, doctors and nurses had worked in shifts around the clock during the complicated procedures. He himself had worked tirelessly, directing, planning, operating and pushing his people to the very limits of their endurance until he was satisfied and almost totally exhausted himself.

First, he had concentrated on the skeletal damage and the complicated fracture of the fibula. He set and pinned it together. He then splinted the fractured tibia and turned to repair torn gastrocnemius and tibialias anterior muscles.

The damage was extensive, but Dr. Strydom was undeterred.

In his reclusive lab at the hospital, he had continued to identify the hereditary determinants of those with AB-negative blood, and through experimental morphology and grafting tests using living tissue of aborted foetuses and embryos, he had met with some success, and amassed a respectable collection of living specimens.

With the confidence that comes with constant practice, Dr. Strydom grafted new embryonic tissue to the mutilated muscles and ligaments of his patient on the table.

Veins and arteries of the lower leg were restored or replaced and the torn and collapsed independent network of capillaries was reconnected under the microscope. Even the minute valves in the lymphatic vessels of the system were repaired to ensure blood flowed in the right direction.

Dr. Strydom's surgical brilliance was clearly demonstrated in the reconstruction of Bred's nervous system, and the correction of the somatic division, which allows voluntary control of skeletal muscles.

Dr. Strydom's staff marvelled at his dedication, his genius, his skill and self-sacrifice.

"Bred Andrews might well have been his own son," they whispered.

But Dr. Strydom was not that noble. He could not and would not tolerate any physical impediment which might in any way misconstrue the responses of the neural systems in his greatest surgical creation — Bred. Simply put, he needed the perfect physical specimen to study; an imperfect specimen might generate false readings.

Dr. Strydom's ego was certainly bolstered, no matter how unjustified, when Dr. Bryce compared him to Robert Louis Stevenson's *Celestial Surgeon,* as he tried to rally the tired team with a poem during a lunch break. Dr. Bryce's clear baritone caused Dr. Strydom to pause, as he was about to enter the room.

> "*If I have moved among my race*
> *And shown no glorious morning face;*
> *…If morning skies,*
> *Books, and my food, and summer rain*
> *Knocked on my sullen heart in vain…'"*
> Dr. Strydom stood quietly, unseen, outside the door.
> "*'Or, Lord, if too obdurate I,*
> *Choose thou, before that spirit die,*
> *A piercing pain, a killing sin,*
> *And to my dead heart run them in.'"*

"And that, ladies and gentlemen, is typical of Dr. Strydom, and the example we must live up to, as well," said Dr. Bryce.

Dr. Strydom nodded approvingly as he walked away, memorizing the lines. He considered the tribute to be quite appropriate.

★★★

Bred had indeed recovered far more quickly than Dr. Strydom had anticipated over the six weeks since Bred was brought to the hospital. Only the persistent infections caused by those bacteria-infested bear claws had prevented him sealing the wound and beginning Bred's physiotherapy.

Dr. Strydom's impatience burned with an ache in his chest. Soon, very soon, he would be able to start an electrical analysis of the neurons in specific regions of Bred's brain. He had already mapped the areas where needle electrodes would be inserted.

He just required one more signature from Mary and Graham Andrews.

One bloody signature, was all that kept him from pursuing his quest, he thought bitterly. He gritted his teeth at the bureaucratic stupidity, careful not to portray his self-righteous anger.

"I'm afraid that we may have to keep him here a little longer than we originally anticipated," Dr. Strydom said, studying the clipboard in his hand thoughtfully. "Now, if you will both please sign this release," he said, smiling sympathetically, "we can begin the procedure immediately." He proffered the documents firmly.

"You understand of course, that this is extremely urgent and that time is of the essence." He said, as Mary hesitated.

Mary took the clipboard he thrust on her and studied the form in a daze; it was incomprehensible. Her family was just beginning to become a happy, cohesive unit again, and now this! Mary hesitated. She glanced at the bed where Bred lay sleeping. He seemed to be doing so well…but the doctor said… She took the pen.

"No!"

A harsh whisper emitted from the bed. Everyone spun around in alarm as Bred raised himself groggily on one elbow.

"Don't sign it, Mary. He just wants to…experiment on me!" Bred sounded terrified, pathetic.

Dr. Strydom moved swiftly to the side of the bed. He bent over the boy and shielded Bred from view with his body.

"There, there, my boy," he said gently, forcing Bred back down on the pillows. Dr. Strydom flipped out his stethoscope and listened to Bred's heart and lungs. When he tried to speak, Dr. Strydom placed his fingers over Bred's lips.

"Shhhh!" he whispered, as Bred slowly faded into unconsciousness again. When all was quiet, Dr. Strydom stood up and carefully put away his instrument.

He studied his patient with a great deal of trepidation and kept his back to the Andrews until his nerves steadied. He would increase the prescribed dosage of medication; he did not want that to happen again.

"He's fine now," the doctor said, turning back to the parents with a reassuring smile. "Let's go to my office where we can take care of the formalities, shall we?"

***

Maude was astonished. "I'm away for six weeks and this is the trouble he gets into?" She asked, her voice rising sharply as Maggie finished her story. "What about Josh Morgan? How's he doing?" Maude needed to think.

She remembered her last conversation with Bred on this very topic, What was it he had said? Maude asked herself, trying to recall the conversation.

"…within days of my being in his clutches…electrodes drilled into my brain…making me jerk like a puppet on a string…." Maude remembered that Bred had been very afraid of going back to City Hospital and falling into Dr. Strydom's hands once again.

***

Maggie had been trying frantically to contact Maude ever since she left Bred at the hospital. She had finally reached her through one of the crew at Namier Lake Lodge. He had reluctantly given her the telephone number of Dobbs' house on the Sunshine Coast in British Columbia.

Dobbs was running a charter to Campbell River at the time and couldn't make it right away, but Maude had flown back to Edmonton immediately. Maggie met her at the airport.

Maggie's pent-up frustration, worry and subsequent relief at seeing Maude again came to a head all at once. Maggie wailed, loud and clear, right in the middle of the arrivals area at the Edmonton International Airport. Startled passengers and waiting families gave her a wide berth.

Patrick was not due to move into 'Maude's Cottage' for another month, so the two had taken a cab back to Bolton. Maggie sobbed all the way back.

When they finally reached the cottage, Maude settled Maggie down in the lounge and made a pot of tea. Though Maggie was still very upset, Maude finally gathered all the details of their encounter at Pine Lake and of Bred's present situation.

It was not good. For the most part, when they visited him, he was so heavily sedated that he could not speak and barely realised that they were there at all.

Maggie told Maude what had happened at the campsite, and of Bred's condition at the hospital.

"Josh is going to be okay," Maggie said through her tears, as Maude prompted her and passed her a tissue. "Dr. Bryce says he can go home next week. He's already bragging and showing off his scars to the other patients — especially the kids." She giggled through her tears at the memory of her last visit when Josh tore around the ward in his wheelchair, growling at people.

"He claimed he had the spirit of the bear in him, and some people actually believed it!" She laughed nervously, then, sobered quickly as her thoughts again turned to Bred.

"What are we going to do, Maude," she asked. "I don't trust that Dr. Strydom, he gives me the creeps."

"What about Mr. and Mrs. Andrews'?" Maude asked. "Can't they do anything?"

Maggie shook her head. "Dr. Strydom has got them convinced that Bred is getting the best care possible. They don't know what else to do," she wiped her eyes.

"It was strange," she said, "after the accident, Bred asked for you first, Maude, he wanted you to know that he was going to Edmonton City Hospital. And he mentioned Dr. Strydom…he was so scared. We have to get him out of there. What shall we do?"

Maude looked at Maggie and for a minute her brow furrowed thoughtfully. "Simple," she said at last, brightening. "We're going to take a page from Bred's book of fairy tales; we're going to steal the golden goose."

★★★

Maude picked up the telephone and made an appointment to see Dr. Strydom the following day, complaining of shooting pains in her chest.

Her conversation with Dr. Petrus Stein and Dr. Thlabati at Good Hope University Hospital in Cape Town earlier that day had been most informative. The doctors had been appalled to learn that Bred had fallen into Dr. Strydom's clutches once again and they promised do whatever they could to help.

Maude sympathised with the doctor's frustration that being so far away really limited their personal involvement. The doctors listened attentively as she outlined her plan on how she proposed to rescue Bred.

She would simply free Bred from the hospital by convincing the nursing staff to take Bred down to the x-ray department. Once there, she and Maggie, disguised as hospital employees, would take Bred up the freight elevator. George would be waiting in the parking lot with Kyle's new armoured truck, and he would whisk them away to freedom.

There was a long, sceptical pause on the line while the doctors considered her plan.

"What specific information do you need from us?" Dr. Thlabati inquired suspiciously. He knew that Maude had not called just to chat.

"You fellows are *so* sharp!" Maude answered.

And so it was, with a little prodding and some occasional swearing, Maude was able to glean a good deal of interesting information regarding Dr. Paul Strydom's '*Achilles 'heel*,' and learned exactly what made him tick.

★★★

Dr. Strydom checked Maude over thoroughly in his office at the hospital the following day, but found nothing extraordinary. Nevertheless, he proposed that she should take an x-ray to be sure. Sitting down at his desk, he began writing a prescription for an appointment that same afternoon. Maude watched him carefully from the corner of her eye.

"I received a call from your Dr. Petrus Stein in South Africa the other day," Maude said conversationally, timing it perfectly as she buttoned her blouse. "He was asking all kinds of peculiar questions about that boy Bred Andrews." She slid off the table and stepped into her shoes, careful to grimace at the effort.

She glanced over at the doctor to see if she had gotten his attention.

Dr. Strydom had stopped writing and was staring down at the paper in front of him. "What kinds of questions?" he asked tightly.

"Oh, all kinds of things…though mostly about how the boy was doing," she continued. "I couldn't help him very much because I have very little to do with the Andrews' family anymore since I moved away." She reached for her coat on the chair.

"Dr. Stein did seem apprehensive though," she said thoughtfully. "Especially after I told him that the boy was back in hospital after being mauled by a bear."

He looked at her sharply.

"It's all over town," she added with a little smile, "what a wonderful job you did, doctor."

"Did he say *why* he needed to speak with you?" Dr. Strydom asked, a little too casually as he inspected his nails.

"Why yes," she answered lightly, "as a matter of fact he did. "He plans to publish a medical journal soon. He needed my permission because it concerns my dear departed husband, Fred." Maude ignored his startled reaction and continued casually. "Apparently, he and Dr. Thlabati have collected a lot of information from some old forgotten research papers stashed in a hospital basement somewhere and have refined some new medical techniques." She smiled feebly at the memory, while taking a deep painful breath for effect. "He claims their report will astonish the medical world." Dr. Strydom's face turned bright red as he rose slowly from his chair.

"Something to do with people with…AB-negative blood," she said, carefully putting on her coat.

The shock caused Dr. Strydom to freeze halfway out of his chair. He stared at her in astonishment, his mind whirling.

All the files had been purged from the computers in his operating rooms at Good Hope Hospital in Cape Town — he had overseen it himself. He had even gone so far as to physically remove the hard drives from nine of his computers and brought them along with him as well.

Everything he had was carefully filed and locked away in safety deposit boxes at the bank, or in the oak filing cabinet at his apartment right here in Edmonton.

Blindly, almost in a panic, he headed for the door.

"I have to go. I have an appointment."

"My x-ray prescription?" Maude said plaintively.

Dr. Strydom spun around impatiently and scribbled his signature on the requisition.

"Just give that to the nurse in x-ray," he called back quickly as he headed out the door.

Maude watched his hasty departure. She sat down at the desk, picked up his pen and carefully altered the x-ray prescription, substituting her and Bred's names. She left Dr. Strydom's office, and on the way out, placed the prescription prominently on the counter at the nurse's station when she thought no one was looking. She left the hospital practically unnoticed.

★★★

Later that afternoon, Maude and Maggie waited patiently in the hallway outside the x-ray department in the lower level at City Hospital. Both were dressed in green-washed hospital scrubs and caps. Masks hung loosely around their necks along with their false identification cards that Maggie had made on her computer.

Patients, nurses and doctors came and left, but no one questioned the two nurses loitering near the entrance. A short time later, as Maude anticipated, a surly hospital porter wearing blue jeans and a black sweatshirt with *'Bullet'* blazed across the front in white letters, wheeled Bred up to the doors of the x-ray department. Maude took a deep breath as he stood beside her.

He was black, and he was enormous!

Maude looked up and read 'Dan' off his nametag.

"Station Six," Maude observed casually, looking down at Bred and the card on his chest. He waved sleepily from the gurney. She looked up at the giant porter.

"We're heading back up there in a few minutes, Dan," she said, matter of fact, "take an early coffee break… we'll bring him back with us." She turned away. Dan hesitated.

"You guys work too hard," added Maggie with her brightest smile, "you deserve a break once in a while."

He shrugged and left.

Maggie watched as he took the elevator to the third floor. She nodded to Maude and they wheeled Bred quickly down the deserted corridor and around the corner to the freight elevator.

Maggie pushed the button for the elevator. Fifteen seconds later, the doors opened. Maggie stood transfixed, her eyes widened in shock.

The biggest nurse she had ever seen filled the opening. Her tawny brown hair flopped down over her wrathful chubby cheeks as her big brown eyes stared down into the depths of hers. She flexed her mighty muscles, sealing the open doorway of the freight elevator and their pathway to liberty.

Maude's plan had been so simple, so conceivable — except for this little glitch.

★★★

Bred had woken in a drug-induced fog two days earlier to find his nurse and Dr. Strydom in a heated discussion.

A highly competent, experienced health care professional, despite her enormous size, she knew the drugs being prescribed were intended to kept her patient in a comatose state; she just didn't know why. Bred was not a high-risk case and she challenged the doctor forthright.

Dr. Strydom was arrogantly adamant that she follow his instructions to the letter and administer the medication he prescribed — without question, or face severe consequences.

Fearful of being removed from the ward, she had sadly and reluctantly complied.

As she handed the little plastic cup with the pills to Bred, with the doctor standing at her shoulder, she quoted a line from Shakespeare's Hamlet:

"'Now cracks a noble heart. Good night, sweet prince; And flights of angels sing thee to thy rest!'"

Bred got the message even in his befuddled state.

"'O, I die, Horatio?'" he said, and tucked the pills away in his cheek like a chipmunk. He took a sip of water and swallowed.

Dr. Strydom ignored the exchange as he once again checked Bred's vital signs. Satisfied, he left the room. Bred immediately spat out the tranquillisers.

She smiled down at him proudly. "I saw *nothing!*" she expounded in a perfect rendition of Shultz from the old sitcom 'Hogan's Heroes.'

That morning, however, she had suspected a mischief when Maude had acted so suspiciously with Bred's x-ray prescription. She had only noticed Maude because normally-honest people always overact when performing criminal activities.

The familiar armoured truck idling in the parking lot near the loading bays all morning had not gone unobserved either. The dutiful nurse had intuitively stowed herself in the freight elevator that accessed the loading bay on that side of the parking lot.

Now, inconceivably, her suspicions of an abhorrent, unequivocal crime had been confirmed, and her blood pressure rose exponentially. She gazed at her hapless victims with narrowing eyes; her lips puckered and she growled her wrath. Her anger knew no bounds — there would be no respite for those who would attempt to kidnap her cubs, the sick, or the dying.

Incredibly swift for a woman of her size, her colossal arms shot out like the tentacles of an octopus. Both Maggie and Maude were trapped, smothering in those cavernous armpits, and under those voluptuous mounds of motherly love.

★★★

"Ilsa! Let them go, Ilsa!"

His voice still small but firm, called out from the gurney. Her anger faded as she turned to him.

"But why, why, Bred?"

"Because, I'm getting in that elevator."

"I don't understand, what about me?" she said.

"You're staying here 'til the elevator gets safely away."

It was a game they played. Bred had discovered her passion for nostalgic classics soon after they cut back on his medication.

She released the women and they fell to the floor gasping. Nobody noticed. She continued the charade.

"No, Bred, no, last night we said…"

"Last night we said a great many things. You said I was to do the thinking for both of us. Well, it all adds up to one thing. I'm getting on that elevator with Maude and Maggie where I belong."

"But Bred, no, I… I…"

"You've got to listen to me. Do you have any idea what I'd have to look forward to if I stayed here? Nine chances out of ten we'd both end up in the psychiatric ward."

"You're saying this only for me to let you go," she pouted.

"I'm saying it because it's true. Inside of us we both know I belong with Maude and Maggie," Bred continued, "maybe not today, maybe not tomorrow but soon and for the rest of your life."

"But…what about us?" she leaned over him, wringing her hands, her face full of anguish.

"We will always have…. Station Six," he said with sweet sadness.

The magnificent mammoth looked up at the ceiling with a gasp. Huge crocodile tears ran slowly down her beautiful round cheeks and splashed onto the floor. She slowly turned away, her arms stiff, fingers splayed at her side.

"'Here's looking at you, kid,'" he said, in perfect Bogart.

Safe in the freight elevator, Maggie was still confounded.

"What was that all about?" she asked shakily, hanging on to the gurney while regaining her strength.

"*Casablanca,*" Maude said, giving the grinning Bred a dirty look, and wondering if he was really worth saving.

"Who?" Maggie asked desperately.

★★★

CHAPTER FOURTEEN
The Escape

George drove the fugitives to Maude's house. He helped deposit Bred on Maude's double bed before rushing the armoured truck back to Kyle's warehouse. As far as anyone was concerned, he had taken it in for a service.

Maggie and Maude entered a state of post-action euphoria as they bounced exuberantly around the room, burning off the last remnants of their adrenaline rush. Finally, they sat down exhausted and bantered light-heartedly with each other about their adventure across the room.

"What do we do now?" Bred asked enthusiastically, amused at their antics. "Make a run for the Yukon?"

Their smiles faded slowly as a new realisation set in.

"Oh, dear," Maude said.

Totally focused on the execution of their venture and the risks of the moment, Maude and Maggie had fallen into the same trap that many criminals had before them; they had failed to plan for the aftermath.

Neither of them had considered the consequences of their actions outside of their own little circle of influence. They had not considered the impact on the Andrews' family, the reaction of the hospital authorities, the community — or of the police.

It suddenly began to dawn on them that the situation might be quite serious.

"We kidnapped a sick child," Maggie exclaimed suddenly, her eyes large and fearful, "From his hospital bed! The police will be searching for us, Maude, with guns and dogs! There'll be a province-wide search!" She was becoming hysterical. "A nation-wide manhunt! House-to-house searches! Radio, TV cameras! — Mug shots!"

Maude was becoming alarmed as well and quickly went over to her and wrapped her arms around Maggie's shoulders.

"Now, now, dear," she said. "I know it looks bad on the face of it, but I'm sure the police and the courts will understand when we explain ourselves." Maude did not sound convincing at all.

Bred sighed and picked up the telephone. He dialled a number while Maggie continued exploring and escalating the worst-case scenarios; her voice rising higher and higher. She would soon have herself convicted and sentenced to the electric chair.

Maggie stopped abruptly and watched Bred open-mouthed as he spoke into the telephone.

"Hello, Kelly?" he said. "Yes, it's me...I'm fine. I've left the hospital and am staying over at Maude's for a little while. Tell mum where I am, I don't want her to worry...Okay...Bye." He hung up the phone and flopped back on the pillows.

The room was very still. The two women sat stunned, holding on to each other in the upholstered Queen-Anne chair. They stared at him, speechless, as he lay on the bedspread with his hands behind his head, grinning at them.

The veil was lifted. One little phone call had turned 'kidnapped' into 'he went home.'

A light breeze ruffled the blue-flowered print curtain as Maude rose quietly and walked over to the bed, fully intent on strangling him to death with her bare hands.

★★★

Mary had been frantic when she first received the call from Dr. Strydom's office notifying her of Bred's disappearance from the hospital.

Child Welfare Services was soon at her door demanding to see Bred, and checked the house to see that he was not there.

"The Andrews' were obviously to blame for the dangerous situation the boy was in, and for not providing proper care and attention to a minor," said the hospital (Dr. Strydom's) attorneys'.

Dr. Strydom had long ago obtained the confidential medical records from a Dr. Brown for just such an eventuality. The documents proved that the Andrews had been unfit parents, 11 years ago.

"Unfit parents?" Mary questioned coldly. She had been there before. She called Graham, and he walked out of a board meeting and raced home immediately.

Graham and Mary had just sat down in the lounge to discuss what to do next, when the telephone rang. Kelly sprinted into the room, unaware of the situation, and picked up the receiver before either Mary or Graham could warn her that it might be from the kidnappers.

Kelly was expecting a call from Josh and was a little disappointed to hear Bred's voice.

"Hi, Bred," she said, in response to his greeting.

"Well, I guess it's okay if Maude and Maggie are looking after you," she said doubtfully. "Want to talk to Mom? Okay…'bye." She hung up the phone, looked up, and was startled at the expressions on her parents' faces.

"What?" she asked.

Mary and Graham ran over to her, the questions tumbling over each other. Kelly was totally overwhelmed and came clean.

"That was Bred. He didn't like the hospital. He's over at Maude's place," she blurted. "He doesn't want you to worry, he'll be home soon."

Maude called a few minutes later to reassure Mary that Bred was fine and resting peacefully. She and Mary had a long chat.

"Oooooh!" Mary said as she hung up the phone, her eyes narrowed, teeth clenched. "He's not getting away with this!"

Graham shuddered at her tone. He was not sure who Mary was talking about, but '*he*', was doomed.

★★★

Dr. Strydom had been totally irrational and abusive after the abduction of his patient. His staff attributed his ranting and raving to concern for the boy, which was only partially true.

On the one hand, Dr. Strydom desperately wanted Bred to be a one-hundred-percent healthy specimen for him to study, and on the other hand, he might very well turn Bred into a vegetable. Dr. Strydom was prepared to take that risk.

The doctor was justifiably concerned that outside of the controlled hospital environment, the infection could spread very quickly and possibly even reach the boy's brain. If that were to happen, the entire experiment would be lost. Dr. Strydom was not about to let that happen to his prized patient without a fight.

After notifying the authorities and the parents, the doctor had privately contacted other sources in the town of Bolton and offered his own reward for information as to the whereabouts of the injured boy.

Slowly, as the days went by following Bred's 'escape' from the hospital, the noose tightened around Bred, as the greedy, the unscrupulous and the nefarious saw an opportunity for easy money. Kyle Bishop, at the bottom of that despicable food chain, finally made the call.

The whole kidnapping thing had actually worked to his advantage after all thought Dr. Strydom. It had given him time to plan, to have a few meetings and to set some legal wheels in motion. He had a strong case now, Child Welfare was behind him.

"The parents were obviously to blame for the dangerous situation that the boy was in," he told them, "and were 'Unfit Parents' — for not providing proper care and attention to a minor," had been his recommendation at a closed-door meeting, and the bureaucrats had nodded in agreement.

Dr. Strydom loved the Child Welfare system: by the time the Andrews regained custody through the courts, he would have completed his 'examinations and procedures' on the boy. All he had to do now was to catch Bred Andrews. The boy was trapped and an ambulance was on standby for his call.

Dr. Strydom would first place the boy in quarantine — with a twenty-four hour guard around the clock. Not even the parents would be allowed to see him alone; and then he could do whatever he deemed necessary — with the court's blessing of course.

And should anything unforeseen happen to Bred while under his care? Thought Dr. Strydom, well, spreading infection, caused by unsanitary conditions outside of the hospital environment, could have lead to super-bugs, which might prove unresponsive to conventional medication.

What a shame.

★★★

Inspector Claude DuBois read the forensics reports again, flopped back in his chair and stared out the window. He took a deep breath and exhaled loudly.

Policemen were not supposed to feel despondent about their cases, but this one was too close to home. He had personally kept track of the Andrews boy since he arrived back from South Africa. Everything he had heard and seen, except for the bear incident, of course, pointed to a well-adjusted teenager interacting with his peers. In fact, the whole family was getting it together and becoming actively involved in the community again.

Grey-white clouds skittered across the sky in the stiff winds high on the edge of the jet stream, promising a positive change in the weather soon. The knowledge did not improve his mood one iota. It was August, it wasn't even supposed to rain at this time of year.

A group of boys were playing rugby in the field across the road, but his view was partially blocked by a Manitoba Maple tree on the lawn outside. He would have that trimmed one of these days, he thought sourly. He hated having his vision blocked.

An agitated robin perched on a branch for a minute, spewing insults at a marauding cat and defecated into the birdbath below.

"Figures," he muttered.

He was a good policeman; his judgement and the facts should coincide. Something was missing. Claude rubbed his face with his hand and turned back to address his waiting officers.

The investigation of the Parker-courier van robbery was now into its fifteenth month, and they had not yet arrested anyone or recovered any of the stolen money. The Mayor was getting impatient.

"So, now we have a situation here," he said, resigned.

Patrick, sitting patiently across the desk from him nodded. He was not happy with the latest findings either.

He and Michelle had followed every lead on the Parker case to each inevitable dead end. They had finally sat down to review their physical evidence again, and had come up with one startling revelation.

"This is conclusive?" Claude asked.

"Yes."

"The fingerprints on the battery inside the flashlight found under the van belong to Brian, a.k.a. Bred Andrews?"

"Yes."

"This possibly places the boy at the crime scene?"

"Yes."

"Bring the boy and his parents in," Claude said with a sigh.

"We have a problem there," Michelle said. "Bred Andrews somehow left the hospital six days ago and nobody knows where he is."

"Well, find him then!" Claude said bristling.

"Yes, Sir!"

Michelle and Patrick rose very quickly and made a hasty undignified exit from the inspector's office.

★★★

Bred didn't know what to do. It was just one week since his escape from the hospital and everything was in turmoil.

He couldn't go home; Child Welfare Services and Dr. Strydom's lawyers would have him back in the hospital again before he could blink.

Despite Maude and Maggie's careful ministrations, his wound had become infected again. Bred shook his head in disgust. Grizzly bear claws harboured some of the most dangerous bacteria known to man.

Bred had spent much of the last evening on the phone with Dr. Philemon Thlabati and Dr. Petrus Stein in South Africa, and they had finally come up with a plan to resolve the whole issue once and for all and hopefully put Bred's world back on an even keel.

The only problem was that Bred had to be in Cape Town the following week. Petrus had already booked the tickets. On top of that, Bred was, for all intents and purposes a minor on the run from Child Welfare Services, and an invalid at that.

Bred explained the plan to Maude, but she was not impressed; the doctors had screwed up before.

"It's a good thing they left you with the little problems," she said sarcastically, "and now your leg is infected again. Do they know about that? No! You didn't tell them, did you? You really need a doctor, and not just for your leg!" She was quite irate. Bred cringed under the tirade.

Maude left the room and made a call to Dr. Thlabati from the living room out of earshot of the bedroom: she didn't care that it was two o'clock in the morning in South Africa, this had to stop.

★★★

A short time later, Dr. Thlabati called Mary Andrews from Cape Town. The call lasted an hour, and only they know what was divulged, but in the end Mary was pale, proud, and not in the least bit surprised.

They discussed the present situation, and Dr. Thlabati suggested that, under the circumstances, the Andrews' should bring Bred to the Good Hope Hospital in Cape Town for treatment.

"Well, I don't know," Mary said uncertainly. "He was mauled by a grizzly bear. Can your people treat those types of injuries over there?"

Dr. Thlabati was hurt. "You do my colleagues and me a disservice," he said, with a catch in his voice. "We treat snake bites, lion bites, leopard bites, crocodile bites, bat bites, slashes from all manner of razor sharp claws, people gored by Cape buffalo and others stomped by elephants. One poor fellow at the local zoo even had a hairy old rhino horn jammed up his ass!" He struggled to regain his composure.

"I assure you we can handle a scratch from your teddy bear," he said coldly.

★★★

Despite Bred's protestations, Maude telephoned Matt Finch. He arrived twenty minutes later in the emergency medical service ambulance with Julie in tow.

Bred watched helplessly as they drove up and prepared himself to do battle.

"Chill, Bred," Matt said with a grin, when he saw the look on Bred's face. "We happened to be going off-duty when Maude called. We're here to help. We're not here to rescue you from your kidnappers." He closed his eyes and shook his head in mock disbelief at Maude when she began her protestations. The story of their escapade was all over City Hospital.

Matt opened his jump bag while Julie peeled the bandages off Bred's leg.

"You need to see a doctor, Bred," Julie said, seeing the black and yellow infected wounds and the progressive infection developing deep beneath the skin. "I can't stop this." She continued. "The wounds need to be opened and drained first, and you need prescribed medication."

"No!" Bred protested passionately, launching himself up on one elbow, his eyes blazing with fever and anguish. "They'll try to put me back in the hospital. I'll fight them to the death." His face was flushed and taut and his hair was plastered to his damp forehead.

Julie was startled for a moment. She had not seen such dogged determination in such a youngster for a long time.

"I just need a twenty-four hour field dressing, so you fix it, Julie...please," he said desperately. "I have a very important exam to write and I need a clear head. After that, I'll do whatever you say." He flopped back on the pillow in a cold sweat, exhausted. He hated lying to her.

"I don't have...." she began, and stopped.

Julie's olfactory senses registered the all-too familiar scent of infection, and with a start, she looked down at the wounded boy. For a moment her blood ran cold as uninvited memories of a different time and a different place flooded through her once more.

She felt the horror surge like molten lava up through her breast and let it go. She knew that she would never be free of the images or of the dreadful emotions her senses evoked, but she also knew that she was strong enough to handle them.

Julie took a deep breath, exhaled slowly and felt her fear recede like the cool frothy waves on the seashore. There was a sense of purpose to it all now. She tightened her jaw and pressed on. Julie looked around for Matt. She nodded and he opened the medical box as she set to work.

Matt watched Julie operate for the hundredth time, still amazed at her deftness and skill as she employed the techniques she had been forced to develop in a war-ravaged place, and now used as the foundation of her profession.

★★★

A half-block away from Maude's house on the opposite side of the road, a police cruiser sat idling in the shade beneath a large elm tree. The vehicle was parked facing the house and was partially obscured by a large green Plymouth sedan.

Corporal Patrick D'Laney and Constable Michelle Monair watched unnoticed as Matt and Julie pulled up in front of 'Maude's Cottage' and unloaded their gear from the EMS ambulance. Julie met Maude and Maggie standing at the gate.

The gusting wind picked up, and a dry twig snapped off high in the elm and fell onto the hood of the cruiser. Patrick leaned forward and looked up through the branches to the bright afternoon sun flashing through the fluttering multi-coloured leaves. Claude was right; fall would come early this year.

Maude and Maggie folded their arms across their chests in the sudden chill breeze and walked quickly back down the cobbled walk. They disappeared into the house.

"He's in there, isn't he?" Michelle said unnecessarily.

Patrick nodded.

"Are we going in?" She asked.

"Not just yet," Patrick said, slipping the car into gear and pulling out into the road. "There's someone we must see first." He drove past the house and turned right at the

stop-sign. A short while later they passed Maude's Donut Shop, drove out beyond the town limits and down the road towards the Andrews' Estate.

★★★

His fever subsided over the next week, but Bred was still uncomfortable and that made him a little cranky.

"What do you mean you don't want to come along?" he growled, looking up from the travel itinerary at Maude.

The flight was scheduled to take off from Edmonton International Airport on Wednesday at 8:45 p.m., which was tomorrow night, fly to Calgary and then on to New York. They would refuel on Cape Verdi Island and fly on to Johannesburg. They would catch a connecting flight to Cape Town after a four-hour layover.

The plan called for Bred to be taken to the airport by Maude and Dobbs masquerading as his aunt and uncle. The Child Welfare Department as well as Dr. Strydom were still keeping the Andrews' residence under close surveillance, so he couldn't go anywhere near there. Bred had to arrive at the airport carrying his own ticket.

Kelly brought Brian's passport from the Andrews home, and had picked up his tickets from a travel agent in Edmonton that morning. She dropped them off at Maude's house before heading over to the donut shop.

In order to travel as a minor, Bred took it upon himself to modify Brian's original notarised travel letter, which was still attached to his passport from his previous trip to South Africa following the courier van accident. Everything had been arranged except for this one little problem with a sceptical Maude.

Dobbs had flown in the night before and was standing in the doorway listening to the exchange.

"International kidnapping has got to be a federal offence!" Maude protested, turning away.

"We're related by an earlier marriage," Bred argued persuasively, trying to reason with her, "Dobbs and I will attest to that." He waved his arm wildly for support from that quarter.

"Besides," she continued, brushing aside his argument. "I don't want you to go to South Africa, with all those wild animals and natives screaming about." She shuddered. "Raping and pillaging throughout the countryside." Her face paled as her eyes flittered apprehensively around the room.

Dobbs chuckled. Maude had a way of bottling things up for ages and then blurting out what was bothering her in a crisis. Maude turned to look at him, a little annoyed at his insensitivity.

"Aw shucks, Maude," Dobbs drawled, "who's been telling you such things? South Africa is a civilised, law abiding country with police and everything; much like Canada." His eyes clouded over with sweet memories.

"Besides, how can we pass up a holiday basking in the sub-tropical sun, sipping exquisite wines, sherry's and brandy and subjugating ourselves to the gentle administrations of the maidens of the 'wine lands.'" He sighed, and nearly choked when he saw the look in her eye.

This is not good, he thought. Dobbs recovered quickly, blabbering on about mountains and ostriches and such, but to no avail. He had seen the fire dancing in her eyes.

"Fred did," she said coldly, pursing her lips and narrowing her eyes, "just before the two of you went off on your six week 'business trip' in '86." She turned to face Bred. She was not done.

Bred stared at her in astonishment. It never fails, he thought. One little exaggeration…one… after all these years …and it comes back to bite me in the ass!

★★★

The one-hour trip to the airport in Dobbs' Buick the following afternoon was uneventful, though unusually quiet. Maude, seated up front with Dobbs, was still incensed and a little distant. She glowered at Dobbs when he began a conversation, and he trailed off to a whimper. Bred gave up and sat brooding in the back seat, hugging his collapsible wheelchair.

The sun was warm and bright in a cloudless, pale blue sky. It was a typical late summer day in Alberta. That morning, the first light frost had blanketed the lawns and vehicles parked along the road and settled the dust from the farmers harvesting in the fields, leaving the air crisp and clear.

The highest leaves on the limbs of some poplars and elms had already begun to change in anticipation of the cold north winds. They fluttered like golden wings in the breeze and flashed prismatic beams of light, announcing the changing season to the world.

As Dobbs pulled up in front of the departure entrance at the airport, Bred gazed to the left and was shocked out of his contemplative mood when he caught sight of Dr. Strydom's Mercedes bathing in the sunlight in the V.I.P. parking lot across the way. He brushed it off. The doctor was probably here on hospital business.

A porter unloaded their luggage onto his cart, and Dobbs helped Bred into the wheelchair. Maude steered him towards the entrance, and Bred pulled the hood of his dark blue sweater up over his head. He slouched down in the chair as they passed through the automatic doors.

The airport was busy, with six international departures within the hour and five domestic arrivals on the level below. Upstairs, the viewing platforms and lounges were packed with passengers and sightseers.

All we had to do, Bred thought, is to keep a low profile.

Bred was quite optimistic that they would go unnoticed in that great sea of humanity.

"Gate Sixteen; two hours," Dobbs muttered, glancing at the boarding passes.

"Maude! Bred!" Kelly came tearing through the crowd with Josh in tow, yelling at the top of her lungs. "Dr. Strydom is here!" she yelled breathlessly. "He's got bodyguards and the police and everything and…and he's looking for you, Bred!"

"What! Where?" Maude said.

"Over there by Gate Sixteen," Kelly yelled, pointing frantically.

Everyone within the sound of her panic-filled voice froze in their tracks. The crowd quietly parted along the route of her outstretched arm and pointing finger, they moved quickly to either aside, creating a clear path, like Moses parting the Red Sea…fifty…sixty yards… right up to a startled Dr. Strydom and his entire entourage. Kelly just stood there, motionless with surprise.

Dr. Strydom's followers consisted of a hospital security guard in uniform and a huge black hospital porter dressed in blue jeans and a black T-shirt with *'Bullet'* blazed across the front in white letters. Maude recognised Dan from the hospital and cringed. Behind them stood a smug Kyle Bishop, and a very sheepish looking George.

Bred sighed.

★★★

"*Hey! Bliksem!*" (asshole!)

Dr. Strydom was the first to recover. But the crowds were no longer interested and surged on about their own business. Like teeth in a gearwheel, the corridor closed shut.

"That was him!" he yelled at the guard. "After them!" He dove into the throng, fighting his way upstream against the flow of people heading for the departure lounges.

Kyle and the hospital security guard followed after him, but Kyle tripped over someone's luggage and sprawled on the stone floor, dragging the guard down with him. In a blaze of flashing colours, umbrellas, shoes and handbags, people everywhere tripped, stumbled and scattered out of their way.

George watched the fiasco developing with some amusement and giggled, then the remorse at what he had done set in again and he was contrite.

"Judas!" he admonished himself miserably for the umpteenth time. It was his fault that they were there in the first place.

George had driven Kelly to the travel agent in Edmonton a few days ago and had almost wet himself hearing about their latest antics. He had really gotten to like that prodigal son, along with his crazy family and his friends.

But later, when Kyle confronted him demanding answers about George's unexplained absences and his jaunts with the armoured truck, George began to stutter and contradict himself. Kyle's suspicions were aroused and he threatened to fire George if he did not spill the beans. George's nerve broke and he confessed.

It didn't take Kyle long to find out who the ticket was for, where Bred was going, and when. Kyle was on the phone to Dr. Strydom before George even left the room.

"Judas!" George admonished himself again, as he reluctantly took off in the wake of the determined Dan the *'Bullet'*.

★★★

Bred flicked up the front wheels and spun the wheelchair around like a paraplegic basketball pro.

"Head for the elevator," he called back to the startled group, "and bring the bags!"

They tore helter-skelter across the floor, following closely in the vacuum created by the hurtling wheelchair. Dobbs grabbed the indignant luggage-porter by the belt and bum-rushed him in pursuit.

Fearing for their lives, people scattered left and right ahead of the careening, whooping, demented boy, just as they must have flown from the path of any normal runaway chariot in ancient Roman times.

Bred cut to the front of the line at the elevator and repeatedly pressed the button for ten agonising seconds until the doors opened. He rammed his chair into the elevator and herded everyone out and would not allow anyone else in except those in his own group. Dobbs hit the 'down' button just as the *'Bullet'* burst into view and slid to a screeching stop ten yards away.

A malevolent triumphant smile contorted his dark features exposing his missing front teeth. His was not a pretty face and it sent shock waves through all who witnessed the startling transformation, but the *'Bullet'* had suffered too much to notice or care about such things.

At the hospital he had been subjugated by the public humiliation, the anger and scathing sarcasm of Dr. Strydom for letting Bred escape. Afterwards he had had to endure the scorn and smirks of his peers and everyone else who knew him throughout the hospital. But now, here at last, trapped in the open elevator and within his grasp, were the very causes of his misery.

'Bullet' savoured the moment. He would not be tricked again; he would be vindicated for having been duped by these weak, devious little white creatures. He charged like an enraged bull, straight towards the closing doors. Josh braced himself for the impact.

To *'Bullet's'* astonishment, a body suddenly lumbered out of the petrified ranks of the startled spectators and exploded like a football tackle in his peripheral vision. He tried to duck.

George's shoulder caught him under the right arm and slammed him sideways into the far wall, twelve feet to the right of the elevator. The *'Bullet'* drove his fist into George's ample belly in frustration, as the elevator doors sealed shut.

Bred leaned over and held the 'STOP' button. He placed his finger over his lips signalling everyone to be still.

"Get down to the lower level!" Dr. Strydom screamed over the drone of the traffic. "Quickly!"

Bred made himself count twenty-five seconds before releasing the button and opening the doors. Almost everyone had left the immediate area except for the one or two Samaritans trying to assist George. He was still on his knees regaining his breath. Bred wheeled over to him, followed by the others. George waved him off, not yet able to speak.

"Go!" he croaked.

"You took a *'Bullet'* for me George," Bred said solemnly, "I won't forget that."

George managed a groan and a weak smile as Kelly clapped Bred smartly behind the head with the palm of her hand.

"Where too?" Dobbs asked.

"Gate Sixteen!" Bred said, wheeling onto the crowded concourse. "Once through security, Dr. Strydom can't touch us."

"Let's go!" Dobbs instructed the porter, who minced quickly across the floor with the luggage, glancing back apprehensively at Dobbs from time to time.

They made their way quickly down through the busy airport terminal to Gate Sixteen and to the relative safety of the security gate.

Bred led the way into the security area and an uneasy silence descended on the group. The room was almost empty as the majority of the passengers had already passed through.

Bred caught a whiff of something distinctly medical, like latex gloves, and stopped so quickly that Josh following close behind was stabbed in the groin with the handle of the wheelchair.

"Bloody Hell, Bred!" he cussed, one octave higher than normal, bending over. "That smarts. I oughta..." he stopped abruptly.

Dr. Strydom stepped out from behind the partition wall ahead of them. The fugitives froze as the 'Bullet' and Kyle Bishop closed in behind them, blocking their exit.

"Did you really think that I would fall for that stupid trick with the elevator?" Dr. Strydom sneered.

Dr. Strydom straightened the sleeves of his suit and smiled paternally at the intellectually inferior creatures he had captured so easily. The outcome had been inevitable; they would come to accept that, in time.

"Let us pass, you crazy bastard!" Josh yelled loudly. "We have a plane to catch!"

Dr. Strydom was startled. "Wh...What?" he spluttered. Nobody had ever called him a crazy bastard before.

The head security guard frowned at the commotion. She walked over and stood beside Dr. Strydom, accompanied by a young police officer. Relieved by the distraction and the official audience, the doctor quickly regained his composure.

"Were you planning to leave Canada with your *nephew* and his phoney documents?" he challenged. He looked down at Bred. "You are not going anywhere except back to the hospital for treatment," he gloated, almost giggling. "Come, come, the ambulance is waiting outside."

He was forgetting himself again in his moment of triumph. A crowd had begun to gather around to watch the show. He took a deep breath and stretched his neck.

"And the rest of you are going to jail for kidnapping and aiding and abetting in the delinquency of a minor." His glee was almost hysterical.

The security guard looked at him with raised eyebrows. "I think that we should all step into the security office," she said, nodding to the officer and led the way through the double doors with the frosted glass windows.

Bred followed her with a groan.

He turned around looking for Maude, but she was clinging to Dobbs, her face hidden in his jacket. Kelly paid him no attention as she helped the injured

Josh limp towards the door. Bred groaned again and followed the guard down the hallway.

The security guard opened a door to an interrogation room and waved impatiently for Bred to enter. They all filed reluctantly through the door into the brightly lit, sparsely furnished room.

Bred was surprised to see that there were other people in the room. He was even more surprised when he recognised Mary and Graham seated at the table, along with Patrick and Michelle. Beth came out of left field, strangled his neck and smothered his cheek with kisses.

"Holy Shit!" he muttered.

There was a moment of silence when Mary rose solemnly and came over to him. She bent down, hugged him and kissed him on the cheek. Then without a word, she walked over to Maude and they hugged like long lost friends and chattered and giggled incoherently for a while.

Mary then turned to Dr. Strydom, who was also apparently surprised speechless by the encounter. "What seems to be the problem?" she asked coolly.

"They...They tries to kidnap him out of the country!" Dr. Strydom stammered, with a thick accent, losing control of the English language.

"Maude Parker and Mister Dobbs? Kidnappers? Don't be ridiculous!" Mary said, with a wave of her manicured hand. "Our friends were kind enough to drive Bred to the airport. We're seeking medical attention for our son, you see... outside the country." She looked at her nails. "That is our prerogative, I believe." Mary looked over at Corporal D'Laney. He shrugged in agreement.

"That's right," Dobbs said with a smile. "Here are your tickets and boarding passes, Graham." He stepped forward and handed them over. Graham took them with a nod of thanks.

Mary then focused her attention on Bred while still speaking to Dr. Strydom.

"We chose to do this since we did not approve of the procedures you proposed at the hospital, doctor," she explained, her eyebrows raised, "and that is why my husband and I did *not* sign your waiver."

Bred scratched the prickles at the base of his skull. He had the distinctly uncomfortable feeling that he'd been had.

★★★

"You can't take him out of the country!" Dr. Strydom yelled in panic. His vision of the future was beginning to blur. His eyes swept the sea of hostile faces in the security interrogation room at the Edmonton International Airport.

This could not be happening! His patient would not slip through his fingers once again!

"He's coming with me! I have a *court order!*" he screamed frantically.

"You do?" an alerted Corporal Patrick D'Laney stepped forward. "May I see it, please?"

"Well, I don't have it here. It's coming!" Dr. Strydom fumed. "It's still in the works!"

"Still in the works, huh? Tsk...Tsk!" the corporal clucked, shaking his head. "We must have the proper documents in order to execute a court order, doctor, you must know that." He turned to Mary.

"No, Wait!" Dr. Strydom cried, desperately searching for some way to regain control of the situation. Was he to lose the greatest medical achievement in history through emotional logic and quasi-rational rhetoric?

"I'm sorry, doctor," the corporal said with finality, dismissing him. He nodded to the security guard. She left the room. Patrick turned to Graham. Dr. Strydom's complexion turned ashen.

"You and your family are free to go," Patrick said officially. Graham nodded. "But you must come down and see me at the precinct as soon as you return." He winked at Mary. She knew that he was bending the rules.

"We promise," Mary said gratefully, squeezing his hand.

"Right oh!" Graham interjected, looking at his wristwatch. "Come on, dear, children. We had better get going or we'll miss our flight." He rose, gathering their hand luggage.

"No!" Dr. Strydom screamed. "He's mine!" He rushed across the room and desperately grabbed Bred in the wheelchair.

The despair and frustration of having to watch his finest creation spiralling uncontrollably out of his grasp once again, forever elusive, fading away like a wisp of fog on a morning pond.. His life's work useless... wasted... too much to bear... too much to be expected of the desperate, whirling mind of the psychotic, dispassionate surgeon.

"I created him! I gave him life!" he cried, trembling violently. He focused his wildly hysterical eyes on Mary. "He's not your son any more!"

In the ensuing stunned silence, Dr. Strydom spun the wheelchair around and headed for the exit. Bred locked the right wheel and kicked hard with his good leg. He and the doctor tumbled onto the floor.

Constable Michelle Monair pounced on the doctor, pinned him, face down, and cuffed him on the spot.

"That's it!" Graham said angrily, stepping into the fray and picking the uninjured Bred off the floor. "I'm pressing charges for assault," he said to Michelle, "and I'll have a restraining order on you, Strydom, before we get back."

He and Dobbs settled Bred back into his wheelchair. Graham turned back to the ashen-faced doctor now sitting on his knees with his hands behind his back.

"If you come within a mile of my boy again," he said coldly. "I'll have you prosecuted to the full extent of the law. You will never practice medicine again!" He ushered the family out of the room.

Mary stood a moment longer in the doorway, looking down at the shattered, sobbing remnants of the man she had once respected and trusted so deeply. This was the man she blessed in her prayers for restoring the life of her son. She had no wish to linger, but she was torn between her own selfish joy and relief, and compassion for the broken man and his tragic loss.

He was moaning what sounded like a prayer. And in the stillness she heard the soft words, swimming in agony, the final vestige of sanity from a brilliant mind:

"'If I have moved among my race
And shown no glorious morning face;
…If morning skies,
Books, and my food, and summer rain
Knocked on my sullen heart in vain…'"
His voice faded away and she strained to hear the rest.
"'Or, Lord, if too obdurate I,
Choose thou, before that spirit die,
A piercing pain, a killing sin,
And to my dead heart run them in!'"
"Obdurate? Unyielding!" In a flash, Mary recognised the
words from *The Celestial Surgeon.*

She turned quickly and rushed down the hallway and onto the waiting aircraft.
The vision of Dr. Strydom's passionate outbursts and the poignant aftermath
would be forever burned into her heart.

"I created him! I gave him life! He's not your son any more!"

She knew that Dr. Strydom had spoken the truth — and she didn't care.

★★★

CHAPTER FIFTEEN
The Finger of God

The last leg of their flight from Cape Verdi took them across the Atlantic Ocean until they reached the coast of Namibia on the southern continent of Africa. There they crossed a narrow strip of desiccated land named the Namib, meaning 'Waterless Land' in the Hottentot tongue. A total desert, one hundred kilometres wide and twelve hundred kilometres long, there is no other place on earth that looks at the sky with such desolation or loneliness than that.

Bred was struck again by the haunting beauty of Namib's red and golden barrens and wondered at the hidden riches still waiting to be found in its bosom. He watched mesmerised through the window as the desert dunes emerged like unreal pink and purple hills in the first light of the new day.

Formerly South West Africa, the area had been claimed and mined by the Germans at the turn of the century, only to be followed by the British, who had also failed to tame the savage land. Fred and Dobbs had journeyed there, by Land Rover and on foot.

On the wall of one abandoned mine in the desolate valley of the Khan River, someone had scratched a prophetic message sixty years before they arrived.

"No rain, no wealth,
We abandon ye therefore to the sun,
The sand and the flies."

He knew it as an arid, hostile place of dense fog, mirages and strange amber skies; and off its western shore in stark contrast, the fertile Atlantic Ocean, teaming with life.

Life and death — side by side. An awesome, ancient, and beautiful land.

He and Dobbs had travelled from Cape Town through Namaqualand to Port Nolloth, having crossed the Orange River, and had driven up through the

Diamond Coast — the forbidden zone — right up to the Kunene River. After setting out on a scheduled three-day trip through the Wilderness of Africa, they had finally arrived in Walvis Bay thirty-four days later. Suspected of diamond smuggling, they were arrested and flown back to Cape Town. Charges were eventually dropped, but not erased from the record.

The rugged mountains of the Namib gave way to the Kalahari Desert, and Bred settled back in his seat and smiled as the sights recalled other memories. He grimaced at the throbbing pain in his leg and he closed his eyes once more.

Mary watched Bred snuggle down beside her and settle into a more comfortable position on her shoulder. She would have given much to read his thoughts at that moment.

She looked around for her family in the growing light of the new dawn. Beth was stretched out sound asleep, her tousled head on Kelly's lap, while Kelly had her hand tucked under her father's arm as she dozed on his shoulder. The family had not been this close for a long time. Mary's soul flushed with pure contentment.

Graham winked at her and she drew a quick breath, but the salty tear still prickled her eye, and she had to blow her nose.

★★★

Dr. Philemon Thlabati greeted them as they emerged from customs at Cape Town International Airport later that morning. Sergeant Frikkie Marais of the South African Police Department accompanied him.

Bred's condition had deteriorated significantly over the last four hours, as the foul poison caused his wounds to become infected once again. The authorities had been notified and an ambulance was waiting outside the airport to rush him to Good Hope Hospital.

Sergeant Frikkie Marais had time for only a few quick questions before they whisked Bred away, and what he had learned was not encouraging. Deep in thought, the sergeant sat quietly in his car in for a long time before signalling his driver to follow the ambulance to the hospital. It was time to put his cards on the table; it was time to meet with Dr. Colin Montgomery once again.

★★★

Later that afternoon, Sergeant Frikkie Marais sat waiting patiently in the comfortable red leather chair in Dr. Montgomery's splendid, opulent office. He had always wanted to sit in that chair, but Dr. Montgomery had always signalled him to sit in one of the less comfortable colonial upright chairs in front of the desk. Actually, the sergeant reflected, he could probably have seated himself anywhere he wished on that particular day.

Sergeant Marais had walked into Dr. Montgomery's office and, without ceremony, placed the file marked 'Confidential — Dr. Paul Jacobus Strydom' on the desk in front of him. Dr. Colin Montgomery opened the file, and thereafter never lifted his eyes from the pages, even once. When he finally did look up, one hour and thirty minutes later, his face was pale and his eyes had red rings around them, like a man who had been too long in the trenches. He stared unseeingly at the patiently waiting Sergeant Frikkie Marais.

"I…I didn't know," he mumbled finally, placing his hand over his eyes. "I will resign immediately, of course."

"With all due respect, sir," Sergeant Marais said seriously, "there is no need for that." The doctor tried to interrupt but the sergeant raised his hand and continued.

"This was an operation underwritten by powerful people at the highest level of our previous administration. You were not *permitted* to know anything, and when they thought that you did, you were incarcerated." He studied the doctor carefully. Even the good ones needed a boost now and then.

"It is only due to your dedication and personal sacrifice that we have progressed this far, doctor," he said, "and now we need your help again — to close this case for good."

Dr. Montgomery stared down at his desk for a while, wrestling with his thoughts, and his conscious.

"I could have done more," he said finally.

"Schindler said the same thing after the war," Sergeant Marais said with a smile, "but nobody else did what he did either."

The doctor smiled wryly at the ridiculous comparison and reached across to the telephone. He called his secretary on the intercom. "Sarie," said Dr. Montgomery, "please locate Dr. Thlabati and Dr. Stein and have them come to my office immediately."

The young doctors arrived in his office ten minutes later, dressed in lab coats, having interrupted their hospital rounds. They were surprised to see Sergeant Marais present in the room. After formal sombre greetings, Dr. Montgomery beckoned them to the desk. He handed Petrus the confidential file on Dr. Strydom.

"Oh, shit!" Philemon said softly, after reading the first few lines over Petrus's shoulder. It was going to be a long day.

"I understand you kept this to yourselves," Dr. Montgomery said coldly, "now you
will tell me everything," he said. "Everything!"

The two penitent young doctors left his office three hours later. Dr. Colin Montgomery looked at his wristwatch. He nodded to Sergeant Frikkie Marais, and placed a telephone call to Dr. Paul Strydom in Edmonton, Alberta, Canada.

★★★

Dr. Paul Strydom rolled the pure-malt whisky over his tongue and savoured its essence, as he focused his mind on the problem at hand. He had done some serious soul-searching over the last few weeks since the airport fiasco.

He was relaxing on his patio overlooking the river valley, watching the early fall colours along the wooded waterway splash across the panorama. It was a typically beautiful warm late September evening. A gusty breeze ruffled the leaves on the potted geranium as the sun went down and he noticed a fresh bite in the air, a hint of the changing season.

Geese in classic "V" formation headed noisily east and west to glean the grain fields and fatten up for their epic journey soon to begin.

He sighed and took another large nip of his scotch and choked as the harsh liquor bit into his throat. In a sudden fit of rage, he threw the glass out into the void, where it curved downward in a graceful arc to shatter on the pavement in front of a startled cyclist.

It was not in his nature to give up a fight, but this Andrews case had become too complicated. Too many people were involved now and his ability to function freely and quietly was becoming severely impaired. Under the circumstances, if anything should happen to the boy while he was in his care, he would have a lot of explaining to do, and the infection excuse would no longer fly.

It was time to leave that theatre and move on. Not literally, of course, his position at Edmonton City Hospital gave him a certain amount of freedom, which would be difficult to re-establish elsewhere. All was not lost. He knew that throughout history, fate had exhibited a way of balancing the books in favour of the tenacious philosopher.

He had his research notes and he had his venue. All that he needed now was a dedicated team to work with him. With Canada's chronic shortage of physicians, it might not be that difficult to recruit most of his old team from Good Hope Hospital in Cape Town, South Africa.

"Patients? Well there was an abundance of neglected seniors around, and the poorer outlying communities would appreciate his *free* medical consultations.

Hell! They might even make me a Member of the Order of Canada, he thought.

Dr. Strydom lay back in his chair and was seriously planning his next move, when the telephone rang. He stood up, lifted the receiver and was surprised to hear the voice of his old colleague, Dr. Colin Montgomery.

"Paul?" Colin said jovially. "A patient of yours just checked into my hospital, one Brian Andrews. He calls himself Bred."

"Yes," Dr. Strydom answered. "I was aware that the Andrews boy was going there for treatment. What of it?"

"I thought that you might be interested," Dr. Montgomery sounded disappointed, "since he'll be undergoing certain neurological tests here."

"What do you mean?" Dr. Strydom asked tightly, alarmed.

"Well, I have a dossier in my possession, detailing extensive research that you and your team conducted here at Good Hope Hospital," Dr. Montgomery said. "Many of the documents pertain to the Andrews boy and ... a Mr. Fred Parker?"

The blood rushed to Dr. Strydom's head. In a daze, he staggered to a chair. His worst nightmare was coming true: someone had stolen his work!

"My.... research journals?" he asked, barely able to speak.

"Copies actually," Dr. Montgomery continued cheerfully. "Right under our noses. Paul, you sly dog!"

He's playing games with me, thought Dr. Strydom. "If you have my journals," he said bitterly, "why are you calling me?"

"Well," Dr. Montgomery said, "it seems that the final chapter is missing."

Dr. Strydom felt a flush of relief. He had written and compiled the final reports himself, right there in his offices in the basement of Good Hope Hospital. Computer print outs, charts, tapes, everything related to the final operations had been locked in his briefcase. Those documents had never left his possession. It would take them years of research to copy his neurological surgical techniques.

"Now, Paul," Dr. Montgomery continued seriously. "To coin a phrase : '*There is enough glory for all.*' You, of course, are the pioneer…the surgeon…the scientist, who single-handedly developed the procedures. I would only like to help to put the icing on the cake."

When Dr. Strydom remained silent, Dr. Montgomery continued.

"All I'm asking, Paul, is that this hospital receive some of the credit. Internationally. Remember Dr. Barnard and the first heart transplant? It would re-establish Good Hope Hospital as a world leader, and bolster universal recognition of the New South Africa."

Dr. Strydom hesitated. He was well aware of Dr. Montgomery's irrational personal regard for the staff, the hospital and its reputation. He had exploited that weakness many times in the past, and now he could add 'love of country' to the list.

"What of the parents?" he asked.

Dr. Montgomery smiled. He nodded to the Sergeant, sitting patiently in the red leather chair.

"They're heading back to Canada as we speak," Dr. Montgomery answered. "The children are due back at school, and Mr. Andrews has a business to run. Mr. and Mrs. Andrews have requested that the boy remain here with us…. Until such time as he recovers… completely." Dr. Montgomery paused to let the revelation set in. "We agreed, of course."

There was a long pause in the conversation.

Dr. Montgomery had one more item:

"I've been told that Mrs. Andrews is ill and will require hospitalisation. She wishes to be at home in Canada with her family," he said.

★★★

Bred swam up through the white mists of consciousness and surfaced in a rush. His eyes focused on the picture of a yellow spotted giraffe on the ceiling with big blue eyes and long, black eyelashes. He had the strangest feeling that he had been there before. There was one major difference: he could not move. He was paralysed.

Fear welled up in his throat until he thought that he might choke. This was an evil place. Bred tried to scream but no words came out. He had no control over his muscles, or even his very breath.

He could see the doorway and the sight of the person standing there shocked him to his soul. Dr. Paul Jacobus Strydom was leaning against the doorframe with a smirk on his face.

He was swinging a stethoscope, back and forth, back and forth.

"Gotcha," Dr. Strydom mouthed the words. "Gotcha."

Bred tried to scream, but the mist swirled around him again.

"Bred! Bred!"

He heard Mary's voice faintly calling his name and he tried to swim up through the suffocating fog. His lungs bursting, he gasped for air and the room burst into view — opening up like a flower before his startled vision. Mary was leaning over him holding his flailing hands, her face filled with concern.

"Wake up, Bred," she said urgently. "Wake up!"

"Deep breaths," the nurse beside her said, "Take deep breaths." She wiped the perspiration off his flushed and frightened face with a damp towel. "Children sometimes have a bad reaction to the anaesthetic," she said, "he'll be just fine now."

Bred was not so sure. He looked quickly around the stark recovery room. There were no pictures of giraffes, and no sign of Dr. Strydom. It had just been a bad dream; a hallucination. Bred settled back on the pillow, still shaken by the experience.

"Let's not do that again," he pleaded. "Okay?"

Mary suddenly left his side and rushed into the bathroom, where she was physically ill. The nurse looked after her, a little concerned, and mentally made an appointment for Mary to see the doctor.

★★★

The doctors had taken one look at Bred's wounded leg and rushed him into surgery. The highly trained team of surgeons and nurses had quickly drained and cleaned the wound.

"We could have healed that infection long ago with maggots and a *madumbi* root poultice," an intern muttered. She had dealt with far worse cuts and bruises in the bush.

The chief surgeon gave her a dirty look, which was somewhat wasted behind his mask. Nevertheless, he understood her scepticism.

She was a Sotho, a medicine woman from the *Thaba Bisiho*, meaning 'Mountain of the Night' in her native tongue.

In the new South Africa, she was required to learn European Western Medicine. But she was not prepared to relinquish her faith in two thousand years of herbal knowledge passed down to her through the generations.

"This boy has shown an allergic reaction to penicillin," noted the doctor later during his rounds. "What would you recommend as an alternative antibiotic?" he asked the accompanying students.

"Erythromycin," one said.

"Ceclor," said another.

"Fermented *marula* fruit," suggested the intern from *Thaba Bisiho*.

★★★

The Cullinan Hotel in downtown Cape Town publishes a fine, hard-covered tourist information book with glossy pages. Like the Gideon Bible, monogrammed notepaper and envelopes, one book was allocated to each room in the hotel. The book weighed about six ounces and makes an excellent Frisbee.

Mary replaced the phone carefully and, with a howl of fury, winged the book thirty feet across the room and nailed Graham under the arm between the fourth and fifth ribs. He yelped and dived behind the sofa as a battery of assorted missiles from the bathroom supplies rained down on him.

"You sanctimonious prick!" she screamed, finding an arsenal of coat hangers. "Deceitful hypocrite!"

Five minutes later, spent, out of ammunition and with tears of frustration running down her cheeks, Mary sank onto the bed talking to herself.

"It'll be okay, he says, I'll be careful...We don't have to worry any more... Just this once...You horny bastard!"

Beth peeked out from the other room where she had been watching television, big eyed and breathing fast. Kelly came out of the shower soaking wet with a bath sheet wrapped around her and her toothbrush still stuck in her mouth.

Graham looked up over the arm of the chair.

"What's the matter, dear?" he asked meekly.

"I'm pregnant!" she howled, flinging a pillow at him.

Graham caught the pillow. There was a moment of shocked silence; then to Mary's amazement, the room erupted in a chorus of laughter and pure joy.

★★★

"He says you must kill him," the chatty little Hottentot beside him said in broken English, referring to the earlier sage renditions of his companion, "with a poisoned arrow."

Bred had been moved from recovery to the children's ward at the hospital. He had woken bathed in sweat and yelling in terror from his reoccurring nightmare. The two Hottentot orderlies dressed in green scrubs had rushed to his bedside, wiped his face with a damp cloth, and tried to calm him down by touching his arms and feet and poking him in the ribs with a stick. Finally the Hottentots became engaged in a solemn clicking-conversation in which the other spoke softly. There were many of their people employed in menial jobs at the hospital.

"You little buggers are so damned bloodthirsty," Bred exclaimed, still edgy from his dreams. "Just how do I kill my demon?"

"With this!" the chatty Hottentot exclaimed, with a toothless grin, holding up a small glass vial filled with a muddy-brown liquid.

"Poison, ground from the stings of scorpions," he said ominously, as he handed it to Bred. "Ten bucks, please."

'Chatty' and 'The Other,' as Bred referred to them, were from the Griqua tribe of the Eastern Cape. They are a subgroup of the Khoikai, 'men of men,' a nomadic people who are believed to be the first aboriginal inhabitants of south-western South Africa.

'Hottentot' was a word coined by early Dutch settlers in South Africa to describe the strange clicking language of the Khoisan.

'Chatty' and 'The Other' lived in a shack in the squatter camp near Cape Town and walked ten miles back and forth to the hospital every day. Every so often they would disappear from civilization and trek off into the Kalahari Desert. Their families lived somewhere in southern Namibia.

In their years of working in the Western Regions, Fred Parker and Dobbs had picked up a smattering of the Khoisen and Herero languages. Not enough, mind you, to hold a conversation, but Bred had learned enough to know that these fellows were not at all concerned about him. They just wanted to scam a few dollars off the 'dam-Amerikan.'

He decided to play along for a while, and handed over the money from his bedside drawer. "I will pay you for the '*mut'i* (medicine) to expel my demon," Bred said solemnly, as they took the money with glee.

"This demon of your dreams," the chatty one enquired. "He is an animal?"

"Yes," Bred replied, "he is the White Baboon from the *Mukurob!*" The Hottentots' faces suddenly became serious as the exorcism suddenly took on a whole new meaning.

Mukurob!, 'The Finger of God' as the Europeans called it (this is as close as Europeans can come to spelling the word. It has a click in the middle.), is a vertical cone of mica schist, topped with a massive pillar of granite rock. The column rises from the desert floor, and towers a hundred feet into the sky near the towns of Tses and Asab, in South West Africa, now called Namibia.

The Hottentots believe that it has supernatural powers. Fred had heard the stories and had seen the extraordinary geological rock structure in South West Africa.

Bred used the name, not only to highlight the mystery of his demon, but to add to the perception of these superstitious people that a higher power was involved in guiding the events in his destiny.

"I'm being a prick," Bred muttered to himself, but he took advantage of their superstitions anyway.

The other little man held out his hands for the vial in a begging fashion, but Bred was having none of it. An exorcism once undertaken, and the potion handed over and paid for, could never be forcibly withdrawn — on pain of having those demons transferred onto you and your family. That was the diktat.

The Hottentots sighed and hunkered down quietly on their haunches beside the bed. Bred had his lunch, and still they sat quietly where they were.

The very happy and boisterous Andrews family visited Bred with the news about Mary. Bred was just as delighted, and the celebrations went on for some time until visiting hours were over. Though they eyed the pair of green-clad orderlies curiously, the family was too polite to ask who they were, and neither Bred nor the Hottentots offered any explanation.

A senior orderly tried to remove the Hottentots later in the afternoon. But after a few tense moments in which they exchanged words made up of strange clicking sounds that Bred could not follow, they calmed the senior orderly and sent him on his way. The Hottentots then settled back down to their vigil once again.

Bred dozed a little, and woke as the shadows danced on the walls in the golden light of the setting sun. He turned to his side and found them still sitting on their haunches, waiting patiently.

The Other was holding a small grey stone on a string, swinging it in little circles above the floor. He was quietly chanting an incantation as if in a trance. He stood up slowly and walked over beside the bed. He took out a small Red Cross pocket-knife, opened it, and cut off a lock of Bred's hair. Still chanting quietly, he returned to his seat where he tied the hair with a piece of red wool and placed it on the floor beside him.

From inside his shirt, he removed a rolled up piece of worn leather, which he spread out like a cloth in front of him. Around his neck, hung a small black pouch on a leather thong. He opened it and emptied the contents onto the cloth. The dying sun glinted off pieces of bone, wood and polished semi-precious stones. He added the lock of hair to the pile and began chanting as he swung the stone in small circles over the cloth once more.

To Bred's amazement, the items seemed to spread out on the cloth all by themselves.

After a while, '*The Other*' stopped and studied the pattern. He jumped back as if startled and began chattering incoherently to his companion.

It was funny.

Bred watched the strange little men and marvelled at the ancient, powerful superstitions that held them. But had they solved the mystery of the White Baboon? '*Chatty*' turned to him.

"The evil one has turned away from you and seeks a thousand others," he said.

"What would you have us do — *Old Man?*"

Bred was suddenly uncomfortable. He decided that the session had gone on long enough.

"How do I trap this White Baboon?" he asked. There was a long silence while the Hottentots studied the patterns on the leather cloth.

"You cannot trap him with food," Chatty said, thoughtfully, "he has enough of that."

"He must be trapped with a promise," '*The Other*' said, speaking directly to Bred for the first time, "a promise that will give him power over all the baboons."

"How do I do that?" Bred asked, intrigued.

"You must restore to him the budding flower, whom he thought lost; And even his ebony shadow."

It was Bred's turn to be startled.

Both men had risen together— and had spoken in unison.

They took back the vial that he offered with sombre faces and left without another word.

★★★

"He won't come," Bred repeated for the third time, "he's lost interest in me."

Philemon and Petrus had dropped in to see Bred in the children's ward the following morning. At Bred's request, they had summoned Dr. Montgomery and Sergeant Marais.

"How do you know that?" Dr. Montgomery asked impatiently. "When I spoke with Paul Strydom earlier, he sounded quite enthusiastic."

"He won't come without a promise that will give him absolute control over everyone," Bred continued uncomfortably. He really didn't have a lot to justify his statement. "They told me..." he hesitated. It was all beginning to sound a little outlandish.

"What did they tell you?" prompted the sergeant gently.

"You must restore to him the budding flower, whom he thought lost; And even his ebony shadow." Bred quoted. "But I don't know what the riddle means."

"Where did you hear that?" Philemon demanded loudly, jumping to his feet.

"From the Hottentots," Bred said, somewhat startled. "Why?"

"Because you spoke in the ancient Khoisen tongue," Sergeant Marais said, rising carefully and looking thoughtfully out the window, his hands clasped behind his back.

The case had just taken on a whole new meaning. Khoikhoi spiritual messages were never trivial.

"They hypnotised you, so that you would not misunderstand the message," he said.

★★★

"So, this is what we have so far," Sergeant Marais said, studying his notebook.

They had assembled in Dr. Montgomery's office after dinner and had been tossing the riddle around for an hour. Everyone was mentally exhausted.

The sergeant went through the riddle one more time.

"One: We have to *restore*, give back, to Dr. Strydom, something that was lost, was taken away, or misplaced. Two: *the budding flower* — indicates a singular, tangible expanding or growing entity. Three: *whom* — a reference used only with regards to a person. Four: *he thought he had lost* — A wife? A girlfriend? A child? Or a friend?

"Or protégé," mumbled Philemon, resigned. He was slumped on the floor, leaning against the wall with his arms resting on his knees.

He looked over at his friend sprawled out in the big red leather chair. "As in Dr. Petrus Stein." He said with finality.

"Wh...What?!" Petrus exclaimed.

"Wake up, Petrus!" Philemon said, exasperated. He rose to his feet, reluctant to expose a truth that should otherwise best lie dormant. "Think back and recall the long philosophical discussions you had with Dr. Paul Strydom. And let us not forget the private lectures. You were soaking it up like a crocodile soaks up the midday sun on a sandbank." Philemon paused to consider his words and decided to be blunt. "Also, your relationship was sympathetic; you moped around for weeks after Dr. Strydom left. You were the wildebeest left behind in the migration. He was your tutor, your educator, and your mentor."

"He was a *genius!*" Petrus yelled back defensively, jumping to his feet to face his accuser.   "He performed an operation like a concert pianist....You saw him, he was an artist, a perfectionist, a philosopher... he...he...oh, shit!" He flopped back in his chair aghast as the realisation hit him. "I was his protégé!"

Dr. Montgomery nodded in reluctant agreement.

"Why didn't you two say anything?" Petrus asked, nearly choking.

"I am your friend," Philemon said gruffly, "not your nursemaid."

"That works," Sergeant Frikkie Marais said studying his notebook and totally unfazed by the revelation.

"We must return to Dr. Strydom the protégé whom he thought he had lost — Dr. Petrus Stein."

"And just how do you propose we do that?" Petrus asked. And then, as everyone looked at him expectantly, it dawned on him.

"I'm going to Canada." he said apprehensively.

"There is one more thing," said Bred quietly as the discussion turned to making preparations. They turned to look at him curiously. "Dr. Philemon Thlabati must go too."

The room was silent.

"Are you suggesting...?" Dr. Montgomery began.

"There's more to the riddle," Bred continued, patiently holding up his hand.

"And even his ebony shadow". In the Old South Africa, in the realm of Apartheid in which Dr. Strydom lived and flourished, black men were subjugated by the whites regardless of their intellectual or academic achievements. Dr. Strydom could not accept the concept of equality, and probably never will." Bred explained.

"Dr. Philemon Thlabati must accompany Dr. Petrus Stein on his quest. He must provide a convincing performance of subservience to Dr. Stein, especially in the presence of Dr. Strydom," Bred said coldly.

Dr. Montgomery gasped at the audacity.

Bred ignored him and turned to Philemon. "You are the *ebony shadow*," he said.

"There is no way that I would subject Philemon, or any man, to that kind of humiliation," cried Petrus, appealing to Dr. Montgomery. "I thought we had gone past that. A man shall no longer judged by the colour of his skin."

"No need to be so damned sanctimonious, Petrus," Philemon laughed, getting to his feet. "People will not abandon their prejudices overnight, but it will come to pass. Even the cheetah gives up her prey to the hyena." (The Zulu people have always been physically and spiritually connected to their natural environment, and children are taught from an early age to compare everyday events in nature with the passage of their own lives.) Philemon turned quickly to face Bred. "You are very wise for your years," he said with a grin. "I will go with Petrus and act as his servant. But heaven help him if he makes me clean his boots." He turned and threw his arm around Petrus's neck.

"So first I'm a hyena," Petrus said indignantly, breaking Philemon's hold and cuffing him on the ear. "And now you want to take it outside? Very well then!" He danced around like a boxer, as Philemon carefully selected a long letter opener from the holder on the desk.

"Just don't cut off my ears, okay?" Petrus pleaded, suddenly perplexed. Everyone laughed. They had all heard the story of the despicable janitor.

Philemon grinned, shook his head and looked at his friend more seriously. "We must play our parts very carefully, Petrus," he said, "to catch this wily *'White Baboon.'*"

★★★

"Where the hell did you get that?" Dr. Petrus Stein asked, turning from checking the contents of his briefcase to stare at Dr. Philemon Thlabati in astonishment. Philemon was standing grinning in the doorway, wearing a dark, ill-fitting suit from the seventies, a white shirt, red tie and patent leather shoes.

"From the *Sally-Anne*." Philemon laughed, referring to the Salvation Army Store. "If I am to play Dr. Strydom's *kaffir,* (lowly servant) pathetically striving to equal his betters, I had better look the part."

It was six o'clock in the evening. Petrus and Philemon had flown into Edmonton International Airport via London the previous afternoon and had checked into the Plaza Hotel. Petrus had contacted Dr. Strydom earlier that morning and the latter was expecting them to arrive at his apartment within the hour.

"That's not bloody funny," Petrus said. "Playing a part is one thing, Philemon, but that is going too far — that's ridiculous!"

Philemon could see that the stark reminder of the reality of colour discrimination in South Africa embarrassed Petrus. "Is it, really?" Philemon pursed his lips thoughtfully. "You and I were raised on the very narrow edge of South African Colonial-Boer *Apartheid* society, protected from a great deal of the realities by our influential families and our own social standing at the University."

"We were *all* influenced by the State," Petrus said. "And by the Dutch Reform Church. Anyone who felt that they should be doing something to change the situation were quickly discouraged by the secret police. We soon figured out that it was better not to be involved with radicals, and we really didn't know any better."

"In those days it was not wise to attempt to change the status quo," Philemon nodded. "And the status quo my friend, is exactly what you see here." He held out his arms and did a pirouette, making himself dizzy.

"Remember, you and I were not always together at school," he said, throwing his arm around Petus's shoulders to regain his balance. "You socialised with your white friends, and I walked with my black brothers and sisters. I know how downtrodden and despised we blacks were by some white people. And even you, my friend, were called a *kaffirboetie,* (a black mans brother) because of me." He took a deep breath and dropped his arm.

"I know," Petrus said sadly, staring reflectively down at the carpet. "But we have a cunning and devious adversary here, Philemon. He will eat us alive if he gets a whiff of deception."

"Exactly!" Philemon said. "So to succeed, we must revert back to the South Africa he remembered — and to the way things were in those days." He studied his friend soberly.

"Petrus," he continued patiently. "A pair of ugly little mongooses will always manage to defeat the mighty King Cobra."

"Not always!" Petrus said in a panic. "Last year the workers killed a ten-foot King Cobra in the sugar cane field back on the farm. When they opened it up, there was a mongoose inside. Do you think it died of natural causes?"

Philemon threw back his head and laughed. "Touché!" he said, when he had recovered. "But it was the way it was back then, until Nelson Mandela came back." He smiled.

White South Africans were the last of the European colonists to relinquish power back to the indigenous people. They followed the Portuguese in Mozambique, the British in Northern and Southern Rhodesia, the French in Ethiopia and the Sudan, the Belgians in the Congo, and on and on. Each African country had paid a price, before and after their independence.

The New South Africans were determined to prosper together, to cherish the prize.

"Yes," Petrus said, grinning back at him and closing his briefcase with a snap. They had had this conversation before.

★★★

CHAPTER SIXTEEN
The Persuader

Dr. Strydom greeted Dr. Stein cordially as the two visitors arrived at his apartment.

"And this is Dr. Thlabati," Petrus said. "You remember him from Good Hope Hospital, of course."

"Of course, of course," said Dr. Strydom, shaking his hand. "Phillip, isn't it?"

"Yas, Sir," Philemon said with a broad smile.

Dr. Strydom led them into the lounge. When everyone was seated, he poured each a drink and sat down across the table from Petrus.

"Dr. Stein," he said. "Can we get right to the point? Why are you here?"

"We heard that you were considering returning to Good Hope Hospital," Petrus said seriously. "That being the case, I wish to set the record straight as to what has transpired since you left."

Dr. Strydom looked at him questioningly.

"It will probably save me a lot of explanations and embarrassing questions later, sir," Dr. Stein added uncomfortably. "So first of all, Dr. Strydom," he continued, regaining his composure and opening his briefcase. "I wish to return something that I found in a file drawer in your office shortly after your departure." He produced Dr. Strydom's missing journal, dated just prior to the operations on Brian Andrews and Fred Parker.

"No one else has seen this, Doctor," he said sincerely, holding it out to Dr. Strydom. "Except for myself of course and… oh…and Dr. Thlabati here. I copied the summary and gave it to Dr. Montgomery to gain his support."

It was partially true, except that all the pages had been scanned into a computer and all concerned had worked from copies.

"Actually," Philemon said proudly, straightening his tie, "I found it and brought it to Dr. Stein." Petrus gave him a hard look. "I was cleaning the cabinet," he said uneasily, "and it must have fallen down the back." He dropped his eyes to his hands and he clammed up.

"Did you read this document?" Dr. Strydom asked, ignoring the interruption and flipping through the once familiar pages. He looked directly at Petrus suspiciously.

"Every word of it," Petrus admitted, nodding. "I have the procedures almost totally committed to memory."

"I, and Dr. Thlabati here," he patted Philemon on the shoulder, "spent nearly six months working with cadavers in the mortuary before we attempted any procedure on a live patient."

"You attempted a human transplant?" Dr. Strydom was shocked.

"Good lord, no! Chimpanzees". Petrus said with a giddy laugh. "Though I… we have inserted a few microelectrodes into specific areas of a human patient's brain and have accumulated some incredible data…" Dr. Stein turned to Dr. Thlabati. "Give me the 'Miranda, AB — Neg.' file please, Doctor," he instructed. Philemon complied hastily.

With the help of Dr. Montgomery and Sergeant Marais's political contacts, sophisticated scientific government computers had been programmed to produce authentic looking charts and data, simulating some of the more complicated procedures developed by Dr. Strydom. The computer had then generated the predicted and rather impressive results. The information was then downloaded onto compact discs.

Dr. Stein displayed these data with pride on Dr. Strydom's computer monitor. A lively analytical discussion ensued in which even Dr. Thlabati participated, though he was careful to display a lesser level of understanding.

"Where did you get these?" Dr. Strydom asked, studying one of the incredibly detailed MIR images displayed on the monitor.

"In your operating rooms on the lower level," Dr. Thlabati said proudly. "Dr. Stein has convinced Dr. Montgomery to reopen the facilities and even to upgrade some of the equipment."

The discussion ran late into the night. Dr. Strydom finally rose and looked down at Petrus thoughtfully. He walked across the room and opened the French doors onto the patio. It was a beautiful fall night, the air was crystal clear and the bright lights of the city of Edmonton twinkled off to the horizon where they blended with the stars.

"Dr. Thlabati," he said. "Would you excuse Dr. Stein and me for a few minutes? Dr. Stein, will you please join me on the patio? I have something I wish to discuss with you privately." Dr. Stein rose obediently and followed Dr. Strydom to the door.

"Phillip," Petrus said, turning in the doorway and looking back at all the papers, glasses and coffee cups scattered around. "Would you mind cleaning up the mess while we're gone? There's a good fellow." He closed the door behind him before Philemon could reply. Dr. Strydom raised an eyebrow but said nothing.

When Petrus had settled comfortably, Dr. Strydom produced two fine Cuban cigars and offered one to Petrus which he accepted with a nod. Dr. Strydom turned away and stood looking out over the city with the unlit cigar in his mouth. He contemplated for a few moments and turned back to face his guest. He cut the end off the cigar and put a match to it. He peered at Petrus with one eye through the curling blue smoke before offering him a light. He sat down opposite Petrus and lay back in the chair, staring thoughtfully at the burning end of his cigar.

Petrus sat quietly, patiently waiting.

"I am not planning to return to South Africa," Dr. Strydom said finally. "I have everything I need right here to continue my research. I have also begun making preparations to engage some of my old team from Good Hope Hospital in Cape Town." He took a puff on the cigar, exhaling slowly. He leaned forward and studied Petrus carefully in the pale light shining on the patio.

"I would like you to join me, Petrus," he said. "Just think about it. You have only read my notebook, and that brought you all the way to Canada. You have barely scratched the surface!"

Petrus was surprised at the emotional forcefulness of the man. "I am flattered, Dr. Strydom," Petrus said, gathering himself. "But my own research on one particular patient has provided such extraordinary results that I cannot possibly leave him at this time."

"And what research is that?" Dr. Strydom asked incredulously, unable to comprehend that any other research could possibly be more important than his own.

"Simultaneous microelectronic stimulation of the parietal and temporal lobes and the amygdala in the limbic system and at the top of the hippocampus," Petrus said, referring to those inner parts of the brain. "I could really use your diagnosis, doctor. I am really concerned that my inexperience may cause irreversible damage," he said regretfully. "There is a growth pattern in certain areas that is beyond my comprehension." He studied his cigar reflectively

"Like what?" Dr. Strydom asked curiously.

Petrus removed a small tape recorder from his pocket. "Like this," he said. "I was able to stimulate some latent memories and emotional outbursts." He pressed the button and the recorder came to life.

"You can't have my money! You can't have my money!" A boy kept screaming, over and over again. Then a male voice interceded. *"Careful, Maude, the water gets very deep. Look out for the waves! Look out for the waves!"*

There was a deathly silence. The two men stared at each other.

"Who…who is your patient?" Dr. Strydom asked tightly, but he already knew the answer.

Those were the unmistakable voices of Brian Andrews and Fred Parker — one and the same.

There is *growth, healing and integration of the two minds* after surgery!

The revelation hit Dr. Strydom like a thunderbolt. The Andrews boy had only shown him one side or the other, Brian or Bred....Now this!

Dr. Strydom had thought it possible but never dreamed... the concept was so astounding that he could barely hear Petrus speaking to him. His mind was in a whirlwind of excitement. He sprang to his feet.

"It is absolutely imperative that I do the diagnosis on your patient," Dr. Strydom said emphatically. He swallowed hard to regain his composure. "Of course, I will be returning to South Africa with you," he added, a little more calmly, placing his hand firmly on Petrus' shoulder. The emotions bubbled up in him again and he shook his head, unable to contain himself.

"This is beyond anything human civilisation has ever experienced before!" Dr. Strydom blurted suddenly waving his arms. He strode up and down the patio, too excited by the prospect to return to his chair. "We are teetering on the brink of the greatest medical breakthrough in human history," he exclaimed.

"Imagine immortality for selected rich and famous patients — integrating the minds of great thinkers, industrial visionaries and philosophers!" His voice rose a little higher with barely controlled emotion, the excitement in his eyes flashed despite the diffused lighting. "We will develop a secret network, a core group of perfect human intellectuals," he continued, "and the greatest prize of all: absolutely untraceable anonymity!"

His face was gleaming, tense, and his voice was barely audible when he turned to face his audience. Dr. Strydom's next words blazed like a fire into Petrus's startled soul.

"In our lifetime we will develop a human *Master Race!*"

Petrus was appalled. Before him stood a man who had reached the pinnacle of his profession, a man who had sacrificed everything, friends, and the love of a family, his private life, everything, for the pure advancement of his knowledge and learning in medicine, for the good of mankind. Or was it for the good of mankind?

Dr. Strydom was a leader among men, a hero, and a mentor. The most brilliant surgeon he had ever known, Petrus thought, and one whom dozens of doctors wished to emulate, himself included. ... and for what? Petrus shook his head as he confronted his own moral dilemma.

The bar had been set by the laws of our society and defined by the Hippocratic Oath, he thought, Dr. Strydom has obviously chosen to cross the bar, to ignore both the law and the oath...or maybe, Petrus' eyes widened as the reality struck him, maybe Dr. Strydom had *never* subscribed to either of them.

It was at that point that Dr. Petrus Stein concluded that Dr. Paul Jacobus Strydom was probably insane.

★★★

The arrivals terminal at Johannesburg International Airport in South Africa, is a dreary, uninviting place at twelve-fifteen in the morning. It was raining, and the international Pan-Am jet from New York disembarked its passengers onto the tarmac a hundred feet from the terminal. From the top of the gangway, Dr. Strydom had a sinister feeling of foreboding as he looked out across the pavement towards the glass doors clearly visible beneath the bright lights of the docking bay.

Inside, the terminal was no better, except for the rain. A grey-painted open warehouse with a luggage carrousel and customs booths at the far end of the warehouse greeted the travelers. Two signs divided the passengers into two rows, 'South African Citizens' and 'None South African Citizens,' a throwback from another era when the signs read: 'Whites' and 'None Whites.' Dr. Strydom did not notice; he was still a citizen. Two officers on each row processed one-hundred and thirty-two passengers in two hours, a new record. There was no customs check.

Sergeant Frikkie Marais accompanied by four constables were waiting for him at the customs exit. Dr. Strydom saw them first and tried to turn back into the luggage terminal. Unfortunately, the airport guards had been alerted and escorted him unceremoniously into the hands of the law.

"Dr. Paul Jacobus Strydom," the sergeant said. "You are under arrest for the murder of…"

"Don't be ridiculous," Dr. Strydom interrupted, unnerved by the sight of Sergeant Marais and his constables — and the feeling of *déjà vu*. "We have been down this path before. I have already been cleared of any wrongdoing concerning the deaths of those *kaffirs*." Dr. Strydom searched the terminal, desperately seeking support from someone in the crowd, but finding none.

"You are under arrest for the murder of Mr. Fred Parker," Sergeant Frikkie Marais repeated coldly. "You of all people should know the difference between a kidney and a brain, Doctor," he added. "We have eye witnesses who will swear that you performed unnecessary experimental surgery, resulting in the death of one, Mr. Parker."

He took the attaché case from Dr. Strydom's trembling hand and passed it to one of the constables. It was unfortunate that just at that critical moment, Dr. Philemon Thlabati strolled casually past, and Dr. Strydom saw the huge grin on face.

Dr. Strydom lost it. And to the great satisfaction of the overzealous arresting officers, Dr. Strydom began to resist arrest.

Dr. Stein relieved the young black constable of the burden of the attaché case so that the latter could participate in the violence, and quickly disappeared into the crowd.

"*You have the right to remain silent,*" Sergeant Marais recited, his hands full with the uncooperative Dr. Strydom. "*You have the right to a lawyer…*"

Sergeant Frikkie Marais was in his element — this was *his* moment of glory!

★★★

A short time later, Dr. Petrus Stein was en route to the hotel in a taxi. Beside him sat Dr. Philemon Thlabati. There was a little raucous horseplay in the back seat, which had the cabby quite perplexed for a few minutes, although a American one hundred-dollar bill calmed him down considerably.

"It was the tape recording that did the trick," Petrus said gleefully. "Good thing Maude had that old video tape of Fred Parker teaching her how to sail."

He opened Dr. Strydom's attaché case and found that it held nothing of consequence besides a few shirts, ties and socks.

"It seemed that Dr. Strydom was not totally convinced by our performance after all," Petrus said thoughtfully. "How did you do, Philemon?"

"You mean while I was cleaning up Dr. Strydom's apartment — like I was told to by the *Master*?" Philemon asked haughtily.

He opened his briefcase and extracted a thick manila envelope and a file folder labelled: *'Operating Procedures & Notes — B. Andrews / F. Parker.'* By Dr. Paul Jacobus Strydom.

"You were maybe looking for something like this?" Philemon inquired with a smile. He repeatedly snatched the file away from the grasping outstretched hand of his companion. Philemon would not let Petrus get near it. Raucous horseplay resumed in the back seat of the taxicab.

***

CHAPTER SEVENTEEN
The Frame

Bred sat staring gloomily out of Mary's bedroom window on the Andrews' estate. He looked out across the once green lawns as they slowly faded to gold in the late afternoon sunshine. A killing frost had pervaded their little sanctuary the night before and the effect on the summer annuals was immediate, and devastating.

It was the middle of September. Fall had arrived early, and the little evergreens stood out in stark contrast to the red, orange and brown leaves of the deciduous trees. Vibrantly green just a few weeks ago, the once colourful bushes and flowers hunched cold and grey in their beds.

Mary walked over to him and silently put her arm around his shoulders and looked out at the gardens with him. The scars of tire tracks were even more plainly visible now in the lawn at the bottom end of the garden, despite the area having been repaired and re-seeded.

It had been a sad, sad day.

Dr. Thlabati and Dr. Stein had been at the airport to bid them farewell. Philemon had turned to Bred while they stood in front of the departure lounge at Cape Town International Airport.

"Go with God, *Old Man*," he said, speaking in his native tongue. "You must come back before you are too much older." He grinned at Bred mischievously. "We will baffle the witchdoctors with your wisdom in the Valley of a Thousand Hills, where the mighty Thukela River ceaselessly searches for the weakest of men and of beasts."

"I will return when bidden by Dr. Philemon Thlabati, the son of the Sub-Chief of the Zulus," Bred said with a bow of his head. "To visit with you and your noble 'White Shadow'," he continued with a grin, to which Petrus and Philemon laughed.

Kelly and Graham just looked at him with puzzled expressions.

"You learned an awful lot of Zulu in a very short time, Bred," Graham said finally, recovering from his surprise, and led the way into the airport lounge. Mary just smiled and said nothing.

Bred had not considered the effect his linguistic acumen might have on the family. He bit his lip.

Fred had not forgotten.

★★★

After an uneventful flight and a few days' rest, a noticeably jubilant Graham and Mary Andrews had casually escorted Bred to the police precinct in Bolton as promised. Beth and Kelly were back in school, having only missed a few weeks of the semester. Bred planned to challenge the mid-terms, return to school after Christmas break, and graduate with his pears next spring.

The Andrews' lack of concern proved premature though and their optimism turned to alarm within the hour.

During a lengthy interrogation, in which Michelle and Patrick reintroduced the evidence against Bred, Graham got mad and demanded his lawyer. Mary was reduced to tears.

Finally, Inspector Claude DuBois, Operations Commander, Fifth Detachment, in the town of Bolton, had formally charged Brian Andrews, alias Bred, of Bolton, with complicity in Kyle's Courier Service robbery, and wanton destruction of property with intent to injure.

Bred had sat there and said nothing since he could not remember any of it anyway, except for some vague memories — almost like waking from a dream. He was most impressed, however, with the assemblage of evidence. Patrick and Michelle had really done a good job. But, after spending a night in an awful, stinking jail cell, Bred concluded that he wanted no part of incarceration.

The facts in the case needed a good 'do-over'

The following morning, a court order released him into the custody of his parents pending trial and Bred had returned to the Andrews' estate to brood.

"The gardens will come back again next year," Mary said reassuringly, reading his mood.

Bred nodded and gave her a quick smile. "What made those tracks?" he asked, pointing towards the marks in the lawn.

"You did, dear," she said, squeezing his shoulder, "just after your fifteenth birthday, almost a two years ago, almost a lifetime ago." She kissed him on the forehead before leaving him to contemplate his fate by the window, and went back to rearranging her linens.

★★★

The following afternoon, Bred sat alone in his favourite seat in Maude's Donut Shop sipping cold coffee. It was not a pleasant day at all. Blustery winds tore through the treetops ripping off dead leaves and their drab broken remnants. They fell to the ground where they collected in sodden wind-driven piles in the odd nooks and crevices of the town. Low grey clouds carpeted the landscape and the odd squall sent sleet, leaves and rain splattering against the glass panes of the solarium.

Mary had given him a ride into town and dropped him off at the door to the donut shop. His leg had healed very well and although he moved slowly, he walked almost without a limp. With physiotherapy, the doctors had told him, the prognosis was for a complete recovery within a year.

The first thing that he had noticed when he walked through the doors of the donut shop, was that people avoided looking at him. Nobody said hello unless they were cornered and they did so, only to move quickly away.

Bred sighed. Word of his arrest had gotten out fast; he was already being ostracised for his alleged crime. Nobody was even supposed to know. I'm a minor for crying out loud! But Bolton was a very small town.

It was time to start undoing what was done.

Bred had a chat with Maggie, to catch up on the news.

"Apart a bus hitting the lamp pole on the street outside and, oh…your arrest last night, nothing else happened in town," Maggie said. Bred could see that she was uncomfortable talking with him in the shop, and asked her to leave when people began looking their way and whispering.

"Better not to be seen fraternising with criminals," he told her sarcastically, "it may impact on the business."

"Totally bogus, Bred!" Maggie cried. "I know that's totally bogus…isn't it?"

Bred sighed again. It was going to be harder than he thought.

★★★

Inspector DuBois was not a happy camper. He sat in his office and glowered at the two officers seated uncomfortably in front of him.

"Based on evidence gathered in South Africa," he said. "The Parker case is officially no longer a homicide." He handed the documents to Patrick and glanced over at Michelle. "It's robbery with intent." He shifted uncomfortably in his chair.

"When something is not right, my stomach hurts," Claude continued with a growl, "and my stomach has been hurting for a long time." He stood up and walked over to the window. It did not matter that the Maple tree had not yet been trimmed, the leaves had fallen off and he could see the park through the branches now. There was nobody there. He turned to the officers.

"Despite your damning evidence, I still think that Andrews kid is innocent," he said. "I feel it right here," he stabbed his belly with his index finger. "Dig deeper, look to your sources again."

Michelle was startled. "We're to look for evidence that our evidence is wrong?" she asked, glancing over at Patrick with a grimace.

The inspector nodded. "That's right," Claude said, knowing that he would have to answer to the captain for that one.

★★★

Patrick rubbed his forehead and placed his finger over his mouth as he leaned with his elbow on the chair. He looked at the photographs lying on the table for the hundredth time, then across at Michelle.

"I don't see one thing that contradicts our findings," he said despondently. They had been at it all morning. She shook her head in agreement, her brow furrowed. They had set up their storyboard in the conference room at the precinct and organised the photographs into categories.

"Brian's truck transported the dressers and mirrors to the dumpsite," he said, pointing to the picture, "and ..."

"Wait!" Michelle said, and Patrick jumped. "But was he driving it?" Her eyes were so wide her eyebrows almost touched her hairline.

"Probably," Patrick said thoughtfully. "Brian considered it his truck and only his. He was very possessive. What made you think of that?"

"I don't know," said Michelle reflectively. "Something Maggie said earlier about that bus accident the other day. She said: '*He was the bus driver, but was he driving the bus?*'"

Patrick rocked back and forth for a minute. "But, then again, Brian was only actually seen driving the truck home the following day," he said with a frown. He stood up quickly. "Let's make some calls," he said, reaching for his jacket.

Corporal Patrick D'Laney and Constable Michelle Monair found Graham standing on the sidewalk outside his department store, staring gloomily at his new green BMW parked on the roadway.

"Fancy new machines," he muttered irritably, looking at his watch. "They're great until something goes wrong." He gestured towards the flat tire. "What can I do for you now?" he turned to Patrick. He was still a little hostile. "I thought you had your man...uh boy," he added sarcastically.

Patrick rubbed his nose. "This case is not closed by a long shot, Graham," he said patiently. "We're questioning the evidence and we'll get to the bottom of it. And right now we need your help."

Graham was somewhat pacified.

"Did you ever lend this truck to anyone before Fred Parker's accident?" Patrick asked producing the photograph.

Graham thought for a minute. "Now that you mention it," he said, "I believe I did lend the old Ford to Fred once. I don't remember exactly when though."

Patrick nodded and they left the shop. He stopped on the pavement and looked up at the sky.

Corporal D'Laney was a good police officer; one who trusted his instincts. A feeling, a hunch, something slightly out of kilter and the alarm bells rang.

The alarm had just rung with one clear ping, like a tiny silver bell at the base of his skull.

Graham was too smooth, too polished.

Michelle was bubbling over at his elbow with new theories. He looked at her and smiled at her exuberance. He shook off his misgivings.

"We must see Maude. She's probably still up at Namier Lake," Patrick said, glancing at Michelle.

Michelle paused, her enthusiasm drained quickly.

Patrick had been professional to a fault since their return from Namier Lake. Once or twice she had tried to open a personal conversation, but he had not responded at all. Her love for him burned deeply in her breast; how could his have cooled so quickly? Or had he actually never loved her at all?

Michelle braced herself and swallowed hard. She was a police officer.

"Okay," she said, tightly.

★★★

Corporal D'Laney and Constable Monair flew into Ft. McMurray the following morning on an Air Canada Boeing 727. The sky was overcast and a freezing wind gusted across the airfield at 40-50 km per hour. Michelle flipped up her hood and walked backwards into the wind. Patrick had to guide her to the air terminal.

Maude and Dobbs met them at the airport and drove them to a local hotel-restaurant on the edge of town for lunch. The interior of the hotel was decorated like an oasis, with a creek and running water, green shrubs, flowers and coconut trees. Someone had made a valiant attempt to block out the bleak grey landscape of the real world outside. Michelle was enchanted.

"It will snow tonight," Dobbs said, as they took off their coats and were seated at their table. "We should have been at the coast by now, but there was an unfortunate family emergency." He looked a little uncomfortable after he said that.

The small talk continued until the conversation got around to Bred. Patrick produced the photographs of the truck and was rewarded with the anticipated response from Maude.

"Fred once borrowed a truck like that one to take some old furniture to the dump," she said. "I remember." Maude peeked over his arm at another picture.

"Yes...yes, just like that one. It was a couple of days before Fred's accident," she said.

Patrick flinched and Michelle nearly swallowed her cucumber sandwich whole.

"What kind of furniture?" Michelle asked, when she had regained her breath.

Maude put her hands over her mouth and looked at the ceiling, concentrating for a moment.

"I don't remember exactly," she said. "Just some junk from the shed out back." Her eyes shifted from Patrick to Michelle and back again. "An old dressing table, some broken mirrors and such, I think," she added quickly. Maude was not a very good liar.

"Maude," Patrick said carefully. "Did you speak to anyone in Bolton on the phone recently?" He leaned forward on the table and looked her straight in the eye. Maude looked very uncomfortable. She would not lie again.

"Yes," she said meekly, "I talked to Maggie."

"About Bred?"

"Among other things…yes." She lifted her chin.

"And did she coach you on what to say when you and I got together?" he asked, not too kindly.

"Look Patrick," Maude said, regaining her dignity in the truth. "I cannot remember exactly what Fred took to the dump that day, but I do know that he borrowed a truck from Graham Andrews to do just that, shortly before the accident." She wrung her hands and swallowed the lump in her throat.

Patrick nodded, sitting back. He really cared for Maude; she had been through a lot.

"What else did Maggie tell you to say, Maude?" he asked gently.

Maude looked at Patrick thoughtfully. "Well, Maggie suggested that I ask you to check the pockets of Fred's old jacket…you know," she said, as Patrick cocked his head, "the one he had hanging in the van. Maggie thinks that there might be a clue there about the accident, though I can't imagine what." Maude shook her head.

"Maggie has been reading too many mystery stories," Michelle smiled kindly. "But we'll check again anyway. Where's the jacket now?"

"Why, I left it in the basement closet next to the dryer," Maude answered. "In 'Maude's Cottage', which you are presently renting from me, Patrick." She seemed a little startled at the coincidence.

★★★

Bred left the red brick Victorian-styled house on the Andrews estate and walked slowly down the gravel driveway towards the gates. It was a beautiful fall day in Bolton, clear and warm with little wind. The weather had mulled itself into a typical Alberta Indian Summer and it was expected to continue throughout the week.

Bred felt the good-pain of his healing muscles and tendons as he stretched out every deliberate step. He felt confident, alive and, apart from being accused of killing himself, he was happy with his new life. His plan to clear himself of that heinous crime was coming together quite nicely. He had anticipated every nuance, every possible scenario.

When he reached the end of the driveway, he absently followed the line of the tire tracks cutting across the lawn to where the truck had turned around. A frown creased his brow when he realised that he had reached the end of the tracks. He looked around puzzled. Why would he, or anyone for that matter, drive down there in the first place?

Bred read the signs.

The truck had apparently backed up to one of the sheds, before tearing off back across the lawn to the driveway. Bred opened the doors of the shed and looked inside. He saw the rusty yellow pails piled randomly to the roof. To one side he noticed five pails, neatly stacked with their lids loosely clipped back on. He removed one of the lids and peered inside.

"Holy shit!" he gasped. Perhaps he hadn't anticipated every nuance, every possible scenario after all!

Bred carefully made his way around to the back of 'Maude's Cottage' and found the shed at the end of the garden. He retrieved Fred's transit level and a long tape measure. He also pulled out an old notebook from a drawer on the shelf.

Since Patrick was now living in the cottage, Bred had first made sure that Patrick was not at home. Having found what he needed, Bred hurried home to the Andrews' estate. He rifled through Graham's desk in the study until he found a pocket calculator in a bottom drawer.

He was ready.

Bred had met with George earlier that morning and had been greeted like an old friend. Bred filled him in on the rise and fall of Dr. Strydom, and George just shook his head in astonishment.

"Bloody hell, Bred!" he said, rubbing his neck. "You sure do see a lot of action for a boy your age. I hear you even got busted."

"Bogus!" Bred said. "Totally bogus!" He had heard that expression somewhere.

Kyle still had the courier service, but his previous activities were under investigation by the Standard Bank.

George still had his old job as the courier driver and agreed to give Bred a ride to Edmonton in the armoured truck that same afternoon. George picked Bred up in downtown Bolton as arranged.

"Where to?" George asked, as they headed down the old road from Bolton to Edmonton.

"Just drop me off at Poplar Creek," Bred answered.

George looked at him curiously. He saw the look on Bred's face and decided not to ask any more questions.

George dropped Bred and his equipment off at the base of the slope a short distance from where Fred had driven off the road. George would return at about seven-thirty that evening to pick him up.

When he was alone again, Bred stood quietly surveying the scene around him.

Basking in the warmth of the pleasant afternoon sunshine, with the creek gurgling below and the autumn leaves rustling softly in the breeze, Bred could think of few more tranquil places. Raindrops from the night before glistened like drops of crystal glass on the olive, yellow and brown poplar leave drying in the sun at his feet.

No one would ever dream that such a place could be the birthplace of the incredible sequence of events that had began right here in that dreadful crash almost a year before.

The guardrails at the edge of the road had been replaced, but the scars of Fred's horrific plunge were still visible on the steep rocky bank and in the flattened trees and bushes below. Bred shuddered at the memory.

Taking a deep breath, he walked along the base of the slope to where the van had eventually come to rest. The creek was only a foot deep now, running clear and swift over the rounded pebbles and rocks. Bred had a sudden vision of another time and shuddered again. He gathered himself and crossed over the creek to the other side. He worked his way fifty yards upstream, to where he could see a small cave cut into the limestone rock in the bank just above the water level.

Bred removed five bank bags from his duffel bag and stuffed them into the cave. He obscured the bags completely by throwing mud, stones and dirt over them. He brushed out his own tracks using a spruce branch and splashed water over everything. Satisfied, Bred returned to the other side of the stream and after selecting a suitable site, began setting up his equipment.

Bred surveyed the entire area and wrote everything down carefully in his notebook. He measured the incline angle, the curve and even the camber of the road. He measured the elevation of the bank, the angle of the incline and the distance from the road to the creek.

He did some rough trial and error calculations. When he was satisfied, he sat down on the edge of the road to wait for George and idly threw rocks into the creek. The rest of the work he could complete at home using his computer.

The ambience settled his spirit and he was at peace with the world. No one had passed that way the whole time that he was there. He thought it was a shame really. More people should see rural Alberta in the fall; it was good for the soul.

The following morning, while Patrick and Michelle were still in Ft. McMurray, Bred slipped around to the back of 'Maude's Cottage' and put all the equipment back in the shed. Climbing carefully up onto the deck, he retrieved the key from beneath the potted *rhododendron* and let himself into the house through the back door. Bred chuckled when he recalled the last time he had done that.

Bred made his way to the basement and found Fred's old jacket in the cupboard. He slipped the notebook into the inside pocket. He left his rubber boots in the basement as well and hobbled painfully back to the Andrews' estate in his bare feet.

★★★

Corporal D'Laney and Constable Monair returned from Ft. McMurray that evening, landing at the Edmonton Municipal Airport since they had caught a flight back on the RCMP Lear jet.

They drove the hour and a half to Bolton and went directly to 'Maude's Cottage'. Darkness had descended on the little town by the time they reached the house. Patrick was not surprised to find the 'clue' that Maggie had spoken of in the inside jacket pocket. He flipped over the pages. The lines and symbols meant nothing to him. He handed it to Michelle. She studied it for a minute and shook her head.

"No idea," she said.

"Me neither," Patrick said thoughtfully. "I'll pass it on to the inspector; he'll know what to do with it."

Patrick was very quiet on the way to the precinct. Michelle looked at him with a concerned look on her face.

"That book wasn't there before, was it Patrick?" she asked.

"No," he answered with a troubled frown, glancing over at her, "and I didn't leave the lights on in the basement either."

★★★

The following morning Patrick and Michelle drove up into the yard on the Morgan farm. As soon as they got out of the cruiser, the two golden retrievers were all over Michelle and she dropped to her knees to pet them. They licked her face and were snuggling right into her arms, as retrievers will, when she suddenly caught a whiff of them. She staggered back, gasping for air.

In shock, she caught sight of a dark mass of putrid buffalo guts and a rancid liver lying in the grass ten feet away — just as the full stench invaded her innocent nostrils and ravished her olfactory nerves.

"Auuuuugh…Auuughhh!"

She dry heaved across the yard in a staggering gallop trying to escape the sticky sweet aroma from beyond the tomb.

"Auuuuugh…Auuughhh!"

Patrick rested his arms on the top of the cruiser and watched her go at it with a half-smile on his face. Pete Morgan stepped out onto the porch and scratched his chin thoughtfully.

"Should maybe head upwind if I was you," he said wryly.

Michelle focused on his voice and stumbled blindly through her tears up onto the deck and into the house, slamming the door behind her.

They could hear her dry heaving through the walls.

"Sorry about that," Pete said, in no rush to go back inside just yet. He nodded to the dogs rolling in their glorious bounty.

"They drag that stuff in from the neighbour's place. I think he has a slaughterhouse over there. Sure does hum though."

"Auuuuugh…Auuughhh!

The men could contain themselves no longer. The laughing-bubbles built up in their bellies and exploded through their clamped lips. They desperately tried to contain them with their hands, but were only partially successful.

They tiptoed uncontrollably up and down the deck like Indians doing a pow-wow in slow motion.

When he had recovered somewhat, Pete wiped away the tears with his sleeve and called Josh over from the barn to get rid of the mess. He and Patrick talked shop for a little while, leaning on the porch rail and pretending not to hear what was going on in the house.

When things had quieted down, Pete cautiously opened the door and they went inside. Michelle was standing in the middle of the room, red eyed, ridged and pale. She had changed her blouse for one of Josh's shirts. Her tunic was safely stashed in a white plastic laundry bag near the door at her feet. Neither man looked directly at her or dared to crack a smile as they shuffled over to the table.

A short time later, Josh walked into the kitchen. He had washed up outside and came in drying his hands. The adults were all seated around the table drinking coffee while waiting for him. He noticed that Michelle was wearing one of his shirts, but he said nothing. He took a deep breath and sat down in the only vacant chair.

"These officers want to talk to us about Fred Parker's accident again," Pete Morgan said, not lifting his head.

"Okay," Josh said, nodding, "but I think I've already told you everything I know about it."

"I know Josh," Michelle said, "but we may have missed something intangible." Seeing his questioning frown, she continued. "Like smoke in the air, dust, a movement out of the corner of your eye."

"Nothing like that," Josh said, shaking his head. "It was a quiet evening."

"You were the first to see the light, Josh," she asked patiently. "What did you think it was?"

There was a long silence while Josh pondered. "I thought it was the reflection of the moon," he said at last, "until I remembered there was no moon that night." He laughed uncomfortably.

Patrick leaned forward. "The light was dim?" he asked intently.

"Yes, Sir," Josh said hesitantly.

"But, when you gave it to us it worked just fine," Michelle said. Her heart leapt as the realisation hit her.

"You changed the battery!" she exploded.

"Well…yeah!" Josh said.

"This changes the whole case. The battery was not at the scene! Bred was…" Wildly excited, Michelle swung around to face Patrick. The words froze on her lips.

Patrick sat there, his face like stone. He had expected to hear nothing less enlightening.

"Ping!" went the little silver bell in Patrick's head.

★★★

Jenny's Department Store was owned and run by Jenny Tabor, a spinster of fifty-four years.

When questioned by Corporal D'Laney, she remembered Bred being in her store around the time of the accident. Josh and his family were also regular customers, but she could not recall them being there at that time.

"How can you remember one customer out of so many from a year ago?" Michelle asked incredulously.

"I remember because he took something without paying for it! I don't forget those things," she replied indignantly.

"Do you remember what it was that he took?" Michelle asked.

"I believe it was a large battery," Jenny said, fussing behind the counter. "I noted it down and charged Ms. D'Laney-Andrews for it afterwards. Here, let me take a look."

Jenny Tabor pulled out an old ledger from under the counter and paged through it quickly. "Here it is," she said concentrating. "*Charge to Mary D'Laney Andrews — One nine volt battery — $12.50.* I remember he spent a long time making his choice. I think he went through all of them," she said, still annoyed by the incident.

"When was that — exactly?" Patrick asked.

"Ms. D'Laney-Andrews paid me back the week beginning September fourth," she answered, looking at the date. "I don't have the actual day."

"The week following the accident," Patrick said.

★★★

Inspector Claude DuBois looked up from the paperwork in front of him, and shook his head in astonishment.

"This is incredible!" he said. "A complete reversal?" He didn't know whether to laugh or cry. "How the hell did that happen?"

The inspector had set up a meeting including Patrick and Michelle in the conference room at the Fifth Precinct, to review the latest developments in the Parker case. The evidence had all been prepared and categorised, and was laid out on the conference room table. Everyone had been briefed.

"This is Dr. Powers, a forensics guru from head office here to assist in the investigation, at my request," Claude said, by way of introduction. "The rest of the people you know." He waved his arm indicating the officers around the table.

"Go ahead Corporal," he said, handing over the floor to Patrick.

"Let's go over the evidence once again," Patrick said, standing up and walking to the end of the table. He held his chin while he concentrated.

"First: With regards to the furniture and the mirrors, we are no longer sure who dumped them there. We have witnesses who will swear that Fred Parker borrowed the truck that is reputed to have transported the mirrors on or about that time." Patrick checked his notes.

"Second: Josh Morgan claims to have purchased a new battery for the flashlight and replaced it prior to handing it over to the department. The battery that was in the flashlight at the scene was taken to a local garbage dump. There is no chance of recovery.

"The fingerprints on that battery inside the flashlight match those of Brian Andrews, but may have been made earlier in Jenny's Hardware Store.

"The storeowner witnessed him handling the batteries on the shelf a few days prior to Josh Morgan's alleged purchase."

"Alleged purchase?" The inspector raised his eyebrows."You're not buying it?" he asked.

Patrick shrugged. "Too many convenient coincidences," he said, sitting down. "It doesn't feel right. All our earlier evidence — trashed?"

Michelle looked at him wide-eyed. "We don't know about the boots yet," she said.

"I can help you with that," Claude said, resting his arms on the table. "The report just came in. Forensics has shown that the boot print moulds taken by Constable Monair at the dumpsite matched the ones found in the basement of 'Maude's Cottage', where Fred Parker was living at the time." He sat back in his chair and rubbed his forehead. "There is not a single recoverable fingerprint on them."

Michelle turned from the Inspector to Patrick and back to the Inspector her mouth open with surprise, unable to speak.

"It gets better." Claude sighed, seeing her expression. He nodded to Dr. Powers, the forensics guru from head office. "Go ahead, Doctor," he said.

Dr. Powers rose hesitantly to his feet and nodded to the inspector. Buttoning his jacket nervously, he walked to the overhead projector and switched it on.

"Well, first," he said, flicking to the appropriate slides. "This is a breakdown of the information in the notebook." He flipped to each page in turn, explaining the markings as he went.

"There is a detailed survey of the entire crash area at Poplar Creek. The tolerances on angled measurements are to within a second, and linear dimensions to within one-quarter of an inch. And even the locations of the larger bushes and trees are shown.

"All calculations utilise probability theory, calculus, differentiation and integration, and are to four decimal places. The author used complex mathematics to solve problems related to acceleration, torque, trajectory, vector analysis, mass, friction and kinetic energy." Dr. Powers switched off the projector. He moved to the computer keyboard and sat down.

"We checked the calculations and simulated the results on a computer," he continued concentrating on the screen, selecting the right file. "Let me show you." He pressed a button and the overhead monitor displayed a computer model of a vehicle travelling along the old road above Poplar Creek in a three-dimensional setting.

"Now," Dr. Powers continued, "the van comes around the bend going at seventy-five kilometres per hour, aimed at this reflector target right here," he indicated a point on the road where a moving white line represented the headlights reflected back to the driver. "The vehicle then zones in on the light like tracking a laser beam," he said, as the vehicle tore up the slope, "and strikes the target!" Dr. Powers narrated the slow motion action on the screen, displaying the shards of the mirror exploding in front of the vehicle.

"The vehicle then leaves the road and becomes airborne, turns 360 degrees in the air and lands like a skier on the down-slope. His fall is broken and his speed is checked by the bushes and the creek at the base of the hill." The film simulation came to an end and Dr. Powers switched off the machine.

"Even the density of the willow trees and bushes were calculated," Dr. Powers continued with glee, getting right into it. "The reflector mirror to keep him on line was a stroke of genius!"

"What would he do that for?" Michelle asked, totally out of her depth.

"To stage a spectacular crash…and survive!" Claude said, standing up. "But, he miscalculated."

"Yes," Dr. Powers said. "He forgot to factor in the weather — the swollen river and the slippery road conditions."

Patrick shook his head. "And who put that extraordinary mathematical notebook together?" he asked sarcastically. "And when?"

"Why, your Mr. Fred Parker, of course!" Dr. Powers said, somewhat taken aback. "The notepaper was at least five years old. He was a civil engineer, quite capable of making those computations."

In the ensuing silence Dr. Powers collected his papers and turned to go, the files tucked safely under his arm. He suddenly remembered something and turned back to Patrick.

"We also confirmed the handwriting in the notebook," he said gravely. "Absolutely no question — it was Fred Parker's."

★★★

Inspector Claude DuBois lay back in his chair and looked thoughtfully across his desk at the two young police officers sitting uncomfortably in front of him. It was the following day, and the telephones had not stopped ringing all morning.

"We dismissed all charges against the Andrews boy this morning," he said, with a somewhat satisfied smile, rocking back and forth. "I think we can close the book on this one. It looks like old Fred Parker staged the whole thing."

"Inspector, I don't think…" Patrick began.

"He had time, place, motive and opportunity," Claude continued, ignoring the interruption and looking up at the ceiling. "Can't prove a damn thing though," he continued. "He could have done the whole exercise for fun." He rotated his chair so that he could see out the window. "Besides," he said, "we're way over budget, and resources are limited."

Patrick tried again. "Sarge, there are too many coincidences. It's been too easy! We need to …"

"I want you two to take a look into that cattle rustling case out at the Beau Meadow Ranch," Claude said thoughtfully.

"Just one bloody minute, Claude!" Patrick demanded jumping to his feet. "We didn't do all this work for nothing, we…"

"You ever hear about the man driving his wagon along the country lane, when he got stuck in a rut?" Claude interrupted again. "Well, apparently he just got off the wagon and stood looking at it aghast and not doing anything, except to yell really loud for some guy named Hercules to come and help him."

Patrick stood stock-still with his mouth half-open.

"Anyway," Claude continued undaunted, looking up at the ceiling again. "As it turned out, Hercules was in the neighbourhood and came over to take a look. When he saw that the wagon-man was just standing there wailing and not doing anything he said, '*put your shoulders to the wheel, man. Goad on your mules and never call me again to help you until you have done your best to help yourself.*'"

Claude rolled his head to one side and smiled tiredly at Patrick.

Patrick looked at him in astonishment. "Claude…?"

Michelle rose quietly from her seat and took the stunned corporal by the arm and steered him gently out of the room. Patrick watched the inspector over his shoulder as he was slowly led away. Inspector DuBois lay back in his chair humming a tune, totally oblivious.

When the door had closed behind them, a bewildered Corporal D'Laney turned to Michelle. "What the hell was that all about?" he asked.

"*Æsop's Fables,*" she said, smiling up at his baffled expression. The unflappable Patrick D'Laney was finally out of his league. "Advice, without our perceiving the presence of the advisor; he disassociated himself from the instruction."

"What instruction?" Patrick was even more confused.

"He was telling us to get on with the Parker case," she said, "and to do so without his involvement."

Inspector Claude DuBois had his orders too.

★★★

"We could try to trace back the footprints of the truck," Michelle said, going through her old notes.

They had gone back to their office at the precinct and were reviewing details and statements from everyone about the case. Their desks were piled high with reports, files and pictures accumulated over the year.

"Bred is the only one that could have known what happened to the truck that night," Patrick said, shaking his head, "and he doesn't remember anything."

"Mary D'Laney-Andrews said that Brian took a long time to come up the driveway," Michelle said, tilting her head thoughtfully, reading her notes. "Maybe he dropped someone off — or something."

"It's been a while," Patrick said doubtfully, "but it's worth a try. Let's go and see Mary again."

Mary was waiting for them in the yard when they arrived. It was a little cooler than the day before, to be expected at that time of year, but apart from a brisk breeze and some high cloud filtering out the full warmth of the sun, it was still a most pleasant fall day.

"Just planting the tulips and daffodil bulbs for the spring." Mary laughed, doing a curtsey in her unflattering gardening dungarees. She was starting to show, and Michelle laughed with her and gave her a hug.

When Patrick eventually broached the subject of Bred's return on that fateful night, Mary remembered the early morning in question quite vividly.

"I couldn't see the gate from my bedroom window," Mary said, recalling the incident with a frown. "It was dark and the yard light obscured my view, but I could see the lights of the truck."

"Did it take Bred long to get up the driveway?" Michelle asked. "Was he parked at the gate for some time?"

"Well no, not really," Mary said. "I could see the headlights of the truck as it cut across the lawn. You can still see the marks…look." She pointed them out and shook her head with a mother's tolerant smile. "Bred was so inconsiderate back then." She sighed. "Would you two like some coffee?" she asked brightly, brushing off the past.

Patrick glanced at Michelle. "I think we'll take a look around first, Mary, if you don't mind," he said, thanking her.

Michelle followed Patrick down the driveway and along the tire tracks to the sheds.

Patrick read the signs as Bred had done a few days before, and opened the old wooden doors to reveal the stacks of yellow pails within. There was a hole in the roof of the shed, originally intended to allow access for a grain-loading spout. The trap door, which normally covered the hole, had long since disappeared.

Fall leaves from the deciduous trees in the garden and other air born litter, had blown in through the hole and covered the floor of the shed with an inch or two of foliage.

Patrick noticed the five pails stacked neatly against the wall. He walked over and lifted the lid off one of them.

It was empty.

He checked the rest of the cans in the stack with the same result. He was just about to call it a day when something among the red, yellow and brown leaves on the floor caught his eye.

He crouched down and picked up a slightly crumpled Canadian one hundred-dollar bill.

★★★

CHAPTER EIGHTEEN
The Beginning

George's Gym had become a popular teenage hangout for Bred and his growing group of friends. They had introduced people individually to their clandestine club, as slowly and as hush-hush as possible.

They need not have bothered.

Bred knew for a fact that George's Gym was currently being administered by a legal firm out of Toronto. They had been instructed to do nothing except pay utilities and taxes for the time being. Apparently, an individual who wished to remain anonymous had purchased the gym for cash. Whenever the question came up in conversation regarding the new owners, Bred inspected his nails carefully and said nothing.

Activities at the gym had been confined to quiet physical workouts, a little subdued music, games and the steam room. Their group had gradually grown to a dozen or so, which was not surprising seeing as how it was a small town. Sneaking in and out of the building unseen was a large part of the fun.

But of course, as soon as Josh found out about it — it was party time! The music got louder and the teen crowd grew, especially on weekends. Most parents didn't seem to mind, they knew where their kids were: not in the city.

The last weekend had been a blast, but Bred knew that their activities would not go unnoticed by the community forever. It couldn't last, and he was therefore not too surprised when Kyle Bishop walked through the door of George's Gym early one Saturday afternoon.

Bred, Maggie and Kelly had had just finishing cleaning up from the festivities of the night before and were relaxing in the steam room when they heard the door open. Bred held up his hand for them to remain where they were and stepped out into the exercise room, buttoning up his shirt.

"Mr. Bishop," he said loudly, warning the girls. "What can I do for you?"

Kyle got right to the point. "Anybody else here?" he demanded, standing at the door and looking around the room.

"No." Bred lied, waving his arm at the empty room.

"Good," Kyle said, striding meaningfully across the room. Bred was unsettled by the big man's look of determination and put a workout bench between them.

Kyle stopped four feet away. He was breathing heavily, his arms hanging loosely at his sides.

"What's your problem?" Bred demanded, becoming alarmed. Kyle was obviously very irate and holding back his temper with a tremendous effort. Kyle bent down and threw the bench aside. It went crashing into the weights and mirrors against the wall. The glass shattered and shards fell on the floor. Bred swallowed hard.

"Andrews, you're going to show me where you stashed that money," Kyle said through clenched teeth. "The cops may have bought your story, but I don't." He reached for Bred, but Bred instinctively stepped back and blocked his arm aside.

"What the hell are you talking about?" Bred yelled hop-stepping away the adrenaline rushed through his system. (He was quite pleased with that block.) He felt that he might be able to ward off his cumbersome attacker and possibly even inflict some damage of his own. He was sixteen and in better shape than Kyle Bishop.

Bred bounced up on his toes, prepared to dance with the big man. He had just raised his hands into the Japanese *shoto-kan* defensive position, when Kyle's straight-right fist caught him right between the eyes.

Bred went down like a sack of beans.

Kyle lifted him up by the front of his shirt, his face inches from Bred's.

"I know all about your little trip to Poplar Creek the other day," he said maliciously. "Did you think that George wouldn't tell me sooner or later?"

He dragged the half-conscious Bred to the door with one hand.

"You're going to show me where you stashed that money," he said coldly. "If I have to beat it out of you."

Bred weathered the fifteen-minute, seven-mile trip to Poplar Creek, on the old Bolton to Edmonton road in a daze. At one point he tried to open the door of the truck and Kyle clipped him roughly on the ear. He slumped down in his seat once more, semi-conscious. This was definitely a turn of events that he had not anticipated.

They reached the base of the hill below the crash site where Kyle's Courier Service's van, driven by old Fred Parker, had left the road. Kyle swerved off the road and into the ditch in a cloud of dust.

Bred was dressed only in gym shorts and a newly-stretched cotton shirt, but Kyle hauled Bred out of the truck and dragged him by the scruff of his neck through the underbrush. Bred stumbled blindly in his grasp. Branches tore cruelly at his bare legs and arms, and he stubbed his toes and ankles on the deadfall. Kyle fought his way through the brushes and rocks to the ploughed up area at the edge of the creek where the courier van had finally come to rest.

"Where?" Kyle demanded, holding Bred with one hand and threatening to slap him with the other.

Bred pointed vaguely upstream. "In that cave… on the ….other bank," Bred said groggily, trying to get his bearings.

Kyle slapped him on the side of the head anyway and Bred fell face down in the water on the edge of the stream.

His ears ringing like an express train, Bred managed to roll over and lift his face out of the water just before he drowned. He watched through a swirling grey fog as Kyle splashed across the stream and tore the bags out of the crevice. Kyle ripped open the bags and howled with rage. He lunged back across the stream his face a mask of fury.

Bred could not move.

"There's not more than ten grand here!" he screamed, grabbing Bred by the shoulders and pulling him deeper into the creek.

"Where did you stash the rest?" He shook Bred like a rag doll.

"Swept away…in the…floods," Bred managed to gasp.

Kyle stared at him for a second not comprehending, and then his wrath exploded as the realisation hit him. "Swept away…?" He was beyond all reason. "You bloody fool!"

Kyle seized Bred violently by the shoulders, and dragged him with brute force deeper into the stream. Using the strength of his powerful arms, he forced Bred under the water. "You bloody, stupid fool!"

Bred was startled but unafraid as the cold water closed over his befuddled head and the sound of Kyle's screams became muffled and unintelligible. He blinked and looked up through the clear, cool water at the sun and the green trees above, as if looking through a distorted mirror.

I, Fred have been in this place before, Bred thought calmly, beginning to see clearly, and someone else also belongs here..Brian?

Suddenly, Kyle's deformed features blocked out the sun, and the images vanished.

Bred panicked.

He fought and he kicked and he even tried to bite, but the power and the insane fury that held him beneath the surface was cruel and relentless. The light slowly started to dim.

Lack of oxygen caused his brain to lower its inner defences. The living brain searched its realm to survive — to find an answer to the threat of oxygen deprivation, unbidden by conscious thought.

The stress activated endorphins, the brains natural opiates. They in turn became neuromodulators, increasing the actions of neurotransmitters. Neurotransmitters short-circuited across natural barriers to other parts of the brain they would never have reached in normal circumstances.

To survive, search the mind, find an answer — any answer! —
There was only one!

In a flash of light, Bred was suddenly made aware of another time, another place. Like sailing in the waves on a clear moonlit night, he rode on a sea of strange shapes and desires, in fear and in loneliness.

In the eye of the beast there is a survival instinct; only now and today, there is no tomorrow — and yesterday's memories are a boiling cauldron of irrational emotions and fear.

This was the House of Brian.

★★★

Maggie and Kelly had heard Kyle Bishop roughing up Bred, and Maggie had had her hands full holding Kelly back so as not to give them away. As soon as Bred and Kyle had left, Kelly called Patrick at the precinct and let him know what had happened.

Patrick and Michelle took off immediately after Kyle in the cruiser, with Michelle hollering for backup cars and the medics on the radio. When they reached Poplar Creek they recognised Kyle's truck. Patrick swerved off the road, braking in a cloud of dust and gravel. Michelle was out of the cruiser and heading in the direction of the commotion before he could stop the car. Patrick was still a good twenty paces behind when Michelle caught up to Kyle Bishop.

Her lithe form burst through the bushes, down the bank and plunged into the stream. She was yelling like a banshee. Kyle released one hand on the boy and turned to face the threat. Michelle flew at him like a wildcat and he backhanded her across the cheek as if he were swatting a fly. The force of the blow knocked Michelle staggering six feet to the side, where she sprawled semiconscious, half-in and half-out of the stream.

Fortunately for Bred, Kyle's momentum, combined with the swirling current, caused him to lose his footing on the rocky bottom of the creek. He fell backwards into the water and was forced to release his grip on Bred at the same time. Kyle leapt up with a fearsome bellow, and splashed downstream grabbing for his elusive victim just as Patrick slid down the bank and plunged into the swiftly flowing water.

The stream was about thirty feet wide at that point; river-stone rocks lined the steep banks for ten feet on both sides. A curve in the stream made the water bank slightly as the clear, cold water rushed swiftly and turbulently, around the bend. Young Birch, shrubs and poplar grew down to the shore; older trees could not survive the swift spring run-off for long. The bottom of the creek was strewn with water-worn pebbles, rocks and boulders of all sizes, causing the water to boil and froth at the surface. Two to three feet of water made it difficult for anyone to stand.

Patrick reached Bred first, grabbed him by the scruff of the neck and hauled him to the surface. At that moment, Kyle sucker-punched Patrick on the side of the head. Bred and his would-be rescuer went for a tumbling down the stream for fifteen yards before Patrick was able to regain his footing. Patrick didn't lose his grip on Bred, however, and managed to drag him into the shallows before turning to face the enraged Kyle Bishop charging down on him again.

Kyle's lust for blood and vengeance had not diminished one iota by the time he reached the smaller, still slightly dazed Corporal D'Laney. Kyle took another vicious swing at his head.

Patrick ducked, and took a glancing blow.

Being cast in the mould of his police ancestry, along with six solid years in the force had tempered the metal of one Corporal Patrick D'Laney. The glint of battle in his eye almost cooled the ardour of the bigger man as he grappled his stoic opponent. Kyle might have been wise to quit right then, but the rage in his soul at being robbed by a sixteen-year old boy pushed him on.

Kyle threw a roundhouse right, striking Patrick on the shoulder and knocked him off-balance; Patrick tripped him up and they both ended up in the water, tumbling about, kicking and gouging, but not inflicting much damage.

They separated. Kyle got to his feet first and charged again. Patrick stepped clumsily aside and nailed him on the ear with a good left hand. Kyle fell flat on his face in the water. He got up quickly, but Patrick put him on his back with a solid right between the eyes. Too late, Kyle realised that he had made a *big* mistake!

With a roar of pain, Kyle tried to grapple and managed to head-butt Patrick over the eye. He tried to stomp his stunned smaller opponent with his boot as he stumbled, but Patrick turned aside and smacked him on the mouth with a straight left jab, and then landed another. Reeling, Kyle raised his arms to protect his face. Patrick punched him in the solar plexus with a short hard left, once, twice — followed by a crisp right uppercut to the jaw that rocked Kyle back on his heels. Kyle flopped back down in the creek once more. Patrick went after him, lost his footing, and the two ended up tangling in the current once more. They scrambled to their feet in shallower water; Kyle, breathing hard, picked up a rock and swung, hitting Patrick on the forearm.

"You want to fight dirty, eh," breathed Patrick, "Ok, let's go."

Kyle tried a weak swinging left hook. Patrick blocked and pounded Kyle with a four punch combination to the body and head, so swift were his fists, it was almost a blur. Kyle went down sideways and rolled to his knees.

Patrick was coming for him again when Kyle rolled over and held up his hand.

"That's it!" he sobbed, gasping for breath through his swollen, split lips. "I've had enough!"

"Not quite!" Patrick growled, and bitch-slapped him across the side of the head, vastly altering Kyle's ruddy complexion. "That's for Michelle," he said.

Patrick grabbed Kyle roughly by the collar, forced him to his feet and dragged him out of the creek. He threw him into the arms of the two uniformed officers who had been waiting patiently on the shore while Corporal D'Laney got the job done.

"No reason why we should all get our feet wet," one of the officers said, grinning.

Meanwhile, Michelle had crawled over and resuscitated the half-drowned Bred. She kept the uniformed backup officers at bay with a glare. Bred coughed up half the creek, but he was still alive — much to his own surprise.

Bred and Michelle were both sitting draped in blankets a few minutes later when the paramedics arrived. Bred was still shivering with shock despite the warm sunshine. Matt Finch and Julie Martins came sliding down the bank of the creek and stood staring down in surprise at the battered pair.

"Hell's Teeth, Bred!" Matt said, shaking his head as he opened his kit. "You ought to be living in a bubble my boy."

★★★

After everybody left Poplar Creek to return to Bolton, Michelle went in search of Patrick. Her heart pounded as she met him coming towards her at the edge of the trees. His face was like granite. The blood had almost dried from the cuts on his cheek and forehead below his unruly hair. He looked like a warrior.

Her Warrior!

She stopped, trembling, not sure what to do.

Patrick too, caught his breath at the sight of Michelle. A gentle breeze fluttered the golden leaves around her and the sunlight glittered off the water droplets in her hair. He stood there gazing at her, trapped by her beauty.

She had been hurt. He wanted to take her in his arms and shield her from the world. He knew then that he loved her with all his heart.

But Constable Michelle Monair was a good police officer with a great future ahead of her. He tightened his resolve not reveal his inner turmoil. To do so would be to show her he loved her, and ultimately, to ask her to give up her career for him; and beg her to marry him. He could not do that to her.

"Are you all right?" he asked hoarsely.

"Ye…yes," she stammered.

He walked slowly down the grassy incline towards her. When he reached her, she held up her trembling hand without looking at him and he stopped by her side.

The warmth of their own proximity intermingled with the scents of the forest and enveloped them. A zephyr of wind blew a halo of falling leaves around them, as uncontrollable emotions as old as time drove them on. Slowly, unsure, and very afraid, they turned to each other. Engulfed by the power of their love, they kissed, as lovers do, for a long, long time. They sank unknowingly to their knees among the fallen leaves on the forest floor.

Then the spirit of the forest blessed another union of its creatures, as it witnessed the passion of their embrace.

★★★

Bred sighed and pressed the button. He was ready.

The biggest nurse he had ever seen rumbled down the hallway and burst into the room with the enema kit in her arms.

Her tawny brown hair flopped down over her elated chubby face, as she stared into his eyes and checked his vital signs. She was beaming from ear to ear and her big brown eyes were moist as she cooed and prodded and tucked him in all over.

"Will you marry me?" he asked her coyly, when she was done.

"You have some visitors," she said, ignoring the question, though he could see by her body language she was tempted. "You will be able to go home tomorrow, but only if you behave," she added sternly.

Bred couldn't help himself. Rupert Brookes came to mind.

> *"'I have been so great a lover: filled my days*
> *So proud with the splendour of Love's praise*
> The pain, the calm, and the astonishment,
> *Desire illimitable, and still content!'"*

She waggled a finger at him, frowning as she left the room. He could hear her tittering as she reverberated down the hall.

Bred smiled.

★★★

Patrick and Michelle had visited with him a little earlier that morning. Michelle had a nasty bruise and a bandage on her cheek. She was still quite swollen, but she smiled happily as she kissed Bred on the forehead. She flashed her engagement ring and Bred made a fuss over it.

"So, he finally asked you to marry him," Bred said with a grin.

"Yes," Michelle said," squeezing his arm, "and I'm transferring to forensics in Edmonton. Inspector DuBois has arranged it all and there won't be any conflict with the department."

Patrick was a bit more formal. "You'll be happy to know that Kyle Bishop is behind bars," he said. "He won't bother you again. He was just infuriated because you left all that money in the cave like that."

"Me?" Bred said innocently. "Why me? It wasn't my fault that the police only searched downstream after the accident." Bred was quite indignant. "I was just lucky to discover the empty bags in that cave. Just good detective work if you ask me"

Michelle joined forces with Bred to protest the insinuation.

"Okay!" Patrick said, holding up his hands defensively. "But there's still the question of the hundred-dollar bill I found in your shed. The bulk of the stolen money could have been hidden in there."

"Or, the bill could have just blown in with the leaves," Bred said, petulantly.

"What would have been the point in stashing it anyway; it was all marked," Michelle said with a puzzled frown. "Unless the money was…" The startling revelation struck her.

"There never was anything wrong with the money, was there?" she asked, wide-eyed. "Inspector DuBois lied?"

Patrick shrugged.   "It's possible that there was a logjam downstream, which flooded the creek and backed up during the first storm," he said thoughtfully, changing the subject. "Those bags might have been thrown out of the van during the crash and ended up in the water. They could have floated back up in an eddy and been left high and dry in that cave. Subsequent floods may have washed most of the bills away," he added doubtfully.

"I'm still not convinced that you did not play a part, young man," he said sternly, sitting on the side of the bed. "There's probably a happy ending to this story, but I want to know the truth, Bred."

You can't handle the truth! Bred thought. He had always wanted to say that, like in the movie 'Men of Honour.' He sighed.

"Okay, Uncle Patrick," he said innocently, looking very serious.

Patrick nodded. "Maggie, Josh, Miss Jenny, (the general store owner) and even Graham were contacted by someone with a masculine voice, warning them that we were still investigating the case," Patrick said, looking at Bred carefully.

"Guilty," Bred sighed with a wince. "Voice synthesiser," he explained. "I was just trying to prove my innocence by refreshing everyone's memory of the days leading up to Fred Parker's accident."

"And the notebook?" Michelle asked.

"I found it in the tool shed behind 'Maude's Cottage'," Bred said. "I put it in Mr. Parker's old jacket pocket in the basement while you guys were up north. Was it a good clue?" he asked brightly.

Patrick just shook his head and Michelle laughed quietly.

★★★

There was not much physically wrong with him. Bred had only sustained a few minor cuts and bruises and a slight concussion during the altercation. But in any event, Dr. Bryce had decided to keep him in hospital for observation for a few days.

Bred had taken the opportunity to enjoy the peace and the freedom to explore the nether reaches of his opening mind. With a little concentration, he could go to a quiet place and recall memories of Brian as a little boy. Faint recollections of a loving family and happy times floated around in the House of Brian.

There was no perception of autism or schizophrenia of course, but in another room Bred could see the growing, unexplainable loneliness and frustration in Brian's later years. At the other end of that room there was a bright light. Bred closed the door; he felt no need to go there.

The Andrews' family filed one by one into the room. Beth ran over and hugged his neck and kissed his cheek, chattering excitedly. Kelly and Maggie held Bred's hands, vying for their share of his attention. Graham and Mary stood arm in arm grinning down at him from the foot of the bed.

Bred settled back down on the pillows with a sigh. This was a vastly different atmosphere from the first time that he had met the Andrew's family in this very room. He had a feeling things would be a lot better from now on.

Bred had checked the papers carefully that morning; his stock portfolio was doing quite well.

THE END

CPSIA information can be obtained at www.ICGtesting.com
Printed in the USA
LVOW11s0422170915

454495LV00001B/36/P